A SEC
THE FAMILY

Nancy Revell is the author of twelve titles in the bestselling Shipyard Girls series – which tells the story of a group of women who work together in a Sunderland shipyard during the Second World War. Her latest books, *The Widow's Choice* and *A Secret in the Family*, feature some of the characters from the world of the Shipyard Girls series in a new County Durham setting. Nancy's books have sold more than half a million copies across all editions.

Before becoming an author, Nancy was a journalist who worked for all the national newspapers, providing them with hard-hitting news stories and in-depth features. She also wrote amazing and inspirational true-life stories for just about every woman's magazine in the country.

Also by Nancy Revell

The Shipyard Girls

Shipyard Girls at War

Secrets of the Shipyard Girls

Shipyard Girls in Love

Victory for the Shipyard Girls

Courage of the Shipyard Girls

Christmas with the Shipyard Girls

Triumph of the Shipyard Girls

A Christmas Wish for the Shipyard Girls

The Shipyard Girls on the Home Front

Shipyard Girls Under the Mistletoe

Three Cheers for the Shipyard Girls

The Widow's Choice

A SECRET IN THE FAMILY

Nancy REVELL

PENGUIN BOOKS

PENGUIN BOOKS

UK | USA | Canada | Ireland | Australia
India | New Zealand | South Africa

Penguin Books is part of the Penguin Random House group of companies
whose addresses can be found at global.penguinrandomhouse.com

Penguin Random House UK,
One Embassy Gardens, 8 Viaduct Gardens, London SW11 7BW

penguin.co.uk
global.penguinrandomhouse.com

 Penguin
Random House
UK

First published 2025
001

Typeset in 10.4/15pt Palatino LT Pro by Jouve (UK), Milton Keynes
Printed and bound in Great Britain by Clays Ltd, Elcograf S.p.A.

The authorised representative in the EEA is Penguin Random House Ireland,
Morrison Chambers, 32 Nassau Street, Dublin D02 YH68

A CIP catalogue record for this book is available from the British Library

ISBN: 978-1-804-94509-4

To my mum, Audrey Walton (née Revell).
Who, throughout my life, has always encouraged me
to follow my dreams.

x

'You never really understand a person until you consider things from his point of view – until you climb into his skin and walk around in it.'

Harper Lee, *To Kill a Mockingbird*

Acknowledgements

As always, a huge 'Thank You!' to all my lovely readers who continue to buoy me up and keep me going with their wonderful words, heartfelt messages, and to-die-for reviews!

To the brilliant Emily Griffin, Publishing Director of Century fiction, who has been such a support and provided invaluable editorial guidance over the years.

To the fantastic 'Team Nancy' at Penguin Random House UK, who work so hard and with such professionalism on each and every book.

To my super copy-editor Caroline Johnson.

To the forever supportive Katy Wheeler, journalist at the *Sunderland Echo*, presenter Gilly Hope at BBC Radio Newcastle and podcaster Julie Pendleton.

To Phil Curtis and Linda King of the Sunderland Antiquarian Society for their ongoing support and amazing archives.

To Ian Mole for bringing the series to life with his Shipyard Girls Walking Tour.

To my cousin, Allison McDonald and her daughter

Chloe, Kath and Ray Thirlwell, Pauline Stevenson and Elena Notarianni, who have all helped me so much, in so many different ways.

And last, but not least, to my husband, Paul Simmonds, and my sister Jane Elias and her wonderful, inspiring family – husband Siôn and children, Ivor, Matilda and Flynn – thank you for your constant love, care, support and encouragement.

Prologue

Sunderland, County Durham

Monday, 7 May 1945

Ida Boulter zipped up her small beige suitcase, carried it out of the bedroom and put it by the kitchen table. She took a deep breath, forcing down the feeling of nausea she had been fighting whilst packing. She was taking the bare minimum. Not that her life's belongings amounted to much.

The magnitude of what she was about to do hit her again and had her rushing to the sink in the galley kitchen. She hunched over and dry-heaved. There was nothing to bring up. Very little had passed her lips these last twenty-four hours. She breathed in deeply, forcing herself to get a grip.

Glancing through to the clock on the mantlepiece in the living room, a shot of nerves needled every part of her. If she left it much longer, it would be too late. She thought of the consequences and hurried back to the lounge. Pulling out the nearest chair tucked under the small wooden table, she sat down and snatched up the pen she'd left there, ready to write the words that would change her world and that of her children forever.

A change for the better?

Dear God, she hoped so.

She thought of her husband and felt nothing as she wrote a brief farewell note to him. It was the note to her daughter, Angie, that she struggled with. Her daughter was twenty-two years old and on the cusp of a new life with her soon-to-be husband, Quentin Foxton-Clarke. By walking out on her family to start a new life with Carl in London, Ida knew full well that Angie would be left to bring up her four younger siblings, Danny, ten, Marlene, eight, Bertie, four, and Jemima, two. *But what else could she do?*

She glanced again at the clock. She had to be at the train station in thirty minutes. There was so much she wanted to explain to Angie, but there was no time to waste.

Why hadn't she done this earlier?

She knew why.

How do you tell your children you're leaving them and never coming back?

Ida forced her hand to stop shaking and start writing.

Angie,

I'm leaving and I won't be back. I love Carl and he loves me. We're going to make a new life for ourselves away from here. Please make sure the bairns are okay. I know you will. Tell them I'm sorry but this is something I had to do.

Love Mam

Ida stared at the words. This was not normal. Fathers leave their children. Not mothers. But as indecision took hold, Ida saw an image of her own mother. The dull look in her eyes showing those who cared to notice that her spirit had been beaten. Her mother had died long before her time on this earth had run out.

Recalling those darkened, deadened eyes, Ida's resolve returned.

Stuffing the hastily written notes into two small brown envelopes, which had previously contained her wage slips, Ida stood up and placed them on the mantlepiece.

Then she picked up her suitcase, grabbed her coat from the stand in the hallway and walked out the front door without a backward glance.

Chapter One

Eight Years Later

Cuthford Manor, Cuthford Village, County Durham

Saturday, 11 July 1953

Angie looked up on hearing her good friend Clemmie Sinclair cough loudly and tap the glass of her champagne flute. It was usually a man who gave the toast, but Clemmie, a tutor at Durham University, revelled in turning the tables on tradition.

'A toast to the happy couple on their first wedding anniversary.' Clemmie's loud, commanding tone sounded out around the grand, high-ceilinged reception room of Cuthford Country House Hotel.

Angie cringed. She hated any kind of fuss or attention, as did her husband, Stanislaw Nowak.

'To my good friend Angie and her incredibly lucky husband, Stanislaw . . .' There were a few chuckles. Everyone knew Clemmie thought the absolute world of her and liked to remind the man Angie had met two years ago and married a year later that he had hit the jackpot several times over. 'May they continue to enjoy the wedding bliss I have witnessed with my own eyes this past year!'

The guests raised their glasses.

'Here! Here!' The robust voices of the couple's family and friends were clearly in agreement. They too had seen how much joy Angie and her husband had brought not just to each other but to those around them. A happiness, it was agreed, they were more than due as both had suffered terrible personal tragedies.

Angie and Stanislaw smiled, but their self-consciousness was still evident. They had originally wanted just a small family affair to mark their first year of marriage, but it had somehow grown to include their neighbours, the Fontaine-Smiths, the village's general practitioner, Dr Wright, the local vicar and the friends Angie had made when Bonnie, her daughter, who was now nearly seven, had attended the local nursery.

'Time for cake, I do believe!' Clemmie pointed over to the sideboard, knowing not to push her luck and demand a speech from either her beloved friend or Stanislaw.

'*Yeah!*'

The excited exclamations of Angie's little sister, Jemima, eleven, made everyone chuckle.

Feeling someone giving her a gentle nudge, Angie turned to see Marlene.

'So, big sis.' Marlene looked at Angie and her brother-in-law, her blue-green eyes shining with mischief. 'You two still not had a change of heart about adding to our tribe?'

'Tribe' had been the word Angie's first husband, Quentin Foxton-Clarke, had used. A term of endearment that had stuck.

'No, we haven't.' Angie scowled at her younger sister, who was sixteen but had always been much older than her years, in attitude as well as looks. Even more so today, with her carefully made-up face and crimson-painted lips. 'You lot are enough to contend with.' Angie had never begrudged having to bring up her siblings after their mam had abandoned them eight years ago, but it had not always been easy. She cocked her head over to her younger brother, Bertie, twelve, and Jemima and Bonnie, who were jiggling about on the spot as they waited their turn for a slice of chocolate cake. Since chocolate was finally no longer rationed, they seemed determined to make up for the years cocoa powder had been akin to gold dust.

'Yes, but we're all getting older,' Marlene said, waving over to her elder brother, Danny, who had just walked into the room with Thomas, the stablehand.

Angie saw the flush of excitement in her sister's already rouged cheeks as Thomas looked over and offered a wide smile.

'And you lot getting older is meant to make it easier?' Stanislaw joshed, making light of a conversation he knew tended to rankle Angie.

'Of course!' Marlene said, flicking her carefully curled blonde hair back over her shoulder. 'Danny and I are all grown-up.'

'Um, I don't think so.' Angie widened her eyes. 'You are

still only sixteen and Danny only just eighteen. Legally, you're not "all grown-up" until you are twenty-one.'

Marlene tutted.

'And no more champagne,' Angie reprimanded her. 'You were only meant to have a few mouthfuls for the toast, and I can tell you've had more.'

Angie heard Marlene mutter a familiar jibe, *'You're not my mother,'* which, as always, was said under her breath as she flounced off, making a beeline for Thomas and her brother.

'That girl gets more headstrong by the day,' Angie said. Marlene had always been a handful. Angie had tried her best bringing her up, but it was hard. And it was true. Angie wasn't her mother. Which had made it harder still.

Stanislaw lowered his head to kiss his wife. 'Don't worry.'

'I know. I just don't want her going off the rails. And I feel that she's teetering on the edge at the moment.'

Stanislaw kissed Angie again, which did not, as he'd hoped, erase the look of concern on his wife's face.

'And what else is bothering you?' he asked.

'Oh, it's silly, but I do wish everyone would stop harping on about us having a baby,' she groused.

'It's what people say, isn't it,' Stanislaw pacified her. 'They expect it. You get married, you have a baby. People can't understand . . .' he paused, wanting to make sure he sounded genuine, '. . . that we're quite happy the way we are – with the family we have.'

Angie nodded. 'I know. I shouldn't let it bother me.' She had told Stanislaw many times over that she felt their family was complete. They had five children aged between six and eighteen who needed their love and attention – as well as a fledgling business to run. The Cuthford Country House Hotel was still in its infancy, and although it was doing well, they could not rest on their laurels. Angie didn't have the time or the energy for a baby.

'Unless,' Stanislaw probed, 'it bothers you because you're having a change of heart?' He tried to keep his tone impartial.

'God, no,' Angie said. 'You?'

Stanislaw shook his head and smiled. He didn't trust himself to speak. The last thing he wanted on their first wedding anniversary was for Angie to see that he did, very much, want to add to their tribe. But he was wise enough to realise the problems it would cause if Angie were to know his true feelings. There was no doubt she would feel obligated. And there was no way he would ever want to have a child under such circumstances.

'Come on, let's go out the back and have a ciggie,' Marlene said as soon as she'd reached Thomas and Danny. 'I'm guessing Lucy-loo's here, skulking out the back with the horses?'

Danny nodded. Lucy Stanton-Leigh, the love of his life, had just arrived. They'd put her horse, Dahlia, in the stall that was kept free for when Lucy rode over from her family home, a very grand estate called Roeburn Hall, a mile north of Cuthford Manor. The two had met two years ago at a local gymkhana. Their backgrounds could not have been more different, but it had been their shared love of horses that had drawn them to one another.

'Honestly, I don't know why she won't come in rather than wait outside like a pariah.'

'She's shy,' Danny defended her.

'Snobby more like,' Marlene retorted.

'God, talk about the pot calling the kettle black,' Danny sniped back, trying to veer the conversation away from the real reason Lucy never came to any of their gatherings. It wasn't Lucy who was the snob, but rather her family. If they got wind that Lucy and one of the Foxton-Clarkes were even fraternising – never mind romantically involved – there'd be another war on.

'I was going to grab some cake,' Danny said.

Marlene rolled her eyes.

'You and your belly.'

'Yeah, me an' all,' Thomas said. 'Mabel's dishing it out, so we'll get an extra thick slice.'

Marlene tutted. She knew that Mabel had a crush on Thomas, although he refused to acknowledge what was blatantly obvious.

'Hurry up, then,' Marlene ordered. 'I'm gasping for a smoke . . . Oh, and Thomas, grab me a glass of champagne and bring it out the back. And don't let Angie see you. She'll know it's for me. I'll meet you both in the stables.'

Marlene slipped away from the party as discreetly as possible as Danny and Thomas went to get their cake.

'You shouldn't let her boss you about like that,' Danny said.

Thomas smiled. Marlene could order him about as much as she liked. It was just her way. She liked to make out she was full of confidence and couldn't care less about anyone or anything, but Thomas knew the real Marlene. He was one of the few people who did. One of the few people to whom she showed her true self.

And the real Marlene – the Marlene that Thomas loved – was quite different to the showy front she put on display.

Chapter Two

Ida Boulter looked out of the window as the train crossed the eleven-arch viaduct that brought those travelling by rail from the south into the city of Durham. She glimpsed a view of the famous cathedral as the rhythmic rocking of the locomotive was replaced by the stuttering of brakes.

This was the first time she'd left the capital in eight years – and it would be the last. The nerves she had been fighting for most of the five-hour journey from London were not because she had left home for good, however, but because of the purpose of her journey.

As the train made its way into the station, Ida thought of Carl. The pain she'd felt leaving him had been like nothing she'd experienced before – other than the day she had left her children eight years ago. The heartache she'd felt then had been insurmountable.

But just as on that day before the end of the war in Europe, Ida was convinced she'd made the right decision. It might have broken her heart, but it was not something she regretted. Not even for a moment. She had to take strength from that.

Standing to get her suitcase, Ida reached up to the overhead rack. As she did so, the sleeves of her blouse fell back, revealing a cluster of fresh bruises on her arms. She grimaced and caught an elderly woman on the other side of the aisle staring at her, or rather at her bruises. Ida saw the judgement in her eyes and bit back a response.

By the time Ida had retrieved her luggage, the train had come to a halt and was hissing and puffing its relief. Stepping onto the platform, Ida took a deep breath to calm the rush of nerves. She had no idea what to expect. She might have heard through an old friend how Angie, Danny, Marlene, Bertie and Jemima were doing, but she'd not had any kind of contact with them since the day she'd walked out the door of her former home on Dundas Street.

After asking directions, Ida made her way to the depot, her scuffed leather suitcase banging against her stockinged legs. She was sweating by the time she got there, even though it was not far, but it was turning out to be a hot summer and the sun was blazing and the air humid. She asked a conductor coming out of the canteen which bus went to Cuthford village and he pointed to a queue of people boarding a green single-decker idling by the kerbside.

After paying the fare and taking her seat, Ida immediately heard the strong north-eastern dialect as a couple of women with their children chatted away behind her. Ida looked out of the window and tried her hardest to distract herself from her conflicting feelings as the bus pulled away. The joy she felt from the anticipation of seeing her children again after such a long time was dampened by how nervous she felt about suddenly turning up on their doorstep. A nervousness that was compounded when she thought of the reason she had come all this way to see them.

13

Forcing herself to concentrate on the passing snapshots of Durham from her window seat, she noticed that something felt different but couldn't put her finger on what. At first, she assumed it must be the overriding sense of history as the bus passed architecturally beautiful buildings and she caught glimpses of quaint cobbled streets, but it wasn't until the city was behind them that Ida realised she hadn't seen any cordoned-off bomb sites or new buildings being erected. Durham had escaped the wrath of war. It was so unlike her ravaged home town of Sunderland, which had paid the price for being the biggest shipbuilding town in the world, or her adopted home, London, which had endured the worst of the Blitz, the aftermath of which was still very much evident.

As the bus made its journey out into the countryside, Ida felt her apprehension grow and tried to distract herself by looking at the breathtaking dark green, slightly hilly land-scape. Passing through the various mining villages, she could see those who lived there were far from well off, but the children she spotted playing in the streets looked well and rosy-cheeked. Seeing them brought her anxiety back tenfold as she thought of her own children. Would she even recognise them?

She reprimanded herself. *Of course she would.* They were her flesh and blood.

But would *they* recognise *her*? The older ones, for sure – but the two youngest, she didn't know. Bertie had only been four and Jemima two when she'd left them.

When the bus finally stopped at Cuthford village, Ida was the only one to alight. She thanked the driver, who eyed her suspiciously. He must think her a southerner. She had actually worked hard at losing her strong Sunderland accent after escaping her marriage and moving down south. She hadn't wanted anyone to find her, or Carl. Nor did she want to bring with her anything of her old life.

As she walked the half-mile from the village to Cuthford Manor, she passed a sign showing directions to the 'Cuthford Country House Hotel'. Ida felt her heart pummelling. Her nerves were taking hold.

Ten minutes later, she reached another, more grandiose sign for the hotel in front of a pair of huge ornate black gates. She stopped to get her breath. The tiredness from the long journey was catching up with her. Seeing the gates were open, she felt relieved. She'd had no way of knowing if Angie and the children would be at home as it was now the summer holidays and she and her new husband could well have decided to go away.

She'd taken a chance – *had* to take a chance – as time was running out.

Walking through the cast-iron gates and seeing Cuthford Manor for the first time, Ida came to a standstill.

It was magnificent.

More than magnificent.

She remained standing, simply staring, taking in the manor's splendour. The grounds were bigger than any park she'd ever been to, the lawns on either side of the gravelled driveway perfectly manicured. But it was the pale sand-coloured stonework and wonderful turreted and tapered towers that gave the place its uniqueness.

15

As Ida continued up the driveway, she saw a number of cars parked out the front, including a beautiful navy blue Bentley and a racing-green sports car she thought might be a Jaguar. Ida slowed down, suddenly feeling completely out of her depth. Her head started to spin, and she was forced to crouch down on her haunches, both hands gripping her suitcase, steadying her. It had been a long journey. And she'd barely slept the night before or eaten much.

Taking a deep breath, Ida stood up and walked with purpose towards the entrance. As she approached the pillared porch, she could hear music, laughter and chatter. The hotel must be hosting an event. A party. She caught sight of balloons in one of the large windows to the right of the entrance. Hopefully, if the hotel was busy, she'd be ushered in and taken through to the back. Ida looked down at her clothes. They were clean but a little worn, just as she was. It was certainly not fitting attire for such a grand residence. They wouldn't want her to be seen by the other guests.

Bolstered by thoughts of being steered to a quiet part of the manor where she would be able to chat with Angie on her own, Ida walked up the wide flagstone steps and pulled on the doorbell.

Chapter Three

Hearing the jangle of the bell, Angie instinctively went to answer it, but was stopped dead in her tracks by the look she'd been shot by Wilfred, their butler-cum-concierge.

Stanislaw noticed and laughed. 'I often wonder who is really in charge of this place.'

'I accepted a long time ago that I am mistress of the manor in name only,' Angie said, smiling as she took a sip of champagne. She rarely drank these days and the Dom Perignon had gone to her head. She watched as Wilfred put his plate of half-eaten cake on the sideboard, straightened his tie, tugged at the cuffs of his three-piece suit, then walked purposefully out into the large, tiled hallway. Wilfred had been given a new lease of life since the hotel had opened a year and a half ago. He was positively fawned over by their American guests, who, in their words, found him 'adorable'. Angie had lost count of the number of times they'd asked, 'Can we take him home with us?' She always laughed, but she had a feeling that they would if they could.

'I wonder who that can be?' Angie mumbled. The hotel had been closed for the weekend. Not just because of their wedding anniversary party, but to give everyone a few well-deserved days off. The hotel might be on the small side, with just seven suites all in the East Wing of the manor, but those suites were more like apartments, each with a bedroom, small lounge area and bathroom. The management and running of the hotel were shared between Angie, Stanislaw, Angie's father-in-law, Lloyd Foxton-Clarke, and his wife, Cora.

The cook, Alberta, who was not getting any younger, was constantly run off her feet, frying up full English breakfasts in the morning and then producing three-course meals of an evening. She'd finally acquiesced to training up Mabel, their former scullery maid, who they'd recently discovered was quite the cook and whose baking almost rivalled Alberta's, not that anyone would dare to admit that. The maids, too, were also run ragged with all the cleaning, the bed linen that needed changing and the mounds of laundry they had to get through on a daily basis.

They all needed a break.

'Just about everyone we know is already here,' Stanislaw said. At six foot tall, he dwarfed his wife as he followed her through the throng of guests.

Angie reached the main foyer just as Wilfred was opening the large oak front door.

On seeing the tired-looking middle-aged woman standing on the doorstep, suitcase in hand, Angie stopped dead in her tracks. She blinked hard. Was she seeing things? Was the champagne playing tricks with her mind? She'd been having a few dreams about her mam of late. Were they seeping into her waking hours, making her imagine that she was here now?

She watched as the woman with wavy blonde hair, a pale complexion and heart-shaped face, who looked the spit of their mam only skinnier and older, talked to Wilfred.

Angie heard Wilfred cough, something he only did when he was put on the spot, and watched as he stepped back to allow the visitor to cross the threshold and into the entrance hall. Seeing Angie standing as still as a statue and looking as though she had just seen a ghost, he announced the visitor.

'Mrs Ida Boulter.'

Behind her, Angie could hear the shuffle of feet as people's curiosity got the better of them while she and her mother simply stood and stared at each other.

'Mam?' Angie asked in disbelief.

Ida nodded by way of reply.

Angie remained glued to the spot, speechless, grappling with the reality that their mother was actually there. At Cuthford Manor. After a hiatus of eight years. After walking out on them the day before her wedding to her first love, Quentin Foxton-Clarke on VE Day. A day that had signalled the end of her time working as a shipyard welder and the beginning of a new life with her husband, her four siblings and her old neighbour, Mrs Kwiatkowski.

'I'm sorry . . .' Ida apologised, putting down her suitcase; it suddenly felt like a dead weight. In fact, her whole body felt like a dead weight. 'I would have written. Told you I was coming . . .' Her voice trailed off. She'd had no intention of doing so for fear she'd be told she was not welcome and they didn't want to see her. And she couldn't risk that. She *had* to see them.

19

Suddenly Ida's attention was drawn to the partygoers.

Angie followed her gaze to see her mother staring at Bonnie, who had just sidled up to her and was now looking straight back at the woman who had brought her mother and stepfather's wedding anniversary celebration to a standstill.

'Oh my goodness!' Ida couldn't help the outburst. 'Your daughter?' She asked the question, but Ida had no doubt of the answer. The little girl with the short blonde hair was the image of Angie – and of her father, from what Ida could remember of her daughter's first husband.

Angie eyed her mother. 'Yes, and *your* granddaughter.'

Ida opened her mouth to speak. To offer up her reason for turning up out of the blue as unexpectedly as she had abandoned them all those years ago. To explain why she had made the long journey from London to come here. Looking around at the crowd of people who had come out of the room where the party was being held, she stopped herself. This was not the low-key arrival she'd foreseen.

Catching movement out of the corner of her eye, Ida found herself looking at her two youngest children. They had pushed their way to the front and positioned themselves next to Angie. *How they had grown.* Jemima looked the same, with her curly golden-coloured hair and blue eyes, only older. But Bertie looked different. He'd filled out and had his father's broad build. Although unlike him, her youngest son, who was wearing wire-rimmed spectacles and was conservatively dressed, appeared very studious.

Before anyone had a chance to speak, there was a sudden

gust of air and the two Bullmastiffs, Winston and Bessie, came bounding out of the corridor and were charging towards the interloper.

'Sit!' Angie commanded. Both dogs skidded slightly on the tiled flooring and obeyed orders, their eyes on Ida, their tails wagging furiously, the usual trail of drool hanging from their jowls.

They were followed by Marlene, Danny and Thomas.

On seeing her mother, Marlene gasped – her look one of sheer disbelief.

'Marlene—' Ida stepped forward but stopped on seeing her beautiful daughter take a step back.

'What are you doing here?'

Ida looked to see where the young man's voice had come from. A well-spoken voice with just the slightest hint of an accent – the soft lilt of their home town.

Ida wrenched her gaze away from Marlene to look at Danny. Her eldest boy.

Seeing her children there – within touching distance – she started to walk towards them. She didn't care that they were all looking at her as though she were the devil incarnate, she just wanted to hold them.

But as she made to walk towards them, she was hit by another dizzy spell and the faces of her children started to swirl in front of her. Their expressions a mix of anger, confusion and concern.

Then her legs buckled, and the floor rose up at her.

She felt a blow to the head.

And then there was darkness.

Chapter Four

Monkwearmouth, Sunderland, County Durham

1905

Ida sidled up to her mam, who was leaning against the big white ceramic sink where she was peeling potatoes. The way her mother was standing, one leg straight, the other bent, her stomach pressing into the side of the sink unit, told Ida she was tired. Ida was five years old, but she had only ever known her mother to be as skinny as a rake, with permanent dark shadows under her eyes and straggles of dark blonde hair around her pale, almost translucent face. And tired. She was always tired.

When Ida was older, her brothers and sisters recalled a different woman – one who smiled and laughed and had roses in her cheeks – but as the youngest child, unexpected and unwanted in her mother's fortieth year, Ida had never been privy to that side of her.

Ida gave another sharp tug on her mam's apron. She thought she might have fallen asleep standing up, her eyes open. She seemed to be lost in another world. A better world? Her mam's chapped red hands, though, carried on their work mechanically.

Again, Ida pulled on the dirty grey apron.

When Mrs Robson eventually looked down at her daughter, she simply stared at the scraggly, scruffy child staring up at her with her father's blue eyes.

'What yer after?' she asked, her attention back on the potatoes she was peeling.

Ida didn't know what she was 'after'. There was such a long list, she hardly knew where to start. Some food for one thing. Some clothes that were clean and not threadbare.

In the end, Ida decided on a cuddle and raised her arms in answer to her mam's question. Her heart lifted when a softness came into her mam's sad eyes and she smiled, albeit wearily, at her youngest child. But just as her mam was drying her hands on her apron, Ida heard the front door bang open and her father's heavy footsteps tramp along the hallway. And at that moment all hopes of a cuddle were quashed. Her father's arrival in their small terraced cottage a short walk from the Wearmouth Colliery equated to the arrival of royalty. Ida was nudged aside by her mam's rush to go to her husband and welcome him home, take his coat, ask how his day had been and then hurry back to the kitchen to make him a fresh brew.

Over the next hour, the rest of Ida's siblings arrived home, either from school or work, and Ida was lost in the melee and the fight for a cuppa, their tea, a place to sit or the use of the outside lavvy. Like a litter of pups, Ida was the runt, pushed out of the way, fighting to get back into the throes of the family, but generally failing.

Chapter Five

Saturday, 11 July 1953

Within seconds of Ida hitting the floor, Dr Wright was by her side, checking her pulse and gently lifting her head to see how badly she'd cracked it on the floor. He hated tiles and flagstones for exactly this reason.

Cora immediately started to move the guests away from the woman who, it would seem, was Angie and the children's mother. She'd seen a little blood on Ida Boulter's blonde hair and she immediately offered up a silent prayer, begging the good Lord, *Please, not again.*

Lloyd ushered Bertie, Jemima and Bonnie into the kitchen, along with the dogs, telling them they had to leave the good doctor in peace to tend to 'the woman'. It didn't seem right to refer to her as 'your mother'. He'd always viewed Angie as mother to all of the children – not just Bonnie.

Angie instinctively went to Ida's aid and crouched down next to her as Dr Wright pulled out a little bottle of smelling salts from his inside jacket pocket. He'd learnt over the years that it helped to have it to hand. Being the only doctor in the village, he was never really off duty. Unscrewing the top, he waved it under his patient's nose for a few seconds.

Angie let out a half cry when she saw her mother's eyelids flutter open and she started to try and sit up.

'Let's get her to bed,' Dr Wright said. 'She needs to rest, and I want to put a dressing on that head.'

As Angie took her mother's arm to help her up, the sleeve of Ida's chiffon blouse rode up, exposing a cluster of dark purple bruises. Angie wasn't the only one to spot them.

'Oh my God!' Marlene exclaimed.

Seeing the anger and hurt on her sister's face, Angie looked at Stanislaw, who immediately herded Marlene, Danny and Thomas down the corridor towards the kitchen. As he did so, the guests collected their bags and coats, each one telling Cora to call them if they could help in any way, knowing that the best way they could be of support at this moment was to leave the family to deal with its latest trauma. They, too, had seen the blood and, like Cora, had thought of Angie's first husband, Quentin Foxton-Clarke, who'd died tragically nearly four years ago when one of the horses at Cuthford Manor had reared in its stall after being spooked. There'd been talk that the manor was cursed after Quentin's death, which had been followed a little more than a year later by the fire that had nearly razed the place to the ground, but people had changed their minds over the last year and a half after seeing the success of its conversion into a small but exclusive country house hotel.

'Let us do the heavy lifting,' Clemmie ordered, nudging

Dr Wright out of the way a little too robustly and causing him to stagger as he stood up. Clemmie didn't notice as her full concentration was on Angie and her 'mam'. They both looked as white as sheets. She got hold of Ida's other arm. 'One, two, three—'

The two friends got Ida to her feet without too much trouble as she was by no means a big woman. They supported her as she slowly climbed the wide, carpeted staircase and then guided her along the corridor to the guest bedroom in the West Wing, where the family lived.

'So sorry,' Ida mumbled. 'Didn't mean to faint.' Her voice was slightly slurred and came out in a whisper.

'I don't think anyone *means* to faint,' Clemmie said, attempting to sound jocular. She too had seen the bruises and instantly felt anger towards the man who must have caused them.

After getting Ida into bed, Clemmie left, telling Angie she'd be downstairs in the lounge if needed. Angie smiled her thanks and fluffed up the pillows, getting her mother to sit up.

Luckily the hotel had a well-stocked first aid kit and Dr Wright was able to check Ida's temperature and clean and dress the wound on the back of her head.

'And some arnica might help those bruises, as well as any others you may have,' he said. There was not a trace of judgement in the doctor's tone; he was merely imparting practical advice.

After hearing Ida hadn't eaten much, Cora, who was hovering in the doorway, went back downstairs, returning ten minutes later with a tray of sandwiches and a cup of sugary tea.

'Right, let's leave Mrs Boulter to rest for now,' Dr Wright ordered. He then looked at his patient. 'I'll come back later and see you,' he told her, 'just to double-check all is as it should be.'

He turned his attention back to Angie and Cora, who he knew shared a closeness more akin to that of a mother and daughter. 'And don't hesitate to call me if you've any concerns. Keep an eye out for any signs of concussion, but my feeling is that Mrs Boulter will be as right as rain after a day or so of bed rest. Rest and recuperation should do the trick.'

After Angie saw Dr Wright to the door, the relief she felt at there being nothing seriously wrong with her mam was quickly followed by the resurgence of long-buried resentments.

Growing up in Dundas Street, whenever Angie had been happily playing with her friends outside, or, as she'd got older, going out with workmates or on a date, her mother had always seemed to put some chore or other upon her. Usually watching the children or getting the tea ready, or nipping to the shops for something or other.

Years might have passed, but today had proved that nothing had changed. Today had been about celebrating her wedding anniversary with Stanislaw and enjoying a much-needed weekend off. But, as was always the case whenever her mother was about, this had been brought to halt.

When Angie went back to see her mam, she knocked gently. As there was no answer, she opened the door a fraction, only to see that her mother was already fast asleep.

But instead of pulling the door to, Angie stayed there, looking at her mam for quite some time, a million and one thoughts racing around in her head.

Marlene took a drag on her cigarette and blew out a long stream of smoke into the air.

She was sitting in the tack room at the front of the converted barn together with Danny, Lucy and Thomas.

'Blow it away from the horses,' Danny told her, frowning.

Lucy was also wrinkling her nose and waving the latest copy of *Horse & Hound* about in an effort to disperse the smoke.

Marlene threw her brother a daggered look. 'My God, our errant mother has turned up and all you're bothered about are the bloody horses.' She took another drag, but this time she blew the smoke towards the open barn doors.

'Why do yer think she's suddenly turned up here?' Thomas asked. He knew more than most just how much anger and resentment Marlene felt towards her mam, who she had not seen hide nor hair of since she was a young child of just eight. Marlene didn't talk about her mam much, but when she did he could see and hear the hurt that had been buried so deep. Eight years had passed since her mam had run off with her bit on the side, but time had not lessened Marlene's rancour.

'Well, judging by those bruises on her arms, she's come running to us for help. Or a place to stay. Probably both,' Marlene said, taking a sip from the glass of champagne she'd refilled before coming out to the stables, declaring that she 'needed it for the shock'.

Lucy threw Danny a horrified look. 'Bruises?'

'Yes, she had some bad bruises on her arms,' he said, taking Lucy's hand and squeezing it. He knew how much any kind of mistreatment of either humans or animals affected her. Lucy was the most gentle-natured, kind-hearted person he'd ever met. 'But that's not to say some bloke's done it. Mam might have had a fall, or some kind of accident.'

'Poppycock!' Marlene said. 'They were the same ones she used to get when she and Dad argued.'

'Gosh, that's awful,' Lucy exclaimed, aghast. Her own mother and father were barely on friendly terms, but they only ever hurt each other with words.

'I wonder if it's that bloke, Carl?' Marlene ignored Lucy. There was nothing to dislike about the girl her brother was besotted with, but her wishy-washy ways didn't half get on her nerves. 'Or someone else she's shacked up with,' she said. 'I'm sure Carl wouldn't have hung around for long. Probably left her for a younger model years ago.'

'So, you haven't heard anything from your mother since she left you?' Lucy asked. Since she had met and fallen hopelessly in love with Danny, they'd got to know almost everything about one another. There was one person, though, Danny rarely mentioned – his 'mam'.

Marlene answered for her brother, first taking another puff on her cigarette. 'Not a dicky bird since she skedaddled off with lover boy Carl and dumped us lot on our Angie the day before she married Quentin. I'm surprised Angie didn't send her packing.'

'Yer mam did faint 'n bash her head. I don't think anyone with a heart could have chucked her out in the state she were in,' Thomas said.

Lucy looked at Marlene and then back to Thomas. If anyone else had said that, Marlene would have ripped their head off. But Thomas, she had learnt, was the only person who could challenge Marlene and get away with it. Probably because they had known each other for years.

'I suppose we'll just have to wait until tomorrow to find out why she's tipped up here,' Danny said, getting up and grabbing one of the saddles and a bridle.

Lucy grabbed her black velvet riding hat and crop and stood up.

'Or why she *claims* she's here,' Marlene said, finishing her champagne. 'I don't trust that woman as far as I could throw her. Anyone who can cheat on their husband like she did, and get away with it, must have lying down to an art.' Her last words were a little slurred.

Danny and Thomas exchanged glances. Marlene was clearly now quite tipsy. Danny cocked his head at his younger sister and Thomas nodded. He would keep an eye on her.

'Come on, let's take the hounds out for a walk.' Thomas nudged Marlene.

'See you later,' Lucy said as she made her way over to Dahlia, an elegant English thoroughbred whose black coat was so shiny it glistened.

'And try not to chew Thomas's ear off too much,' Danny shouted over his shoulder as he headed towards the stall of his favourite horse, a speckled grey gelding called Ghost.

'God, if ever there's a time to *chew someone's ear off*, it's now,' Marlene huffed as she stubbed out her cigarette.

Thomas chucked a ladle of water on the cigarette to make sure it didn't set the place alight. He'd listen to Marlene until the cows came home. He just wished he could tell her that he felt the same way about her as he knew she did about him. But it was impossible. A while back, Stanislaw had warned him to stay clear of Marlene – orders he knew had really come from Angie. And there was no way he could go against the wishes of his employer. Not if he wanted to keep his job. And he did. He couldn't imagine a more perfect place to work.

As they both made their way over to the kitchen to fetch the dogs, Thomas struggled to keep his feelings for Marlene under wraps. He knew, though, that he had to. It wasn't just the risk of losing his job that had him holding back from declaring his true feelings. Marlene might well be sweet on him now, but in time she'd want to be with someone who was of equal social standing – and, more importantly, rich.

Marlene had told him many times over that having spent the first eight years of her life in poverty, she intended to live the rest of her life like a queen. A very rich queen.

Recently she had declared she was going to be an actress. And a 'fabulously rich' one at that. Thomas knew that becoming a Hollywood star might be pie in the sky, but marrying someone who could give her a movie-star lifestyle was certainly achievable.

And money was something Thomas did not have. As the son of a poacher, he had never been rich. And never would be.

Chapter Six

After checking on Ida for the umpteenth time, Angie had gone to say goodnight to the younger ones and chat a little more about the impromptu visit of their mother – a mother they knew about, but of whom they had no real memory. She'd then gone out to see Danny in the stables, where she knew he'd be grooming the horses and listening to his little transistor radio. She'd asked him if he wanted to chat about their mam's sudden appearance, but he'd just shaken his head and mumbled that he was 'fine'. Angie knew not to push and had trooped back indoors to seek out Marlene. She'd found her in the study, chatting on the phone to her best friend, Belinda.

Angie mouthed 'Are you okay?' with a genuinely concerned look on her face, but was shooed away by her younger sister, who didn't stop to draw breath as she relayed how the party had been brought to a sudden end by her 'cow of a mother' turning up on the doorstep.

When Angie walked into the living room, where she knew Stanislaw, Lloyd, Cora and Clemmie to be, everyone stopped talking and looked at her expectantly.

Slumping down on the sofa next to her husband, who immediately pulled her close for a cuddle, Angie looked at the dogs lying in front of the marble fireplace. They didn't move from their prime position but lifted their heads and gave their adored mistress a doleful look, having sensed the change in her mood.

'Are the children all right? Or as all right as can be?' Cora asked.

'Yes and no,' Angie sighed. She kissed Stanislaw on the cheek, then leant forward and poured herself a cup of tea from the pot on the art deco glass table. The front reception room had been cleared of decorations and balloons. The day no longer felt celebratory.

'It's a lot for them to take on board,' Angie said, blowing on her tea. 'Jemima and Bertie seem intrigued, and dare I say it a little excited at having their mother suddenly appear out of nowhere.' She shook her head. 'I just wish she hadn't sprung herself on us like that. She should have written and told me. Then I'd have at least been able to chat to them all and prepare them.'

Stanislaw muttered his agreement. He was fighting hard to keep his thoughts to himself. He'd never understood how Ida could have abandoned her children on the eve of her daughter's wedding, especially as four of them were still so young. He knew Angie had taken on the role of her siblings' stand-in mother without a second's thought, and when he had talked to Angie about her husband's death, she had told him that in many ways her younger siblings, and of course her daughter, had been her salvation. Caring for them had forced her to claw her way out of her pit of grief and start living again. But, despite this, Stanislaw was still of the

33

opinion that his wife's mother had committed a terrible and unforgivable wrong by leaving her family.

'Would you have allowed her to come here if she'd written ahead?' Lloyd asked. The feeling he and Cora had shared was that Ida Boulter had been well and truly consigned to the past. Along with her husband, despite him living just ten miles away in Sunderland.

'I don't know,' Angie said. She thought for a moment. 'I'd have probably suggested we meet somewhere in town – or even that I would go to her – so we could leave if we wanted to. I don't reckon I'd have agreed for her to come here and stay.' She took a sip of tea; she felt parched. 'Anyway, she's here. And it looks like we haven't got any choice but to let her stay.'

They all murmured their agreement.

'And if I'm right in why I think my mam has just turned up unannounced and without any forewarning, it would not be a situation where she had time to write ahead and tell us she was coming for a visit.'

'The bruises . . .' Clemmie murmured.

'You think she's come here seeking sanctuary?' Lloyd asked.

Angie nodded. 'I do. I think it's obvious, don't you?' She looked askance at everyone.

'Possibly,' Cora said.

'Seems more than likely,' Stanislaw agreed.

They were all quiet for a moment.

Clemmie broke the silence. 'Did Bertie or Jemima recognise her?'

Angie shook her head. 'Jemima definitely didn't. Bertie said he thought he had a vague memory of her. But neither of them remember much about living with Mam and Dad in Dundas Street.' There was a time when Angie would have referred to the little terraced cottage in one of the poorest areas of Sunderland where she had been born and brought up as 'home', but not any more. Cuthford Manor was now very much her home. After Quentin died, she'd wanted to leave. But since Stanislaw had come into her life, and after the place had nearly been burned to cinders, she had realised that the saying was true: home is where the heart is – and her heart was here, with her daughter and siblings and the people with her in this room, who might not be blood but were most definitely her family.

'Bonnie, of course,' Angie relayed, 'was jumping up and down on the bed all excited at having a *grandmother* suddenly appear out of nowhere.' Everyone smiled. Bonnie was a ball of energy and endless inquisitiveness.

'That child is going to have such a warped vision of what a grandmother is like,' Lloyd said wryly.

'Isn't she just,' Angie agreed. 'She proudly tells anyone who asks that one of her grandmothers went AWOL before she was born, and her other grandmother is "locked up in a place for crazy people".'

Clemmie couldn't help chuckling. 'The funny thing is, if they're not from the area, they just think she's got a vivid imagination and is making it all up.' She had heard Bonnie tell some of the hotel guests, who had smiled at the sweet little girl who lived there, but clearly hadn't believed a word she'd said.

'If only that were the case,' Lloyd said, swirling his single malt around in his glass. Bonnie's grandmother, his former wife, had not only set the West Wing alight, but had also been responsible for killing Quentin, their only child, after orchestrating an 'accident' in the stables that had been meant for their daughter-in-law.

'Dare I ask how the two eldest took it?' Cora asked. She knew Danny and Marlene had gone out to the stables with Thomas, but hadn't seen much of them since.

Angie let out a long sigh.

'That good?' Clemmie said.

Stanislaw squeezed Angie's leg.

'Well, you know Danny. Silent night when it comes to anything to do with *feelings*. He's spent most of the afternoon out riding with the elusive Lucy.' Angie didn't keep the vexation she felt about Danny's unofficial girlfriend from her voice. She had tried to welcome the girl into the fold, but not once had Lucy attended any of the dos she'd been invited to. Angie had confessed to Stanislaw that it was her belief that Lucy's family thought it unbecoming to mix with the likes of a 'coal miner's daughter', which she knew was how many in the area still referred to her.

There had been a time when this would have infuriated Angie, but not any more. She just accepted the fact that England's social strata was, and always would be, multifaceted, which often went hand in hand with prejudice and snobbery. It was one of the reasons she loved Lloyd and Clemmie so much, as they had never shown even a drop of bias or discrimination. Either to her or to Stanislaw, a Polish refugee who had been unable to return to his homeland after Stalin had taken it over following the Second World War.

'It's Marlene I'm most concerned about,' Angie admitted. 'She's always felt a lot of bitterness towards Mam.'

'Which is understandable,' Cora said. 'From what you've said.'

'It is,' Angie agreed. 'And Mam turning up like this is going to make her worse still. Guaranteed.'

A few hours later, Angie was the last to turn in for the night, after checking on her mother one final time.

'Come here.' Stanislaw threw the covers to one side and beckoned Angie to bed. 'Your mother will be fine. And if she's not, it won't be your fault.' He tried to keep the hardness out of his voice. This woman had only been under their roof for a matter of hours and already she'd caused upset and angst. *And* had everyone running around looking after her.

Angie clambered into their double bed and snuggled up.

'I know. I just feel I need to check on her in case she has some kind of delayed reaction. It was quite a crack on the head.'

'I think if anything were to happen, it would have done so by now. Dr Wright doesn't seem overly concerned. And you're not going to be of any use to anyone tomorrow if you're walking around in a sleep-deprived haze.' He had a feeling that tomorrow would be busy, and that Angie would be needed and stretched thinly between the children.

Again, Stanislaw felt a surge of anger at Angie's mother, who was clearly morally bankrupt and totally self-centred, and was now expecting her daughter to come to her aid at the drop of a hat. Ida Boulter had done a good job of reversing the mother-daughter roles, and the pattern seemed set to continue.

'What are you thinking?' Stanislaw asked. He could only imagine what it must be like to have had an upbringing like Angie's. His own parents had been loving, kind and caring. Despite all the evil and human atrocities he had seen in the war, and during his time in a Siberian gulag, he was still stunned by the heartlessness and harshness of human behaviour, particularly when it came to children.

'I'm too exhausted to even think,' Angie said. She was quiet for a moment. 'I guess as long as the children are all right, then so am I.'

The truth was that since Angie and her siblings had all started their new life at Cuthford Manor, she'd been too busy to give much thought to her mam. There'd been idle moments when she'd wondered where Ida was and if she was still with Carl, but that was all. Angie knew more about her dad thanks to her old shipyard workmates, who kept her up to date with any news during their regular get-togethers. The last Angie had heard was that her father had given up the booze after meeting a Liverpudlian woman who, according to her friend Gloria, was 'a bit of a God-botherer'. God might have replaced the liquor in her dad's life, but there'd still not been any room left for his children.

Stanislaw kissed the top of Angie's head as he felt her fingers trace the raised scarring on his arm. He knew what she was thinking. Since the fire two years ago that had nearly killed the people she loved, life had been relatively smooth. There had been a happy, stable atmosphere.

Ida Boulter's arrival, though, Stanislaw was convinced, was going to cause ripples, if not waves. The period of calm they had all enjoyed since the trauma of the fire was about to come to an end.

Chapter Seven

Sunderland, County Durham

1911

As soon as Ida saw the elderly ticket lady turn in her seat to talk to one of the usherettes, she bobbed down so that she could not be seen and scurried into the Coronation Picture Palace. Ida was smaller and skinnier than most other eleven-year-olds and had her strategy of gaining free admittance to the local cinema down to a fine art.

For Ida, the single-storey building within spitting distance of the Wearmouth Colliery, and only five minutes' walk from her home, was where she was transported to another world. A world far different to the one she inhabited.

Tonight, Ida had been particularly determined to see a film called *Her Child's Honor* as it starred an actress called Florence Lawrence. Tiptoeing down the left side of the auditorium, Ida slipped into the first free place she could see, immediately sliding down so that her head was leaning on the back of the wooden seat. The cinema was dirty, and the air permanently infused with stale cigarette smoke, but Ida paid no heed. Instead, her senses were focused on the film and the sound of the piano, which was to the right of the screen and was being played by an old man who had the longest, boniest fingers Ida thought she'd ever seen.

The film was what was known as a 'short', but despite being just twenty minutes long, from the moment the projectionist cranked up the first reel, Ida was sucked into a world of make-believe.

Entranced, she watched the heroine run away from home, unable to bear the abuse of her drunken soldier husband. Ida could feel her own heart lift as the wife liberated herself and travelled to the city, to a better life. She took in every detail of each flickering scene and, by the time the credits rolled, the tears were snaking their way down her cheeks.

As she dawdled back to her home in Barclay Street, her tears dried and she began to imagine what it must be like to be a famous actress like Florence Lawrence. *What an exciting, glamorous life she must lead.*

Ida twirled and danced her way home, occasionally stopping and checking for trams before jumping into the middle of the tracks and turning to an imaginary audience.

'Thank you, thank you!' She waved her hand at her adoring fans. Catching an invisible bunch of flowers, she smelled them, copying the wide, coquettish smile and fluttering eyelashes of the film's heroine.

Reaching the turn into Barclay Street, Ida immediately stopped her theatrics and brought herself back to the real world.

She narrowed her eyes to look down the long line of terraced houses on the left-hand side of the street.

It was gone ten o'clock. The coast should be clear.

She could just make out her house. There was a street lamp directly opposite and the small circle of yellow light it emitted enabled her to make out her front door.

Ida started to walk tentatively down the street. Her uncle Evan had usually left by now, but it was always better to be safe than sorry.

On hearing his distinctive booming voice, Ida stopped dead in her tracks.

'Righty-ho! Night all!' He always sounded so cheery. Such a 'happy chap', she'd heard people say of him. But her mam's brother was not such a 'happy chap' with Ida, who in her head called him 'the snake'. A two-headed snake, like the one coming out of the wicker basket belonging to a flute-playing Indian in one of the films she'd seen.

Two heads because her Uncle Evan had two sides to him.

Ida pushed her small body up against the black wrought-iron railings outside one of the houses, not moving a muscle and barely breathing. She saw a glimpse of her uncle as he pulled the door to. When it shut, the smile dropped from his face, which was replaced by the one Ida knew. A dark, cruel face. He looked angry. Ida knew he'd be mad that she'd not been there and had once again managed to give him the slip.

She waited until he stepped out onto the pavement and walked away in the opposite direction, back to his own home within a stone's throw of J.L. Thompson's shipyard on the north dock of the Wear.

When Ida could no longer hear his footsteps on the

pavement, she breathed a sigh of relief and hurried the rest of the way home.

Walking through the front door, Ida made her way to the kitchen, passing her dad, who was nodding off in the armchair by the range. She didn't need to see the brown bottle of beer or the empty pint glass to know he'd been drinking as she could smell it, along with the distinct odour of coal and colliery. In the kitchen, she found her mother stooped over the sink. She gave Ida a cursory glance before carrying on washing the pots and pans, too tired even to acknowledge her daughter's presence with the effort of words. Ida looked to the adjoining utility room, where there was a pile of dirty laundry. Her mam had started to take in washing from the hotel down the road to try and earn a little more money to add to the pittance her husband gave her. The few coins he left on the mantlepiece every Friday after he'd been paid were enough to pay the rent man, but not enough to keep all the children her dad had sired from going hungry. The bulk of his wages was spent either down the pub or at the bookies. Ida's deep dislike of her father was exacerbated by his belief that it was his God-given right to be waited on hand and foot by her mam. She knew most of her friends' dads were the same, and that it was the way of the world, but that didn't mean Ida didn't still inwardly rail against the injustice.

After grabbing a glass of water and tearing off a hunk of bread and spreading it with beef dripping, Ida headed off to the back bedroom she shared with those siblings who still lived at home. Making sure she didn't drop a crumb for fear of attracting the rats from the butcher's next door, Ida said her usual prayer to the good Lord for her uncle Evan to die a long and painful death, or any death, for that matter, as long as it was soon. Then she let her mind drift to happier thoughts, replaying her favourite parts of the film she'd just watched.

Drifting off, the image of the runaway wife was replaced with an image of herself, escaping her home town and travelling to the city – to live a new, happy and carefree life.

Chapter Eight

The morning after Ida's arrival at Cuthford Manor, Angie knocked on the door of the guest bedroom with a tea tray and was surprised to hear a robust 'Come in!'

Opening the door, she was even more surprised to find her mother up and dressed.

'Dear me, Angie, you look terrible.' Ida squinted as her daughter entered the room with the tray. 'You always were prone to dark circles under your eyes when you were tired.'

Angie stared in disbelief at her mother, who, as Dr Wright had predicted, now seemed as right as rain.

'That'll be because I've been up all night worried about you,' Angie said, putting the tea tray on the little round wooden table in the middle of the room, which was more like a bedsit as it was large enough to accommodate a wardrobe, vanity dresser, a standalone sink unit and a double bed. She didn't know whether to feel relieved her mam was all right or angry that she was sat there large as life, telling her she looked awful.

As Angie poured the tea, adding milk and sugar, the way her mam liked it, she glanced down and saw that Ida's suitcase had not been unpacked. Again, she felt torn between two completely opposing emotions. Fear that her mam was going to go as quickly as she had come. And relief that her mam appeared to have no intention of staying.

'So, come on, Mam, put me out of my misery. Why now? Why, after not hearing a peep from you for years, have you suddenly graced us all with your presence?'

Ida took a sip of her tea. 'Ahh, you still make a good cuppa.'

Angie waited, her teeth clenched.

'Well,' Ida said, putting her cup back on the saucer. 'I wanted to see how you were all doing.'

Angie creased her brow. 'Really? Nothing, not a letter, phone call, visit, nothing for nearly a decade—'

'Eight years,' Ida corrected.

'Eight years and two months, if we're going to be exact,' Angie said. She'd done the maths while she'd lain awake most of the night. 'So, are you telling me that you just woke up one morning and thought, I wonder how my children are?'

Angie stared at her mam.

'And what about Liz? Have you any idea where your eldest child even is?'

Ida sighed. She had expected this reaction. Would probably have been more perturbed had Angie been any different. She'd always loved Angie's fire. She only wished she'd told her that when she was smaller.

'For your information, Liz is now in Australia,' Angie relayed. 'She emigrated there shortly after the war. She's getting on just fine, if you're interested. Happily married and doing well for herself.'

Ida wanted to tell Angie that she knew this, and more, as

46

she'd kept tabs on all her offspring since she'd left the north-east, thanks to her old friend Niamh O'Reilly. But she didn't. It wouldn't have made any difference to the hurt Angie and the rest of the children felt.

'I'd ask where you've been since you upped and left us,' Angie said. 'But I'm guessing you've been in London, because you sound like a cockney now.'

Ida bit back a retort that Angie and the children now sounded like they had blue blood running through their veins, rather than the blood of a coal miner and a factory worker, but held back. She needed to keep the conversation on track.

'Like I said, I really just wanted to see you all. See how you're all getting on.'

Angie gave her mother a look of pure scepticism. 'Come on, Mam, pull the other one, it's got bells on it.'

Ida knew this was going to be hard. She needed to be here a week at least – ideally more – to do what she had come here to do. There was no way she could let Angie chuck her out today. With hindsight, Ida wished that she'd played up the bash on her head more.

'Okay,' Angie said. 'I was thinking about this last night, in between checking up on you every hour.' She now felt resentful she'd sacrificed her sleep when there was nothing wrong with her mother other than something a good kip and a bit of food wouldn't remedy. 'I know you, Mam.' She looked down at her mother's arms, which were covered up. 'We all saw your bruises yesterday. You've obviously decided you've had enough of being used as a punchbag and thought you'd come here, knowing we'd have room and that it was far enough away from Carl – I'm guessing it *was* Carl you were living with?'

Ida nodded.

Angie continued. 'Far enough away from Carl for you to feel safe. There's no way he'd come here to find you. You're not stupid. You knew that. Just as you know that I'm a soft touch and I wouldn't be able to say no.' She looked at her mother. 'Am I right?'

It seemed an age before Ida spoke and when she did, she had tears in her eyes.

'Yes, Angie, you're right.'

It hurt Ida to say it, almost as much as it had hurt her to leave Carl, knowing she would never see him again.

Chapter Nine

'*Oh. My. God!*'

Angie smiled. Only her best friend Dorothy could make her chuckle like this in the direst of circumstances.

'So, she just turned up like Little Orphan Annie on your doorstep? In the throes of your wedding anniversary party?'

Angie felt guilty for waking up her friend at the crack of dawn. New York, where Dorothy now lived with her husband Bobby, was five hours behind.

'Sorry for calling so early, Dor, I just had to speak to you before we went out for a *family* walk with the dogs.' Angie shuffled in the leather swivel chair in the study where the phone was. She smiled again on hearing Dorothy's dramatic gasp of disbelief.

'Well, I never thought I'd hear those words said in relation to your mam. Ever,' she declared. Angie detected the hint of an American accent, which Dorothy had been fighting against as her English accent had people practically worshipping at her feet and she didn't want to lose it. Plus, her editor was keen to maintain Dorothy's 'Britishness' since it was fundamental to her very popular weekly column in the *New Yorker*.

'Yes, "family" and "walk" are not something you'd ever

expect to hear in relation to the Boulters – that's for sure,' Angie said. She was so glad she'd rung Dorothy. Her friend from her days doing war work at Thompson's shipyard in Sunderland was the only person who really knew – and had actually met – her mam. Even her other former workmates had never met Ida in the flesh, although they'd heard enough to form an opinion of her. An opinion that was only fractionally better than the one they had of Angie's dad.

'Blimey,' Dorothy said, her voice muffled as she lit up a cigarette. 'I'm still in shock here.'

Dorothy had been with Angie the day before her wedding to Quentin, when she'd been dragged back to Dundas Street after they'd clocked off from their shift at Thompson's. Angie had wanted to check on her mam as she was worried about how her dad would react when Ida told him about her bit on the side. But when they walked into the house, all they'd found were two old wage packets propped up on the mantelpiece – one addressed to Angie and one to her dad. Dorothy had watched the blood drain from her best friend's face as she'd pulled out a scrappy piece of paper and read the note from Ida. Dorothy couldn't believe that Angie's mam had done what she'd done – and on the day before her daughter's wedding too.

'Yep,' Angie whispered, as she didn't want anyone listening in to her conversation. 'We're going for a walk so Mam can get reacquainted with her children. She said it would be better than sitting in a room together in an awkward silence.'

Angie could hear her friend blowing out smoke.

'Well, she's certainly thought it through,' Dorothy said, an image of that afternoon eight years ago flashing to the forefront of her mind. The dirty faces of Angie's siblings staring up at them silently. Intuition telling them that something was badly wrong.

'And she doesn't want Danny or Marlene to go on this "family walk"?' Dorothy asked, recalling the beginnings of panic on the children's faces as it dawned on them their mam had done a bunk.

'She wants to chat to them separately,' Angie said.

'I'll say it again, *she really has thought this through*,' Dorothy said through pursed lips.

'A case of leaving the *worst* until last,' Angie said, checking her watch. It was nearly eleven.

'Makes sense – I can't see either Danny or Marlene giving her anywhere near a warm welcome,' Dorothy said. 'So, you reckon she jumped from the frying pan into the fire with this Carl bloke?'

'It would appear so,' Angie said, inwardly cringing when she recalled the dark purple bruises.

'How long you going to let her stay?' Dorothy asked. If it had been her, Ida Boulter wouldn't have made it over the threshold.

'I reckon a week will do it. Let her get back on her feet and find somewhere to live. Something tells me she doesn't want to go back to London.'

'Really?' The incredulity in Dorothy's voice was nothing to do with Ida not going back down south, but because of her best friend's charity in spite of everything her mam had done.

'Yeah, something tells me she's come back up north for good,' Angie mused.

Hearing the children clattering down the stairs, Angie told Dorothy she had to go.

Dorothy wanted to say so many things, but she only had time to tell Angie to call her whenever she needed. Day or night.

After putting down the phone and stubbing out her cigarette, Dorothy made a pot of fresh coffee.

That day – the day before Victory in Europe had officially been declared – would be forever etched into Dorothy's mind. She'd felt so sorry for Angie back then. Her best friend should have been whooping it up and enjoying her last day of being a single woman, but instead she'd spent it in a state of shock. She'd told Dorothy that she would never have imagined her mam leaving them all like that – and running off with her younger lover. Perhaps if the children had been all grown-up it would have been different, but they weren't. *Jemima was only two, for God's sake.* Thank goodness for Lily, the madam of a bordello, who ran her business discreetly from a beautiful four-storey terrace in the upmarket area of town. Lily had opened her home and her heart to the children. Danny, Marlene, Bertie and Jemima had been fed, watered and scrubbed clean by Lily, ready for their big sister's wedding the next day.

As Dorothy stared out of the window of her apartment onto the New York skyline, her focus came back to the present. This was the last thing Angie needed at the moment.

She had a young daughter to bring up, made especially tricky by Quentin dying when Bonnie was just a toddler. And she was also bringing up her four younger siblings and working full-time.

Angie had explained to Dorothy that the running of the Cuthford Country House Hotel had been divided up so that Lloyd concentrated on the accounts and finances, Cora oversaw the domestic staff, and Stanislaw managed the estate and those who worked it, which left Angie herself, as the actual owner and therefore the hotel's figurehead, to deal with the guests, making them feel welcome, ensuring they had what they needed, and if they hadn't, then sorting it out in a timely manner. No wonder her best friend didn't want to have any more children.

And now her selfish, good-for-nothing mother had turned up without notice seeking out her daughter's help.

Dorothy took a sip of black coffee. But there was a niggle at the back of her mind as to the reason for Ida's sudden reappearance. Ida had been one of the well-known 'Craven's Angels' working at the local ropery on the north side of the river. They were a familiar sight, walking to work in groups, laughing and joking and smoking like troopers, their hair always tied up in colourful headscarves and their language turning the air blue. Ida was a tough, strong-minded woman. If she had decided she'd had enough of Carl, Dorothy would have thought she'd have either booted him out or simply left. Just as she'd left Angie's dad.

And that was the other thing which didn't sit right. Dorothy had once caught a glimpse of Carl when she and Angie

53

had been walking back to Thompson's. They'd spotted Ida and Carl having a quick kiss before disappearing into one of the backyards along St Peter's View. First impressions could be wrong, but Carl just didn't look the violent type. He was young, slim, good-looking, with a mop of brown hair that flopped forward, giving him a rather bohemian look. He looked more poet than someone with a propensity for violence.

Dorothy reprimanded herself. Just because someone looked a certain way, it didn't mean they couldn't be a nasty bastard behind closed doors. But instinct told her otherwise. Besides, it sounded as though Ida had been seeing Carl a long time behind her husband's back before she'd eloped with him. Surely she would have got a hint that he might be free and easy with his hands?

Dorothy poured Bobby a cup of coffee, adding two sugars and a good splash of milk. She'd be interested to hear what he thought.

As she made her way to their bedroom, she shook her head again, thinking of the 'family walk'.

She still couldn't imagine Ida out striding through fields and climbing over stiles with her two younger children, granddaughter and a pair of dappy dogs, each the size of a mountain lioness.

Life was certainly full of surprises.

Chapter Ten

'Isn't it lovely here? It's like a painting.' Ida stopped for a moment and took a deep breath, admiring the miles of emerald-green and rapeseed-yellow patches of countryside that ended where the sky, clear but for a few wisps of clouds, began. She looked at Bertie, Jemima and Bonnie, who were walking next to her. They all nodded. Angie knew the children were always like this with strangers initially. *Strangers.* How awful that your own mother could be a stranger.

Angie was walking just a few steps behind. She wanted this time to be about Ida and the children. But she also wanted to observe her mother. She appeared to have changed a lot and Angie wasn't sure if it was genuine or if she was putting it on.

'The entire estate consists of forty-two acres,' Bertie chirped up as they continued walking, pushing his steel-rimmed spectacles up his nose. Angie knew it to be his tick when he was a little anxious or meeting someone for the first time. It might not be the first time Bertie had met his mam, but he'd told Angie that he'd 'given it much thought overnight' and he had no memories of 'the woman who had given birth' to him. The memories he thought he had were of Liz, which made sense, as Angie's older sister had been tasked with looking after the children when their mam was working.

'What's it like where *you* live?' Jemima asked, stumbling a little as her big blue eyes were fixed on her mother and not on watching where she was walking.

'Oh, very different from here,' Ida said. 'Buildings instead of fields. Concrete instead of grass. Cars and buses instead of horses and tractors. And the air . . . well, the air is awful.'

'In what way?' Bertie asked.

Angie saw Ida suppress a smile and knew why. Bertie spoke the Queen's English perfectly, and he was as inquisitive as he was intelligent.

'Well, London has what are known as *pea-soupers*.'

Jemima and Bonnie chuckled. Bertie's face told Ida he needed a more scientific explanation.

'It's a thick fog, but not like the sort you get here – this fog is caused by the smoke and soot from coal and other things which pollute the air. It can be quite dangerous for babies and old people and those with breathing problems. It's so thick, you can hardly see one foot in front of the other. Last December it was so bad it became known as the "Great Smog".'

Angie, who was just managing to overhear the conversation, could remember the newspapers reporting on it. Thousands of people had become ill or died.

'Sounds awful,' Bonnie said.

'We'll have to tell Marlene as she thinks London is *marvellous*,' Jemima said, impersonating her big sister. 'She reckons she belongs down there more than she does up here.'

'Does she?' Ida asked with interest.

'Not that she's even been there,' Bertie added. 'She just knows about it because she's always asking Clemmie.'

All of a sudden, Winston and Bessie came charging back through the long grass towards them. They headed straight for Ida, which surprised Angie. They also seemed to find her fascinating. When they had met her properly for the first time this morning, they hadn't stopped sniffing her. In the end, Angie had had to shoo them out into the yard to enable her mother to put on some boots Angie had found for her.

'They like you!' Bonnie laughed as she ran ahead and shouted for the dogs, trying to distract them. They were covering Ida in saliva and looked on the verge of flooring her.

As they continued their walk, Angie observed how Ida's concentration was one hundred per cent on the children. Watching them. Listening to them. Asking them questions when she got the chance. And answering the barrage of questions they had for her.

By the end of the walk, the children were laughing and joking and bouncing around – the dogs too.

Angie saw her mother's eyes were alight with wonder and pride. She had never seen her look at any of her children like that – ever.

It also made Angie view the children through a different lens and realise just how much they had all changed since their mam had last seen them.

As they all headed back to the house, Angie felt a confusion of emotions. She knew she should be pleased – relieved even – to see how happy the children were. Pleased that they were getting to know their mother. But part of her felt disappointed that they hadn't given Ida a harder time.

Then she thought of Marlene and Danny and felt guilty, as she knew without a shadow of a doubt that their initial meeting with their mother would not be in any way joyful.

Nor would they be as easy to win over as Bertie, Jemima and Bonnie.

After the walk, Ida told Angie she was going to have a little lie-down. The journey and the knock to her head had taken more out of her than she'd thought – but she'd be refreshed and looking forward to having dinner later with Angie, Danny and Marlene, as planned.

Angie first insisted she have something to eat, having been told by Dr Wright to make sure her mother had three meals a day. Angie also thought it a good idea because her mam was looking a bit thin, which she put down to the stress of leaving her abusive fella.

Cora took up a tray of sandwiches and a pot of tea for two, then stayed for a little while, chatting. The women were around the same age and both from working-class backgrounds. Before Cora had married Lloyd Foxton-Clarke, she had been the housekeeper of Cuthford Manor. The two women were wily enough to know what was really going on. Cora was checking her out. Ida would bet the little she had that after finishing her tea, Cora would go and report back to those closest to Angie – Stanislaw, Lloyd and the eccentric academic called Clemmie who seemed to half live there.

After Cora left, Ida lay on top of her bed. She was quite exhausted. But also extremely happy. The walk with the little ones had been wonderful. Better than she could ever have thought possible. Not only did they like her, they had also opened up to her. They had been themselves. Shown their true characters. And what amazing characters they were. *And how they had grown. How well they looked. How well they spoke. How educated they were.* She had wanted so much to give them all a hug when they'd finished the walk, but had held back. Too much too soon.

As Ida drifted off to sleep, she felt so proud of her children. Bertie was as bright as a button. You'd never think he was his father's child. Jemima seemed full of mischief and life. And her granddaughter Bonnie was like a bouncing ball. Quite tomboyish. Very like Angie at that age.

As sleep took hold, she forced herself to simply revel in the joy she felt.

She pushed back all thoughts of Carl, although it was hard.

Just as she also pushed back her anxiety about how Danny and Marlene would react when she saw them later at dinner.

'Tatham Inn, Pearl Lawson speaking.'

'Hi, Pearl, it's Angie here.'

'Alreet, hinny,' Pearl said, dropping back into her usual

59

strong north-east dialect once she realised she was speaking to Angie. 'How yer deeing?'

'I'm all right, Pearl, thanks. Do you mind getting a message to Polly and the rest of the gang, please?' The Tatham Inn was where Angie and all her shipyard workmates used to drink. It had continued to be the centre of their social world after the war and they still met there every few weeks for a good natter and catch-up.

'Course. I'm all ears,' Pearl said. Angie could hear her lighting up a cigarette. She didn't think she had ever seen Bel and Maisie's mam without either a smoke or a drink in her hand.

'Can you just tell them that I won't be able to make it tonight? I'll try and ring again later when they're all there to explain why.'

'You sure you're alreet? You sound a little – I dinnit knar – not yerself.'

Angie let out a slightly strangled laugh. 'Well, my mam's suddenly turned up out of the blue, that's why I'm not coming over.'

'Well, I never,' Pearl gasped. 'Nee wonder yer dinnit sound like yerself. I won't probe and ask yer the whys and wherefores of it all, but I'll tell Polly and the rest of yer mates when they're in later on.'

'Thanks, Pearl. Tell them I miss them.' It was at times like this that Angie really did miss her old workmates from Thompson's. Missed them being just around the doors for a quick chat.

'They're here fer yer if you need them, yer knar that, dinnit yer?'

'I do, Pearl. I do.'

Angie's former boss, Rosie, and her old workmates Polly, Gloria, Martha and Hannah had always been there for her, and Angie knew they always would be.

'So, Mam,' Marlene said as Angie started ladling out the shepherd's pie Alberta had cooked for supper, 'looks like you made quite an impression on your youngest son and daughter and your granddaughter during your walk today.'

Angie threw Marlene a warning look. She had made her sister promise to behave; their mam might well deserve whatever was thrown at her, but Angie didn't want any kind of a scene. Seeing Marlene's demeanour, though, Angie also realised that pigs might fly.

'Jemima and Bonnie came to see me to tell me all about it,' Marlene continued. 'Apparently, even the dogs were all over you.' She took her plate off Angie and ignored her warning look.

Angie handed Danny his plate. He mumbled 'Thanks' and immediately tucked in. Angie glowered at him. They always waited until everyone had been served. She didn't want their mother to think she hadn't brought them up to watch their manners. As soon as the thought went through her head, she felt like slapping herself. *Here she was, having brought up her mother's offspring, worried that it might appear she hadn't done a good job of it.*

Danny had promised Angie he'd have dinner but would not be sticking around to play 'happy families'. Angie had said she didn't think there would be any chance of that.

'Yes,' Ida said, smiling as Angie put down a plate in front of her. 'It was lovely. They seem happy.'

Marlene mumbled something that sounded like 'No thanks to you' as she took a drink from her glass of water.

'It was a nice walk,' Angie said, trying to add a degree of warmth to the atmosphere. 'Nice for the young ones to get to know their mam a little. And Bonnie. The nearest she's ever had to a grandmother was Mrs Kwiatkowski.'

'Your Polish neighbour from Foyle Street?' Ida asked.

'That's right,' Angie said, surprised her mam remembered. When Angie had left home and moved in with Dorothy during the war, her mam's only concern was that she'd lost her childcare.

'And what about Quentin's mother? I think Bonnie was going to tell me about her, but was shushed by Jemima.' Ida glanced at Marlene and Danny, who were looking to their older sister to answer.

'That's a long story,' Angie said. 'Perhaps for another time. Let's just say that Bonnie's other nana doesn't live in the area any more – but even before she left, she was never keen on spending any time with her granddaughter.'

Ida didn't let on, but she knew all about Bonnie's other grandmother, Mrs Evelyn Foxton-Clarke, who had unwittingly killed her own son, then tried to burn down this beautiful manor, and was now incarcerated in the notorious high-security Rampton hospital.

'So, Mam,' Marlene said after forcing down a mouthful of mince, 'Angie says you've come seeking sanctuary. That you've left Carl?'

Ida nodded, noticing her daughter staring at her arms, which she'd made sure were well covered up.

'So, what are you going to do? Angie says she's allowing you to stay here for a week, but after that you're on your own. Like we were on our own when you upped and left us.'

Angie sighed. Well, at least she'd managed to serve up before the first stone was thrown. She looked at Danny, who seemed to only have eyes for the food on his plate.

'I'm going to Whitby,' Ida said, taking the first verbal blow on the chin. She expected there to be plenty more.

'Not back to London?' Angie asked. So, her suspicions must have been right. Her mother had come back to the north-east to stay. Whitby was not a bad choice.

'No, definitely not back to London,' Ida said.

'How you gonna afford a place in Whitby?' Danny perked up. His dark eyes challenging his mother. 'You know there's no money to be had here. This place might be huge and make us look like we're loaded, but we're only just managing to stay afloat.'

Angie looked at her brother and gave him the faintest of smiles. Unlike Marlene, Danny really was 'all grown-up'. And with that maturity had come a fierce protectiveness towards those he loved. The Cuthford Country House Hotel was doing a little better than simply making ends meet, but Angie knew Danny was ensuring that their mam wasn't going to take a lend of her, as she'd always done in the past.

'I've not come here with my begging bowl,' Ida said, knowing that this was what they would surmise. 'I have my own money.' Ida was being intentionally economical with the truth; she wasn't going to tell them she only had enough to keep her going for a month or two. 'Enough about me,' she said, forcing herself to eat the shepherd's pie, which was delicious, but her appetite was non-existent. 'Tell me about yourselves. Danny, I hear you have your own riding school.'

Danny nodded in acknowledgement but didn't offer up any information.

Ida wanted to ask if he had met a girl, but she didn't want to push it. Bertie had mentioned someone called Lucy when he'd been telling her about Danny and his love of horses.

She also really wanted to ask Angie why she hadn't had a baby with Stanislaw yet. Her daughter and her new husband had been married a year. Angie had fallen with Bonnie not long after she'd got married, and she knew that Stanislaw's first wife had been pregnant, so she wouldn't have thought there'd be problems in that department.

Ida instead turned her attention to Marlene, who, she guessed, would probably have a few boyfriends on the go, along with a trail of admirers. Not only was Marlene a beautiful young woman with her blonde hair and blue-green eyes, she also had much of her father in her.

'Any idea what you might want to do after you leave school, Marlene?' Ida asked.

Angie looked at her younger sister – she too would love to know the answer to this question. Marlene had mentioned some airy-fairy idea of becoming an actress, but nothing serious. She'd decided to stay on for the sixth form, but Angie had a suspicion this was purely because her friend Belinda had. And because it meant she didn't have to get a job.

'Well, I've got it all worked out,' Marlene said, looking at her sister. 'And I know you think it's just some passing fad, Angie, but I'm dead set on becoming an actress. I've been looking into it and reading up on how stars like Marilyn Monroe started their careers and they were models first and that was how they got noticed. That's how they got into the movies. So, as soon as I've turned seventeen, I'm going to go down to London and get signed up to a modelling agency.'

Ida and Angie looked at Marlene, horrified. But for different reasons. Ida saw acting as the road to nowhere; Angie as a total waste of a top-notch, and very expensive, education.

The pair started to speak at the same time and stopped.

Danny scraped back his chair. 'I've got to go and check on the horses.'

Ida looked at her son. He seemed so serious, so quiet, so *angry*. Angry at her. She didn't blame him, but she wished he wasn't.

'Perhaps you can show me the stables in the morning?' she asked.

Danny looked at his mother. His expression giving nothing away.

'Yeah, sure. I'll be free at eleven.'

Not wanting to be left alone with her mother and Angie, Marlene also stood up and said she had to ring Belinda.

65

Chapter Eleven

Eventually the elderly ticket lady, Edna, told Ida that she was tired of pretending not to notice her sneaking into the cinema. She suggested that instead Ida should come and get a ticket like the other cinemagoers, only unlike them she would not have to pay. Ida didn't think she could love anyone quite as much as Edna – and the usherette, Rosalind, who she learnt was actually Edna's daughter.

And so the cinema became Ida's second home, providing her with an escape from her life – and from the two-headed snake that was her uncle.

Ida saw many more films over the next few years at the renamed Cora Picture House, but none of them affected her in quite the way that *Her Child's Honor* had. It had opened a door in her eleven-year-old mind, allowing many dreams and ideas to come and go – one of which remained steadfast. Like the wife in the film, Ida had resolved that she too would run away to the city. She would leave her home town, leave the misery of her home life, and escape to the capital.

She had since watched many films that had been set in London and had decided this was where she wanted to be.

After turning thirteen, Ida left school and started work. By now most of her other siblings, who were much older than Ida, had left home, but that didn't mean her mam wasn't still working herself to the bone, day in, day out. Besides taking in a mountain of laundry from a few local hoteliers, she'd also got a job as a cleaner in one of the posh houses in Roker, where the family of a shipyard owner lived.

It was around this time that Ida's prayers concerning her uncle Evan were, in part, answered. She was not granted the joy of watching him shuffle off this mortal coil in an agonising fashion, but he did move away from the region. It was all very hush-hush, but Ida wasn't too interested in the reasons. He was gone. That was all that mattered.

On her first day working at Craven's Ropery, Ida felt like skipping to the factory gates. This was the start of her new life. And, more so, the start of her being paid a wage, which would enable her to turn her dream of escaping into reality. She just had to save up enough money for the train fare to London and have enough to put down a deposit to rent a room. Enough money to keep herself going until she was able to find a job and support herself.

Some of her girlfriends just wanted to get married and have babies, but Ida did not. She couldn't understand why anyone would want to tie themselves down to a bloke and feel the constant pull of children on their apron strings. *Why would you want to spend your life living on the meagre scraps your husband gave you, and in deep dread of being in the family way – again?*

Her mother had fallen twice since Ida was born and had miscarried on both occasions. Ida often wondered if her mam had somehow caused the miscarriages as she seemed so relieved afterwards, despite becoming quite poorly due to the amount of blood she had lost. Ida had seen just how bad it was, for she had helped her mother scrub the wooden floors before her father returned.

No, Ida wanted to be like actresses Florence Lawrence or Mary Pickford – independent women. She had read about them in the newspaper and seen photographs of them as they attended yet another fancy do or got married again. Both women seemed to enjoy getting married.

But most of all, Ida vowed with every part of her being that she would never – not ever – follow in her mother's footsteps. She would never be a slave to a man, because that's how she saw her mother: at the beck and call of her husband and a skivvy in her own home.

Ida was grown-up enough to realise that she would probably not be able to become rich and famous like the Hollywood stars she adored, but she could move away and become something – anything – other than a replica of her mother.

Her wage at the ropery was meagre – she earned less than those over eighteen and her pay was further docked because she was female, despite working the same long hours and doing the same hard toil. But, again, Ida told herself that this was just the way of the world, and at least she was able to squirrel a little away every week after paying her mam and dad for board and lodgings.

It took almost a year for her to be within reach of her target amount. And with each month she became more and more excited.

But then, in June 1914, shortly after Ida had turned fourteen, Archduke Franz Ferdinand of Austria was assassinated – and his murder catapulted the country into war. A war that soon became known as the Great War – not that Ida saw anything great about it. She knew it was selfish to feel the way she did, especially when the local newspaper was filled with lists of those who had been killed in combat, but Ida was angry that the war had caused her plans to be put on hold. She'd been within touching distance of her dream, only to have it snatched away.

Ida might have been bitterly disappointed that her escape to the city had been thwarted, but she refused to give up. She would keep working, and keep earning, and then, as soon as the war was over, she'd be jumping on the first train headed for the city where the streets were paved in gold.

Chapter Twelve

Monday, 13 July 1953

The Cuthford Country House Hotel reopened its doors after the weekend break.

Lloyd, Cora and Stanislaw told Angie that they would manage the running of the hotel without her so that she could take the week off to concentrate on her mother's stay, or rather, to concentrate on the children and their reaction to having their mother suddenly plunged back into their lives.

They were all relieved to see that Bertie, Jemima and Bonnie seemed happy about Ida's impromptu visit. Angie knew that this was helped no end by it being the summer holidays, which tended to be a bit of a drag as it wasn't as though they had other children nearby they could play with, Cuthford Manor being a half a mile away from any other kind of civilisation. As a tutor at the university, Clemmie shared the same holidays as the children and normally tried to spend as much time as she could with them, but after Ida's arrival she had told Angie she was going to 'butt out' for the duration of their mam's stay so they could be together as a 'family', though she was persuaded to still come over and have her evening meal with them.

Ida was, therefore, the young ones' main attraction – particularly as she would only be there for the week. Ida couldn't have been more overjoyed and agreed to just about everything they suggested doing, which generally involved playing games inside, playing games outside, taking the dogs out, going to the sweet shop in the village, and listening to *Children's Hour* on the wireless at teatime.

Danny had shown his mother the stables and introduced her to all the horses as he'd promised, but after that he avoided her, which was easily done as the holidays meant that the riding school was booked up solid. On a few occasions, Ida had seen Lucy at the stables with her Black Beauty horse, but they hadn't been introduced.

Marlene was by far the unfriendliest, speaking down to Ida and getting in the odd jibe when they were having dinner. Ida tried to catch Marlene on her own so they could talk, but so far had been unsuccessful.

Angie was easier and could be drawn into a conversation, but she obviously had her guard up, and Ida did not know how to break through.

Lloyd and Stanislaw were polite and courteous, as was their way, but Ida could sense their judgement of her.

Cora, on the other hand, grabbed Ida for a cup of tea whenever the opportunity arose. She had given Ida the grand tour of the manor – both the East Wing, which was where the guests stayed, and the West Wing, which was for family and friends.

Apart from the children, Cora was the only one who was really getting to know Ida. She understood why everyone was keeping the woman at arm's length – it was unfathomable that a mother could run off and leave her children. Cora, however, was not one for judging others. She knew she herself had been judged by many as a 'gold digger' after becoming romantically involved with Lloyd and then marrying him. Rather than playing judge and jury on how someone conducted their life, Cora was more interested in what made people tick. She also felt it important to ascertain that Ida was friend not foe.

'I can't work Ida out,' Cora told Lloyd when they were getting ready for bed. 'My gut tells me she's genuine, but also that she's hiding something . . . She's a strange one.'

Lloyd made a huffing sound. 'Anyone who can desert their children like she's done has to be "strange". There's no other explanation.'

'Mmm,' Cora said, sitting down at her dressing table.

'What do you think she's hiding?' Lloyd asked, propping up his pillows.

'I'm not sure. But I'm going to find out,' Cora said, rubbing cream into her face.

'Is that why you've been spending time with her?' Lloyd asked.

'Partly.'

Cora screwed the top back on her pot of moisturiser. 'I reckon she's changed a lot since she left the family home – although having said that, she still seems like the hard and unsentimental woman Angie has described in the past.'

She picked up her brush from the top of the dresser.

'I was telling her how much trauma Angie had been through with Quentin's death and she didn't really empathise – far from it. Instead, she'd said that there were lots of women who'd had to deal with their husband dying, but that her daughter was a "toughie" and she'd been lucky to meet Stanislaw.'

'Dear me, no wonder Angie's a "toughie", being brought up by a mother with an attitude like that,' Lloyd said as he climbed into bed.

'Yes, but then in other ways she's very soft-hearted. You should see her when she talks about the little ones. Her face radiates joy. There's not the least bit of hardness there.'

Lloyd threw back the bedding and patted his wife's side of the bed.

'Unlike Danny and Marlene,' he said. 'I'm not seeing any joy there.'

'Mmm,' Cora agreed. 'Too much water under the bridge, I think.'

The next day, Thomas sacrificed his lunch break to give Marlene a riding lesson. She had told him that she had just read in *Picturegoer* magazine how some Hollywood starlet was a horse lover and had put her amazing figure down to being an avid rider all her life. The article had gone on to say that the actress's perfect posture had come from training to do dressage and circus tricks. Marlene had told Thomas that was what she wanted him to teach her. And so Thomas had forsaken his break and was presently eating his corned beef sandwich whilst shouting out instructions to Marlene as she rode Starling around the paddock.

'Head high, and gently squeeze with both thighs,' he instructed.

As Marlene trotted by, her back ramrod straight, her chin slightly tilted up, Thomas smiled. Marlene was the only person he'd seen arrive for a horse-riding lesson with bright red lipstick on. He knew Angie had cut her some slack this week and that Marlene was taking full advantage.

After the lesson, as they walked Starling around the ring to cool off, Thomas looked across at Marlene as she gently stroked Starling's face, muttering to her that she was a clever girl.

'You don't think it might be worth trying to talk to yer mam,' Thomas suggested. 'Get to know her a bit.'

Marlene rolled her eyes heavenward. Eyes that felt tired and looked a little bloodshot due to the sleepless nights she'd suffered since her mother's arrival.

'I do not understand why people appear to be on Mam's side.' There was anger in her voice. 'I think people forget that *she* left *us*. Not the other way around.'

'I know,' Thomas placated. 'But she's here now.'

'Yeah! Only because she's got nowhere else to go,' Marlene snapped back.

'Perhaps,' Thomas conceded.

As Marlene took off her cardigan, he had to avert his eyes from her low-cut top.

'But still, it might be good to at least try to get to know

her a bit while she's here. You were just eight when yer mam left. Yer will have both changed a lot.'

They stopped to let Starling graze for a moment and sat down on one of the bales of hay used as makeshift seats.

'A leopard never changes its spots,' Marlene said, tying the arms of the cardigan around her small waist and raising her face up to the clear, sunny sky. 'She might be trying to come across as all maternal with the little ones, but it doesn't wash with me. She's up to something. I can sense it.'

'What do you think she's up to?' Thomas asked. In his opinion, Ida seemed to be genuine. He'd watched her with the children and seen her play an extra game of hide-and-seek even though she'd looked like she was about to drop.

'I don't know, but I'll find out,' Marlene promised.

'Well, it might help to talk to her, if that's the case,' Thomas said.

Marlene tutted.

'Do yer think she'll go back to her bloke?' Thomas asked. 'My mam said out of all the women she'd known over the years who left husbands like this Carl bloke, they'd all gone back.'

'Well, if she does, she does. I don't care. Just as long as she doesn't stay here.'

'Surely you don't mean that.'

'I do.'

Thomas looked at Marlene. She liked to make out she was thick-skinned – that her years living with her mam and dad and brothers and sisters in Dundas Street had made her

75

hard – but she wasn't anywhere near as tough as she liked to think. She'd arrived at Cuthford Manor when she was eight years old, which meant that she had now spent half her life here, and it had softened her, whether she liked to admit it or not.

'Right, I'd better get on,' Thomas said, standing up and brushing hay off his jodhpurs.

If he stayed sitting next to Marlene for much longer, he didn't trust himself not to try and kiss her.

A temptation made worse by the fact he knew Marlene would not object.

Later on that day, when the last group lesson had finished and the horses had been fed, watered and groomed, Lucy rode over from Roeburn Hall on Dahlia to see Danny. Any visit to Cuthford Manor was always the highlight of her day.

After a walk interrupted by a number of pauses for embracing and kissing, the pair headed back to the barn and climbed the wooden steps up to what Danny called his 'digs'. Helped by Stanislaw and Thomas, he had converted what had once been the hayloft into a small living and sleeping area.

Since Ida's dramatic arrival at Cuthford Manor, Lucy had been encouraging Danny to open up and chat about his mother. It had not been easy. She'd even told him a little about her own family, hoping that by confiding in him how there was no love lost between herself and her own mother, he would follow suit. But that had only ended up with Danny asking questions about her family. And if she thought there was any chance he could meet them so that they could come clean about their courtship.

Just the thought of it made Lucy feel sick with nerves. She knew that day would come, just as she knew exactly what the reaction of her parents would be.

'You don't think it's worth spending a little bit of time with her?' Lucy asked, bringing the conversation back to Danny and his mam. 'She's only going to be here for another few days.'

'Not really,' Danny said as they both collapsed onto an old sofa that Danny had managed to drag up there with the help of groundsmen Ted and Eugene. 'I suppose I don't feel like I have any time for her cos she never had any time for us.'

'Didn't she work, though?' Lucy asked. None of the women in her family had ever worked.

'That didn't mean she couldn't also be a mam to us,' Danny said, pulling Lucy close and inhaling her perfume, which was infused with the smell of hay and horses. 'She dumped us on our Liz and Angie whenever she got the chance. And then dumped us with Angie permanently when she ran off with that Carl bloke.'

'And your father couldn't look after you?' Lucy asked. This was the most Danny had said about his life before he'd come to Cuthford Manor and she intended to make the most of it.

Danny let out a short, mirthless laugh. 'God, no. Our dad was the one that needed looking after . . . Now I'm older, I realise that Mam would have known Angie would never leave us with our dad. She likes to act hard-faced, but she's a big softie at heart.'

Lucy wasn't so sure about this, but kept quiet. Danny's older sister frightened her a little. Especially knowing she'd worked as a welder in a shipyard during the war. She'd also picked up that Angie didn't approve of their relationship, which struck Lucy as so ironic. Danny's family thought she was too well-to-do for him, and hers that Danny was too working class.

'Angie's been all right with your mam, though, hasn't she? She's been spending time with her?'

'Mmm,' Danny mused. 'I think that's just because of the little ones. Anyway, enough about my mam.' He gently tucked a strand of Lucy's blonde hair behind her ear and pulled her close, kissing her gently.

As always Lucy could not resist and kissed him back – just as gently and just as passionately.

Chapter Thirteen

On Thursday evening, Ida retired to her room early. She'd had a lovely day with the children, but she was exhausted. She also needed some time to think.

It had been agreed that she'd leave on Saturday, which meant her week was nearly up and she'd made absolutely no headway with either Marlene or Danny.

Ida sighed as she opened her sash window a little and closed her eyes, feeling the lovely warm evening breeze on her face. So different from the flat she'd shared with Carl, where the windows were rarely opened as the smells from the market and the neighbours' cooking could be overpowering. Ida again had to push thoughts of Carl away. God, how she missed him. She still couldn't quite comprehend that she would never see him again. But she knew she had done the right thing by leaving.

Settling herself in the armchair she had positioned so she could sit and look out at the stables and the rolling countryside beyond, Ida thought about how she was going to orchestrate sitting down with Marlene, Danny and Angie. As she watched the sun go down and her eyes started to feel heavy, she resolved to simply ask them to give her an hour of their time before she left.

As she imagined how it would feel to tell them what she wanted – needed – to impart, she again felt doubt gnawing away in her mind. She had never told another soul what she was about to share with her three eldest.

Was it definitely the right thing to do? Especially for Marlene? She was the youngest of the three and this would affect her the most.

She knew, though, in her heart of hearts that it *was* the right thing. Marlene could handle it. She was old enough. And she would have Angie and Danny to support her if she did take the news badly.

Why was it that the right thing to do was often the hardest and most painful?

When Ida woke the next day, though, her plans were scuppered. Her throat felt so sore it hurt even to swallow, and from her brow it was clear she had a temperature.

When Angie popped her head round the door to say her usual *good morning and did she want to join them for breakfast?* she was not surprised to see her mam looking so poorly.

'Bonnie's glands are up and she's got a temperature as well,' Angie said, sitting on the side of Ida's bed and putting her hand to her mam's sweaty forehead. 'Looks like she's passed it on to you . . . Fingers crossed you're the only ones to catch it. Everyone else seems to be feeling okay.'

Dr Wright was called and after giving the poorly patients a good checking over, he instructed them both to stay in bed, drink lots of fluids and try to eat little and often, and hopefully the 'lurgy', as the children were calling it, would be gone in a few days.

He told Angie that her mother might take a little longer to get back on her feet, and that he didn't like to intrude in familial affairs, but Ida had told him she was leaving on Saturday, which he thought was too soon for a full recovery. Angie's heart sank at Dr Wright's words. The thought of her mam staying with them for longer made her wilt. The constant mix of emotions her mam's presence was stirring up each and every day was draining. On top of which she felt guilty pushing her workload onto Cora, Lloyd and Stanislaw for yet another week.

When Angie told Ida that the doctor thought it best for her to stay longer, she saw relief on her mam's face, which made Angie even more convinced that she didn't actually have anywhere to go. Every time Angie had tried to find out more about where Ida was headed after she left Cuthford Manor, she'd been vague and had been quick to change the subject. Whitby might well be her chosen destination, but Angie suspected that her mam had not secured any kind of board or lodgings there.

Later that day, when she took her mam some of the cook's home-made chicken and vegetable soup, Angie caught another glimpse of her mother's bruises when the sleeves of her cotton nightie rode up. She was surprised that her bruises hadn't gone yet, or at least started to fade; arnica, she'd found, usually did the trick.

Glimpsing the bluish-purple bruises, Angie again felt a

mix of emotions. Anger that her mother had let someone do this to her – and sadness that her mother had spent her married life being treated badly by their dad, only to then spend another eight years enduring the same maltreatment.

Angie's whole being seemed to be in a state of conflicting emotions, as she explained to Stanislaw that evening over a cup of tea in the kitchen with the dogs.

'I feel angry at my mam and then sorry for her. I feel happy that the younger ones are enjoying Mam's company, then resentful as I don't think she deserves their appreciation. I feel sad Danny and Marlene won't be nice to her, then glad because it's what Mam deserves – then guilty for being so horrible and unforgiving.'

'Well, there's a lot to forgive,' Stanislaw said, trying hard to keep the judgement out of his voice. 'She *did* walk out on you all. Left her children in your care. She's been here nearly a week and she's not even said how sorry she is for leaving you all.'

'No, she hasn't, has she . . .' Angie mused, recalling that Dorothy had said the same when they'd spoken the other day. 'Perhaps she's *not* sorry . . .'

Stanislaw stopped himself from saying what he was thinking. *Well, she bloody well should be.* He had no doubt that his opinion of Ida was justified, but he had to admit that the anger and frustration he felt about her had been inflamed by her turning up at a time when he had decided to start tentatively broaching the subject with Angie of possibly having a child together.

Angie had claimed they didn't have time in their busy

82

lives for another addition to their family, but he wasn't convinced this was the case. Either way, he wanted to get to the bottom of it and find out why his wife seemed set against having a baby with him.

He'd initially thought that not having a child with Angie wouldn't bother him; that he could be content with just her and the children. He was, after all, as good as a father to Bonnie and to Angie's siblings. But as the months had passed, he couldn't shake the desire to have his own child. Was it some kind of innate primal urge to reproduce? Or because his unborn child all those years ago had not had the chance of a life? He wasn't sure. What he did know, though, was that Ida's arrival had put the mockers on any attempts to bring up the matter, certainly for the foreseeable. And it looked as though Angie's mam was going to be here a good while longer.

When Angie told everyone over breakfast that their mother was going to stay longer so that she could 'get back on her feet', Jemima and Bertie clapped their hands. Ida's room was only a few doors down from their bedrooms in the West Wing and they had started going to see her when she was there, usually armed with a pack of cards or one of their many board games.

'Do you think she'll be well enough to play Monopoly?' Bertie asked. This was his favourite as he was able to grill Ida about all the properties.

'Oh my God!' Marlene dramatically dropped her half-eaten slice of toast and marmalade onto her plate. 'Am I the only one who seems *not* to have amnesia?' She looked around the table at everyone. Out of the corner of her eye, she saw Alberta grab her tobacco and papers from the side and hurry quietly out of the kitchen.

'Our so-called mother did leave us all eight years ago!' Marlene exclaimed as she looked at the little ones. 'And even if you can't remember it, I've reminded you enough times of what she was like. *What she did.*'

Marlene glared at Danny for support, but he simply shrugged his shoulders. He hadn't forgotten. How could he? But his mother's return had not sparked any great feelings of love or loathing in him. Unlike his younger sister.

'We haven't forgotten,' Angie said, putting down her teacup. 'But I can hardly chuck her out when she's poorly.'

'Well, I don't see why not.' Marlene picked up her plate. 'I'm going into town to meet Belinda today,' she announced as she shuffled off the wooden bench and tossed her toast into the bin. 'We're going to the Globe.' The Globe was a cinema in Durham that had become Marlene and Belinda's latest haunt.

'As long as you're back for teatime,' Angie said. This time Marlene didn't mutter her usual retort of Angie not being her mother.

Marlene could have sweet-talked her way into sharing a car into town with a couple of the guests, but she couldn't face talking to them and putting on a happy face. So, instead, she got Thomas to take her into the village on his motorbike and then caught the bus to Durham. Within minutes, as she looked out of the window, she could feel her eyelids becoming heavy. Since her mother had turned up she'd hardly slept a wink. And when she *had* managed to fall asleep, she'd been plagued by dreams. Nightmares. Disjointed snapshots of her life before Cuthford Manor. A life which had been a living hell, not that her mother or her father were aware of it. Nobody had been, apart from Danny. Thank God she'd at least had her older brother watching her back.

Chapter Fourteen

Over the following week, as Ida got better, aided by a bottle of tonic Dr Wright had given her to help with anaemia, the anxiety she felt worsened. And once again she fell into the same internal dialogue of checking and cross-checking that what she was about to disclose to her elder children was right. That any harm or upset it might cause would be outweighed by the benefit of knowing.

On Thursday morning, two days before she was due to leave Cuthford Manor, Ida forced herself out of bed, got dressed and asked Angie if she could have a word with her and Marlene and Danny in private.

Because the front living room was now used by the hotel residents to sit and read the papers or to wait for Jake to chauffeur them to wherever they wanted to go, and was therefore presently full of chatter and cigarette smoke as the hotel was fully booked, Angie took Ida to what had become the 'family room' towards the rear of the house. It had originally been the music room, but as none of the children had shown any great yearning to learn instruments, it had been converted into a lounge, with a big comfy sofa and chairs. The floor-to-ceiling windows looked out onto the back of the manor, and were framed by long velvet curtains that served them well in the winter when the temperatures often dropped to freezing and strong winds created draughts.

Today, though, the sun was shining, and the large inglenook fireplace was filled with a floral display Mabel had created from the abundance of flowers growing in what Angie called 'the Italian gardens'. Bill the gardener had cultivated an amazing array of flora, which grew around the stone statues of men and women dressed in togas, which Quentin's late grandfather, Leonard Foxton-Clarke, had brought back from one of his many trips to Europe.

Angie and Ida were followed into the room by one of the maids carrying a tea tray, which she set down on the thick oak coffee table. The maid was a relatively new employee, a young girl from the village, and every time she came to this room, she couldn't take her eyes off the little television that stood on a nest of tables in the corner of the room and had recently been acquired by the family.

When the maid left, Angie started pouring their tea.

'Do you still keep in contact with anyone from Sunderland?' Ida asked, by way of breaking the silence.

Angie noticed that, like herself, her mam no longer called the place they had been born and raised 'home'. It was one of the very few things they had in common.

'Yes, all my workmates from Thompson's. I meet up with them every few weeks in the Tatham,' she said, handing her mother a cuppa. 'Dor's in America now with her fella, but we chat on the phone regularly.'

Ida nodded. 'I'm guessing they've all got families now?'

Angie gave her mother a look, wondering if this was her

way of getting onto the subject everyone seemed determined to bring up with her.

'Well, Rosie's not got any children, but I'm not sure she wants them. Hannah and Olly are thinking of adopting a brother and sister from Prague, and I think it'll only be a matter of time before Dorothy starts a family. Oh, and Polly's brood is growing and shows no sign of stopping,' Angie said. 'She's on to number six now. Still trying for a girl.'

'Five boys,' Ida shook her head. 'She'll have her work cut out there.'

Angie nodded.

'So . . .' Ida shuffled in her cushioned chair. 'I'm surprised *you've* not fallen yet?'

Angie took a sip of tea and put her cup back on the saucer.

'You might be even more surprised, Mam, to hear I might not *want* to fall.' Angie felt herself bristle. Her mam didn't have any right to ask her something so personal. But that was her mam. She might have changed a lot since Angie had seen her last, but she was still blunt and to the point. She'd never been one to mince her words.

'You *might* not want to fall or you *don't* want to fall?' Ida asked. She was genuinely interested.

Angie huffed. 'Why is it that as soon as you get married, everyone starts asking when you're going to start churning out babies?'

Ida laughed. She'd missed her daughter's spirit. 'That's always been the way. Always has and probably always will be.' She blew on her tea, which was in a very pretty rose-patterned china cup.

As Angie hadn't answered her question, Ida asked again. 'Seriously, though, do you not *want* to have children with Stanislaw? You've been married a year . . .'

Angie looked at her mother. 'Not that it's any of your business – or anyone else's . . . But, *no*, I don't want any more children. Not only have I got Bonnie, but thanks to you, I've also got four more, and as you can see, I have a hotel to run. I don't have *time* to have another child – or the energy.' When she finished what was becoming a set response, Angie felt annoyed that she had – yet again – fallen into the trap of feeling as though she had to explain herself.

'But what about Stanislaw? Doesn't he want to have a family with you? From what I've picked up, he's not got any of his own children, has he?'

Angie hesitated. Stanislaw had been married and his wife had been expecting at the start of the Second World War, but she had been killed – executed – by Soviet soldiers who had stormed their village in Poland.

She was saved from answering the question when Marlene and Danny's muffled voices could be heard as they walked down the corridor.

Angie heard Marlene snipe, 'What do you reckon she wants?'

Danny mumbled something that conveyed he had no idea.

As soon as they walked through the door, Angie said, 'Tea?' And without waiting for a reply, poured them each a cup.

'Remember, no sugar,' Marlene said, seeing that Angie was about to drop a lump in her cup.

Angie threw Ida a look. 'Your daughter has an obsession with having a twenty-inch waist.'

'Well, if you do, Marlene, you'll also lose your fulsome chest,' Ida said. 'When you lose weight, you can't dictate where it goes from – and sod's law it comes off the places you don't want.'

Marlene tutted, but Angie saw her mind ticking over.

'And from the photographs I see of these actresses in the papers, they have very shapely figures,' Ida added.

Marlene plonked herself down on the sofa, followed by Danny.

Angie handed them their tea.

'So, come on, Mam, why did you want to talk to us this afternoon? I'm taking a group out trekking soon and I need to get the horses ready,' Danny said, not trying to hide his feelings, or lack thereof, for his mother.

Ida felt the physical hurt of her son's rejection; not that she blamed him.

'I'll be going on Saturday ...' Ida began. Hurt now replaced by nerves.

'That's a relief,' Marlene mumbled under her breath.

'So,' Ida continued, pretending not to hear, 'I wanted to chat to you before I go. In private. Just the three of you.' She pushed away any residual doubts, telling herself that she had made her mind up. It was the right thing to do. Regardless of the fallout. And she had to do it now or it would be too late.

Just then, the dogs came bustling in as Marlene had left the kitchen door open. They headed straight for Ida and seemed intent on sniffing her, their tails just missing the tea tray.

'Come here,' Angie said, putting on her stern voice. She pointed to the rug by the hearth.

Winston and Bessie obeyed, glad not to be ordered back out. They slumped down, eyes fixed adoringly on Angie.

'So, Mam, what do you want to talk to us about?' Danny asked again, impatiently.

Ida looked at her three children, who weren't children any more, and suspected that what she had to say initially would not make much of an impact, but she needed to say it anyway.

'I wanted to tell you that I'm sorry.'

Marlene let out a harsh laugh. 'So sorry that it's taken you nearly two weeks to say it!'

Angie threw Marlene a look. They needed to let their mam speak.

Marlene ignored her. 'So what are you sorry for? There's a long list.'

Ida viewed her daughter. She was so like herself – very headstrong and outwardly self-assured – but she was also very like her father.

'I'm sorry for the way that I've been. For the kind of mother I've been to you all,' Ida said. Taking a deep breath, she continued. 'In the past I tried to tell myself I hadn't been *that* bad.' She paused and took stock of the fact that she had never beaten any of her children – just the occasional smack to keep them in check. 'But I've come to realise what has been more devastating for you was my inability to love and care for you as a mother should. I know that now, but back then I didn't.'

Or perhaps she'd simply refused to acknowledge it. Refused to face up to it.

'I worked all hours God sent – taking any extra shifts I could, which gave me the perfect excuse to push the care of the smaller children onto the eldest. Convincing myself that I needed to work, that we needed the money. Your dad's wages were not enough to keep us all fed and clothed with a roof over our heads. But deep down, even if I didn't have to work, I still would have. Anything to avoid being a mother.'

Anything to avoid being her mother.

'And I knew your dad rarely bothered with you all, which makes my behaviour even more unforgivable.'

No-one spoke. Angie waited, expecting her mam to follow up her diatribe of self-condemnation with an apology for leaving them all for her fancy man. And, having become his punchbag, realising that she'd made a terrible mistake.

But she didn't.

'I've learnt a lot during these past eight years – since I left you,' Ida said.

'*Left*? I think it was more than *leaving*. Abandoned us more like.' Marlene spat out the words. Her long-harboured resentment was finally able to reach its target.

'What did you learn, then?' Danny asked.

Ida looked from Angie to Marlene to Danny.

'I learnt – or perhaps it's more accurate to say that I finally faced up to the fact – that I have been a terrible mother.'

'God, Mam, you needed eight years in London with your Don Juan to work that one out?' Marlene's face was flushed with anger.

Ida wanted to say so much that she should never had had children, but she had to pick her words carefully.

'I was selfish,' she admitted. 'I should have looked after you all properly. Loved you all. I should have cared for you all. But I didn't.' She wanted so desperately to tell her story. To share with them her past and also to be honest about the present and what would happen in the near future – but this was not the time or place. It was unlikely there ever would be a right time.

'So,' Marlene said, narrowing her eyes. 'Why are you saying this now? What's caused you to have this sudden pang of conscience?'

'You're both at an important age,' Ida said, knowing that she could only tell Marlene the partial truth. 'I want you to know that I have recognised my mistakes and my failure as a mother, and want to make amends for that. At the very least give you an apology.'

Marlene glared at her mother. 'So you expect us to just forgive you for being an awful mam? For leaving us all the time with Liz or Angie, and then getting me to look after the little ones when I was barely able to look after myself? Do you expect us to forgive you for not making sure we were fed enough or washed and dressed properly?' Marlene was becoming increasingly worked up.

'Do you know that my life was hell at school because you couldn't be bothered to make sure I got a bath – or had clean clothes to wear?' Marlene put her finger to her mouth, as though thinking. 'Oh, no, that was because you were either too busy pandering to Dad's every need, at work with the other "angels", or off with your fancy piece!'

Ida remembered her own childhood torment. She felt wretched hearing that her own daughter's early years had been a near repeat of her own. *God, the guilt was overwhelming.*

'I'm so sorry,' Ida said. 'I truly am.' *More than you will ever know.*

'Well, sorry doesn't cut it, Mam. Sorry doesn't make up for the fact that, thanks to you, there was not one day I didn't get picked on at school. Every day, the same group of boys would tell me that I was dirty, smelly, ugly. They'd hold their noses when I passed. No-one wanted to sit next to me because I always had nits. They made my life a living hell.'

'Why didn't you tell me?' Ida asked, aghast. Suddenly all thoughts of what she had really wanted to say went out the window. She had not expected to hear this.

Angie was also shocked, wanted to ask the same questions, but held back; she and Danny had become bystanders.

'I didn't tell you, Mam, because you were never there!' Marlene's voice was raised. 'And obviously I didn't tell Dad. He made it quite clear to us all that he'd prefer it if we were neither seen nor heard.

'The thing is,' Marlene continued, her face flushed and her voice shaky, 'it wasn't just about being dirty and unkempt – it was about *you*.'

Ida looked surprised.

'Yes, *you*, Mam! My tormentors knew about you and

your "loose ways". So, you can imagine what ammunition that gave them. And they made it clear they believed it was a case of like mother, like daughter.' Marlene swallowed hard. The memories of that time replaying in her mind on a loop. 'I was only eight, Mam! Eight years old! I didn't even know what a "loose woman" was. But by God, they sure wanted to show me.'

Marlene wanted desperately to cry and cry. But she wouldn't let herself.

Angie was horrified. She looked across to Ida and saw a reflection of her own alarm.

Both went to comfort Marlene.

'Don't!' Marlene said. 'I don't want comforting now. It's too late.' She wiped away a tear that had escaped and was trickling down her face. She turned to Danny, who looked incredibly sad. He, too, hated going back to that time, and rarely did.

'If it wasn't for Danny, God only knows what would have happened. He was the only one there for me. Always watching out for me. Always chasing them off if he saw them coming for me. Always getting into fights for me.' Marlene smiled at her older brother, her expression one of both love and sorrow.

'So, Mam, you can see why you *saying* sorry now doesn't even touch the surface.'

Marlene got up.

Ida opened her mouth but didn't know what to say. Instead, she merely watched her daughter walk out of the room.

Nothing about their chat had gone as expected. She had been so focused on what she wanted to disclose to them that she had failed to anticipate how talking about the past, apologising for her behaviour, would reopen so many old wounds.

It was going to make finally telling Marlene the truth so much harder.

Chapter Fifteen

As most of the guests staying in the hotel that night had decided to eat out in Durham or at the Farmer's Arms in the village, Angie, Stanislaw, Lloyd, Cora and Clemmie had their evening meal in the dining room. Ida had asked if she could just have a bowl of soup in her room as she felt exhausted and was hoping for an early night.

After Mabel had brought in their plates of pork chops, mixed vegetables and new potatoes, Angie relayed how, as a child, Marlene had been targeted by a gang of older lads at her school – and how she'd been lucky that Danny had kept an eye on his younger sister and had made sure the bullying and name-calling hadn't been taken to another unmentionable level.

Clemmie put down her knife and fork. Solid silver cutlery clattered against the bone-china plates. There was very little that quelled her appetite, but hearing about Marlene's vulnerability as a child had not just put her off her food, it had made her feel quite queasy.

'This is shocking. Truly shocking!' she exclaimed.

Everyone murmured their agreement.

'And you don't think they ever got to her when Danny wasn't there?' Stanislaw asked, jaw clenched.

'That's what I was wondering,' Lloyd said, taking Cora's hand and squeezing it. His low tone was evidence of his own ire, just as his wife's stillness told him she, too, was seething.

'Well,' Angie said, 'she *said* they didn't.' She thought for a moment. 'To be honest, I did wonder that myself – whether she would have said if they had succeeded in doing what they wanted, but my gut instinct is that they didn't. She looked at Danny with such intense gratitude. I really think he managed to keep them at bay.'

'You think so?' Clemmie asked, needing reassurance for her own peace of mind. Since she had been in a relationship with Barbara, whose life was dedicated to the fight for women's rights, she'd heard such terrible stories about the sexual exploitation and abuse of women. She couldn't bear to think of Marlene – a mere child – suffering in this way.

'Yes, I do,' Angie said. 'The one thing our dad taught Danny – as the eldest boy – was how to throw a punch. Danny's always been able to look after himself from when he was knee-high. After one playground scuffle with him, I'm sure those boys wouldn't have wanted a second round.'

'Thank goodness you brought them all here,' Cora said, taking a sip of her wine. She too had given up on eating.

Angie looked around the table at her husband, her friend, and the two people who had become like parents – and who she knew viewed herself and her siblings as their own flesh and blood.

'Come on, try and eat something,' she said, cutting into her pork chop. 'Mabel will be distraught if we leave our food. And I'll have to convince her that it's not her cooking that's at fault.'

As they forced themselves to eat, Angie told them that before Marlene's disclosure, Ida had apologised to them for being a 'terrible mam'.

'She said she was "selfish", and that she should have looked after us properly. Loved and cared for us.'

'Well, I suppose that's something,' Cora said. 'She's admitted her failings. It sounds like she wants to make amends.'

'I think she does,' Angie said. 'Although the cynical part of me wonders if she'd have said anything at all had she not needed somewhere to stay.'

'I'm sure she could have found sanctuary elsewhere,' Cora countered. She was still convinced that Ida was keeping something from them all. And she was determined to find out what it was.

Angie felt unusually rankled by Cora because she seemed to be going out of her way to spend time with Ida. And the little snatches of conversation Angie had overheard between the two indicated that they seemed to get on. Angie might be putting up with her mother's presence, but she didn't want anyone else making her feel at home.

'I'm guessing that apology was also for leaving you all?' Lloyd asked.

Angie shook her head. 'No. I'm still waiting for that one.'

'Now that Marlene has told us about the bullying she suffered . . .' Clemmie mused, sitting back and pushing her plate away; unlike Angie, she was not worried about Mabel's feelings, '. . . so much about her makes more sense.'

99

'In what way?' Stanislaw asked. Marlene had always caused Angie the most angst, even more so of late as her behaviour was becoming more unpredictable. Angie was sure her younger sister was drinking alcohol whenever she got the chance, and had started to smoke, although Marlene thought no-one knew. And she seemed to enjoy dumping her boyfriends more than actually dating them.

'Well, she's always so pristine,' Clemmie answered. 'I don't think in all the time I've known her I've ever seen her with a speck of dirt on her – which is quite some feat, living out in the country, and with two pony-sized dogs forever leaving their drool on anyone who goes near them.'

'You're right there,' Angie agreed. 'When we first arrived here, she was obsessed with having baths. She'd only ever get out when the water had gone cold. I put it down to the novelty of an indoor bathroom.' She paused for a moment as more memories of that time came to the fore. 'And she went through an obsessive stage of making me check her hair for nits too.'

'Her love of fashion and make-up also makes sense,' Clemmie continued.

'And her wanting to be a glamorous actress,' Angie tipped in.

'Exactly,' Clemmie agreed. 'She's like a peacock with its feathers out. *All the time*. If I was Freud or Jung, I'd say she's trying to adjust the balance for all the years she spent wearing second-hand rags. And wants constant attention and adulation to make up for the neglect she suffered.'

Angie nodded her agreement, not that she knew much

about psychological theories, but what her friend said made sense.

Like Clemmie, Angie gave up on her food and put her knife and fork down on her plate.

'And perhaps it's why she never seemed to mind when we used to joke about her being the "offspring of some air-head toff",' she said.

'Because she loves the thought of being different,' Cora mused.

They were all quiet for a moment.

'When did this awful victimisation start?' Lloyd asked.

'I asked Danny and he thinks it was about a year or so before we moved here,' Angie said. She'd asked her brother more about that time, but it had been like getting blood out of a stone. 'So, Marlene would have been about seven.'

'So young,' Cora said, speaking everyone else's thoughts.

Later, when they were in bed, Stanislaw gave Angie a cuddle.

'And how are *you* feeling?' he asked. Sometimes he felt as though his wife was so concerned with everyone else's feelings she forgot to consider her own.

'Oh, I don't know,' Angie sighed. She ran her hand through his short, light brown hair. 'I suppose I should feel angry with Mam. What she did was hard on us all. We had to grow up quickly. My older sister Liz was tasked with bringing me up, and then when I was old enough, I helped her bring up the younger ones. But I didn't think anything of it. I suppose when you're young, you don't know any different. But I didn't get bullied like our Marlene.' Angie snuggled up closer. She felt his skin on her own. 'I just wish I'd realised how vulnerable the younger ones really were.'

'And you don't think you were also vulnerable?' Stanislaw asked.

'Not really,' Angie answered honestly. 'Looking back, I think Mam got worse after I started work. And after the war started, Dad began to drink more, which meant he was either down the pub, or if he was home, he was two sheets to the wind or asleep.'

'And you don't feel resentful towards your mama?' Stanislaw asked. There were still some words he said in his home tongue. 'Or your dad, for that matter?'

'I suppose I did in the past. Not a lot, but a bit. When I was younger, Mam wanted me to babysit or do chores instead of going out to play, and when I was older, she always seemed to need me to do something or other when I wanted to hit the town with my mates. But it didn't eat me up,' Angie said. She paused for a moment. 'To be truthful, I haven't given much thought to how I was brought up. To how we've all been brought up. Until now.'

'And now,' Stanislaw asked, 'what do you think?'

Angie sighed. 'I don't think I'd say I feel resentful. Probably just a bit hard towards Mam. I'm also wondering why she feels the need to apologise to us all now.'

She thought for a moment, wondering whether to be honest about what was dominating her feelings.

'I think,' she said eventually, 'more than anything, after hearing what happened to Marlene, I feel guilty.'

Stanislaw shifted a little so he could see his wife's face. 'Why would you feel guilty?'

'Because,' Angie said sadly, 'I also abandoned them – I moved out and it was after that point that Marlene started to get bullied. She'd have told me if I'd stayed at home. If I hadn't got a flat with Dor. And when I left, I only went back once a week. On a Sunday. I'd see the young ones, make a meal and give Mam and Dad some of my wages. If I'd stayed at home, or at least been around more, I'd have known what was going on.'

'They weren't your responsibility,' Stanislaw said, turning Angie's face so that she would look at him, see the veracity of his words.

'But they *were*,' Angie said. 'Oh, I know, in a perfect world they were Mam and Dad's responsibility, but our world was far from perfect and Liz and I were responsible for them. And when Liz left to join the lumberjills in Scotland, they became *my* responsibility.'

Angie swallowed her emotions and looked away.

'I knew what Mam and Dad were like, but I swanned off regardless, whooped it up with Dor. My joy at moving out – my own liberation – came at their expense. At the expense of their welfare, safety and happiness. It's clear Marlene's life became unbearable after I moved out – she got lumped with the little ones at home and hounded by those sadistic boys at school.'

Angie shifted around so that she was facing Stanislaw. She knew that sometimes he found it hard to understand her family, as his own upbringing had been so different.

'The funny thing was, when Mam left and Quentin and I agreed to take care of them and bring them back here, it was a relief.'

'A relief?' Stanislaw was genuinely puzzled. 'I can't imagine many brides being *relieved* when their mother went AWOL the day before they were due to get married.'

'I know, it sounds strange,' Angie said, 'but I'd been feeling increasingly worried – and guilty – in the run-up to the wedding. Whenever I saw them all, they seemed to be scruffier – skinnier. Dor thought so too. And I know Quentin was shocked.' Angie turned so that she was lying on her back, looking up at the ceiling. 'We'd resolved to keep an eye on them, but I'd been feeling more and more uneasy about leaving them and going off to live in a big house with a rich husband. So, when Mam left, in a funny way the guilt went, because Quentin and I decided that they'd come with us.'

'He was a good man,' Stanislaw said. He'd never met Quentin, who had died many months before Stanislaw had come to work at Cuthford Manor, but he felt he knew the type of man he was. Lloyd also often talked about his son, and whenever anyone else mentioned Quentin, they always did so with a smile on their face. He had been much loved. And from what Stanislaw had been told, he'd been deserving of that love.

Angie smiled, recalling the looks on her siblings' faces when they had turned up at Lily's flamboyant house in the posh part of Sunderland the night before Angie's wedding. They'd been agog at the magnificence of the place and entranced by Lily, with her auburn-coloured hair and her two 'girls', Maisie and Vivian, who looked as though they had just stepped out of the silver screen.

Angie turned over and cuddled up to Stanislaw, trying to keep the vision of their awestruck faces in her mind. But as soon as she started to relax, the image of Marlene as a small child, being taunted and picked on, returned.

Her younger sister might have escaped a horrific ordeal at the hands of the older boys, but she had still been traumatised by the bullying she'd endured – and even more by the fear of what had been threatened.

Chapter Sixteen

1914–1936

Ida told herself, as most people in the country did, that the war would soon be at an end. But they were wrong and the war went on and on. Everyone had to do their bit. And so Ida continued working at the ropery. Later in life, she often wondered, if the First War hadn't happened, would her life have been different?

Two years into the war, aged sixteen and having worked her way up in the factory to be a splicer, Ida fell madly in love, as only those who know little of the world do. The object of her infatuation was a miner called Fred Boulter.

Ida had literally bumped into him on her way home from the Cora Picture House, having seen Mary Pickford in a romantic comedy called *Hulda from Holland*.

Fred had been coming out of the Wheatsheaf Inn and was chatting to some of his friends, not looking where he was going. He'd sent Ida flying and gone to help her up and apologise.

As soon as she clapped eyes on this tall, dark and hand-some stranger who had literally bowled her over, Ida was smitten, comparing him to the Hollywood actor Max Linder with his dark hair swept back from his face. The only difference being that Fred was a little broader and did not have a moustache – that would come later.

Ida reflected in years to come that when she met Fred, she'd become interested in boys at a time when most of the town's young men were off at war, with the ones left working either down the pits or in the shipyards.

Fred talked often about his resentment at not being 'allowed' to serve his country because he was in a 'reserved occupation', which Ida consoled him about.

In many ways, Ida was very grown-up and independent for her age – she'd had to be, she'd practically brought herself up – but in other ways, she was naive and innocent. Until she met Fred, she'd never had a boyfriend or been kissed. What her uncle Evan had done to her did not count.

In her vision of the world, Ida saw that there were two diametrically opposing views of what love was: the kind of 'love' she had seen at home between her mam and dad, and the romantic love she had seen played out at the picture house.

And Ida knew exactly which one she wanted to find for herself.

The feelings she had for Fred were, she was sure, just like those she had seen projected onto the cloth screen at the Cora – and which she and Edna and Rosalind had all swooned over and chatted about endlessly.

Ida would have her happy-ever-after ending. Fred was her first love and he would be her only love. Of that, she was certain.

She still went to the pictures, of course, most of the time taking Fred, who she introduced to Edna and Rosalind. And for the first time, Ida paid, or rather Fred did.

Ida told Fred all about her dreams of moving to London when the war ended. 'We can be free spirits,' she said one night when he was walking her back to Barclay Street. 'Doing what we want. Beholden to no-one.' Ida believed Fred when he told her that he also wanted to leave their home town and embark on an adventure down south. Just like he said he enjoyed the films Ida dragged him to see.

What he should have said was that he enjoyed the make-believe of Ida's plans for a new post-war life in the country's capital.

After they had been courting for some time, Fred, who was three years older than Ida, coerced her into making love, promising that she could not get pregnant; he would do it in such a way that she'd be fine. And like the young fool she was, Ida believed him. She trusted him. He was her forever love.

Ida would never forget the feeling of horror when she missed her first period.

By the time she'd missed the second, she knew she was pregnant. Her body was changing. Something her mother had also noticed.

'Yer've got yerself in the family way, haven't yer,' she said, viewing her daughter with sorrowful eyes.

Ida tried everything to cause a miscarriage – but nothing worked.

When she realised her baby wasn't going anywhere and

seemed determined to be born, she married Fred just a few weeks before the end of the war. Six months later, Ida gave birth to a daughter, Elizabeth, in May 1919 – a time Ida couldn't help thinking was meant to have marked the start of their new life in London.

But Ida was not without hope, as Fred continued the pretence that they would move down south when the country had found its feet after the war and their baby was a little older.

It wasn't until she was older that Ida realised Fred had never really shared her dream, but had just gone along with everything she said. She also realised with bitterness that she had been trapped into marriage. Fred had known exactly what he was doing and had taken advantage of her youth and naivety.

Shortly after Liz was born, Ida's mam died. She was found on the floor of the kitchen, next to the sink. The doctor said she'd had a heart attack. Ida knew different. Her mam had died because she'd had enough of her life of drudgery. The irony of her death next to the sink in the small kitchen where she must have spent most of her life did not escape Ida. Nor did it surprise her when, a year later, her father married again. He needed a replacement skivvy and had found a woman foolish enough to agree to take on the role. Ida did not go to the wedding, and the little contact she'd had with her father up till then came to an end.

By the time Ida's second child, another daughter, Angela, came along in 1922, Ida tried to tell herself that they could still move to London. Fred was continuing to go along with the charade that this was their plan. 'We just need to save up a little more money,' he'd tell her. His argument being that they would need a financial buffer as it would likely take him a while to find a new job down there.

But over the next few years the country dropped into a recession, which saw unemployment rise sky-high, with many collieries and shipyards closing. A move to London was out of the question. As Fred often told her, they were lucky he had a job and worked at the north-east's biggest colliery; there were no concerns about it being shut down – unlike many of the smaller pits in the county.

When the Great Depression hit in 1930 Ida realised her dream was just that. It was never going to happen. She often wondered if this was why she felt so unmaternal. She went through the motions with Liz and Angie, but as soon as they were old enough to go to school, she went back to her old job at the ropery. She desperately tried not to fall pregnant again, which was difficult as she had learnt early on in their marriage that when Fred wanted to take her to bed, she went. It was her duty as a wife.

Generally, though, she managed to create dramas or distractions when she knew it was the time of the month that she was most likely to fall. Over the years she fell pregnant twice, but miscarried on both occasions, for which she was eternally grateful, although she never admitted as much. Both times she remembered her mother and the relief she had seen on her face after she had also miscarried. The parallel frightened Ida, as did the parallels she was starting to see between her own marriage and that of her mam and dad. The only difference being that Ida was not as down-trodden as her mother and dared to set her lip to her husband. Their shouting matches would have the neighbours banging on the walls. Ida was not one to back down, but knew when to stop. Fred had a heavy hand. His slaps across the head or face felt more like punches. And when he grabbed her around the wrists or arms, he left his mark. He was a strong man and had become even more muscular over the years as his work down the pit demanded.

When Ida fell pregnant a fifth time in 1934, she again hoped and prayed for another miscarriage, but this time she went full term and much to Fred's joy she gave birth to a boy, Daniel, the following year.

His arrival though, brought no joy to Ida. Instead, she felt the tentacles that seemed to have slowly wrapped themselves around her over the years tighten. Even worse than the demise of her dream was realising that her life had become the one she had always vehemently promised herself she would never have. Her life had become a duplicate of her mother's. She had stepped right into her shoes.

Ida often thought of the film she'd seen when she was a child. She had become the wife acted by Florence Lawrence, married to a man who cared only about himself and having a drink; although, unlike the film's main character, Ida had children. Running away to the city was easier when you only had yourself to think of.

More disturbingly, though, Fred had become the mirror image of her own father. He did his shift at the Wearmouth Colliery, then went to the pub for a few pints before returning home, where he expected a meal to be ready. He shared very little of his wages with Ida and paid his three children little heed.

Ida's only escape was to the cinema or the theatre with Niamh, her friend from work.

She told herself that at least this was something her own mam *hadn't* done.

Chapter Seventeen

Friday, 22 July 1953

Ida woke the day after her 'chat' with Angie, Danny and Marlene. A chat that had not gone as she'd hoped or planned. After hearing about her daughter's trauma at the hands of the school bullies, it would have been too much to carry on with what she'd wanted to say in that moment. Marlene had been too upset and angry.

As Ida got up, washed and put on her clothes, she did so with a growing sense of dread. She would have to do it today or not at all. She was due to leave tomorrow. It was now or never.

After Ida had forced down a light breakfast in her room, the little ones came in to see her and Ida plaited both the girls' hair and listened to Bertie telling her all about a book he was reading called *Casino Royale*.

Steeling herself, she sent the children off to see Bill, who was planting some vegetables, and went down to find Angie in the study to ask if she could have another chat with her, Danny and Marlene. She wanted Angie and Danny there to support their sister.

'I just need to speak to them properly before I go,' Ida said, trying to hide her anxiety.

Angie agreed. Not for her mother's sake, but for her brother's and sister's. She did not want their mam leaving a cloud over everyone's heads. And since their 'chat' yesterday, a thunderstorm had appeared. Angie presumed Ida wanted to smooth the waters before her departure. She certainly hoped so. Although sometimes it was hard to second-guess her.

As long as she didn't cause any more upset.

Bribery persuaded her two siblings to see their mam after lunch in the family room. Danny had been given the green light to purchase another pony for the stables, and Marlene was allowed to go to Newcastle with Belinda to buy herself a new outfit.

Angie was already sitting with Ida when Marlene and Danny reluctantly entered the room.

'I'll be gone soon,' Ida said to Marlene, seeing the look on her face.

'When?' Marlene demanded. 'You were only meant to be staying a week and here you still are – two weeks later.'

Angie threw her sister a look, which she ignored.

'I'll be leaving tomorrow. I promise,' Ida said, fighting back the intense pain her words caused her. The pain of leaving her children once again. And this time for good.

Marlene emitted a slight huffing sound.

'So, what is it you wanted to tell us?' Danny asked. 'I thought you'd got everything off your chest already.'

Ida looked at her three children. She really had no idea

114

how they were going to react, but was preparing herself for the worst-case scenario.

'Not everything, I'm afraid. There's something else I need to tell you.' Ida turned her attention to Marlene.

'Actually, it's something I need to tell *you*, Marlene.'

Angie and Danny turned to look at their sister.

'Me?' Marlene's expression turned from surly to surprised.

Ida nodded and shuffled forward in her seat in an attempt to lessen the gap between herself and her daughter. Marlene instinctively leant back.

'What have you got to tell me?' Marlene suddenly felt suspicious.

Ida hesitated.

'God, Mam, just spit it out!' Danny demanded. He was not normally an impatient person, but his mother had a way of instantly making him feel irritable and restless.

Angie looked at her mam, but couldn't read her at all. She used to able to, but not any more.

'There's no easy way to say this,' Ida began, 'so I'll just spit it out . . .'

Another hesitation.

'Well, go on, Mam,' Marlene gasped.

Ida took a deep intake of breath.

'Your dad isn't your dad,' she said simply.

Marlene's face creased up.

'What do you mean, *my dad isn't my dad*?' Marlene asked. Granted, she had never felt she'd really had a dad – particularly since they'd been at Cuthford Manor. But still, she couldn't believe what she was hearing.

Ida took another breath.

'I had a brief affair with another man. And I fell pregnant with you,' she explained matter-of-factly.

There was a stunned silence.

Ida felt three pairs of eyes staring at her in disbelief.

Angie looked at Marlene, then at her mam. 'And you're sure about this?'

Ida nodded. 'I am.' *How she wished she wasn't.*

'So, who is he?' Marlene asked, her excitement growing.

Ida had thought long and hard about how she would answer this inevitable question, and had decided in the end to be as truthful as possible.

'His name is – or rather, *was* – James Midgley.'

'He's dead?' Marlene asked.

Ida nodded, hoping she looked convincing and that the flush on her cheeks was not as obvious as it felt. Unlike Marlene's real dad, she was not very good at lying.

'So who was he? Did he know about me?' Marlene asked, her head spinning with questions. The past twenty-four hours had been an overwhelming emotional rollercoaster.

Ida shook her head. 'No, he doesn't – didn't – know about you. By the time I realised I was pregnant, he'd left town.'

'So, he didn't live in Sunderland?' Marlene asked.

Ida shook her head. She glanced at a shocked-looking Angie and Danny.

'So, where *did* he live?' Marlene asked.

Ida was surprised her daughter seemed more intrigued than angry. Perhaps she shouldn't have been so surprised.

Fred had really been a father to Marlene and their other children in name only. From the start of their marriage, he'd made it quite clear to Ida that children were the woman's responsibility.

'He lived in London, I think,' Ida answered. 'Although he travelled around a bit.'

'Why? Was he a Gypsy?' Marlene asked, thinking of the Travellers Danny had bought some of his horses from.

'No,' said Ida. This part would be easier, because it was the truth. And it was why she was telling Marlene. She was a young woman now and Ida wanted her to have a sense of her own identity. Of where she'd come from. Of the man who had helped create her.

And also because if she didn't tell her now, she never would.

'He was an entertainer. An actor,' Ida said.

'An actor!' Marlene's eyes were wide with incredulity.

'Yes, but not like one of these actors you see in the films. He acted on the stage. In theatres.'

'An *actor*,' Marlene repeated, her excitement growing. *It was in her blood.*

'Well, more of a stage actor,' Ida said. 'He liked to say he was a *thespian*.'

Marlene nodded. Of course. Everything was falling into place. It felt as though she'd found the missing piece of the jigsaw. *This was why she had always felt a little different to her siblings.*

'And he really didn't know about me?' Marlene asked again.

Ida shook her head.

'So, he didn't know I existed?' Marlene reiterated.

'No, but—' Ida stopped herself. She didn't want to tell her daughter outright that James Midgley would not be interested in knowing if he had a daughter. Ida was sure that he had other illegitimate children the length and breadth of the country, about whom he had no desire to know either. Ida had learnt too late that James was a no-good philanderer.

'But what?' Marlene asked. She glanced at Angie and Danny, who had become spectators in this real-life theatre.

'But . . .' Ida struggled to find the right words '. . . I don't think he was the kind of man who was interested in having children.'

'You don't think he had a right to know about his own daughter?' Marlene asked, now feeling resentful that her mother had not given her the chance to meet him when he was in the land of the living.

Ida looked up at her daughter. 'Marlene, it was a brief affair. He was in a variety show playing at the Empire. He charmed me. I was flattered. But when he left, that was it. Even if I'd wanted to tell him, I'd have had no idea how to find him.'

Marlene turned to Angie and Danny, who were still looking shell-shocked, and then back to her mother.

'God, I wish I could have met him,' Marlene said with longing.

Ida had thought her daughter would be angry and upset

118

because she was illegitimate, because those awful boys at her school had been right – her mam was a 'loose woman'.

'And he's definitely dead?' Marlene asked again.

'Yes, I'm afraid he is – I found out after I'd moved to London,' Ida confirmed. 'His lifestyle wasn't a particularly healthy one. He smoked like a trooper and drank like a fish. Even back then I could see he wasn't one to make old bones.'

She flashed a look at Angie, wondering if she could see through her deception.

'I just wanted you to know, Marlene, in case you ever felt different to your siblings. I just wanted you to know the truth.' Ida paused to pick her words carefully. 'I wanted you to know – especially seeing how you are now, so full of life, so glamorous, so gregarious – that you are very like him in many ways.'

Marlene felt a swell of joy at her mother's words. That was how she liked to be perceived – 'gregarious' and 'glamorous'. God, she tried hard enough.

For the next hour, Marlene grilled her mother about her father.

In what ways did she look like him? Did she have a photograph? Ida didn't. If she did, she would have burned it by now. Not that she told Marlene that.

What was he like in the show she saw? Ida said he was very good. She didn't say that she didn't think he'd ever be in line for any awards, his employability being due more to his handsome looks and charisma. Ida felt pleasantly surprised, though, by how well Marlene had taken the news. All the nerves and worries she'd felt about telling her had been unfounded.

When she had drained her mother of every last detail she could recall about her father, Marlene got up and looked at Angie. Before she had a chance to ask, Angie told her that, yes, she could ring Belinda, but she didn't think it would be a good idea to be telling 'all and sundry' about what she'd just found out.

Marlene rolled her eyes at Angie.

'Of course, I won't! Belinda and I keep each other's secrets.'

After Danny had followed Marlene out, leaving Ida and Angie on their own, there was an uneasy silence.

Angie looked daggers at her mother. She wasn't sure if she was angrier about the effect this might have on Marlene or because something like this was just what she'd feared – her mam dropping a bombshell and leaving Angie to sort out the mess.

'Do you think that was a good idea?' she asked, the edge in her voice razor-sharp. 'Marlene's already going off the rails as it is. This is going to make things much worse.'

Ida sighed. 'I just felt she needed to know. She needs to know that Fred is not her father.'

'But why now?' Angie asked.

'She's old enough to know,' Ida said. 'She's practically a woman.'

'She's still young and mixed up for her age,' Angie bit back. 'She's had a different life to me – and you. Marlene's

120

still at school. We'd been working for three years by the time we were her age.'

Angie gave her mother a slightly puzzled look. Something didn't sit right.

'So, the reason you've told Marlene now – after all these years – is because you think she's *come of age*?' she queried.

Ida nodded but didn't say anything. There was no way she could tell her daughter the truth.

Angie gave her mother a frosty look. 'You might have pulled the wool over Marlene's eyes, but you haven't fooled me.'

'About what?' Ida asked, suddenly afraid that Angie had rumbled her other secret. The one she was most definitely not going to disclose.

'About the fact that this James Midgley bloke is not six feet under, but alive and kicking.' Angie sighed. 'You're a terrible liar, Mam. It was written all over your face. I'm surprised Marlene didn't pick it up. God knows how you managed to keep your affair with Carl under wraps.'

Ida sighed, relieved it was just Angie who had realised she was lying.

'Keeping Carl from your dad was easy,' she said, sitting back in her chair. 'All he was bothered about was himself. Being fed. Having enough money for his beer. And being listened to if he was in the mood to chat.'

Angie had to agree. Her father was too wrapped up in himself to consider anyone else. Let alone notice anything about anyone else.

'So, why did you lie?' Angie asked. 'If you felt the urge to tell Marlene the truth, why not tell the whole truth? Why not tell her that he's still alive?'

Ida shuffled in her chair.

'If there was the remotest chance that James would want to meet Marlene, I'd have told her. But I know for certain he would not be interested. He'd probably deny it, for starters.' Ida had felt such a fool when she'd realised that all his sweet-talking, fancy words and loving ways were as much an act as the persona he was playing on stage. She'd learnt the hard way on the final day of the show, when she'd gone to see him.

'I didn't want Marlene going off in search of him and, if she found him, being devastated that he wasn't interested in her being his daughter.' Ida looked with sadness at Angie. 'Your sister more than anyone has suffered because of me. And because of your father. He's not been much better. He's not even been in contact since you all came here, has he?'

Angie nodded. She'd written to him and invited him to visit or for them to all go and see him, but he'd never replied.

'I didn't want Marlene to suffer more rejection,' Ida said.

Angie was quiet. She could understand her mother's reasoning, but she still felt Ida shouldn't have told Marlene this at all. That all she'd managed to do was prod an already buzzing hornets' nest.

'So, how do you know he's still alive?' Angie asked.

'About a month or so ago, I saw his face on a poster advertising a show he was in at some theatre in Soho. He's calling himself Jacques Kaplan now, but it was definitely him.'

*

After ringing Belinda and being told to call back in ten minutes, Marlene sat thinking about her father.

Her father who was an *actor*. James Midgley. She wondered if there was any way that she could get a picture of him. See what he looked like. See how much she looked like him.

Did she have the same eyes? The same nose? Mouth?

Feeling her wrist for her gold bracelet, a habit she had developed whenever she was nervous or excited, Marlene sat up straight and looked around her on the floor and on the desk by the phone.

'Bugger,' she murmured to herself. She needed to get the clasp fixed. This was the second time it had come loose. At least she knew where it would be. She'd been fiddling with it when she was sitting on the sofa, listening to the news about her real father.

An actor who had performed at the Empire.

Getting up from the leather chair, she left the study. She smiled at a couple of guests, who she presumed from their attire were going out hunting, and straightened her shoulders. It was childish, she knew, but she wanted to say, *Do you know my father was an actor?* Obviously, she didn't, but her smile was wide and full of confidence and stayed with her as she headed back to the family room.

As she approached, she could hear her mam and Angie talking. She'd have thought they would be gone by now. Angie might have been civil to their mam these past few weeks, but they were hardly at that stage of sitting and having cosy chats together.

She tiptoed along the corridor and stood next to the door, which was slightly ajar.

They were talking quietly.

Marlene caught something about being rejected. Was her mam talking about herself? Why would she be surprised they all rejected her? At least she knew what it felt like.

'So, how do you know he's still alive?' Angie asked.

Marlene froze. *Still alive? Was she talking about her father?*

She stood stock-still, hardly daring to breathe in case she missed a word.

Oh my God! He's still alive! My real father is still alive! The words screamed in her head. Her heart was thumping so loudly she struggled to hear Angie's response. Something about it being 'a good thing she'd lied' otherwise 'Marlene wouldn't rest until she found him'.

Tiptoeing away, Marlene's breathing returned to normal only when she was back in the main hallway, which was busy with people coming and going. Not that Marlene was aware. She was oblivious to everyone and everything around her.

She hurried up the stairs to the West Wing, the words of her sister looping in her head – *she wouldn't rest until she found him.*

She marched into her bedroom.

'Too right I won't rest!' she declared.

Chapter Eighteen

1936

Ida and her friend Niamh became regulars at the various cinemas and theatres around the town, although there was one place Ida couldn't bear to go to – the Cora Picture House. It had been renamed and revamped since Ida was a child, but it still brought back too many memories of the dreams and aspirations she'd had that had come to nothing.

As winter turned into spring posters started to go up in town, advertising a special variety performance by 'The West End Theatre Company'.

'Tell him yer've a late shift,' Niamh told Ida one day at work. 'Get Liz or your Angie to mind yer little 'un. Tere's no way we can miss this one.'

Ida agreed. It had, after all, been weeks since she had done anything but work at the factory, then go home to cook and clean and pander to Fred's every whim and look after the children. At least Liz and Angie didn't need looking after now they both had jobs themselves.

'All right, I'll go,' Ida said. 'Will yer be able to get us tickets?'

'Is ta Pope not a Catholic,' Niamh laughed.

And so that Friday night, the two women met up in the Dun Cow pub next door to the Empire for a drink before the show.

'Look at the state of yer?' Niamh said, grabbing their drinks and marching Ida to the toilets.

'I couldn't do myself up,' Ida explained, 'for fear one of the nebby neighbours saw me 'n said something to Fred.'

Niamh was thankful her own husband was not in any way like her friend's old man. Her bloke was far from perfect and loved his drink a little too much, but he had no objections to her going out on an evening. Especially as it put his wife in such a good mood. Whenever she got back after a show, they'd pack the children off before heading to bed themselves.

'Beautiful!' Niamh declared after Ida had put on some lipstick, mascara and a dab of rouge. Her friend was indeed an attractive woman. 'Yer'll have all the men chasing yer!'

'Behave!' Ida scolded. 'One is more than enough.'

'Well, if they want yer, they'll have to get to the front!' Niamh couldn't contain her excitement any longer. She waved two tickets that were for the middle of the third row.

Half an hour later, the two women were in their seats and watching the huge red velvet curtains being drawn to either side of the stage.

'Welcome to the show, ladies and gentlemen!' the handsome compère announced, his eyes sparkling in the spotlights as he gave his audience a theatrical bow.

His eyes scanned the gods, then the circle and finally the stalls.

Ida caught her breath as his attention focused on her for the briefest moment, but it was enough for her to feel a flush – part embarrassment, part excitement. Niamh nudged her. 'Told yer you'd have all the men after yer.'

Ida tutted, but over the next two hours she was transfixed, not by the acts but by the very debonair compère. His blond hair, piercing blue eyes, wide smile and white teeth made him look more like a movie star than a master of ceremonies, although the jokes he told between acts and his confidence and storytelling while the stage was rearranged for the next performance were just as captivating.

When the curtain finally came down, Ida and Niamh were in seventh heaven, although for different reasons.

'Doesn't it make yer feel full of the joys of spring,' Niamh said as they made their way out, shuffling slowly up the aisle behind those they'd been sitting in front of.

Ida smiled, though her thoughts were not on the joys of the season but on the man who had made a point of surreptitiously catching her eye whenever he'd had the chance.

When they finally made it out of the front entrance and down the steps, they were amongst the last to leave. They had just started to make their way down High Street West when they heard a now familiar voice shout out.

'*Excuse me!*'

They automatically turned and saw the compère, now changed and in civvy clothing, jogging towards them.

'I'm sorry,' he said breathlessly, drawing to a halt. He looked at Ida as though she were a goddess sent from above.

'I couldn't help but notice you—'

Ida thought his eyes even more blue and sparkling than when he'd been on stage; his face even more handsome up close.

'—you both!' he corrected, finally tearing his eyes away from Ida to look at her friend. 'I hope you don't feel that this is an imposition, but I could see how much you enjoyed the show and I wondered, as it is such a beautiful building, if you would like to come and have an after-show drink with me and the rest of the performers. It's our first night. We always have a little knees-up to mark the start of the show's run.'

Before either of them had a chance to reply, he suddenly hit his head with the palm of his hand. 'God, I'm such an idiot! I haven't even introduced myself. I'm James. James Midgley.' He stretched out his hand.

'Ida – and this is Niamh.' As soon as Ida felt his warm hand on hers, she sensed her entire body tingle in a way it never had before. Not even when she had first met Fred.

Hearing the slow grind of one of the corporation buses making its way up the slight incline of the High Street, both women turned.

'You stay, Ida!' Niamh said. 'Go to the party! Enjoy!'

And before Ida had a chance to argue, her friend had hurried off, making it to the bus stop just in time to catch her transport home.

'Well,' James said, putting out his arm for Ida to take hold of, 'I do believe you don't have a choice.'

For the next hour, Ida felt as though she herself was in a movie. Everything was more colourful, more exuberant, more fun than anything in real life. James was charming, the antithesis of the man she had spent the past eighteen years with. He was attentive and courteous, introducing her to the rest of the performers as though *she* were the real star of the show. He gave her a glass of champagne, which Ida sipped slowly, relishing every drop.

When James saw her looking at her watch, he begged her to stay just another few minutes.

Taking her by the hand, he made her close her eyes as he led her down a corridor. Ida heard the click of a switch and the swish of heavy material, followed by the faintest breeze on her flushed cheeks.

When they came to a stop, James whispered in her ear, 'Now, open those gorgeous eyes of yours.'

Ida had never been told her eyes were gorgeous. Nor had she felt such a gentle touch as James continued to envelop her hand in his.

She let out a gasp when she saw where James had brought her.

She was standing in the middle of the stage. The lights had been switched on so that she was able to see the beauty of the empty auditorium. The plush red and gold cords. The intricate cream plasterwork on the ceiling and walls.

'It's beautiful,' she said.

James took both hands in his and turned her slightly so that she was now facing him and not the auditorium. 'No, *you* are beautiful.' And before Ida had a chance to respond or bat away the compliment, he kissed her. Gently at first. And then more passionately.

And Ida didn't stop him. She was no longer in the here and now, but in another, more wonderful world.

Ida remained in that surreal world over the next four weeks while the show played up to the Easter break.

Every night she would meet James when the curtain went down, entering the theatre by the stage door at the side of the building.

As soon as she stepped over the threshold, James would be there to envelop her in his arms, drawing her away from reality and transporting her into the world of make-believe.

Ida saw those weeks as a gift she had unexpectedly been given. A gift of love and laughter. Of a kind of lovemaking she had never experienced before. She felt that they were truly making love. *She* certainly was. And she believed James was too.

As they lay in bed afterwards, James smoking a cigarette, his arm around Ida, still holding her close, as though loath to let her go, they would talk about the future. James had declared himself to have fallen truly, madly and deeply in love with Ida. To be incapable of being parted from her for more than a night.

In turn, Ida told him of her dream to move to London – that initially it had been to escape the unhappiness of her childhood, but more recently to escape the unhappiness of her marriage.

'Run away with me!' James said.

At first, Ida had taken his words as folly. But the more he implored her, the more she believed him. 'You must follow your heart. Your dreams!' he declared.

And so Ida's long-buried visions of a new life started to take shape once again. *She could take Danny, and Liz and Angie could come if they wanted to.*

James had told Ida that he was unable to have children due to a childhood illness, and she felt relieved that more children was something she wouldn't have to worry about again if she went with him.

As the days went by, it became harder and harder to leave her lover. Fred believed she was working late shifts and was always sound asleep when she returned. He had stopped taking much notice of his wife, so Ida's subterfuge was easily maintained. It surprised her that she did not feel any guilt, which in turn made her realise that there was no love left between them.

On the day the show was due to end its run at the Empire, at which point the cast would return to London, where they had been booked to do an Oscar Wilde play in the West End, Ida turned up at the theatre as usual, but was surprised to find that James was not there to greet her. She asked one of the actresses where he was, and she directed her to his dressing room.

As Ida walked along the corridor, she could hear him talking.

'What can I tell her?' James implored.

'The truth,' the other man's voice replied.

Ida slowed to a halt.

'Really?' James said. 'Tell her that we've had a wonderful time, but it's now the end of the road, that it wouldn't work out if she came with me back to London? Especially with three children in tow. Really, I was foolish to suggest it.'

'But I thought you loved her?'

'I thought I did,' James admitted. 'But how do I tell her that I don't feel that way any more? That I have a terrible character flaw of easily falling in love – just as I easily fall out of love. I honestly thought it was different this time. I really believed she was The One.'

Ida had to put her hand on the wall to steady herself. Her legs had started to shake, and her heart felt as though it was beating so violently she would surely pass out – or simply collapse and die like her mother had, because she no longer had the heart for life.

When she realised she had neither fainted nor died, Ida turned slowly and walked back along the corridor. Back out through the stage door. And back into the real world.

Little did Ida know then – or even now – but the dialogue she had overheard was as much an act as James's purported love for her. It had been a little scene that James and his friend had re-enacted many times over the years as a way to dump the women they'd seduced. Mostly it saved them the confrontation, as most of the women they charmed into their beds would simply turn and go. Their hearts broken but their dignity intact.

Which was certainly the case for Ida.

She forced herself to be thankful that no-one, not even Niamh, knew of her affair or her heartbreak, or of the unbearable depression she was plunged into.

But if Ida thought that her life could not become any more insufferable, she was to be proved wrong when, the following month, she felt the tenderness of her breasts. She knew the early signs. She was pregnant.

As she and Fred had not slept together during the month of her 'late shifts', there was no doubting the paternity. James, another of life's two-headed snakes, had not only lied about his love for her – he'd lied about his inability to have children too.

And now Ida not only had to deal with the emotional repercussions of being duped, used like a rag and tossed away, but also the physical ones.

She didn't know who she hated most – James, or herself for being so stupid.

Ida made sure she and Fred were intimate so there would be no doubting that he was the father.

And, every day, she prayed for a miscarriage, to no avail.

Nine months after her affair with James Midgley, Ida gave birth to a baby girl she named Marlene.

Chapter Nineteen

Seeing how white Ida looked after her chat with her three eldest children, Cora said that she would bring some food up to her room. Not giving Ida time to argue, she bustled off to the kitchen, where she tasked Mabel with making some sandwiches.

When Cora brought the tray to Ida's room, they shared a pot of tea and nibbled on the finely sliced beef and tomato sandwiches, made with freshly baked bread and a thick pasting of butter.

Ida liked Cora. And she sensed that Cora liked her too. Although she wasn't sure whether it was more a case that Cora felt sorry for her, which Ida hated the thought of. But still, Cora had become a friend of sorts. She didn't judge Ida, or if she did, she was good at hiding it.

Ida told Cora what she had disclosed to Marlene and they talked a good while. When Cora could see that Ida was tired, she left her to have a nap, telling her that she'd send the young ones to wake her up in an hour or so, which pleased Ida. It would probably be the last time she got to braid Jemima's hair, listen to the next instalment of the spy story Bertie was reading, and smile at Bonnie as she practised her wobbly headstands and half splits.

As Ida drifted off to sleep, her mind replayed the conversations of the past two days. She'd experienced such an onslaught of feelings after Marlene's awful admissions yesterday – outrage and anger at the sadistic bully boys, an even greater rancour at herself as she should have been there for her daughter, followed by unbearable guilt.

She'd had to push aside her self-recrimination in order to concentrate on today's conversation. At least she would leave here knowing that she had been able to give her daughter the truth about her parentage. And even though her apologies for failing them as a mother had fallen on deaf ears yesterday, she had at least done her best to show them she was truly sorry.

A part of her just wished she could have had more time with them to talk – and to make them understand her reasons for leaving them all those years ago.

But still, she had to be content with what she had been able to impart.

And thankful that she had been given these two weeks with them all.

Feeling the need for a ride and some fresh air so as to digest the news her mam had just divulged, Angie headed out to the stables. She'd just checked on Marlene, who was on the phone to Belinda, and had been given a dismissive smile by her sister as she'd carried on excitedly chattering away.

Angie would have given anything to chat to Dorothy and resolved to call her as soon as she had the chance.

As Stanislaw saddled up Ghost and Starling, he noticed the expression on his wife's face. He knew that look. Just as he knew it would have something to do with her mam.

Twenty minutes later, they had galloped together cross-country to Angie's favourite spot, where, on a day like today, when the sky was clear and the sun was shining, the tops of Durham's famous cathedral and castle could be seen to the south and the shimmer of the North Sea to the east.

'That felt good!' Angie declared as she swung her leg over Starling's broad back end and dismounted She walked her horse over to the shade afforded by a huge oak tree. Stanislaw did likewise, dropping the reins so that Ghost could also bow his head and munch on the still dewy grass.

'So, come on, tell me all,' Stanislaw said, taking her by the hand and walking over to the spot on the brow of the hill where they usually sat.

As Angie told him all about James Midgley – or the actor now known as Jacques Kaplan – Stanislaw felt his temperature rise.

'Why did she tell Marlene? Let sleeping dogs lie. I don't see what good it will do *at all*,' he said, not hiding his exasperation.

'I know,' Angie agreed. 'I just hope this doesn't spur Marlene on even more in her determination to become an actress.'

'You would have thought that might have occurred to your mam,' said Stanislaw.

'To be fair, the picture she painted of this bloke wasn't exactly glamorous. If anything, it was the opposite.'

'Mmm,' Stanislaw said, not wanting to say what he really thought. Angie was happy to denigrate her mother, but she was defensive when others did.

They were both quiet.

'I just hope she never finds out this man is still alive,' Stanislaw said, putting his arm around his wife and pulling her close. 'Then there *will* be trouble.'

As they rode back to the manor, Stanislaw let his wife take the lead on Starling. Watching her canter on ahead, he thought of the irony that Ida had been off having babies with different men, not giving two hoots about the children she'd spawned, whereas her daughter wouldn't even have a child with her own husband – a child on whom there was no doubt Angie would bestow an endless supply of love and care.

Was Ida the reason that Angie didn't want another child? Had her mam somehow turned her against having more children?

Stanislaw shook his head. Nothing made sense any more.

When Angie got back from her ride, she headed indoors to find Marlene. She wanted to have a chat, to make sure her younger sister really was all right. Marlene liked to play the drama queen when she had an audience, or to make out that nothing in life fazed her, but there was a depth to Marlene that she rarely allowed others to see.

Hurrying through to the kitchen, where Angie found Alberta kneading dough and Mabel stirring a huge bowl of cake mixture, she asked them if they'd seen her sister.

Both women shook their heads. Angie felt for them having to work in this heat. The windows were open, but even the slight breeze drifting through was warm. It was so hot and stuffy even the dogs had left their usual spot by the Aga in favour of a cool, shaded area outside in the yard.

Hurrying down the corridor, Angie almost crashed into her sister.

'There you are!' Marlene stopped in her tracks. 'I was just looking for you.'

The pair walked back to the main entrance hall. It was, as usual, chaotic, with hotel guests milling around and chatting. Angie overheard one group talking about John Reginald Christie, who had been given the nickname of 'the Notting Hill Mass Murderer'. *Only in London*, Angie thought.

'Are you okay?' Angie asked, scrutinising Marlene for any signs of upset. She found none. Just a perfectly made-up face and a slight fizz of excitement.

'Yes, honestly, I'm fine. I was just coming to find you to see if it's all right if I stay over at Belinda's tonight?' Marlene's face was convincingly earnest and her tone as though she really was asking her sister's permission, when in reality they both knew she was going regardless.

'This is all a bit sudden?' Angie asked.

'I know,' Marlene said, 'but Belinda has just had her heart broken.'

'Again?' Angie said.

'Yes, poor thing. She doesn't have much luck with the boys. I've told her a hundred times, "Treat 'em mean, to keep 'em keen".'

Angie exhaled.

'And this is not because of what you found out this afternoon?' Angie asked.

'What? That, as well as abandoning me, to add insult to injury Mam's lied to me my entire life about who my real dad is?' Marlene shot back.

'Yes,' Angie said, drawing on her depleting reservoir of patience.

'No,' Marlene lied, 'but I'll be able to take Belinda's mind off her treacherous wannabe Mickey Rooney by telling her my shocking news.'

Angie thought that Marlene liked to live her life as though she were in a movie. Finding out that the man who had fathered her was an actor would, she was sure, exacerbate this even further.

'Mam's going tomorrow – don't you want to stay and say goodbye? Maybe wait and go to Belinda's tomorrow?' Angie asked, even though she had a good idea what the answer would be.

Marlene gave a bitter laugh. 'What? Like she waited to say goodbye to us all when she left us for Casanova Carl?'

Angie sighed. Her sister was determined to hang on to her resentment with a fierce grip. She couldn't blame her, though. Angie didn't know how she would feel if she'd been in eight-year-old Marlene's shoes when their mam just up and left. Or indeed in her shoes as a sixteen-year-old having just been told her dad was in fact some now-deceased stage actor.

'Okay,' Angie said. 'Perhaps when Mam's settled into her new digs in Whitby we can all go and pay her a visit.'

Marlene made a sound which told Angie that she and the rest of the children would be going on their own. She certainly would *not* be going – and Angie doubted Danny would either.

Angie saw Wilfred open the front door for some new arrivals – a rather timid-looking couple who, judging by their accents, hailed from Scotland. As Wilfred welcomed them in, Angie saw that Marlene had already packed a small, overnight case, which she'd put by the coat stand in anticipation of leaving. Again, Angie mused how she was head of the family in name only. Everyone always ended up doing what they wanted, regardless.

'I knew you'd say yes,' Marlene said.

'Mmm,' Angie murmured, thinking Marlene's bulging overnight case equated to what most people would take for a long weekend away.

'Oh, and don't worry if I'm not back until late tomorrow,' Marlene informed her. 'I think Belinda and I might go shopping in Newcastle and then catch a movie.'

Angie watched her sister hurry across the hallway, her shoes clip-clopping on the tiles. She was surprised to see that her sister was wearing heels, but there was no time to say anything.

Picking up her little suitcase, Marlene turned to wave goodbye and left.

*

Jake was surprised that Marlene had asked if he could take her to Belinda's house in the Austin rather than the Bentley. It must have been a first. Marlene loved the best of everything and normally would have kicked up a fuss if he'd suggested he chauffeur her in anything but their best carriage. He was glad, though, as being in the Bentley could sometimes feel like driving a tank, albeit a very beautiful shiny blue one.

As he drove along the winding country roads to Durham, Jake noticed Marlene was unusually quiet. She normally chatted away, usually some kind of tittle-tattle she'd read about a Hollywood movie star, but not this afternoon. Jake put this down to her mam's presence at Cuthford Manor.

Perhaps Marlene's unusually quiet mood was because Mrs Boulter was leaving tomorrow. Angie had told him to keep one of the cars free to take her mother to the bus station, from where she was travelling to Whitby. Jake had told Angie that he was happy to take her mam to her new digs in the picturesque fishing village in North Yorkshire, which was only an hour or so away, but his boss had shaken her head and told him that she'd already asked and Mrs Boulter had refused her offer.

As they approached the outskirts of the city, Jake glanced in his rear-view mirror. Marlene was staring out of the window. She looked to be in her own world.

As they drove across Elvet Bridge and headed towards the west of the city, Marlene leant forward.

'Just drop me off here, Jake, I can walk the rest of the way,' she said.

'Don't be daft,' Jake said. 'Your friend's house is only a few minutes from here.'

Marlene looked as if she was about to object, but didn't.

A few minutes later, Jake was pulling into the kerb outside a grand three-storey Georgian townhouse.

'Do you want me to pick you up tomorrow?' he asked.

'No, I'll ring – or I might just get the bus home,' Marlene said.

Jake was again taken aback. When had Marlene ever wanted to use public transport?

Before Jake had time to get out of the car and open the back passenger door, Marlene had jumped out and yanked her little suitcase off the back seat.

'Don't worry about waiting until I get in. If you leave now, you'll miss the traffic,' Marlene urged.

Another first. Marlene being considerate.

Jake nodded and smiled before pulling away. As he turned at the end of the street, he saw Marlene standing on the top step, watching him go.

As soon as the Austin had disappeared from view, Marlene turned on her heel and walked back down the steps. Her heart was hammering as she knew Belinda's mother was at home and there was a chance she might spot Marlene from the front lounge. Hopefully, as it was still sunny, she'd be in the back garden tending to her roses, which were her pride and joy.

Marlene continued as fast as she could down the road with her case. She kept on hurrying even when she was clear of the house, as she was also worried that she might bump into someone she knew – or who knew Angie, or anyone else at Cuthford Manor. Since the manor had become a country house hotel, the family had become quite well known countywide. Durham itself might be classed as a city because of its cathedral, but it was more akin to a parochial market town – with everyone knowing everyone else's business.

Ten minutes later, after hurrying along various cobbled streets and across the bridge, Marlene's case felt as though it had grown heavier. And the heat of the day was making her sweat. Which she hated. She glanced at her watch. She couldn't take a break, though, as she was running out of time.

When she finally reached her destination – Durham railway station on North Road – Marlene put her case down, straightened her skirt and took a deep breath. *She'd made it.* Now she just needed to find Belinda.

Walking up the front steps and through the main entrance, Marlene spotted her friend looking anxious and standing on the southbound platform on the other side of the station. As she made her way over the bridge walkway, she saw a train approaching. By the time she'd got to the other side and down the flight of wooden steps, the train was drawing to a standstill and Belinda was running towards her.

'Oh my God!' Belinda reached her friend. 'I thought you were going to miss it.'

'I know. There was so much to do – pack, speak to

143

Angie . . .' Marlene said as Belinda handed her a train ticket, as well as a five-pound note.

'Are you sure you won't get into trouble for this?' Marlene looked down at the crisp banknote and freshly stamped train ticket. She had the money Angie had given her for her new outfit, as well as the money she'd been saving up from her allowance, but this extra five pounds would mean she could get somewhere decent to stay overnight.

'You'll need it. London's so much more expensive than here,' Belinda said, stepping aside as one of the porters opened the door to the first-class carriage. 'Especially if you end up staying a second night.'

'Thanks, Belinda, you're the best friend anyone could want! I'll pay you back when I return.'

'Are you sure you're doing the right thing?' Belinda asked.

'Absolutely. I've never been surer of anything in my life,' Marlene declared. 'And if I've got the time, I'm going to go to that modelling agency I told you about.'

Marlene's last words were obliterated by the stationmaster's whistle piercing the air as doors started to slam shut and loved ones embraced each other and kissed goodbye.

Belinda grabbed her friend and gave her a big, ungainly hug.

'I'll ring!' Marlene told her as she climbed aboard.

The porter closed the carriage door.

'You'd better!' Belinda said.

The train juddered and started to move.

'Good luck!' Belinda shouted above the hissing and the clunking of metal.

Marlene leant out of the open sash window and waved goodbye until her friend was just a dot in the distance.

Only then did she feel the first burst of nerves.

Chapter Twenty

After a rather stressful last dinner together before Ida's departure the next day, Angie headed to the study, closed the door and sank into the soft leather chair. It was just after nine o'clock. With the five-hour time difference, she'd catch her friend Dorothy before she finished work.

After speaking to the usual string of operators, Angie was finally put through to the receptionist at the *New Yorker*, who then connected her to Dorothy's phone, which was answered by one of the secretaries working in the features department.

'I'll just go and fetch her for you, ma'am,' the young woman said in an American drawl.

Angie could hear the tap-tapping and pinging of typewriters in the background and the general buzz of the large open-plan office. Dorothy had told Angie that her editor had offered her a swanky office of her own as her rise in popularity as one of New York's leading columnists continued, but she'd declined because she said she liked to be 'in amongst it all'. How her friend could concentrate on writing her columns with everything going on around her was beyond Angie.

When Dorothy came to the phone, Angie got straight to it and told her about her mam's scandalous secret.

'Oh. My. God!' Dorothy exclaimed down the phone. 'Although I don't know why I'm surprised, given everything. But, gosh, hearing it, well, it's shocking.'

'The ironic thing is,' Angie said, swivelling the leather chair around so that she was looking out at the long driveway and the expanse of lawns that were becoming yellow in the unseasonably hot summer temperatures, 'we used to joke about Marlene being the offspring of some airhead toff, which she never minded. She always wanted to be different.'

'And I'll bet she loves the idea of being the offspring of a famous actor even more,' Dorothy said. Angie could hear her scribbling. It was a habit she had when she was on the phone. 'I think you can safely say she's inherited her father's theatrical ways.'

'Hasn't she just,' Angie said. 'Although "famous" feels a stretch. He wasn't particularly well known. Mam said he liked to consider himself a "thespian".'

'So he thought a bit of himself, by the sounds of it. The so-called "thespians" I've met here spend most of their time waiting tables and seducing women as a sideline.'

'Yes, I think that's the idea Mam was trying to get across, but you know Marlene – the only word she heard was "actor".'

'And her imagination did the rest,' Dorothy said.

Angie could hear Dorothy stop scribbling to light up a cigarette.

'So, this must have been what your mam was holding back,' Dorothy said. The two friends had agreed during their last telephone conversation – which had been cut short as Dorothy was on a deadline – that Ida wasn't being totally honest with them. But neither of them could fathom why.

'Well,' Angie said, 'I don't know what I thought she was hiding from us, but I'd never have guessed it was this.'

'Nor me,' Dorothy agreed.

'Anyway,' Angie said, her tone changing to a pained groan, 'we've just all had our *last supper* together.'

'Awkward?' Dorothy asked. Angie could hear her friend exhaling smoke and someone shouting in the background.

'Just a bit,' Angie said. 'Danny hardly spoke. And Marlene was conspicuous by her absence. I could tell Mam was upset she wasn't there, as she kept asking about Belinda and what we thought Marlene might end up doing for work'

'Which I'm guessing was met by silence?'

Angie laughed. 'It was, until Cora chipped in that she didn't think Marlene really had any idea what she wants to do when she does leave school.'

'Other than become Hollywood's next young starlet,' Dorothy added grimly.

'And then Lloyd and Stanislaw were making their usual forced conversation.' Angie sighed. 'And every time it was mentioned that Mam was leaving tomorrow, you could see the relief on their faces.'

'And I'll bet they're not the only ones,' Dorothy emphasised.

Angie let out a sad laugh. She would be relieved when

her mam went. But there was also another feeling lurking in the background that she couldn't quite make out. Guilt, perhaps? Which was preposterous. She had absolutely nothing to feel guilty about.

'I'll bet you'll be glad to get back to normal,' Dorothy said.

'I will,' Angie agreed. 'Although I think Jemima, Bertie and Bonnie will miss having their new playmate around.'

'I'm sure Clemmie will be back to fill that role,' Dorothy said. She knew that – other than having her evening meal with them all – Clemmie had kept out of the way to give Ida more quality time just with her children.

'So, what excuse did Marlene give not to be there?' Dorothy asked, curious.

'Oh, Belinda's had her heart broken again,' Angie sighed.

'Oh dear,' Dorothy commiserated. 'The joys of being young.'

'I don't recall you having your heart broken much – if at all,' Angie laughed, remembering being two young, free and single women during their time working in the shipyard during the war.

'Well,' Dorothy said, 'I'm relieved for your sake that Marlene believes her "thespian" of a father is dead and buried, or else I think your mam's revelation would have had the potential to cause far greater devastation.'

'God, that's a scenario I don't even want to even think about,' said Angie.

Chapter Twenty-One

As the train screeched and huffed its way into King's Cross Station, Marlene wasn't sure if she felt more anxious or excited. She had barely left the county since they'd moved there – other than a trip to Harrogate in Yorkshire with the school, and to Edinburgh with Stanislaw, Angie and her siblings to see Wojtek, the famous 'soldier bear', in the city's zoo.

As she applied a layer of her Helena Rubenstein 'heart-shaped' lipstick, Marlene couldn't recall a single trip out that she'd had on her own. Even when she went shopping, Belinda would always go with her.

She wished her best friend had been able to come. She was desperate to speak to her, but she knew she had to find somewhere to stay first. The train had been delayed at Leeds and it was now gone nine o'clock. She couldn't leave it too late to ring, though, as Belinda's mother might get suspicious.

Stepping down from the comfort of the first-class carriage and onto the noisy platform, Marlene was temporarily taken aback. The warm, acrid air caught her throat and she coughed. As she started to walk, she was suddenly jostled, repeatedly, as those in the second- and third-class carriages hurried past her, many of them knocking her case and causing Marlene to stagger a little in her heeled shoes. She picked up her pace and breathed a sigh of relief when she'd made it out of the noisy, dirty railway station.

But walking onto the main street, she was hit by how busy it was – and the smell of the fumes from the traffic, and the cigarette smoke stagnant in the air. The warm air. She'd never felt so warm so late at night. At home, it was always crisp and cold by this time – even in the summer.

As she headed to the taxi rank to the right of the station, she now realised why everyone had been in such a dash getting off the train. By the time she reached the pickup point there was only one cab left and that, she was told, had been booked.

As she waited, with others starting to queue behind her, Marlene took in her immediate surroundings.

First impressions were not what she had expected of London. Clemmie had described the capital as vibrant, full of colour, culture, life and laughter. But the only colours Marlene could see were blacks and greys, with the odd dash of red from the passing double-decker buses.

Marlene reprimanded herself. It *was* night-time, after all.

Finally, a black cab pulled up and Marlene climbed in without waiting for the driver to open the door. Her feet were already hurting and she was now seriously reconsidering her choice of footwear. She wore flats for school and at home; her feet weren't used to heels.

'Where to, love?' the cabbie asked, barely turning his head to look at Marlene.

'The West End,' Marlene said.

The cab pulled away. 'Whereabouts in the West End, darlin'?' The man looked briefly into his rear-view mirror.

'Take me to where all the theatres are,' Marlene replied, trying to keep her voice upbeat and not betray the first stirrings of concern about where she was going to spend the night. She hadn't had time to book ahead and hadn't been too worried as she thought she'd have plenty of time to find somewhere. She hadn't banked on the train being delayed.

It was getting late. She'd have to find a bed for the night sharpish.

Chapter Twenty-Two

In the middle of the night, Ida woke with a start. She was covered in sweat and felt sick as a dog. But that was nothing compared to the malaise in her heart, knowing that tomorrow she would leave – and never return.

She kept telling herself it was for the best.

She would write them all letters and explain why.

Getting out of bed, Ida walked over a little unsteadily to the sink unit and grabbed the towel from the rack. Peeling off her nightie, she wiped herself down and got out a clean one from her suitcase, which she had already packed.

God, she missed Carl. She wondered how he was feeling without her. She hoped he was all right, that he was managing.

It's better this way, she reminded herself.

As Ida climbed back into bed, she thought about Marlene. How she wished she hadn't gone to her friend's. Ida knew that Marlene was punishing her. That she wanted to hurt her as she herself had been hurt. Ida understood that. She just wished she'd been able to talk to her more.

And explain.

Chapter Twenty-Three

Marlene looked at her little travel clock. It was half-past one. So far sleep had evaded her.

The cabbie had dropped her off outside the London Casino on Old Compton Street, which he'd informed her was in the heart of Soho. She'd felt a rush of excitement when she saw the huge banner advertising a musical comedy called *Wish You Were Here*. Clemmie had told her bits and pieces about Soho and about this theatre in particular. Its most recent show, she'd told Marlene, would be set in a holiday camp and have a *real* swimming pool on stage. Marlene had resolved to bring Belinda with her when she returned to visit her father. He might even be able to get them backstage to meet the stars. And, more importantly, he might well be able to introduce her to the director, who she would then charm into giving her a part in his next production.

Marlene's high spirits at being in the heart of the West End, though, had dropped significantly and her initial anxiety had returned as she tried and failed to find somewhere to stay. All the hotels and B & Bs seemed to be full.

'This is our busiest time of year, love,' she'd been told repeatedly.

Marlene wished that Angie's friend Kate, a successful

designer with her own label, Lily & Rose, wasn't presently out of town. Kate had her studio not far from here, in Carnaby Street, but Angie had told Marlene after her latest get-together with her old workmates that Kate was presently in Paris preparing for some big event that would showcase up-and-coming haute couture designers.

And so Marlene had stood, not knowing where to go next, while passers-by tutted and manoeuvred around her. She knew Maisie and Vivian, who had looked after her and her siblings the night before Angie's wedding and who had stayed in touch with the family, also worked in Soho, managing an exclusive gentleman's club that Lily owned. But she could not remember where it was, or even if she'd been told, come to think about it.

Marlene had continued her search for a hotel or B & B that didn't have the 'No Vacancies' sign in the window and had finally ended up in a hotel back where she'd initially been dropped off. She'd been so relieved to find somewhere, she didn't care that it looked a bit run-down and dirty.

She'd been so shattered, she'd expected to go out like a light as soon as her head hit the pillow, but she couldn't relax enough to drift off. Which wasn't surprising with all the noise and shouting, banging and clashing. She'd thought it might quieten down after midnight, but there still seemed to be a never-ending stream of guests, chatting and laughing, coming and going, up and down the stairs, opening and shutting doors.

She thought of her room at Cuthford Manor and of how peaceful it was at night. How the only sounds she would hear were the soft hooting of the night owl or the shrieks and yelps of the foxes as they defended their territory or sought out a mate.

She thought back to earlier in the day when her mam had told her about her real father. It seemed like days ago rather than hours. She turned over in the bed, trying to get comfortable. Some of the metal springs in the mattress were poking through.

She *really* wished more than anything that Belinda was with her now, and hoped she wasn't worried, as it had been too late to call her without raising suspicions.

Lying on the springy bed, looking at the ceiling, which had paint flaking in the corner, Marlene wondered for the first time if she had not been a tiny bit impulsive in coming to London. And that perhaps she should have waited and planned the trip more thoroughly.

At least then she'd have found a better place to stay than this dive.

She'd never known a hotel to charge by the hour.

Chapter Twenty-Four

Angie was up at the crack of dawn. She too hadn't slept well, which meant that Stanislaw had not slept well either. He could always sense when his wife's mind was not at ease, which wasn't surprising, given the dramatic events of late. He knew Angie's feelings towards her mother were conflicted. It was as if her mother had become two different people – the one who brought her up, and the one who had returned on the day of their wedding anniversary.

'You'll be glad to get back to normality,' Stanislaw said as they got dressed. *He* was certainly looking forward to getting back to normality. And with it the chance to chat to Angie about adding to their family.

He also knew that Lloyd and Cora and the rest of the staff would be pleased since they had been working extra hard, and longer hours, to cover for Angie while she dealt with her mam's impromptu and longer-than-expected visit.

'Mmm,' Angie said. 'That's what Dor said too. I'll be glad to get my head back into work again – it's far less exhausting than dealing with family dramas, that's for sure.' She pulled on her shirt and slacks. 'The problem is, I'm wondering if we can ever go back to the way we were before Mam's arrival. Her coming back into our lives has affected everyone.' Angie dragged a brush through her short bobbed hair. 'I dread to think how Marlene's going to be.' She picked up her compact of mascara and quickly brushed it on. 'And how long it will take for me to coax Danny out of his shell of silence.'

Stanislaw, who had finished getting ready, sat at the end of the bed and watched his wife as she reached for her powder puff and dabbed it on her face.

'And I predict the young ones will be surly as anything after their new playmate goes,' she added, putting on a slash of lipstick, which Marlene had told her was smudge-proof and would stay on all day. 'And they'll be on at me to go and see Mam in Whitby before she's even had a chance to settle there herself.'

Angie sighed and turned round to face her husband.

'You see, this is exactly the reason I don't want any more children. Just because they are all growing up, it doesn't make it any easier. If anything, quite the reverse.'

Stanislaw's heart plummeted. Just as his frustration skyrocketed. He made the sounds he knew Angie needed to hear, somehow managing to keep to himself the growing ill will he felt towards Ida, who had single-handedly cemented his wife's decision not to have another child.

Damn that woman, he cursed inwardly.

Afterwards, Angie and Stanislaw took the dogs out for a walk, before the place came to life and the weather got too hot. She then went to see her mam in her room.

As she approached, she could hear Cora's voice, her tone sounding unusually harsh. It wasn't clear what was being said, but it seemed as though the two women were having words with each other.

'Everything all right?' Angie asked, opening the door, which had been left ajar.

'Yes, yes, of course,' Ida reassured her daughter. 'I was just saying what a lovely day it is to travel. And how much I'm looking forward to being by the sea.'

Angie looked at Cora, who did not seem to agree. She picked up Ida's breakfast tray and walked out of the room.

Angie felt Cora would have stomped if her hands hadn't been full.

Chapter Twenty-Five

When Marlene woke after finally falling into a restless sleep just as dawn was breaking, she couldn't wait to get out of the awful hotel she'd been forced to spend the night in. Seeing her small room in the harsh light of day, she subconsciously started to itch. It was filthy. She'd be surprised if there weren't fleas in the bed.

'Chin up!' she told herself as she observed the rim of dirt around the little ceramic washbasin in the corner of the room. 'This is but a minor blip.'

Wanting just to get out of there pronto, she decided not to bother washing her face, but merely added more make-up on top of the old. The clothes she had put on the back of the chair had fallen onto the floor during the night, so that when Marlene put them back on, they were creased and had a few marks from the dirty wooden flooring. She tried to rub them off, but only made them worse. She looked out at the street below, but the glass was so dirty she could barely see out of it.

She resolved to check into a better hotel, freshen herself up and redo her make-up; then she would start her search for her father.

She had learnt last night whilst traipsing around Soho that it wasn't actually that big. It was probably no bigger than the grounds of Cuthford Manor, so she felt confident in her mission. Although that confidence dropped a little as she squeezed her aching and swollen feet back into her heeled shoes.

Leaving the hotel and walking out onto the busy street, the heat hit her. At home, there was always a breeze, even on the hottest days; the benefit, Thomas had told her, of the manor having been built on elevated land.

As Marlene looked around, getting her bearings and deciding which way to go, she found herself being stared at by the men and women who were walking past. The men were looking at her as though she were on display in a shop window, and the women as though she were the lowest of the low. She could swear some of their lips actually curled downwards in disgust.

She looked down at her creased skirt and blouse. *She didn't look that bad, did she?*

As she started to make her way towards one of the posh hotels, she geed herself up, once again telling herself that her trip had just got off to a bit of a bad start and that there was only one way it could now go – and that was up.

Chapter Twenty-Six

Angie was glad that Ida was leaving at mid-afternoon as it was always the quietest time – most of the guests usually went out for the day. Looking out of the entrance of Cuthford Manor, she saw that Jake was waiting by the car, having already put her mam's little suitcase in the boot. Ida had gone to say goodbye to Danny, knowing that it was unlikely he would feel like waving her off. As she'd admitted, 'Goodbyes aren't really the family's forte.' And she'd rather there be no pretence. Despite her words, though, Angie could tell that her mam was disappointed Marlene was not going to be back in time to see her off.

Hearing Ida's voice, Angie looked up to see her mam walking down the stairs, Bertie, Jemima and Bonnie buzzing around her. Noticing Ida's pale complexion and dark eyes, Angie guessed that she had not slept particularly well either, which caused the feelings of guilt she'd had about letting her mam leave so readily rise to the surface once more.

'You all set?' Angie asked, telling herself they would see her again soon.

'Yes, all set,' Ida proclaimed brightly, looking down at the children. 'So, do I get to give you all a hug goodbye?' she asked.

Three solemn faces nodded and in unison the younger children flung their arms around her.

Angie was suddenly hit by an intense feeling of grief, as this was what they'd used to do with Quentin when he'd arrive back from work.

'Now, promise me you won't be sad,' Ida told them. 'We've had such a good time, haven't we?'

They nodded.

'So, you just remember that,' Ida said, desperately holding back the tears, before turning her attention to Angie.

They looked at each other.

'Well, we'll come and see you when you're settled in,' Angie said.

Ida would have loved to have embraced her daughter, but it was obvious by Angie's body language that she did not feel the same.

Ida nodded. 'Of course.'

And with that she turned to go.

Ida had just reached the open doorway when Angie heard a bustling behind her and the sound of footsteps coming from the kitchen. She turned to see Cora and started to smile, but stopped on seeing Cora's deadly serious expression.

'I'm sorry . . .' she began as she hurried into the main hallway.

Angie looked at her mam, who was giving Cora a look that should have stopped her in her tracks but didn't.

Cora reached the children a little out of puff. 'Cook's made you all some of your favourite crispy cakes.'

The children's faces lit up. They looked at Ida.

'Go on!' Ida said. 'Before Danny and Thomas get wind!'

Her words did the trick and the three raced to the kitchen.

Cora took a deep breath.

She looked at Ida and then at Angie.

'Your mam can't leave!' she proclaimed.

'Why?' Angie asked. Her feelings of guilt replaced by both curiosity and concern.

Ida waved her hands as though to dismiss Cora's words. 'It's nothing. Now come on, wave me off! If I don't go now, I'll miss my bus.'

With that Ida made to leave.

'If you don't tell her, then I will!' Cora exclaimed.

'Tell Angie what?' Danny asked. He'd just come in from the stables after being cajoled by Lucy to wave goodbye to his mam.

The dogs, who had followed him from the kitchen, made straight for Ida and, as usual, started sniffing her and demanding her attention. She patted them, unable to move even if she'd wanted to.

'Yes, tell me what?' Angie repeated, thinking her mother looked like a rabbit caught in headlights.

Ida seemed unable or unwilling to say anything.

Angie shifted her attention to Cora and gave her a questioning look.

Cora stared at Ida, giving her the chance to speak.

When she didn't, Cora drew in a deep breath and expelled it slowly as she looked at Angie and Danny. She wished Marlene were also here.

'Your mother,' Cora said, 'is dying.'

Chapter Twenty-Seven

Marlene had been wrong in surmising that her trip couldn't get any worse.

She'd spent the rest of that morning doing exactly what she had done the previous evening – with exactly the same result.

Everywhere was fully booked.

In the end, she found a café that wasn't too busy and ordered herself a cup of tea and a sandwich. She was exhausted, having not eaten anything except an apple since leaving Durham on the train the previous day. Blisters were developing on her heels. She'd be pounding the streets of Soho in her bare feet if they got any worse. And her small overnight case felt heavier by the minute. She stretched her tense neck.

She'd tried to ring Belinda, but hadn't been able to get through to her. The first time, the line had been engaged. She'd kept trying, but there was no change, making Marlene wonder if the phone had been knocked off the hook. In any case, it occurred to her that if Belinda's mother answered, she'd hear loud cockney accents or the chaotic cacophony of the street – honking horns, music drifting out of nearby pubs and venues, screams of laughter or stallholders selling their goods. She'd know for certain that her daughter's friend was not in Durham.

Munching on her sandwich, Marlene looked out of the

café window. There was so much to take in – so many people, young and old, so many fashionably dressed women, so many different nationalities. The criss-crossing roads were jam-packed with nose-to-tail, slow-moving traffic – motor cars, delivery vans, even the occasional horse and cart.

Marlene tried to feel more cheerful and to remind herself of how lucky she was. After hearing so much about London, she was here, finally, seeing and experiencing it for herself.

But it was hard to keep her sense of wonder as she was finding it all so overwhelming. It was busy. Which seemed obvious, but *knowing* it was a busy place and *experiencing* that were two very different things. Especially when the weather was hot and the air felt so dry and lacking in oxygen. She'd been bumped and bashed into so many times, she felt dazed – and was getting more and more irritated. She told herself she'd feel better now she'd had something to eat and a refreshing cup of tea. Although she'd have to shelve the idea of getting herself signed to a model agency.

By the time Marlene had finished her tea, she had decided to abandon her search for a hotel and find her father instead. She might even be able to stay the night at his place.

When the waitress came to clear the table, Marlene asked, 'I don't suppose you've heard of an actor called Jacques Kaplan, have you?'

The pretty young girl shook her head. 'No. I'm not so good with names, though. Better with faces.'

Marlene thanked her, left a tip and walked out of the café to begin her search.

Chapter Twenty-Eight

'Is that true?' Angie asked, shocked. 'Are you really dying, Mam?'

Ida threw Cora a look. They had argued about this earlier in the day. She nodded. She couldn't deny it. The cat was out of the bag.

'I am,' she said.

Angie and Danny were standing still, staring at their mother, waiting for an explanation.

When none was forthcoming, Cora walked over to the woman who had become a friend and gently pulled up her sleeves.

There were fresh bruises on her arms.

'Your mother has cancer of the blood,' Cora explained. 'That's why she bruises so easily.' She had suspected this to be the case when she'd noticed that it was taking a while for Ida's bruises to fade. This combined with the tiredness that Ida tried to hide, her lack of appetite and the bouts of feverishness she was prone to. Cora had had a friend many years ago who'd suffered the same disease.

'So, they weren't caused by Carl?' Angie asked. Her mind seemed to be struggling with what she was hearing.

'No, it wasn't Carl,' Ida said, finally finding her own voice. *How it had hurt her to let them all believe that.*

There was another moment of stunned silence before Danny found his voice.

'Great! That's just great!' he said, his tone one of anger, but the tears in his eyes betraying his sorrow. 'Why turn up? Knowing you're going to die?' He shook his head angrily. 'So, you come here, tell us what a terrible mother you were – as if we didn't know that already – and say you're sorry . . .' Danny took a deep breath. 'Then you drop a bombshell on Marlene without any thought of what effect it might have on her. Thank God this actor bloke you had it off with is dead, otherwise your wayward daughter would be hopping on a train to London to track him down and have some kind of wonderful make-believe Hollywood reunion with him.' He shook his head. 'This is so typical of you, Mam! Selfish to the last. No thought for anyone else but yourself.'

And with that he turned on his heel and stomped back to the stables.

The silence in the high-ceilinged entrance hall was deafening.

'I think a cup of tea is in order,' Cora said. 'Why don't you two go into the lounge. No-one's in there at the moment. I'll go and get us a tray.'

Ida and Angie walked into the lounge without saying a word.

Slumping into the armchair, Ida let out a long sigh.

'Maybe Danny's right. Perhaps deep down my motivations have been selfish. But they weren't meant to be. I just wanted to . . .' Ida paused.

'Just wanted to what?' Angie asked, leaning forward from her seat on the sofa. Her mother was mumbling, as though speaking to herself.

Ida looked up and stared at Angie as though just realising she was there.

'Oh, I don't know, Angie,' she said. 'I suppose I just wanted to acknowledge that I know I have been a terrible mother. I wanted to apologise to you all.' She looked back down at her hands clasped together. 'I wanted you all to let go of the anger and resentment I knew you would feel towards me. Which is why I didn't want you to know I was dying. Because then you'd feel sorry for me and those feelings that really needed to be expressed would get buried. And I didn't want that.'

Ida sat back in her chair.

'And I felt strongly that Marlene had a right to know who her real father was. I didn't want to take that secret to the grave. It didn't feel right.'

Angie sighed.

'I don't know what the right thing to do would be, Mam. Marlene's a tricky one. You never know how's she's going to react to things. I don't think it upset her, though – if anything, I think she felt quite excited by the prospect that her father was an actor.'

They were quiet for a moment.

'So,' Angie said tentatively, 'how long have you got?'

Ida gave her a sad smile. 'Two or three months – possibly more. Possibly less. Dr Wright says it's very hard to tell with these things.'

'So Dr Wright knows?' Angie was surprised.

'He guessed,' Ida said. 'As Cora did.'

Angie thought of how Dr Wright had been to see her mam quite a few times. The tonic he'd given her. The suggestion that she stay another week to get over her throat infection.

'He's a nice man. You've got a lovely set-up here, Angie. Some really decent people around you.'

Ida sat up and her face become serious. 'But I need you to know that I do have somewhere to go.'

'But not Whitby?'

'Not Whitby,' Ida said. 'Although I think that would be a lovely place to see your last days out.' She paused. 'No, I've got a place in a home in Fife in Scotland for people who are dying. They call it a convalescence home, but it's mainly for people like me.'

Angie thought for a moment. 'That's why you didn't want Jake to take you to Whitby – just into Durham. You were going to get the train up there.'

Ida looked at her watch. 'And I still am. The train isn't until later.'

Angie looked at her mam.

'No, you're not catching any train, Mam. And you're certainly not going up to Fife – if for no other reason than Cora would have my guts for garters.'

Just then they heard the tinkle of china.

'Tea for three,' Cora announced.

Seeing Angie start to get up from her chair, and knowing exactly what she was thinking, Cora put the tray on the coffee table.

'Don't worry about Danny. I went to check on him and he's okay. Lucy's there. They're going out for a ride. I think he just needs time to digest everything.'

She started pouring the tea.

'We can tell the young ones later. They're quite happy in the kitchen being fussed over by Alberta and Mabel. And as Marlene is presently shopping in Newcastle with Belinda, it means . . .' Cora looked at Angie '. . . there's no-one for you to worry about just now.'

Chapter Twenty-Nine

Marlene felt as though she had been in every theatre, every café, even shops and restaurants, asking if anyone knew her father. She'd become so desperate she'd even stopped those on the street she thought looked like actresses or actors to ask if they knew of an actor called Jacques Kaplan – also known as James Midgley – who would be around fifty.

Her search had become interspersed with regular short breaks in cafés, forced breaks because the backs of her heels were now red raw, and her case felt as though it was filled with bricks. The only positive from having to stop and rest so much was that she'd been able to quiz those who brought her refreshments. One of the waiters told her to keep an eye out for posters advertising shows in some of the smaller theatres and venues and to check any noticeboards she might come across. Marlene kicked herself. Of course, she should already have been doing this. Her mam after all had first seen his face on a poster.

Marlene spent the next hour examining every poster and every advert, which was no mean task, as it seemed that there were posters and adverts plastered everywhere you looked – in windows, on walls and lamp posts.

She stopped at every newsagent, each time getting crushed trying to read the noticeboards outside. After finding no more leads as to the whereabouts of her father, Marlene decided to go beyond the boundaries of Soho.

As she made her way up Frith Street, she saw two young children begging. They looked like chimney sweeps and were holding tin cups, their eyes desperately trying to catch the attention of those walking past. As Marlene neared them, she could see their pinched little faces and could tell they were brother and sister. Her heart missed a beat. For a second, she was looking through a keyhole into the past and was staring at herself and Danny, dressed in rags, sitting on the pavement. They had never openly begged, but often those walking past would put a few pennies in their dirty hands. Neither she nor Danny had ever objected.

Pulling her little leather purse out of her jacket pocket, Marlene stopped and gave them a few coins. Enough for them to get themselves something to eat, with a little left over. Their woebegone faces lit up.

'Ah, ta very much, missus,' the young boy said.

His younger sister gave her a tired smile.

Walking on, Marlene felt flat. How little society had changed from when she was a child. Not for the first time, she felt indebted to her sister for taking them all with her to Cuthford Manor.

Thinking of Angie and the sacrifices she had made for her and her siblings, Marlene felt guilty for lying to her about coming to London. It now looked unlikely she'd find her father in time to get the five o'clock train back to Durham. With hindsight, she had probably been overly optimistic that she'd locate him so quickly.

She'd get the first train back tomorrow whether she found him or not, and no-one would be any the wiser.

Finding herself in Soho Square, Marlene walked across the road and into the smallest park she'd ever come across – she thought it more akin to a garden – with an octagonal, Tudor-style hut in it. She made her way over to one of the benches and sat down, glad of a rest. As she sheltered in the shade of the only tree she'd seen since arriving in the capital, she spotted a flyer that had been partly pasted over by another, more recent advert.

She could just make out the word 'Kaplan' – and another which she thought said 'musician'. *Her mam had never mentioned her father being a musician as well.*

Thank God, he was definitely here. She had been starting to worry that perhaps her father no longer worked and lived in London.

She could just make out the words of the venue where he had been performing. The Lido Theatre. It was one she'd not heard of, nor come across, which was surprising as she was sure she had been in every theatre within a half-mile radius in her quest to find her father.

Marlene immediately got up from her resting place feeling rejuvenated, although her shoes were still killing her. Grabbing her case, she headed to the little-known theatre, which, according to the poster, was off Great Windmill

Street. She'd already been to the well-known Windmill Theatre, but hadn't seen a smaller one called the Lido.

Looking at her watch and seeing it was gone half past four, she hoped her father might have just finished a matinee and would be in his dressing room.

It took Marlene longer than expected to find the theatre as it was tucked away down a little side street and was jammed between a rather unusual bookshop, which had a neon sign saying 'Book Mart' above it, and a club called The Flamenco.

Marlene's heart dropped. The theatre had clearly closed down. The windows had been boarded up and a 'To Let' sign was hanging above the door.

She stared in despair at the shabby building that had once been a theatre. As she stood wondering what to do, a young, heavily made-up woman came out of the club, bringing with her a blast of smoky air and the sound of a saxophone being played. She was followed by an older man who was dressed to the nines, with greased-back black hair. They both stopped on seeing Marlene. The way they looked her up and down made her feel uncomfortable.

'You all right there, sweetheart?' the woman asked.

'Yes, yes, I'm fine,' Marlene lied. She saw the man's eyes go to her case, which she had put down on the ground.

'You want to keep hold of your belongings, darlin'. Anything not stapled down round here is guaranteed to be snatched and gone before you've had time to blink,' said the man, who was dressed in a pinstriped suit and polished black shoes.

Marlene immediately picked up her case. Even her hand was starting to blister where she'd been carrying it for so long.

'You new to the Big Smoke?' The woman, who was wearing a low-cut blouse, knee-length pencil skirt and impossibly high heels, took a step forward.

Marlene nodded.

'You looking for work?' The man followed his escort's lead and stepped closer to Marlene, who was feeling increasingly uncomfortable at their continued scrutiny.

'I'll bet she scrubs up well,' the man said out of the corner of his mouth.

'No, no.' Marlene couldn't get the words out quickly enough. 'I'm actually here looking for my father. Jacques Kaplan?'

The demeanour of her inquisitors immediately changed. The woman laughed.

'Ah, Jimmy.' She cast her companion a look. He immediately seemed to have lost interest in Marlene and was now stepping away and lighting up a cigarette.

'Do you know him?' Marlene asked, her heart lifting.

'Of course I know Jimmy.' She narrowed her eyes and again inspected Marlene, although this time it didn't make her feel uncomfortable. 'Yes, I think I can see the resemblance. Not so much now, perhaps, but in younger days.'

Marlene felt like bursting. *She even looked like him.*

'Do you know where I can find him?' Marlene said, feeling renewed hope.

The man, now impatient, grabbed the woman's arm and tugged her a little aggressively.

'He'll be at the Revue Club. He's usually there from about half-seven, eight o'clock—' She yanked her arm away from the man's grip, but obeyed his unspoken command and followed him, staggering a little in her high heels on the uneven cobbles as she tried to catch him up.

Chapter Thirty

As she sipped her tea with Ida and Cora in the front lounge, Angie didn't know what she was feeling, which seemed to be her new state of being since her mam had turned up. Sad, angry, guilty and worried all at the same time. Sad that her mam's life was being cut so short. Angry that Ida had brought this sorrow to Cuthford Manor, and that she would leave them as quickly as she'd come back into their lives. Worried about how it would affect the children. And guilty, as although she had welcomed her mam, she hadn't been particularly loving towards her.

As Ida explained more about the cancer she had and that it was called leukaemia and affected the body's ability to fight infection, Angie thought about Dr Wright and how he would be able to help them care for her mam.

'Is that why you've lost weight?' Angie asked.

Ida nodded.

'And why you fainted when you arrived?' Everything was falling into place.

'Possibly,' Ida said.

'And I'm guessing it makes you tired?'

Angie had thought it unusual for her mam to have afternoon naps, but had put it down to her need to have a respite from the intensity of being with her children after such a long time apart.

Ida nodded.

'And it knocks your appetite?' Angie pictured her mam picking at her food, something she'd never done when they'd all lived at Dundas Street.

Ida smiled. 'Which is so annoying, as I've never enjoyed such lovely dinners.'

Angie was quiet for a moment, taking in her mother's terminal illness before she snapped herself out of her jumble of thoughts and looked at Cora and Ida.

'Well,' she declared. 'If there was ever a reason to indulge in a stiff drink in the afternoon, then this is it.'

'Yes,' Ida agreed. 'The one good thing about impending death is that it can be rather liberating. A good excuse to break the rules.'

Angie felt her heart lurch. Her mother's bravery was making her feel even sadder and even more guilty. She got up and poured them each a cognac from the cabinet in the corner of the sitting room. She put the three bulbous brandy glasses on a silver tray and carried it over to the coffee table.

'I don't know what we're toasting,' she said, her voice wavering with emotion, as she handed a glass to her mam and another to Cora before raising her own.

'Well, I'd like to make a toast to thank you for having me here,' said Ida. 'And for having me a little while longer, although we shall argue about the length of my stay later.'

Angie was about to dispute her mam even considering

179

leaving them, but was silenced by the looks Ida and Cora were giving her.

'Okay, later,' Angie conceded. They chinked glasses and took a sip of their large brandies.

'So, Mam, I'm confused about Carl. Just so I've got this straight in my head, he was never violent towards you in any way?'

Ida laughed. The idea that the man she had shared her life with these past eight years could in any way be physically abusive was absurd. 'Oh, Carl wouldn't – couldn't – hurt anything or anybody. He's vehemently opposed to any kind of violence. I don't think I've ever even heard him raise his voice. He's a very gentle man.'

Angie heard the love in her mam's voice and felt a slew of feelings. She would have liked to have known her mam when she'd been living with Carl. She was still finding it hard to reconcile the mam of the past with the woman she was now.

'I don't understand why you're not with him. Why you want to go off to this place in Scotland and leave him?' Angie asked, genuinely perplexed. *Had the relationship waned? Or perhaps Carl hadn't wanted to care for Ida?*

'I can be as stubborn as an old mule, as you know, Angie.' Ida put her glass on the table. She would enjoy it later, but she wanted to remember every moment she had with her daughter, unsullied by the effects of alcohol. 'I told him that I didn't want his last memories of me to be of illness and death. I knew I couldn't control this cancer, but I could control how I lived what remained of my life. And I wanted Carl to remember the woman he loved – was in love with. The good times we've had. The love we had.'

'I don't know what to say, Mam.' Angie felt the first prick of tears. 'It sounds very romantic. In theory, anyway. But in practice, it sounds very lonely. Not having the person you love there with you at the end.'

Cora muttered her agreement.

'But I would have my memories of our time together, so I wouldn't be lonely,' Ida said, smiling as she thought of Carl. They had argued over her decision, but in the end he'd had to respect Ida's wishes. When she had left their little flat for the last time, she had refused even to allow him to see her off on the train. She wanted her last image of him to be in the place that had been their home. Their happy and loving home.

'It must have been hard to do,' Cora said. 'I don't think I could be so strong. I think I'd have to have Lloyd there every step of the way.'

Angie nodded. 'Me too with Stanislaw.'

'It wasn't easy,' Ida admitted. She could still feel the pain of that final goodbye. She didn't think there had been a moment since leaving that she had not missed him. 'But I'm glad I did it.'

'So, you don't even write to him?' Cora asked.

Ida shook her head. 'No. No phone calls. No letters. It had to be a clean break. I told him that the people at the home would write and tell him when I'd gone.'

Angie could see the pain on her mother's face. Just as she could imagine the pain it must have caused her to lie and say that the reason she was here was because Carl had been violent to her.

'I'm glad Carl wasn't abusive towards you,' Angie said. It was an image she was relieved to be rid of, and which had played on her mind, much as she had tried not to let it.

'Carl's one of the good guys.' Ida looked at Angie. 'Like your Stanislaw.'

Wanting to divert the conversation away from death and towards life – particularly to a subject she had wanted to chat with Angie about in more detail – Ida threw Cora a conspiratorial look.

'Which is why,' Cora said, understanding what Ida was asking of her, 'your mam and I can't understand why you don't want to have a baby with him?'

Angie groaned. 'Not you too.'

Ida and Cora exchanged glances. Neither believed Angie's claims that she was too busy to have another child.

And both women had agreed on what they believed to be the real reason.

Chapter Thirty-One

The relief Marlene felt at having found her father – or rather his whereabouts – was immense. Her original excitement on learning she had an actor father returned to its peak level. She now also didn't have to worry about finding a hotel as she'd be able to stay over at his place.

Everything was working out just dandy – as she knew it would!

Marlene hurried over to a grocer who was starting to move crates of fruit and vegetables that had been stacked up on the pavement.

'Excuse me. I'm trying to find a club called the Revue. Do you know where it is?'

The olive-skinned man with dark hair gave her a curious look.

'It's on the corner of Dean Street,' he said, giving her the once-over.

His slightly lecherous appraisal, so soon after the man and woman she'd met outside the defunct Lido Theatre, made her feel uneasy

There was no need to ask directions as Marlene could now probably draw a map of Soho from memory, so she started walking away.

A piercing wolf whistle followed her. Normally, Marlene might have been pleased with the attention – an affirmation of her good looks. But this time it made her feel unusually vulnerable.

It was a feeling she only just managed to shrug off by the time she reached Dean Street, where she immediately spotted the Revue Club on the corner. It was a Victorian building, with a grey awning over the door. Walking to the entrance, she saw blinds had been drawn down, blacking out all of the windows. A notice on the bright red front door told her the club opened at seven thirty.

She felt a kick of adrenaline from knowing that in just an hour or so she would be meeting her father. *Her real father.*

In the meantime, she needed to find somewhere to sit before she collapsed. Her mind might be buzzing with the rush of expectation, but there was no denying her body felt shattered, and her feet were almost numb with pain.

Seeing a man walking into a pub just a little way up the street, Marlene took a deep breath and checked herself quickly in the reflection of the club's window. Content that she could easily carry off being eighteen years old, she headed without further delay towards the brightly painted Rose and Crown.

Walking through the front door and into the pub's main lounge area, Marlene was surprised it was already so busy. The clientele appeared to be a mixture of those who had just finished work – she recognised a few faces from the shops she'd been in – and young women who looked as though they were at the start of an evening out. They were well dressed, which made Marlene feel self-conscious as her clothes looked even more creased and marked after a full day roaming the streets of Soho.

Reaching the bar, which was three-deep, Marlene only just managed to squeeze her way to the front to be seen by the barman. Feeling the need of a reward for making it through the past twenty-four hours, and perhaps also a little Dutch courage as she had never been to a pub on her own before, she ordered a vodka tonic, despite the early hour and the fact that she should really be having something to eat instead.

Marlene relaxed a little when the barman barely batted an eye at her. She'd passed the age test. She hadn't been in many pubs before, unless it was with Angie and Stanislaw, or very occasionally with Belinda when they'd managed to convince the landlord they were most definitely of legal age.

Taking her drink to a small table by the window, Marlene sat down and immediately eased her swollen feet from the confines of her shoes, making sure that no-one could see.

Bliss!

Chapter Thirty-Two

Angie was sitting on the swivel chair in the study. She wanted Marlene back home as soon as possible. Knowing her, she'd likely swan in later on this evening – leaving it until the latest she was allowed to stay out.

This was a time when the whole family needed to be together.

She looked up Belinda's phone number in her address book and dialled. The phone barely had a chance to ring before it was answered.

'Hello, the Beauchamp household!'

Angie thought Belinda sounded serious but was just glad Mrs Beauchamp hadn't answered. She was not in the mood for small talk and pretending that they liked each other when Angie knew full well that Mrs Beauchamp did not approve of her daughter's friendship with Marlene.

'Belinda, it's Angie here, can I speak to Marlene, please?'

'Oh ... mmm,' Belinda stalled. 'Actually, Mrs Foxton-Clarke – I mean Mrs Nowak ...'

Angie rolled her eyes. She'd given up telling the girl just to call her Angie.

'... Marlene was going to ask if she could stay over another night?' Belinda's tone was almost pleading.

'Sorry, Belinda, not tonight. We need Marlene back here.'

There was silence down the phone.

'Belinda, are you still there?'

'Yes, sorry, Mrs Nowak . . .'

Angie sighed. Belinda was such a ditherer. It was normally quite amusing, but at this moment in time it was very irritating.

'Why don't you go and get her, Belinda. Let me have a quick word with Marlene,' Angie ordered.

Another silence.

'Belinda, what's wrong? Is Marlene there?'

Another short silence. 'Well . . . you see—'

' "You see" what?' Angie demanded.

'Mmm, well . . .' Belinda stuttered. 'Marlene's not actually here.'

'Well, where *actually* is she?' Angie asked, now starting to feel annoyed. Her guess would be that Marlene was out on a date with some boy and had got Belinda to cover for her.

'Mmm—'

'Put your mother on the phone, Belinda,' ordered Angie.

'No, no!' Belinda panicked. 'She doesn't know.'

'Doesn't know what?' Angie asked through gritted teeth.

'Where Marlene is . . .' Belinda let her voice trail off.

'So, where *is* Marlene?' Angie demanded.

A long pause.

'London. She's in London,' Belinda admitted, her voice now trembling.

'London?' Angie's head started to swirl. She wished

she'd not had the brandy. 'Why on earth would she go to London?'

'Well . . .' Belinda decided to plunge in with the truth. She had no other choice. 'She said she wanted to find her father. Her real father. Jacques Kaplan. The actor.'

It took a few seconds for Angie's brain to register Belinda's words, which had been fired out nineteen to the dozen – as though speaking faster would somehow lessen the impact.

And then Angie's heart started to gallop as she realised what had happened.

Marlene must have been earwigging in on Angie's conversation with their mam.

'When? When did she go?' Angie forced herself back into the here and now.

'Yesterday. Late afternoon. She caught the four o'clock train,' Belinda said.

Angie recalled her sister's demeanour, her little suitcase – the way she'd turned and waved goodbye. She'd just thought Marlene was excited, but now she realised there'd also been a hint of guilt there.

'And where's she staying?' Angie demanded. The thought of her sixteen-year-old sister alone in London made her feel sick with worry.

'I . . . I don't know,' Belinda admitted, her own concern for her friend now coming to the fore.

'What do you mean, you don't know? She didn't tell you?' Angie asked incredulously. The pair of them told each other everything. No matter how insignificant.

'Well, she was going to call me when she arrived and tell me where she was staying,' Belinda said.

'And she didn't?' Angie asked, her tone low and deathly serious. 'You've not heard from her since she left?' If Marlene hadn't rung her friend, then something was wrong. Very wrong.

'No, I haven't. Nothing,' Belinda admitted. 'I'm so sorry. I've been in such a pickle. I've not known what to do. She swore me to secrecy, but then when she didn't ring, I didn't know what to do.'

Belinda had convinced herself that her friend was whooping it up and had simply been having too good a time, but now, hearing how worried her sister was, she knew deep down that Marlene would still have called her, even if it was just to tell her about the fabulous time she was having.

Now that she was speaking about it, the angst Belinda had been forcing back suddenly took over. 'Oh God, what if something's happened?'

Angie wanted to lambast Belinda for not calling sooner, but knew it wouldn't help matters.

'So,' Angie began, 'Marlene got the train to London after leaving here yesterday afternoon?'

'Yes. And she said she'd ring me when she'd checked into a hotel.' Belinda was now on the verge of tears.

'So, she hadn't booked up anywhere beforehand?' Angie tried to keep her tone neutral. She needed Belinda to think straight and not dissolve into tears of self-recrimination.

'No, that's why I wasn't too worried at first,' Belinda said. 'If she hadn't found somewhere until late, I knew she wouldn't ring because it would make my mother suspicious.'

Angie took a deep breath. 'And where was she going to try and find somewhere to stay? Which area of London?'

'Soho. She said that's where she'd find her father. Because he'd been in a show there . . .' Belinda was only just keeping the tears at bay. If she started, she knew she wouldn't stop. They'd been brewing all day.

'And no calls today?' Angie asked. 'No missed calls?'

'I've been in all day, waiting,' Belinda informed her. She had told her mother that she was feeling unwell and was going to just sit and read on the sofa. It wasn't really a lie as every hour she'd felt increasingly nauseous, with the same question going round in her head. *Why hadn't Marlene rung?*

'There was only one time she could have called – when my mother was on the phone to her friend for a while.'

'And when was that?' Angie asked.

'This morning. Just after eleven o'clock.' Belinda knew the exact time as she'd tried every excuse to get her mother off the phone, but with no success.

'Right, Belinda,' Angie began, resisting the urge to castigate her for her misplaced loyalty. 'Ring me straight away if Marlene telephones you. You understand? You ring me straight away!'

'Yes, of course, Mrs Nowak, I will. Straight away—' The last few words were spoken to dead air as Angie had already hung up.

Angie stormed out of the study, nearly bumping into a couple who had returned from a walking tour around

Durham. Not that she was aware of them. She was oblivious to everyone and everything around her.

Seeing the disgruntled look on the guests' faces, Wilfred quickly left his spot behind the reception desk and offered to take the couple's coats, asking them if they had enjoyed their tour, and if they wanted a tipple before dinner.

'I don't believe this,' Angie said as soon as she walked into the living room and saw Cora and Ida.

'What's wrong?' Ida asked. Her daughter's face always turned sallow and gaunt whenever she was worried.

'It's Marlene,' Angie said. 'She's gone to London to find her father.'

After Angie had relayed what she had been told by Belinda, Ida asked to use the phone.

Cora went to find Lloyd.

And Angie stomped to the stables to interrogate Thomas.

Chapter Thirty-Three

The next hour wasn't as restorative as Marlene had hoped. It seemed, as a woman on her own, she was fair game, even though she was keeping herself to herself and her attention firmly fixed on the street outside. She lost count of the number of times she was approached and asked if she'd like some company or another drink.

After going to the Ladies to freshen up, Marlene reapplied her lipstick, powdered her face and combed and puffed up her hair, which she'd recently had cut into a shoulder-length bob.

When the barman came to collect her empty glass, he smiled. 'Same again?'

Marlene had been going to ask for just a glass of tonic water, but instead found herself saying, 'Yes, please.'

The barman returned a few minutes later, slapping a fresh coaster on the table and putting her drink down.

'Compliments of the gentleman at the bar,' he said.

Marlene looked up to see a young man smiling over at her.

Instinct told her to reject the man's kindness – no-one gave you anything without wanting something in return – but she didn't want to cause a scene or seem rude and so she smiled her thanks. She felt relieved when the man nodded, smiled and then turned back to face the bar and carry on his conversation with a ginger-haired young man sitting on the barstool to his right.

Checking her watch and seeing it was nearly half-past seven Marlene felt a rush of nerves. *Soon she would be meeting her father.* She would explain to him that she was his daughter. They would chat and rejoice. And she would tell him all about her life – as he would tell her about his.

When she looked back up, she saw the bloke who had bought her a drink climb off his stool and manoeuvre his way through the now packed pub to reach her. He brushed his hair back on reaching her table and then extended his hand.

'I hope you don't mind,' he said. 'But I just wanted to come over and say hello.'

Again, Marlene wanted to say that she did mind, that she just wanted to be left alone with her thoughts, but instead she found herself shaking his hand and not objecting when he moved her small suitcase to free up the chair opposite her and sat down.

'I'm John. Pleased to meet you.'

Marlene forced a smile.

'I haven't seen your face around here before,' said the man, who looked to be in his early twenties. 'You just visiting?'

Marlene nodded. She didn't want to draw him into conversation and tell him that this would soon be her second home as her actor father lived here.

'Where are you from?' her admirer persisted.

Out of the corner of her eye, Marlene noticed the ginger-haired bloke squash through the throng of drinkers, heading in the direction of the Gents.

'Up north,' Marlene replied.

'Ah, I've family up north. Whereabouts?'

Marlene told him, all the while working out how she could get shot of him and concentrate on meeting her father.

'My relatives are in Manchester . . .' he said.

Any more chatter ended when Marlene felt someone stagger into her.

'Oh, mate! Watcha!' It was the ginger-haired bloke. He'd just saved himself from falling by grabbing the back of Marlene's chair.

'Sorry, mate, I didn't see yer there . . .' The man was genuinely apologetic. 'It's like a bleedin' tin of sardines in here.'

'So,' John said, drawing Marlene's attention away from the exchange, 'where you off to now?'

'I'm meeting someone,' Marlene said, looking at her watch.

'I'll leave you to it then. But lovely to meet you. Hope to see you in here again.'

Marlene smiled. This time it was meant. She was glad he'd realised she was not interested in him.

As she finished her drink, Marlene noticed the ginger-haired man leave the pub. He looked to be in a hurry. A few minutes later, John also left.

Not wanting to get to the club the moment it opened, Marlene held back and finished her drink before forcing her feet into her heeled shoes again. When she stood up, she felt unsteady and grabbed the table edge. She really should have eaten something. The two vodka tonics had gone to her head. Pulling her jacket from the back of the chair, she resolved to have a quick bite to eat before going to the club. She didn't want to appear tipsy seeing her father for the first time.

She looked down at the floor for her suitcase.

It wasn't there.

She scanned the beer-stained wooden flooring with a growing sense of panic.

Still no suitcase to be seen.

Calm down, she told herself. It had probably just been pushed under the table after the scuffle earlier.

Bobbing down onto her haunches, Marlene looked under the table.

Her suitcase was not there.

Marlene felt her stomach turn as she was hit by a wave of nausea.

The words of the man in the pinstriped suit outside the defunct Lido Theatre came back to her in a flash.

Anything not stapled down round here is guaranteed to be snatched and gone before you've had time to blink.

Marlene hurried to the bar. Her last hope was that someone had handed it in, but that was soon dashed with a shake of the barman's head.

And it was then that Marlene knew.

She'd been conned by John and the bloke with ginger hair. Buying her a drink had been a ruse. A distraction so that they could steal her suitcase.

How could she be so stupid?

She did a quick itinerary of what was in there. Mainly clothes and toiletries.

At least her purse hadn't been in there.

'No, no, no!' Marlene's words were lost in the increasingly loud chatter of the pub.

She rifled through her jacket pockets.

She remembered the ginger bloke nudging into her. Grabbing the back of her chair.

Her purse!

He'd stolen her purse as well!

Chapter Thirty-Four

Ida's hands were shaking as she dialled the number she had desperately wanted to call ever since leaving London.

She checked the time. It had just gone seven o'clock. Carl would have got back from work and would probably be making himself something to eat. Her heart was thumping as the public telephone in their building rang out.

It seemed forever before Annie, the old woman whose flat was nearest the phone, answered.

'Annie, it's Ida. Sorry to be rude, but there's a bit of an emergency and I need to speak to Carl. Don't bother going up the stairs to knock on the door – just shout up for him.' Ida knew if Annie climbed the stairs, she'd be waiting for evermore.

Hearing her bellow out Carl's name, Ida was grateful the old woman's lungs were in better working order than her legs.

'It's your Ida on the blower – something about an emergency!' Annie's strong cockney accent sounded out loud and clear.

Ida listened, her ear pressed against the black Bakelite receiver, for the sound of Carl's hurried footsteps clomping down the staircase.

As soon as she heard Annie handing over the phone, Ida started speaking.

'Carl, it's me. I know I said I wouldn't call, but this is an emergency – which has nothing to do with my situation. It's Marlene. I told her about James, like I told you I planned to do, but she found out he's still alive. She left Durham yesterday teatime, which means she would have got into King's Cross late. Her intention was apparently to go straight to Soho, find a hotel and then look for her father. But no-one's heard a whisper from the moment she stepped onto the train. She was meant to have called her best mate when she arrived, but nothing.'

Ida stopped and swallowed hard, trying to keep her emotions in check.

'It's all right,' Carl said reassuringly. 'We'll find her.'

At that moment Ida missed Carl more than ever. If there was ever a problem, it was *their* problem – not just *her* problem. He was by her side even now – when she was hundreds of miles away from him.

'Oh God . . .' Ida let out a sob of fear and self-recrimination. 'This is all my fault, Carl. If anything happens to Marlene . . .' She let her voice trail off. *Couldn't she do anything right as a mother?* She should have let them all be. They'd have been better off. She should have stayed on the train and gone straight to Fife.

Ida was quiet for a moment and Carl knew she was drowning in blame and regret.

'Nothing's going to happen to Marlene. We're going to find her,' Carl reassured. 'First off, I'm going to go straight to

Soho and find that no-good waster James Midgley, or whatever name he's going by at the moment. Best-case scenario, Marlene's found him already. But if she hasn't, he can call us if and when she does. But hopefully we'll find her before then.'

Carl waited a beat.

'Now, where are you at this moment? I'm guessing you're still at Cuthford Manor – that you've not left for Fife yet?' Carl had wondered how long Ida would stay there. It had been two weeks since they'd said their final heart-wrenching goodbyes.

'Yes, I'm still here. I was just about to leave, but they found out about the cancer. I'll tell you more later. Just, please, Carl, find Marlene. I feel sick thinking about her in London on her own – never mind trooping around Soho. Talk about easy prey.'

Carl agreed but didn't say so. Ida sounded out of her mind with worry. He hadn't heard her like this since she had walked out on her family when they had left for London. He'd never forget the state she'd been in. She'd not been able to eat or sleep for two days until she had managed to speak to her friend Niamh and been told that, as hoped, Angie and Quentin had taken Danny, Marlene, Bertie and Jemima to live with them at Cuthford Manor.

'Marlene thinks she's tough and worldly-wise, but she's not.' Ida's words broke through Carl's thoughts. 'She's far from it.'

'Right,' Carl said, pulling his jacket off the hook in the communal hallway while jamming the receiver between his neck and shoulder, 'give me a good description of Marlene.'

'Oh, Carl.' Ida's voice cracked with emotion. 'She's so beautiful. So vibrant.'

Carl could hear the love Ida had for her daughter. She was wrong in thinking that she had been born without a maternal bone in her body. But this was not the time to tell her.

'She's got naturally blonde hair, which has been cut into a bob. She looks much older than her age, which is what worries me most of all—'

'Go on.' Carl encouraged Ida to stay on track.

'She's a good few inches taller than me. Angie says she was wearing heeled shoes, but that's not to say she didn't have flats in her suitcase. She had a skirt and blouse on, but again, that's not to say she hasn't changed her outfit. Oh, and she speaks the most perfect Queen's English.' Ida swallowed hard again. 'She's amazing, Carl. So full of life.' Ida felt her panic growing. 'Please go! As soon as you have any news, ring the Cuthford Manor Country House Hotel.'

'I'll call the minute I hear anything,' Carl reassured her. 'And Ida?'

'Yes?'

'I love you.'

'I love you too, Carl.'

And with that she hung up.

'Thomas!' Angie shouted as she strode across the yard towards the stables. Winston and Bessie were by her side, having sensed all was not well with their mistress.

Before Angie reached the converted barn, Thomas appeared, his grooming brush still strapped to his hand.

'Everything all right?' he asked.

'No, everything's about as far from all right as you can get,' she replied tersely.

She heard a horse's hoofs on the cobbles and turned to see Stanislaw returning from a ride out on Ghost.

On seeing his wife's deathly serious face and that the dogs' ears were up and their tails down, he quickly dismounted and walked Ghost over to the stables.

'What's happened?' he asked.

'Marlene's gone to London to find her father,' she said, directing her attention back to Thomas. 'She left yesterday and hasn't been heard from since.'

'Oh God,' Stanislaw muttered under his breath.

'Thomas,' Angie began, 'I need you to be honest with me. No defending Marlene . . . Did you know about this?'

'No, I swear.' Thomas looked from Angie to Stanislaw. 'I'd never have let her go if I'd known.'

Angie looked at Thomas and, seeing the shock and concern on his face, knew he was not lying.

'Okay, I believe you,' she said. 'Did she say anything at all – even just in passing – about her father? Anything which might give us a clue as to where she could be?'

Thomas thought hard.

'She came to see me – but just briefly – to tell me that her real father was some kind of actor. She seemed excited. More than excited. A little manic.' He paused. 'But that's not so unusual for Marlene . . . I asked her where he was.' Thomas inwardly berated himself. He should have guessed she was lying. 'She said he was dead. And then she just sort of flitted off in that way of hers, saying she was going to see Belinda 'n was staying the night.'

Angie looked at Stanislaw. Their expressions were easily readable. *What to do next?*

'I'll go,' Thomas said. 'I'll get the next train and go find her,' he said, pulling his hand from the paddle horse brush and making to leave.

'No,' Stanislaw said, 'that won't be necessary. That'll take too long. We need someone who's there now.'

'I know who to ring!' Angie declared, striding off back indoors, the dogs hot on her heels.

Angie reached the study just as Ida was hanging up.

'Carl's leaving now for Soho. He won't stop looking until he's found her,' Ida said, getting up out of the chair. As she did so, she was hit by a dizzy spell.

Angie ran to grab her before she toppled over. Her own head was spinning, but for different reasons.

Her mam was dying.

Marlene was missing.

Angie took hold of her mam's arm and was just about to speak when Ida beat her to it.

'Yes, I'm going to go upstairs to rest, but before I do, I'm going to get the little ones. I'll tell them there's been a problem with my lodgings – that's why I'm still here. I can keep them occupied. We don't want them picking up that something's wrong.'

Ida stood up straight and took hold of Angie's hand, which was still gripping her arm, and patted it. 'Carl will ring here as soon as he's got any news.'

Angie nodded. Her mam looked as white as a sheet. 'You sure you're okay?'

'Yes,' Ida answered. 'Now call whoever it is you're going to ring. There's no time to waste.'

By the time Ida had left the study, Angie had got through to Rosie. The former head welder of their squad was married to a high-ranking police officer who, Angie hoped, might be able to use his contacts to help. And there was also Rosie's old friend and former business partner, Lily, who ran a gentlemen's club in London.

'Marlene's gone missing in London,' Angie blurted out as soon as she heard her old boss's voice. She quickly relayed the chronology of events, giving Rosie both the real name and the stage moniker of the father Marlene had gone in search of.

'I'll ring Lily – see if she can help – and Peter will ring the Met and get them looking.'

'Thanks, Rosie. God, I don't know what I'll do if something's happened to her.'

'It won't have. Marlene's more streetwise than you think.'

But Angie wasn't so sure.

Chapter Thirty-Five

Marlene stood outside the Rose and Crown, her head spinning. She was in the middle of London. At night. With no money. Just the clothes on her back. And a pair of shoes she'd give anything not to be wearing.

Tears stung her eyes, but the panic racing around inside her head kept them at bay.

Looking down the street, she could see a small group of men going into the Revue Club.

'Everything is going to be fine,' Marlene mumbled, trying hard to convince herself.

You'll find your dad and he'll take care of everything. He'll sort it all out.

She'd be all right just as soon as she found him.

Marlene was just about to cross the road when a small two-door Austin A30 – she knew the make as Thomas was obsessed with cars – pulled up. The driver, a bald man who looked to be in his forties, leant across the passenger seat. He said something Marlene didn't catch, so she stepped nearer and ducked her head down to the open car window.

'How much, darling?' he asked, his gaze fixed on the V-neck of her blouse.

Marlene stood up and staggered back, pulling the lapels

of her jacket up to her neck. She hurried away from the car and down the street, now oblivious to the pain caused by her shoes rubbing against her swollen and chafed feet.

The car passed her again, slowly. She sensed the man's eyes on her, but she walked on, staring resolutely ahead. As the Austin continued down the road and turned left, Marlene slowed down and forced herself to breathe properly.

When she reached the club on the corner of Dean Street, she saw a small queue had now formed. She felt a mess, but on checking herself in the reflection of the club's blacked-out window, she was relieved to see she didn't look too bad. Her outer appearance did not reflect her inner turmoil.

Passing the doorman, she gave him a smile and said a silent prayer of thanks when he welcomed her to the club without asking her age or why she was on her own. She uttered a second prayer of thanks that there was no entry fee.

Having handed her jacket in at the cloakroom, she gave herself a quick brush down. She was glad it was dark as it disguised the marks on her blouse and the creases in her skirt.

Now all she had to do was find her father.

A shot of excitement boosted her flagging energy levels.

He was here.

She knew it.

Her luck was about to change.

Walking through the main doors to the club, Marlene was hit by a frantic cacophony of trumpet, saxophone, piano and drums, which seemed to be whipping those on the small dance floor into a frenzy.

205

Contending with a cloud of cigarette smoke, Marlene scanned the room, looking for her father, even though she had no idea what he looked like. She'd presumed she would somehow just know him as soon as she saw him. Looking at all the faces sitting at the small tables around the perimeter of the dance floor, she realised, not for the first time, how foolish she'd been. It was unlikely she would recognise him even if he was standing right in front of her. She needed to find someone who worked there.

Spotting a waitress weaving her way from the bar towards a table of four young men, her arm raised high as she balanced a tray of drinks, Marlene made a beeline towards her, which was easier said than done. It felt as though she was swimming against the current as she was jostled and nudged with every step she took. The young men, each one sporting the same quiffed hair, were vying for the waitress's attention. She gave them a forced smile before turning and renegotiating her way back to the bar at the far end of the room.

Marlene forced herself through the throng of revellers, her ears accosted by the loud voices of those who were having to shout to be heard and by the occasional shriek of laughter. She felt overwhelmingly aware of the irony that she had dreamt of being in such a fashionable club in London's West End, but now she was actually here, all she wanted to do was to leave. Which she fully intended on doing as soon as she found her father. She had a fleeting vision of her and her dad sitting in his flat, her feet in a bowl of warm salted water, a cup of tea to hand, as she relayed her quest to find him. There had never been any doubt in

Marlene's mind that her father would be forever thankful she had sought him out and that he would be truly over-joyed to learn he had a daughter.

'Excuse me!' Marlene said, tapping the shoulder of the petite waitress, who was now carrying the tray under her arm like a baton.

The woman turned around.

'I'm sorry,' Marlene shouted into her ear, 'I'm looking for someone and hoped you could help.'

The woman looked Marlene up and down. 'Who yer looking for, love?'

'A man—' Marlene began, but the rest of her words were blotted out by the sound of a trumpet solo.

The woman laughed. 'Aren't we all?' Her voice was low and at odds with the way she looked.

'No,' Marlene raised her voice, 'not like that. I'm looking for my father. He's a regular here.'

The woman moved to the side and tugged Marlene's arm so they were away from the main hub. It was a fraction quieter.

'What's his name?'

'Jacques Kaplan.' Marlene felt like hugging the woman for giving her the time of day. 'That's his stage name. His real name is James. James Midgley.'

Marlene scrutinised the waitress's expression, holding her breath, hoping beyond hope that she would see a flicker of recognition.

The woman's face was momentarily impassive. Then suddenly it lit up.

'Jimmy!' she said. 'He gets called Jimmy.'

Marlene felt like jumping for joy.

'Do you know if he's here tonight? Or might be coming in?'

The waitress laughed witheringly. 'When is he not here?' She turned towards the bar and pointed at the figure of a man who was sitting with his back to them. 'Good job you've come early. You might get some sense out of him.'

The words went over Marlene's head.

For her ears were roaring with her own:

I've found him.

I've found my father.

Marlene's heart was hammering. She could no longer hear the jazz or the loud chatter of the beboppers; nor did she notice those in the periphery of her vision. Her focus was solely on the man she knew to be her father, sitting on a stool next to the bar.

A couple fresh off the dance floor had squashed up next to him. Marlene could see his hand was wrapped around a glass tumbler of what looked like Scotch on the rocks. He was neither broad nor slender. His hair was blond but thinning. This much she could tell from behind.

Seeing the couple turn away from the bar with their drinks, Marlene slipped into the gap before it closed up again.

Turning, she saw her father for the first time.

Her vivid imagination had painted a picture of her father as a tall, handsome man, with twinkling blue eyes and a debonair demeanour. William Holden in *Sunset Boulevard*.

The reality of what she was confronted with, though, could not have been more different.

The man she was now staring at appeared old and worn out. His skin was pale and wrinkled, with spidery red lines covering his cheeks, his nose bulbous.

Marlene forced back her first instinctive feeling of disappointment.

It didn't matter what he looked like, did it?

Sensing he was the focus of attention, Jimmy turned his head slightly to see who it was. He had many friends, but he also had many he owed money to.

Seeing the pretty blonde standing next to him, his face lit up.

'Hello there, gorgeous,' he said. 'What's a beautiful thing like you doing in a dive like this?'

Marlene immediately felt uncomfortable. And it was made worse by the way he was looking at her.

He turned his attention back to the barman, who was busy making a cocktail. He nodded to Jimmy to show he would see to him next.

'Don't worry about getting me a drink—' Marlene began.

'No, no, a pretty young thing like you can't get her own drink.'

Marlene heard a slight slur in his speech. The words of the waitress boomeranged back to her. *Good job you've come early.*

'I've not come here to drink,' Marlene said.

'What's that, my pretty?' Jimmy asked, putting a hand on Marlene's shoulder and pulling her closer so as to speak into her ear.

Marlene was immediately hit by the smell of stale sweat, cigarettes and booze. She tried to step back but wasn't able to as the bar was jammed with bodies.

'I said,' Marlene began, 'I've not come here to drink.' She took a deep breath, deciding to just spit it out.

'I've come to tell—' she began. But Jimmy wasn't listening. He was too busy looking at her, and in a way that made Marlene feel more than a little queasy.

'You remind me of someone,' he said, his hand now dropping from her shoulder to her arm. His touch was gentle, but not in a fatherly way.

Marlene tried to free herself but merely ended up elbowing the person behind her.

'Oh, and she's a feisty one.' He laughed at Marlene's lack of success at liberating herself from his unwelcome advance.

Marlene felt a surge of disgust that a man his age was trying to come on to a girl her age.

This slimeball was her father!

Just then, she felt his hand sliding down her back and at the same time pulling her close.

Marlene managed to twist round and snatch his hand before it went any further. She held it so tightly his face creased in pain.

She took a deep breath and shouted in his ear.

'I'm not *your pretty*, or a *feisty one*, or a beautiful *thing* – I'm your daughter!'

She chucked his hand down, unsteadying him on his stool.

People had started to look at the pair as Marlene had shouted her revelation just as the band stopped for a break.

'And my God, have I *wasted* my time and energy trying to find you.'

With that, Marlene turned and pushed her way out of the club, not caring that she was leaving a trail of disgruntled revellers, spilt drinks and shouts of rebuke in her wake.

The four young men with the quiffs had been watching Marlene from the moment she had tapped the waitress on the shoulder. Their attention had originally been focused on the young barmaid, but on seeing Marlene, their interest shifted.

'Look at *her*,' said Tony, the youngest of the group, nudging his older brother, Enrico, who was sitting next to him.

The other two at the table, Jerry and Ricky, saw the interaction and took in the very attractive blonde from her heeled shoes to her shapely behind.

'A young Doris Day,' Tony volunteered.

'Or Monroe,' Enrico added, lighting his cigarette without taking his eyes off Marlene.

'Nice ass,' Ricky whistled as they watched Marlene follow the waitress to the bar.

'I reckon she's younger than she looks,' Jerry said.

'Girls like her generally are,' Tony surmised.

'Jailbait,' Ricky added.

'Only for those who haven't got the plod wrapped around their little finger,' Enrico said, demonstrating his point by wriggling his own, which was adorned with a chunky gold signet ring.

The young men continued to watch Marlene as she chatted to a bloke at the bar. They could only see their backs, but body language told them all they needed to know. Seeing Marlene push away the man's hand as he tried his luck, the four burst out laughing.

'She's a spirited one, that's for sure,' Jerry said, taking a swig of his vodka cocktail.

As Marlene turned and pushed through the crowd of revellers, the four men exchanged knowing glances, downed their drinks in one go and got up to leave.

A few moments later, when the waitress went to see if Enrico and his boys wanted another drink, she was glad to see they were gone. Two couples were now sitting in their places.

Good riddance to bad rubbish.

She just wished she didn't have to put up with their quips and wandering hands, but her boss had told her not to make a fuss.

'You don't argue with blokes like that. They're untouchable,' he'd told her. 'Just put up and shut up. They'll find a new haunt soon.'

'Not soon enough,' Maggie had bit back.

The slightly exasperated look her boss had given her said that he felt exactly the same. Only for him it was not for the sake of his female staff, but because they never paid for a drop they drank. They were parasites – as well as predators. But everyone knew not to mess with them. Just as everyone knew they got away with murder.

Literally.

Chapter Thirty-Six

Marlene staggered out of the club and onto the pavement in desperate need of air. Breathing in deeply, though, all she inhaled was warm smog. How she wished that this was just a bad dream and she could wake up at Cuthford Manor, where she'd open her bedroom window and breathe in the clean scent of the countryside. She closed her eyes momentarily, hoping that when she opened them again, she would somehow have magicked her way back there.

But this was not a film with an assured happy ending. It was the real world.

As if to prove the point, she saw the penniless boy and girl from earlier. They had found themselves a new spot near one of the pubs, clearly hoping that those coming out would feel more inclined to give them some coins after they had enjoyed a few pints.

Seeing them made her think of Danny again.

For the first time ever, she knew what it felt like to be homesick.

As she stood looking up at the night sky, which was obscured by clouds and the glare of the street lights, she knew that she had to get home by hook or by crook. Even if that meant sneaking onto a train and avoiding the conductor, like she had done as a child. What else could she do? She didn't have a penny to her name. She had lost everything.

'*Damnation!*' She cursed aloud.

She had left the club without her jacket.

As she turned to go back in, she bumped into a dark-haired young man wearing an expensive black suit.

'I believe you have lost this!' Enrico declared holding up her jacket. 'The cloakroom assistant was just about to leave her post to reunite you with your coat when I told her I would oblige.'

'Oh, thank you. I was just about to go back in and get it,' Marlene said, stepping forward to take it.

Enrico held the jacket out of reach and pasted a playful look on his face.

'But,' he said, looking into Marlene's blue-green eyes, 'a favour for a favour. As I have rescued your jacket, you must rescue me from a night of boredom and join me for a drink.'

'Well,' Marlene began uncertainly, 'I'd love to, but I have to catch a train.'

'Really? At this time?'

'Yes, trains do run after dark,' Marlene replied with a hint of sarcasm.

'I'll tell you what,' Enrico said, crooking his arm in a gentlemanly manner, 'come and have a drink with me and I shall arrange for a cab to take you directly to the station.'

Marlene's head was telling her no, but her feet were screaming for her to say yes.

Pain scuppered principles.

'Okay,' Marlene said. 'One drink and then a taxi to the station.'

Enrico's face lit up with delight. His charm and innate magnetism never let him down.

'There's a lovely little place just a few doors down from here. None of that screeching jazz. Just a nice, relaxed private members' club.'

As they started to walk the short distance to the club, Marlene turned around to see three other men, all similarly dressed.

'Oh, don't mind them,' Enrico said. 'They're just a few friends who've come along for the ride.'

Marlene thought the good-looking bloke's words strange, but before she knew it, she was being ushered through the doors of the private members' club and didn't see the others snickering at their boss's double entendre.

Chapter Thirty-Seven

Within minutes, Rosie had called her husband, Chief Constable Peter Miller of Sunderland Borough Police, who was working late. He took down the details of Marlene's father as well as a description of Marlene herself. The last time he'd seen her had been at Angie and Stanislaw's wedding a year ago.

He immediately dialled the Metropolitan Police switchboard and asked to be put through to their West End Division. He hadn't said anything to Rosie, but his hopes were not high. The description of Marlene could be just about any young woman with blonde hair. And he knew the coppers would not take the case of a missing sixteen-year-old terribly seriously. He thought that Lily might have a greater chance of success. But only marginally. Soho was a busy place, with an eclectic mix of residents and workers – as well as its fair share of crooks and those existing beyond reach of the long arm of the law.

After speaking to Peter, Rosie rang Lily at her home in West Lawn, which overlooked the Ashbrooke cricket ground. Lily's house in Sunderland had formerly been a very exclusive and thriving bordello, but it had become too well known by the town's boys in blue and she had shut up shop. Not to be defeated, however, she had opened up the legitimate Gentlemen's Club after buying the property next door, and had also grown her London bordello, La Lumière Bleue, named after the infamous French establishments that had a blue rather than a red light outside to show that they were high-end – and, therefore, highly priced.

Lily, who had a soft spot for all of Angie's younger siblings after temporarily taking them under her wing when their mother deserted them, dialled the number for La Lumière Bleue, which was located on the edge of Soho. The opulence and decadence of the bordello was in direct contrast to its location in Carnaby Street, which was a shabby backstreet consisting of rag trade sweatshops, locksmiths and tailors on one side, and the depot for the Electricity Board on the other. It was the perfect location for a house of ill repute – tucked away from prying eyes and fulfilling its clients' need for discretion.

Having talked to Maisie, a former escort who now ran La Lumière Bleue with a rod of iron, Lily felt confident that if anyone was to find Marlene, it would be Maisie and her deputy manager, Vivian. They were a formidable pair and knew anyone who was anyone, along with every nook and cranny of the square-mile patch of Soho. Like Lily, they too were very protective of the children who had turned up looking like street urchins the day before Angie and Quentin's wedding. They had clucked around them, fed them fish and chips, scrubbed them clean and made sure they looked just the part for their roles of bridesmaids and pageboys the next day.

During the eight years since, they had followed the progress of their temporary charges and inwardly rejoiced on hearing how well they were all doing, how educated they had become and what great prospects they now had in life.

As soon as Maisie heard the news from Lily that Marlene had not been seen or heard of since arriving in London yesterday evening, she immediately marched up the stairs to one of the VIP rooms.

She banged on the door. They were in luck. One of their regulars, Detective Chief Inspector Dick Hollis, had dropped by. Maisie had let his tab grow, knowing that it would prove useful at some point in the future.

That time had now come.

As soon as Carl jumped off the back of the red double-decker, he ran through the criss-cross of streets he had got to know well since arriving in London with Ida. They lived in a flat south of the river, but Carl often met friends at the Colony Room Club, a place where poets and artists gathered. It would be his first port of call. A few of the older members had lived in and around Soho most of their lives. There was little they didn't know about this part of the capital – and very few people they didn't either know or know of.

Reaching the bottom of the street, he slowed down to catch his breath and walked the last hundred yards to the familiar faded green door, which had been wedged open. Taking the narrow staircase two at a time, he walked through the main door and into the club, which was simply a room kitted out with a small bar, its walls crammed with paintings.

Along with the warm and chatty atmosphere, the feel was of a rather smoky and cluttered sitting room.

Carl's heart leapt on seeing two Soho seniors sitting at the bar, having an animated discussion, no doubt, about the latest art exhibition they had seen or the most recent literary novel to have been published.

Noticing Carl, they broke off their debate and waved him over.

'I'm not here for a drink,' Carl began saying as soon as he was within arm's reach of the two men he knew to be veterans of the First War, though they never spoke of it. 'I'm trying to find a bloke called—'

Maisie ploughed her way through the list of pubs and clubs in the area, all the while praying that Marlene had made it as far as Soho and had not hung around in King's Cross.

When Detective Chief Inspector Hollis came into the downstairs office, Maisie hung up and explained the situation. She didn't need to tell him what she wanted from him, just as he didn't need to say that he would do so on the understanding his slate was wiped clean.

Maisie listened as 'the Chief' tried not to slur his words and ordered all those on shift from the West End Division to get their backsides off their chairs and their feet pounding the pavement in search of a young girl called Marlene Foxton-Clarke. Maisie had given Angie's first husband's surname as she knew it would inspire those looking to be more robust in their search; someone with a double-barrelled name might well mean a financial reward.

While Vivian brought the Chief a cup of tea to counter-act the brandies he had swigged back during his evening under their roof, Maisie continued down her list of licensees, hoteliers and anyone else she could think of who had a phone.

Detective Chief Inspector Hollis had just finished his second cup of tea when Maisie banged the phone down and looked at Vivian, who had been sitting on a chair by the desk, anxiously watching her friend's face for some good news.

'Bingo!' Maisie declared. 'She was seen at the Rose and Crown earlier. Javier said she was there a while and left sometime after half-seven. He said something about her looking for her overnight case. He wasn't sure if she'd found it or not.'

'I'd bet on "or not",' Vivian said. 'That girl would have been a sitting target somewhere like the Rose.'

'Right, let's go!' said Maisie.

Detective Chief Inspector Hollis reluctantly put down his teacup and pushed his portly girth and his own substantial 'backside' out of the comfort of the cushioned armchair to follow the lead of the two madams.

After Vivian had nipped into the Rose to check that Marlene had not returned, and to ask if Javier or anyone else knew where she had been going, she came back out to find Maisie asking passers-by if they had seen a young blonde girl wandering around.

'Nothing,' Vivian said, shaking her head. 'But Javier did

say that it seemed like she was waiting for someone – and that she kept looking out the window.'

It was on the tip of the Chief's tongue to say that she could be anywhere by now, but he didn't. This was turning out to be a good earner. Shame he couldn't do the same with some of his gambling debts. Then again . . .

'She was here, looking for her father,' Maisie surmised. 'The fact she left the Rose tells us that this was just a pit stop, and more importantly, that she believed this Jacques Kaplan bloke was here somewhere nearby.'

'Let's check out all the pubs, cafés and clubs – say within a few hundred yards. And if no joy, we'll fan out further,' Vivian said.

'You two have missed your calling,' the Chief jested. 'I could do with you on my team.'

'You couldn't afford us,' Vivian quipped, her Liverpudlian accent becoming more prominent, as it always did when she was in a panic.

They crossed the road and walked towards a lively Italian restaurant called La Traviata. Reaching the entrance, Maisie and Vivian stepped aside. The Chief nodded his understanding, pulled open the door and strode towards the maître d', demanding to speak to the manager.

Walking out a few minutes later, he shook his head.

They carried on past a jeweller's and stopped at a bar. Again, the Chief entered and asked to speak to the person in charge.

Again, he came out and gave Maisie and Vivian the same shake of the head.

When they reached the Revue Club on the corner, Marlene and Vivian stopped the Chief from going in.

'We'll do this one,' said Vivian.

The Chief took that to mean the manager was a regular at La Lumière Bleue.

'Fine by me,' he said, digging into his inside pockets for his packet of Chesterfields and the engraved gold lighter his wife had given him for their twenty-fifth anniversary.

The Chief had been wrong in his supposition that Maisie and Vivian had gone to question someone who frequented their 'house of ill repute' – the term favoured by Vivian.

The pair had actually gone to see Maggie, the head barmaid, who did the occasional shift at La Lumière Bleue when she needed to boost her wages. Neither Vivian nor Maisie could understand why she worked at the club when she could earn so much more if she came to work for them. But Maggie had explained that she loved music more than money and occasionally she was allowed to step in and take the stage to sing a few of her favourite Judy Garland songs. Vivian and Maisie always tried to come to the club if they knew Maggie was performing. They both agreed that 'If you closed your eyes, you'd lay money that it really was Judy Garland.'

'God, I hate jazz,' Vivian muttered to herself. It was pointless to even attempt to make herself heard as she and Maisie manoeuvred their way through the packed club.

'Excuse me!' Maisie shouted angrily as a middle-aged man practically pushed her over in his haste to get out of the club. She wrinkled her nose. The man smelled of sweat, smoke and whisky.

Seeing Maggie dispensing a drink from an optic, they waved to catch her attention.

As soon as they reached the bar, Maggie finished serving the customer and went over to see what her two 'other bosses' wanted. She thought they looked unusually serious. And as they both hated jazz, it had to be important for them to 'endure the assault to their ears', as Maisie was prone to saying.

The trio talked. Or rather, Maisie and Vivian fired questions at Maggie, and she did her best to answer.

When they had drained her dry of every last detail of Marlene's short time at the club, Maisie and Vivian hurried out as fast as they could.

Immediately they came face to face with the Chief – and the rude man who had barged past them both inside the club.

As soon as the Chief saw Maisie and Vivian, he tossed his half-smoked cigarette to the ground. 'If you'd told me you were looking for Jimmy here –' he nodded at the dishevelled man standing next to him '– it would have saved us all a lot of time and effort.'

Maisie looked from the man called Jimmy to the Chief, her mind quickly drawing the dots.

'*This* is Marlene's dad?' Vivian practically spat the words out; like Marlene, she had imagined a handsome, rather rakish actor. But this man just looked like a washed-out has-been.

'I am,' Jimmy said, annoyed that he was being talked about as though he was either not there or an imbecile.

Having been told by Maggie about the man who had tried to come on to Marlene, Maisie stepped forward and slapped Jimmy hard across the face.

The Chief looked aghast. Maisie was after all the more reserved of the two madams. She could be vicious with her tongue, but he'd never seen her be physically so.

Vivian looked at Maisie and then at Jimmy before she too stepped forward and unleashed another, more brutal slap across the other side of his face.

'That's for messing with our Marlene,' she said. 'You dirty old man.'

Holding his hand to his reddening cheek, Jimmy defended himself against the accusation. 'I didn't know she was my daughter. For God's sake. Don't you think I feel sick to the very core of my being? Trying to chat up my own daughter?' If the shock of finding out he had a daughter hadn't totally sobered him up, the double whammy of slaps certainly did the trick.

'Even so,' Maisie glowered at him, 'a man of your age – trying it on with a young girl,' she said, the corner of her lips turned down to accentuate her disgust.

The Chief blinked hard, taking in the absurdity of the situation. La Lumière Bleue made its money from older, richer men who liked to enjoy the pleasure of much younger women. He himself being one of them.

'There's more at stake here than me being a dirty old man,' Jimmy said, straightening his tie, 'which I'm not.'

'Which is?' Maisie asked impatiently.

'Marlene – my daughter . . .' Jimmy paused, taking in the mind-blowing meaning of his own words. *He had a daughter!* 'Marlene left the club after my terrible faux pas – but just after she made her departure, so did some other . . .' Jimmy hesitated '. . . *people* . . . Of course, it might just have been a coincidence—'

'What other *people*?' Maisie demanded. The feeling creeping up inside her was not a good one.

Jimmy looked at the Chief.

'It was the Rossi brothers and two of their flunkeys,' he said, his expression intensifying the seriousness of his tone.

Chapter Thirty-Eight

Enrico handed Marlene's jacket to the woman in charge of the cloakroom. The pretty brunette with a figure like Venus clearly knew Enrico and his friends as she smiled and didn't give him a ticket.

The entrance to the main part of the club was a pair of thick red velvet curtains. On seeing the group approach, a young man dressed like a porter from a fancy hotel pulled one of the curtains back to allow them to walk through.

Marlene felt the slight breeze as the curtain fell back into place behind her, together with a sense of unease.

The club was like nothing Marlene had seen before – not that she had many to compare it against. But she had seen plenty of photos of the capital's most fashionable clubs and she certainly hadn't seen any that matched this one.

It was probably the same size as the jazz club, but not half as hectic. The place had a relaxed atmosphere. The air was smoky, but it wasn't just cigarettes she could smell; there was something else, something that reminded her of home. It took a few seconds for it to come to her. *Bay leaves and thyme.* It reminded her of the manor's herb garden.

Looking around, Marlene could see that curtains were a theme of this club, which had a small dance floor in the middle; unlike the Revue, though, it was only half full, and those dancing were far more sedate. As was the music. Down each side of the club, there were small booths with circular leather seats and a little round table with an ashtray in the middle. Each booth had the same velvet curtains, which had been swept to the side with thick gold rope tie-backs.

'What you having to drink, my lovely?' Enrico asked, lathering on the charm.

'Vodka tonic, please.' Marlene knew she should just have a glass of water as her head was all over the shop, but damn it, she'd just found out her father was a lecherous old man – and a drunk to boot.

'I'll get the drinks in,' Enrico said, nodding to one of the free booths. 'Tony, show our guest to the table.'

Sitting down in the low seat, Marlene resolved to tell Enrico when he came back with the drinks that she couldn't stay long. She just hoped he kept his word and organised a taxi to take her to the station.

Judging by the notes she's seen him pull out of his trouser pocket as he went to the bar, he could afford it.

Chapter Thirty-Nine

Hearing the name of the Rossi brothers, Maisie and Vivian paled.

'Oh God,' Maisie said.

'Jesus, only Marlene—' said Vivian. She'd always said that out of all Angie's siblings, Marlene would be the one to cause the most worry. She took no pleasure from being proved right.

'Where would they have taken her?'

'That's presuming they would have taken her somewhere – it might just have been a coincidence that they left at the same time,' Maisie said, but even her own words of hope sounded without substance.

'They've got a private members' club just down the road,' the Chief said gravely. Suddenly the hunt for a runaway had taken an unexpected and menacing turn. The Rossi family, who hailed from Malta, were not people you wanted to mess with. The Chief had never had any direct dealings with them himself, but he knew the family were well connected. And some of those 'connections' reached to a few high-ranking officers in the Metropolitan Police Force.

'Right then, let's go there,' Maisie said. 'Lead the way, Chief.'

They were just about to leave their spot outside the Revue when they heard the sound of someone running – the metal tips of shoes tapping rapidly on the pavement.

'*Jimmy!*'

They all turned on hearing the man shout.

'Are you Jimmy? James Midgley?' he asked, slowing down as he got to them, his eyes going between the man he hoped to God was Marlene's father and two stunning young women and an overweight, balding man who had an air of the Old Bill.

'I am,' Jimmy said, eyeing the tall, dark-haired man with suspicion. 'And who are *you*?'

Maisie pushed past Jimmy. Lily had told her that Ida had got her fella out looking for her daughter.

'Carl! It's Carl, isn't it?'

He nodded.

'We were told you'd be out looking,' Vivian said.

'Any news?' Carl looked at the two women who seemed to be in charge, and who he guessed must be friends of Angie's who had been called on to help find Marlene.

'Yes, we think we might have tracked her down,' Vivian said.

'That's brilliant news,' said Carl, bringing his breathing back to normal.

'You mightn't say that when you hear where we think she is . . .' Maisie said gravely, '. . . or rather, *who* she's with.'

Chapter Forty

After bringing Marlene her drink, Enrico sat down next to her.

Marlene now had a brother on either side.

Shuffling forward, uncomfortable with their proximity, she took a sip of her drink.

'Give us a little privacy,' Enrico told Ricky and Jerry, who were sitting across the small table from them.

Picking up their cigarette packets and lighters, the pair stepped out of the booth.

Marlene watched the taller of the men loosen the tie-back and pull the curtains to.

'You know,' she said, taking another gulp of her drink, 'I didn't realise just how late it is.' She cursed the tremor in her voice, betraying her nerves. 'I think I should get going. I don't want to miss my train.'

Enrico shifted himself so that he was sitting at an angle and able to view Marlene from top to toe.

'No, of course you don't,' he said, taking a rolled-up cigarette that had been tucked behind his ear. Marlene couldn't remember seeing it before he went to the bar.

'We'll get you that taxi as soon as you've had your drink,' he said, lighting the roll-up.

Marlene wanted to down her drink in one, but didn't want to betray the fear creeping into every fibre of her being. Instead, she took another mouthful, resolving to get the vodka down her as quickly as possible without seeming panicked, part of her still wanting to believe that they would be true to their word and get her a cab to the station.

'So,' Tony said, 'tell us about yourself.'

Marlene was trying to think of something to say that might make them back off, but she suddenly found herself in a cloud of smoke which had the same fragrant smell she'd noticed on entering the club. She couldn't help but breathe it in, which caused her to cough.

She watched as Enrico handed the rolled-up cigarette to his brother, who inhaled deeply and then blew out another plume of smoke. Marlene felt it sting her eyes and again was forced to breathe in the sweet-smelling smoke.

'You don't really want to go back up north, do you?' Enrico asked, a smile playing on his lips. 'London's the place to be. Where it's happening.'

Marlene was about to tell him that yes, she *really* did want to go back up north and never return – ever. But before she could get the words out, she was hit by a wave of dizziness. Nausea followed.

'Take another drink,' Tony said, picking up her glass and handing it to her.

Marlene stared into the tall glass, but didn't do as she'd been told.

Had they put something in her drink? A couple of swigs of

vodka did not normally have this effect on her. *Was she being paranoid?*

Then again, she'd been on her feet all day and had barely eaten.

'You could come and work for us?' Enrico suggested, gently touching her shoulder.

'You could earn a lot of money,' Tony added, edging nearer.

'No, no,' Marlene stuttered. 'I haven't decided what I want to do yet.'

She put her drink down and stood up. Her legs felt like jelly, but she forced herself to remain on her feet.

'No, no,' Enrico tutted as he too stood. 'We're not done here.'

He threw his brother a look before putting his hands on Marlene's shoulders and forcing her back down.

'Yes,' Enrico said, slowly pushing her back onto the red leather seating, 'you could earn good money.'

Instinctively Marlene fought back, grabbing Enrico's arms in a fruitless effort to force him to release his hold. Her world had gone from vertical to horizontal. She was strong but nowhere near as strong as Enrico, who laughed at her attempts to break free.

Grabbing her hands, he forced them back behind her head.

'Hold on tightly,' he told his brother. 'She's a lively one.'

Tony pinned Marlene's wrists behind her. He squeezed hard, taking out his bitterness on her that he always got sloppy seconds.

'No!' Marlene managed to scream. There was only a curtain dividing them from those on the dance floor and in the other booths. Someone would hear her and come to her rescue. *Wouldn't they?*

Enrico gave a short bark of a laugh.

'No-one will come,' he said, reading her thoughts. 'But I also don't want to upset the other punters.'

Marlene felt a sudden blow to her head. For a split second there was darkness. As she forced her eyes open, through blurred vision she saw Enrico shaking his fist as though he had hurt himself.

Her mind felt sloth-like, and it took her a moment to understand that she had been punched in the face.

She sucked in air, determined to make herself heard. To let others there know she needed help. She started to scream, but Enrico's hand slammed down across her mouth. He held it there, not only silencing but suffocating her.

Marlene's nose felt blocked up and she started to thrash around as she desperately tried to get air into her body.

She caught sight of Enrico undoing his belt with his free hand, heard his trousers land softly on the carpet.

For a moment she was back in time. A young girl. The gang of bully boys had pushed her to the ground. *Was she back in one of her nightmares? Reliving her childhood trauma?*

Suddenly the wind went out of her as she felt the weight of him on top of her. One hand was still on her mouth, but she could feel the other grappling for her skirt, tugging at it with increasing urgency.

Once again, she was a child, remembering Danny's

233

instructions to her – telling her what to do if she ever got cornered when he wasn't there.

With all her might, Marlene wrenched her knee up, trying desperately to gain enough momentum to do the damage she knew would save her.

Which had saved her as a child.

But this time the weight of her attacker was simply too much.

Try as she might, she could hardly move, never mind defend herself in the way her brother had taught her.

Sick with the feeling of powerlessness, she screamed.

Only this time it was silently in her head.

Chapter Forty-One

'I'm afraid this is as far as I go,' the Chief said.

Maisie turned on him. 'What do you mean, *this is as far as you go*? You'll go in there and get our girl. There's no way the Rossi brothers are going to pay any heed to Vivian and me if we go marching in there, making demands. They'll flick us away like bothersome flies.'

She looked at Jimmy and Carl.

'And no offence, but they'd make mincemeat out of you two. And I'm not necessarily speaking metaphorically.' Maisie shivered. She had heard terrible rumours of the way the Rossi gang dealt with those who crossed them.

Jimmy and Carl made to object, even though they knew the words Maisie spoke to be true.

'Exactly my point!' the Chief exclaimed. 'Besides, I don't think I'd be a fat lot of good because Mr Rossi senior has got some major players in the job well and truly in his pocket.'

Maisie felt the urge to slap the Chief even harder than she'd slapped Jimmy and insist he go in and get Marlene, but she didn't. For starters, he'd probably enjoy it from what her girls had told her, and, secondly, she could almost smell his fear. And if *she* could, the Rossi boys would too.

'Okay, Chief,' Vivian said, glancing at Maisie as she

stepped forward and opened her arms to embrace the man her girls called 'King Dick', which in no way referred to his anatomy. 'You've been a great help tonight. We really do appreciate it.'

She enveloped him in an embrace.

'And don't worry,' she whispered into his ear, 'we'll make sure your slate is wiped clean.'

Then she slowly moved away from him.

The Chief smiled his thanks.

'Go on,' Vivian said. 'Get back to that lovely wife of yours.'

The Chief walked away as quickly as he could without breaking into a run, and Jimmy and Carl turned on Vivian.

'Bloody hell, you mightn't have made it so easy for him,' Jimmy lambasted her.

Carl didn't say anything, but the expression on his face said that he felt the same way.

Maisie, on the other hand, was giving her best friend a knowing look.

'Did you get it?' she asked.

Carl and Jimmy looked at Vivian, their expression changing from outrage to puzzlement.

Vivian smiled.

Quickly checking that the Chief was out of sight, she put her hand out and turned it over to reveal a small leather wallet. She opened it up to show that it was not for the purpose of carrying money – it was the Chief's Metropolitan Police warrant card.

Jimmy and Carl stared at it.

'Well done!' said Maisie.

'Old habits die hard,' Vivian chuckled.

'That's all well and good, but what are we gonna do with it?' Jimmy asked impatiently. *Time was ticking*.

Maisie and Vivian exchanged another conspiratorial look.

'You, *Jacques Kaplan*, are about to play the most important role of your life,' Maisie declared, as Vivian handed him the stolen warrant card.

Chapter Forty-Two

Marlene was vaguely aware of a voice that was loud enough to be heard above the music.

'Sorry, boss, but it's the law. They wanna have a word.'

It was one of the two lackeys standing guard on the other side of the curtain.

Marlene's heart soared. *It was the police. They were here to save her.*

'Well, tell them to bugger off!' Enrico snapped. 'We'll be out when we're done.'

Marlene tried to scream. To tell the police she was here. That it would be too late if they waited. She tried desperately to cry out for help. But it was no good. Enrico's hand was clamped firmly across her mouth; she could barely breathe, never mind speak.

On the other side of the curtain, Jimmy puffed out his chest as he flashed the stolen warrant card.

'We've not come here for your boss,' he said with authority, rocking back and forth on his heels. 'We've come to arrest a young woman called Marlene Foxton-Clarke. The daughter of *Sir* Foxton-Clarke.'

Jimmy cocked his head over his shoulder at Carl. 'My

sergeant is with me in case she causes any trouble. Which I believe is very likely, if what I've heard is true.'

Ricky and Jerry looked askance at one another.

'The girl's not right in the head, gentlemen.' Jimmy tapped his head to demonstrate his point. 'We're here to take her back to the asylum. She caused some poor bloke serious injuries with a knife.' Jimmy looked down at the two henchmen's nether regions so there was no room for doubt as to the kind of injuries that had been inflicted.

'Boss!' Ricky called out, this time with more urgency. 'Plod are here to get the girl. She's dangerous. A nutter. Just escaped from the loony bin!'

There was some muttering behind the curtain.

Jimmy was stepping towards the sound, unable to hold back any longer, when it opened just before he got there.

He was met by the vision of Enrico standing and doing up his trousers and belt.

Marlene was pushing herself up to a sitting position on the leather seat, pulling down her skirt; mascara streaked her face, her hair was like a bird's nest and there was congealed blood around her nose. One of her eyes had puffed up as though she'd just been stung by a bee.

For a brief moment, Jimmy forgot he was in character and made to comfort Marlene, but caught himself just in time. *He just hoped to God that they'd got to her before—*

'Move!' Jimmy demanded, throwing himself back into character.

Ricky and Jerry stepped aside.

'Sergeant Holmes, apprehend Miss Foxton-Clarke,' he

ordered, all the time keeping his eyes glued on his daughter. He could see confusion in her eyes and willed her to keep quiet.

Carl stepped forward and grabbed Marlene's wrist. It hurt him to do so, but he scowled whilst swallowing down his horror at seeing her battered face.

'No trouble now!' he said as convincingly as possible. 'Back to Bedlam for you!'

As planned, Carl took Marlene's arm and marched her quickly out of the club.

'Sorry to spoil your evening, gentlemen,' Jimmy said as he started to back away, 'but that woman is very dangerous. A wolf in sheep's clothing.' He eyed Enrico and Tony. 'You've both had a lucky escape.'

And with that, Jimmy turned and strode as fast as he could out of the club.

Carl walked out onto the pavement, his arm now around Marlene's waist as he tried to keep her upright. She had started to shake uncontrollably and her legs kept buckling involuntarily.

'*Over here!*'

Carl looked up to see Maisie standing next to a black cab, holding the passenger door open. He could see Vivian's face peering out of the back as she waved frantically at him to hurry up.

'Quick!' she shouted out.

Carl practically dragged Marlene the short distance to the getaway car idling by the pavement.

Maisie helped to guide Marlene into the back seat, her heart breaking on seeing the state of her face and her ripped tights.

'Jesus,' Vivian said when she saw Marlene's bloodied nose and swollen eye. 'Come here.' She put her arm around Marlene's shoulders. 'You're all right now. You're safe.'

Maisie turned to Carl.

'Get in!'

He looked back for Jimmy.

'Come on. We can't wait!'

Carl climbed in, followed by Maisie.

'Drive!' Maisie commanded.

The cabbie, who had been sitting quietly, looking straight ahead, knowing when to keep his nose out of other people's business, stamped on the clutch and pushed the gearstick into first.

As the cab started to pull away, a flush-faced Jimmy barrelled out of the club. He looked around before he spotted the taxi with Carl, Maisie, Vivian and Marlene in the back.

'Stop!' he shouted, waving his arms about.

The cabbie braked and Jimmy wrenched open the front passenger door and jumped in.

'Well, thanks for leaving me there!' he said breathlessly.

'Drive!' Maisie repeated, anxiously looking at the club's entrance, half expecting the brothers to have cottoned on to their deceit and to be coming for them.

The cabbie did as he was told, moving through the gears as fast as he could, then breaking and turning left into the first side road they came to. He knew the club the girl had just staggered out of was owned by the Rossi family. There was no way he wanted them clocking his number plate and tracking him down.

As soon as they were out of sight, the atmosphere inside the cab eased.

They'd made their escape without being seen.

Maisie leant forward and tapped Jimmy on the shoulder.

'Warrant card!' she demanded.

The look of outrage at nearly being left behind turned to heartbreak and guilt at seeing Marlene. He handed Maisie the Chief's identification, all the while taking in the pitiful state of his daughter.

'I'm so sorry, Marlene,' he said. 'This wouldn't have happened were it not for me.'

She moved her head, which was resting on Vivian's shoulder, and he could see she was looking at him through her one good eye.

'Good job you can act,' she said, her voice thick and muffled due to her blocked nose.

As they turned onto Old Compton Street, the cabbie glanced in his rear-view mirror.

'You still want dropping at King's Cross Station?'

Vivian caught his eye and nodded at him.

'Why King's Cross?' Jimmy asked.

'Because,' Maisie said, looking at Marlene, 'we need to get this one up north and back home as soon as possible.'

'Those Rossi brothers might be heavy on the brawn and somewhat lacking in the brain department, but they're not that dumb,' Vivian added. 'And when they find out they've been made a fool of – likely sooner rather than later – they'll be out for blood.'

'Great!' said Jimmy, knowing it would take them all of five minutes to find out who the fake detective chief inspector was. He'd be first on their list, having been the main culprit conning them – and stopping them from having their way with Marlene.

His heart beat faster.

He certainly hoped that they had got there in time. That they *had* stopped them.

'I've an idea,' Carl said. They were the first words he'd spoken since hauling Marlene out of the club. Everyone looked at him.

'I'll take Marlene up to Durham on the train. Make sure she's all right. She can't travel up there on her tod. Not in this state. Not after what's just happened.'

'Oh, that's right, you do a bunk up north, make sure you save your own skin,' Jimmy griped. 'Don't worry about little ol' Jimmy here. Just feed me to the wolves, why don't ya?'

'You'll survive,' Maisie said. She'd come across plenty of Jimmys in her time and they were always very good at looking after number one.

'Why don't you,' Carl said, shifting in his seat and delving into his trouser pocket, 'go and lay low at my place for a while.' He pulled out a set of keys.

Jimmy's face lit up at the prospect of avoiding a good hiding and being given free accommodation.

Carl pulled out a pen and small notepad from his inside jacket pocket and wrote down his address.

'It's on the other side of the river,' he said, tearing out the page and handing it over. 'Well away from this Rossi scum.' His eyes flickered to Marlene. He felt the anger rise again at what they had done to her. And even more at what they *might* have done to her. He, too, was unsure if they had rescued her in time.

'When you get to the ticket office,' Maisie instructed Carl, 'tell them to charge the fares to my account. Miss Maisie Hardwick of Carnaby Street. And go first class. It'll be quieter and more comfortable. And they've got a decent buffet carriage.'

As the cabbie pulled up at the station, Carl opened the door and jumped out.

'You 'n all,' Vivian told Jimmy. 'You can get the Underground from here.'

Jimmy reluctantly climbed out of the cab. He looked at Maisie and Vivian and pulled out both his trouser pockets in the style of Charlie Chaplin.

Both women rolled their eyes.

Vivian pulled out a couple of notes from her cleavage and handed them to Jimmy. His eyes lit up when he saw they were two one-pound notes. He tipped an imaginary cap.

Maisie and Vivian then took it in turns to give Marlene a hug. Both telling her that she was a strong young woman and that she would be okay. Marlene hugged them back, not wanting to let go. She nodded at them both. Wanting to believe them.

Maisie looked at her watch and then at Carl, who was

helping Marlene out of the cab, thankful to see that she was much steadier on her feet than when they'd left the club.

'You best hurry. The overnight train leaves at quarter past – that only gives you ten minutes to buy tickets and get on board.'

Maisie saw the looks on Carl's and Jimmy's faces.

She nodded in answer to their unspoken question.

Yes, they had got to her in time.

Still in shock, and in the rush to catch the train, Marlene didn't have the wherewithal to object to Carl accompanying her back to Cuthford Manor. Her mind felt like a projector rapidly clicking through images: Enrico's face as he'd beared down on her; the figure of Jimmy – *her father* – as he held out a warrant card; Carl's horrified expression as he'd led her away from her attackers; the relief on Maisie and Vivian's faces on seeing her coming out of the club.

But overriding all the thoughts and feelings those images conjured up was the sense of relief that she was going home. Back to Cuthford Manor. Back to her family. To those she loved.

'I'm waving you off!' Jimmy insisted as they hurried from the ticket office to platform 12, which typically was at the far end of the station. 'And your address. I need your address.' Jimmy pulled out the piece of paper with Carl's address on it.

Marlene nodded and Carl wrote the address for Cuthford Manor on the back of the piece of paper, then handed it back.

When they reached the first-class carriages, the porter was holding the door open.

Carl stood aside, allowing Marlene to board first.

'Wait!' said Jimmy.

He looked at Marlene, grimacing as he took in her swollen eye.

'I can't say how sorry I am, Marlene. I hope you will be able to forgive me. If not now, in time.'

He opened his arms to give her a hug.

Recoiling, Marlene took a step back. She shook her head.

Jimmy could not remember a time in his life when his heart had caused him physical pain. But he understood why Marlene had rejected his embrace. He dropped his arms to his sides.

'I hope to see you again,' he said, a smile on his face showing his words were meant.

The conductor's shrill whistle made Marlene flinch again, and she turned and climbed onto the train. Followed by Carl.

The long line of carriage doors slammed shut like felled dominoes.

Marlene stood at the open sash window and stared at her father.

He looked different to the person she had seen for the first time in the club.

'I'm going to write to you.' Jimmy waved the piece of paper with the two addresses on it in the air, shouting to be heard above the hissing and puffing of the locomotive. 'And I hope you might write back to me!'

Marlene stood at the window of the carriage and looked at the man who had caused her such upset – but who had also come to her rescue when she'd needed it the most.

As the train pulled out of the station, Jimmy waved.

Just as they were about to lose sight of each other, Marlene raised her arm and waved back.

Chapter Forty-Three

As soon as Maisie and Vivian got through the front door of La Lumière Bleue, they headed straight to the office. Vivian went to pour them both drinks while Maisie dialled Lily. She picked up on the first ring.

'She's fine,' Maisie said without introduction. She knew Lily would have been sitting by the phone since they'd last spoken.

'*Dieu merci!*' Lily exclaimed down the phone. Her croaky voice told Maisie that her boss had been chain-smoking her Gauloises. Despite being born and bred in the East End, Lily was a Francophile. She loved everything about the country, and most who met her believed her when she told them she was a Parisian.

'*They've found her!*'

Maisie moved the receiver away from her ear as Lily shouted to her husband, George, who was evidently not in the room.

'And she's okay?' Lily demanded. Maisie could hear her lighting up a cigarette.

'Mmm, yes . . .' Maisie hesitated. Marlene was going to have one hell of a shiner when she woke up tomorrow.

'What do you mean, *mmm*?' Lily asked, her nerves frayed. The two hours since she'd called them had felt like an eternity.

Maisie relayed what had happened and Lily puffed on her cigarette, occasionally interjecting with questions or exclamations of outrage. George was now clearly in the room as Lily kept breaking off to repeat the salient points to *'mon cher'*.

When she had drained Maisie of every last detail, she hung up so that she could call Rosie.

Maisie was just taking a sip of the gin and tonic Vivian had made for her when the phone rang.

'Five pounds it's the Chief,' Vivian said.

Before Maisie had the chance to even say 'Hello', she heard the panicked voice of Detective Chief Inspector Hollis, whose whispering told Maisie he was calling from home.

'I've lost my damned warrant card,' he hissed down the phone.

'Oh, really?' Maisie said, with faux surprise.

'Did I leave it there?'

'If you did, I would have thought one of the girls would have handed it in. But hang on, let me go and see.'

She put the phone down and walked over to where Vivian was sitting on the chaise longue.

'Told you,' Vivian mouthed as Maisie sat down next to her.

'I think we'll make him sweat,' Maisie said, barely whispering.

Vivian chuckled quietly.

The two women raised their cut-crystal glasses in joyful self-congratulation.

As soon as Lily had conveyed the good news to Rosie, she told her that she was hanging up as she knew Rosie would want to tell Angie *tout de suite*. Which was exactly what Rosie did – feeling beyond thankful that the news was good. It sounded like Marlene had had a very lucky escape. And just in the nick of time too. Rosie had suffered a similar assault when she'd been a little younger than Marlene, and she'd not been so fortunate. She would never want any girl or woman to endure such an attack.

When Angie put the phone down, she felt her body sag with relief and an exhaustion born of extreme anxiety hit her.

Looking out the window to see a group of American hotel guests climbing out of the Bentley, and not wanting to get caught up in a conversation about the beauty of Durham Cathedral or the historical significance of the city's castle, she hurried out of the study and up the stairs to the West Wing.

Just before she reached Ida's bedroom, she heard Jemima's voice cry out, 'Snap!' Ida had been keeping the children distracted and in ignorance of the drama surrounding Marlene's whereabouts.

Standing in the doorway, Angie saw Jemima sitting cross-legged on Ida's bed, a pile of cards between them. Bertie was in the chair by the window, reading a book. And Bonnie was doing a headstand against the wall.

Ida jerked up her head and stared at Angie. The look her daughter gave her told her all she needed to know. Marlene was safe. It was a good job she was sitting, as her legs would otherwise have given way.

'Right, you lot,' Angie said, waving her hand as though directing traffic. 'Out you go! If you hurry, and ask nicely, Mabel will make you all a mug of hot chocolate, but then it's straight to bed for you all. It's *way* past your bedtime.'

In the blink of an eye, Jemima was off the bed and out the door, followed by Bonnie, albeit on the wobbly side, having just righted herself from her headstand. Bertie put his bookmark in place and brought up the rear.

As soon as they were gone, Angie shared the good news. 'They've found her!'

'Oh, thank the Lord!' Ida muttered. 'And she's all right?' she asked, seeking reassurance. 'She's not come to any harm?'

Angie sat down on the side of the bed, depleted of energy, and told Ida what she'd heard over the phone.

'She's had a close shave, by all accounts,' Angie said. 'From what I can gather, it could have been a lot worse. An awful lot worse. But she's safe now. Thank God.'

Chapter Forty-Four

Marlene woke up in her first-class cabin on the night train after sleeping solidly for three hours. The pains in her body had brought her out of the bliss of a deep slumber – and back to reality. Her head was throbbing and she could barely see out of one eye. She clambered out of the narrow bed, the sway of the train causing her to stagger, and stepped carefully towards the compact vanity unit, which had a small handbasin and mirror. She stared at her reflection, not quite grasping that the face looking back at her was her own.

She automatically flattened down her hair, which resembled a scarecrow's. She could see the bracelet of bruises around each wrist. Picking up a neatly folded face flannel, she wet it under the tap and gently tried to wipe her nose clean of dried blood. The effort of doing so exhausted her.

She dropped the cloth, now a faded crimson, back into the basin and steadied herself by placing both hands on the side of the porcelain sink. Looking at her right eye, she knew there was nothing she could do. The lower part of it had swollen more than the upper lid and had turned a reddish-purple colour.

She stumbled back to her bed and sat down, leaning forward with her elbows on her thighs and her head in her hands. She looked down at her bare feet, which were chafed and blistered. Seeing her heeled shoes, she fought the urge to grab them and chuck them out of the train window.

A few moments later, there was a gentle knock on the cabin door.

'Yes?' she called out. Her voice sounded croaky, and it was only then that she realised how dry her throat felt and how thirsty she had become.

Carl popped his head around the door. 'I heard you were up. Do you fancy a cup of tea?'

Marlene nodded. She'd never wanted anything more.

As Marlene stepped out into the passageway, Carl shook out a blanket he had taken from his own compartment and put it around her shoulders. He tried not to show his distress at seeing her eye, which now looked even worse.

'Follow me,' he said. 'The buffet car is just in the next carriage. And the last time I checked it was devoid of humans, bar the one member of staff they have on duty. A very pleasant young woman called Miss Wren.'

Marlene eyed Carl. She was still struggling to align the man she'd imagined Carl to be with the real-life version.

Pulling the blanket around her, she followed him as he walked ahead. Her bare feet felt heavenly on the carpeted floor.

Entering the dining car, she was relieved it was still 'devoid of humans'. Carl, she thought, spoke a bit like Clemmie, only without the plummy accent.

She sat down on a cushioned wooden chair at the nearest table by the window. The blind had been pulled down.

Feeling a sudden sense of claustrophobia, Marlene yanked it open and looked out at the dark outlines of the passing countryside.

As soon as Carl sat down, Miss Wren came over and asked what they would like.

'Can we have a pot of tea for two, please, and perhaps some sandwiches, if you have any?' Carl asked.

If the waitress was shocked by the state of the young woman sitting staring out into the darkness, she didn't show it.

'Of course, it won't take long.'

True to her word, the waitress was back in five minutes with a tea tray and a plate of crustless sandwiches cut neatly into triangles.

Neither Carl nor Marlene had spoken a word since sitting down and both seemed content to remain quiet while they drank their tea and ate.

When the pot was empty and the serving plate speckled with crumbs, Marlene tore her attention away from the darkness of the landscape at night and looked at Carl.

'Mam said you beat her,' she said.

Carl looked shocked.

'Did she?' he asked, not knowing what else to say.

'I saw the bruises,' Marlene stated, watching his reaction.

'Oh,' Carl said, sitting back, his look now one of comprehension.

'That's all you've got to say, "Oh"?'

Carl took a deep breath. *There would never be a good time.*

'The bruises you saw . . .' he began carefully, 'I didn't cause them.'

254

Marlene tried to raise her eyebrows to show her disbelief, but all she managed to do was cause herself pain and exacerbate the thumping behind her swollen eye.

'So, who did?' she asked, pouring herself a glass of water from the jug on the table. Her thirst seemed to be unquenchable.

'It's not a case of who caused them,' Carl explained, 'but what.'

Marlene swallowed, then put down her glass.

'I don't understand. Do you always talk in riddles?' she asked, suddenly worried that the blow she'd had to her head had affected her brain.

Carl took another deep breath. *He just had to spit it out.*

'Your mam's bruises are down to a disease she has.'

'A disease?' Marlene asked, confused. Nothing seemed to be making sense to her. She'd spent the last few weeks believing that Carl was a wife-beater and that was the reason her mam had turned up at Cuthford Manor. To seek sanctuary. Now she was being told her mam had a disease.

Carl nodded.

'A disease which causes bruises?' Marlene asked.

Another nod.

'So what's the disease?' she asked, sounding sceptical.

Carl looked at Marlene. She looked so like Ida. Mother and daughter were similar in so many ways. He could only imagine the kind of reception Ida would have received from the strong-headed young woman opposite him.

'Cancer,' he said. 'Cancer of the blood.'

'Cancer?' Marlene asked, shocked. A sudden feeling of

foreboding started to creep its way from her gut to her head.

'Yes,' said Carl. 'The proper word for it is leukaemia.'

Marlene stared at him, her brain struggling to cope with the gravity of what she was hearing.

'But she'll get better, won't she?' she asked, willing Carl to give her the answer she wanted. Needed.

Carl shook his head, his brown eyes pooling with such deep sorrow that Marlene could almost feel his heartache.

'I'm afraid not,' he said simply.

Marlene stared hard at Carl, as though struggling to comprehend what he was saying.

'I'm sorry, Marlene, but your mam's dying.'

And with those words, Marlene's world was turned upside down for a second time.

Only this time there was no putting it right.

Chapter Forty-Five

Rosie had warned Angie that Marlene looked bloodied and battered, with a swollen eye that would probably have turned black and blue by the time she stepped off the train. She'd explained that Maisie and Vivian had not had time to get her cleaned up or give her new clothes to wear. It had been more important to get her on a train as quickly as possible for fear that the men who had attacked her would get wind of their ruse and try to finish what they had started. Angie felt a shiver go down her spine when Rosie said that the men were part of a well-known gang in the West End, and as such were 'well connected' and 'above the law'.

'It sounds like something you'd see in a film – or read in a book,' Angie told Stanislaw after telling everyone that Marlene was safe. They had all shared the same feelings of relief that Marlene was on her way home, but also of distress on hearing about the ordeal she had endured.

'Who in their right mind would want to go to London?' Angie said, climbing into bed.

Stanislaw murmured his agreement, but was soon asleep, leaving Angie with her mind racing with a myriad of thoughts and worries about her younger sister.

Leaving Stanislaw in their bed as soon as dawn broke,

Angie got dressed, tiptoed downstairs and took the dogs for a walk. She would have given anything to be able to chat with Dorothy, but it would not have been fair to call her in the middle of the night, especially as she worked such long hours.

Later, over breakfast, Angie told the little ones that Marlene had been accidentally elbowed in the eye.

'It seems she might well have the beginnings of a black eye,' she told them. 'But it looks worse than it is.' They started to bombard her with questions just as Ida arrived in the kitchen. She told Angie to get herself to the station and she would tell the little ones about Marlene's adventure in London over a nice cup of tea and a slice of toast. Three pairs of wide eyes stared at Ida. No-one had told them that she had gone to *London*.

Angie arrived at Clemmie's terraced cottage by the cathedral and felt guilty for being glad that her partner Barbara had left 'ridiculously' early to go to Edinburgh for a conference at the university on 'The Political Rights of Women and the Rights of Women in Marriage'. Angie liked Barbara but found her a tad overbearing. She didn't think she could have coped with an outpouring of feminist outrage from her today.

As Angie chatted with Clemmie before leaving for the station, she felt thankful for the easy friendship they shared. Clemmie might be the polar opposite to Angie's friends from Thompson's, but she was a carbon copy when it came to her loyalty. Clemmie had supported her after Quentin's death, and through all the dramas that had ensued, so it was no surprise that she was here again for Angie at the drop of a hat. A constant in times of trouble. Always a support. And, most importantly, she knew what support to give.

Angie and Clemmie arrived at the train station with plenty of time to spare. There was no way they would not be there for Marlene the moment she set foot off the train, but Angie had insisted Ida stay at Cuthford Manor and rest. She'd looked exhausted and her complexion was almost grey. Angie wondered if the doctors had been overly optimistic about the amount of time her mam had left.

Initially Angie hadn't wanted anyone to come with her to the station for fear that Marlene might feel overwhelmed, but when Clemmie had insisted, she'd given in. Clemmie knew of the world outside of the north-east with her work in Europe and her time living in London. She would know the areas Marlene had been, plus Clemmie was the most broad-minded, unshockable person Angie knew. Marlene would feel able to tell Clemmie anything – especially anything she might feel she could not tell her older sister.

As they stood on the platform at the station, waiting for Marlene's train, Clemmie was quiet. It was a comfortable silence and it was what Angie needed, for she had much to reflect on. Two shocking events had happened in tandem. She had been told that her mam was dying, only minutes later to discover Marlene had gone missing.

Looking down the tracks in expectation of the arrival of the sleeper train, Angie was still unsure how to tell Marlene about their mam. It would be a huge shock, compounded by the heinous attack she had just suffered. Marlene could very easily get crushed by the weight of it all.

A mother with a baby in a pram and two small children on either side of her walked past them. As they had no luggage, Angie guessed they were there to welcome home a loved one, or perhaps greet a visitor.

'It's at times like this,' Angie said, still watching the mother and her children make their way along the platform, 'I'm so glad I've made up my mind not to have any more children.'

Clemmie followed Angie's gaze. The young woman had stopped to take the baby out of the pram and was holding her up high, then bringing her back down and kissing her on both cheeks.

'Why's that?' Clemmie was genuinely curious.

'Because of the worry. Going through this with Marlene has made me dread having to go through anything similar with the younger ones. Adding another child to the list of lives I'm responsible for might just finish me off.'

Clemmie was about to argue the point when she saw a faint puff of steam in the distance.

Chapter Forty-Six

As the train pulled into Durham station, Marlene was hit by a flash of remembrance – leaning out of the carriage window of the train to London, waving goodbye to Belinda, her nerves jangling with a mix of apprehension and excitement. Her devil-may-care rush to find her father. Her *actor* father.

It was incredible that just two days had passed since then. It might as well have been two years. For she was returning home a very different person to the one who had left.

As Marlene gazed out of the window at the steam billowing up from underneath the girth of the locomotive, she felt a cloak of grief wrap itself around her.

She grieved for the girl she had been.

And she grieved her mother's imminent mortality.

Last night in the dining cabin, Marlene had questioned Carl at length about her mam – and the terminal illness that was going to take her away as quickly as she had come back into their lives. Marlene had desperately wanted to hear that there was a shard of hope her mother might live. She was a fighter, after all. If anyone could beat this illness, she could. *Surely.*

Carl had given Marlene the saddest of smiles, which

betrayed the contradictions of his innermost feelings – sorrow that the woman he loved had very little time left in this world, but a warmth in his heart on hearing the deeply buried love Marlene had for her mother as it started to make its way to the surface.

Marlene was learning that Carl was a forthright man. He was a truth-teller even if his honesty had the power to cause extreme hurt. He might speak eloquently, but he also did not mince his words. He'd told her there was no hope that Ida would survive this cancer of the blood. He had learnt, he said, that sometimes the only way to carry on was to accept that there was no hope.

Marlene's knee-jerk reaction had been to argue the point, but she didn't. Instead, she had listened quietly as Carl told her how Ida wanted to die alone in a home for other people like herself, and that place was in Fife, Scotland.

Marlene had been outraged. 'Don't you want to be with her?'

'Yes, more than anything,' Carl had told her. 'I argued. And argued. Believe you me.' The exasperation he'd felt was still very fresh. 'But in the end, I had to accept that it was about what *she* wanted. And not what *I* wanted.'

Marlene had looked at Carl. Her mam could not have picked a man more different to her husband.

Having exhausted herself and Carl with her questions, Marlene had gone back to her cabin and lain on top of her bed, going over everything she had learnt.

She thought of how her mam had seemed since she'd arrived at Cuthford Manor. It all made sense. She had wanted to make amends, to say she was sorry, but the main reason she'd come had been to tell Marlene about her real father.

Knowing that made Marlene feel the tiniest bit loved. And she was glad her mam had told her, because she might have joked about it in the past, but she had always felt different to her siblings and could never understand why.

Now she did.

And although her anger towards her mam remained – and the neglect she had suffered as a child was far from forgotten – her opinion of her mam went up a fraction on realising that she had not turned up on their doorstep to use their home as a place to stay after running away from a violent man. The little Marlene had got to know of Carl in the short time they'd spent together was enough to tell her that this could not be further from the truth.

As Marlene had started to drift off to sleep – her mind wandering involuntarily from memories of Soho to anger at her stupidity and how easily she'd been manipulated into such a dangerous situation – she thought of her father. She still didn't know how to feel about him, but he had risked his own safety to rescue her. That had to count for something.

She recalled how her heart had lifted at seeing Maisie and Vivian and remembered their words to her as they'd said their farewells. That she was a strong young woman and she would be okay. She still wasn't sure if she believed them.

She thought back to her mam. Her mam, who was going to die alone in some godforsaken place in Scotland.

Carl said that Ida had still been at Cuthford Manor when she had called and told him to find her daughter.

But would she have gone by the time they arrived back?

If her mam really didn't want Carl to see her, if she really did want to die alone with strangers looking after her, she might have already left.

Marlene panicked at the thought.

She *needed* her mam to still be at Cuthford Manor.

How ironic that she had not even wanted to be there when her mam left, but now she was desperate for her to stay.

The physical assault she'd just endured had been brutal but short-lived.

The pain she felt on hearing about her mam's impending death, though, would be long and sustained.

Chapter Forty-Seven

On seeing Marlene's battered face looking out of the window of the train as it slowed to a halt, Angie's hand went to her mouth.

'Oh my God,' she muttered. Tears immediately pricked her eyes.

Clemmie squeezed her arm.

'Time to be strong, Angie. Your sister needs you to be the strong one.'

Clemmie repeated the mantra to herself. For just as Angie needed to be strong for Marlene, so Clemmie needed to be strong for Angie.

As they walked the few yards to the door of the first-class sleeper, which was now being tugged open by the station guard, Angie tried her hardest to wipe the look of shock from her face.

Stepping out onto the platform, Marlene suddenly realised she still had one of the train blankets wrapped around her. She handed it over to the guard. Turning and seeing Angie striding towards her, she let out a choke of laughter.

'Oh God. That bad?' Her hand went to her face, and she gently touched her puffed-up eye, out of which she could barely see.

As soon as she reached her sister, Angie threw her arms out and pulled her into a bear hug. She then promptly burst out crying. All the stress and anxiety, shock and sadness of the past twenty-four hours suddenly came thundering to the fore and there was no stopping the glut of gulping sobs.

Clemmie looked at Marlene and shook her head.

'So much for me telling your sister to be the strong one.'

They both smiled.

'It's good to see you, Clemmie,' Marlene said as Angie continued to hold on to her, unable to stop the tears. 'I'm fine, Angie, really,' she said into her sister's mop of strawberry blonde hair. 'Honestly, it looks worse than it is.'

Hit by the irony that she had said the same words to Bertie, Jemima and Bonnie, Angie let loose another bout of gut-wrenching sobs.

'Come on,' Clemmie said, rolling her eyes comedically at Marlene, 'let's get this one to the car and back home.'

Marlene smiled with relief. *God, it was good to be back.*

Seeing a tall, dark-haired man loitering near them, Clemmie gave him a hostile look.

'Can we help you?' she sniped. 'Or do you just want to watch the sideshow?'

'Oh God, sorry,' Marlene said, turning around. 'Clemmie... Angie, this is Carl.' She smiled. 'Mam's *fancy bit*. He came with me to make sure I got back all right.'

Angie stopped crying, unclamped herself from her sister and stared gobsmacked at Carl. As did Clemmie. They had assumed Marlene would be travelling on her own, having not been told anything different. Maisie had told Lily, but Lily being in such a state, she'd forgotten to tell Rosie.

'Come on, you two,' Marlene said, shaking her head. 'Pick your jaws up off the ground and let's go home. I don't think I've ever been so desperate for a bath in my entire life.'

Carl drove the Austin 8 back to Cuthford Manor as Angie could barely see out of her eyes she'd cried so much.

'You're just trying to compete with me,' Marlene deadpanned on seeing her sister's red, puffed-up eyes. Her stoicism brought on another wave of tears.

Clemmie was sitting in the front passenger seat, giving Carl directions to Cuthford Manor and firing a volley of questions at him regarding yesterday's dramatic events. When she mentioned Ida and that she'd be shocked to see Carl, there was a sudden awkward silence in the car.

'It's okay,' Marlene said. 'I know about Mam. Carl told me.'

Clemmie shuffled round in her seat and looked at Marlene. 'I'm so sorry.'

'Are you all right?' Angie asked, inspecting her sister's face to try and gauge how she had taken the news.

Marlene didn't trust herself to say anything, so simply nodded.

The four were quiet as they drove the last mile to Cuthford village and then half a mile to the manor. Angie realised that her sister and her mam's *fancy piece* had shared a long journey and that they must have got to know each other a little; certainly enough for Carl to have felt able to tell her about Ida, for which Angie would be eternally grateful. She had been worried sick about Marlene's reaction to the news. She still had to tell the children, but not yet.

As they passed through the gates, Carl broke the silence.

'How is Ida doing?' he asked.

Angie sighed sadly. 'She's tired. I left her resting in bed, although she's probably not getting much peace as Bertie, Jemima and Bonnie have claimed her as their new playmate. God knows how many games of Monopoly and Snap Mam's had to play since being here.'

Carl smiled, his heart lifting as he knew how much it would mean to Ida to spend time with her two youngest and her granddaughter.

As they pulled up at the front of the house, Angie saw the manor's large front door open and Winston and Bessie impatiently squeezing their muscular bodies through the gap. Bertie, Jemima and Bonnie followed. They were all down the stone steps and charging to the car by the time Marlene had got out of the back passenger seat.

On seeing Marlene's face, Bonnie let out a sound that in no way hid her horror at her swollen eye. Jemima made a similar sound of repulsion.

'Cor!' Bertie said, his face scrunching up in disgust. 'That is going to be some shiner!'

'It certainly is!' Marlene forced herself to sound upbeat for the younger ones.

'So, what's been happening since I've been gone?' she asked, realising that this was the longest time she had been separated from her siblings.

'Mam's staying!' Jemima gushed.

'But "only for a little while",' Bonnie relayed.

'Is she now?' Marlene said, their happy faces informing her that they didn't know about their mam's and grandmother's prognosis.

'The place Mam had in Whitby fell through,' Bertie added by way of explanation.

'Ah,' Marlene nodded. 'Any other news I've missed?'

'Yes!' Bonnie exclaimed. 'Lucy's been crying today. A lot.'

'Really?' Marlene threw a quizzical look at Angie, who simply shrugged her shoulders in response.

'Yes,' Jemima said. 'And Danny's in an awfully bad mood.'

'Is he?' Marlene said. 'That's not like Danny.'

Angie was glad that the children weren't too perturbed by their sister's battered face and seemed more intent on filling her in on what had happened since she'd been gone.

'And Mabel's been making Eccles cakes,' Bonnie piped up.

'And we've been the tasters!' Jemima declared, proud that their opinion was being held in such esteem.

'Well, then,' Marlene said. 'I better try one too with a nice cup of tea.'

'Yeah!' Bonnie and Clemmie chorused.

'Before you all run off . . .' Clemmie quickly interjected. She too had been watching the children's welcome and was relieved to see they had not been as traumatised by Marlene's appearance as their older sister had. 'I want you to meet Carl . . .' Clemmie hesitated, realising she didn't know his surname.

'Farley – Carl Farley,' he said, stepping forward and shaking the children's hands.

They each told him their name as he did so.

'Carl is Mam's . . .' Angie began, not knowing what to call him. He wasn't her husband. He wasn't merely a friend. Lover didn't seem appropriate.

Jemima solved her dilemma.

'Mam's fancy man?' she asked.

Everyone laughed.

'Yes,' Carl said. 'I'm your mam's fancy man.'

Just then, everyone's attention was caught by Ida's appearance in the doorway.

There was a tense moment when Carl thought Ida might tell him to go away. That he had to keep his side of the bargain. But Ida smiled, and immediately he knew all was well. Or as well as can be when the person you love more than anything is dying.

Oblivious to his captive audience, he strode towards Ida, his heart soaring that he'd been given this opportunity to see her again before she was taken from him.

Unaware of anyone or anything around him, Carl took the stone steps two at a time.

Reaching Ida, he wrapped his arms around her and kissed her gently on the lips.

The love between the two of them was as clear as the blue skies, which today stretched as far as the eye could see.

Angie stood with Clemmie, Marlene, Bertie, Jemima and Bonnie and watched the reunion between Ida and Carl with intense fascination. Her mam's face had changed in an instant on seeing Carl. Her cheeks flushed with colour and the expression on her face was one of pure love for the man now pulling her into his arms and stooping to kiss her.

In all the time Angie had lived under the same roof as her mam and dad in Dundas Street, she had never seen her being kissed, let alone in such a wonderfully romantic way.

She glanced across at Marlene, whose good eye was glistening with the first sign of real emotion Angie had observed since she had stepped off the train.

Seeing a shiny Aston Martin appear at the top of the driveway, and guessing it was the young couple from Carlisle who had made a last-minute booking this morning, Angie shooed everyone inside. Marlene led the way to the kitchen for tea and cakes, purposely not paying Ida much heed; not because she didn't want to, but because she knew that if she did, the children would cotton on that something was amiss.

Knowing that Ida and Carl had much to catch up on, having had no real contact since Ida had left for the north, Angie suggested they go to the family room and she'd ask one of the staff to bring them a tea tray.

Everyone had dispersed by the time the young couple climbed out of their car and did what everyone always did when arriving at the Cuthford Country House Hotel: they stood and looked up at the unusual architecture with its tapered and turreted towers and exclaimed how 'simply amazing' the place was.

Angie, with Wilfred by her side, fell into hostess mode,

joking that she looked as though she'd been crying her eyes out when, in fact, she suffered from terrible hay fever.

The couple had no reason to doubt the owner of the hotel for she seemed genuinely happy, which she was.

Angie had her sister back safe and sound.

And Carl's arrival boded well for persuading her mam to cancel her one-way trip to Fife.

Marlene, Clemmie and the children polished off just about all the Eccles cakes. Then, seeing that the beginners' riding lesson had finished, Marlene took a deep breath and walked out of the back door, towards the stables.

Spotting Thomas returning from the paddock, she waved over to him.

He immediately broke into a jog, his expression turning from one of joy at realising Marlene was back to a look of concern when he was near enough to see her swollen and bruised eye.

'Are you all right?' he asked when he reached her. He wanted so much to put his arms around her and hold her tight, but something about her demeanour stopped him.

'*Marlene!*'

They both turned to see Danny and Lucy walking towards them from the new stables, which had recently been built nearer to the paddock to accommodate the extra horses Danny had bought. His riding school continued to grow in popularity.

'Thank God you're back!' On seeing his sister's face, his own darkened. For the briefest of moments, Marlene saw the young Danny who had scared off her attackers, his face like thunder and his fists balled.

'I wanted everyone to see me so they could get over the shock and then perhaps treat me as normal – or at least manage to stop themselves from viewing me with revulsion, pity or anger,' she said.

Thomas let out a guffaw.

'Well, your face might look different, but it's great to have the old Marlene back!'

She wanted to tell Thomas that the old Marlene had gone, and had been replaced by an older, more tarnished version of herself.

'Come on, I'll stick the kettle on,' said Danny, cocking his head towards the tack room where there was a little area given over for the making of tea and a cupboard with a supply of digestives.

Marlene eyed Lucy as they made their way to the stables. 'A little birdie told me you'd been crying?' she probed.

Lucy didn't say anything. What Danny had told her about Marlene's ordeal in London was awful; her black eye looked horrendous. But Lucy would have exchanged her own woes for Marlene's at the drop of a hat. At least Marlene was home and could carry on living her life the way she wanted. Something it was looking increasingly likely that Lucy would not be able to do.

Marlene gave her brother a questioning look as to why he and Lucy both seemed so down in the dumps. He responded with a slight shake of the head, which Marlene took to mean he'd tell her later. With that, Marlene recounted her 'two days of hell' in the country's capital, her flea-bitten hotel room that charged by the hour, and her poor feet, which were probably now disfigured for life. Lucy's eyes widened as Marlene told them how she'd been conned by sharks who had stolen her suitcase and her purse. She glossed over her initial meeting with her father, simply saying he was drunk, and gave a sanitised version of what had happened in the private members' club.

'The whole drama has made me think about going over to Clemmie's lot,' she declared.

Danny tutted.

Thomas looked horrified.

'She's not being serious, silly,' Lucy said, nudging Thomas.

Lucy, who was an incorrigible romantic, wondered if perhaps what had happened might finally bring Marlene and Thomas closer together. They'd been dancing around a courtship for as long as Lucy had known them; she'd never seen a pair better suited to one another.

'Maybe I'm not being totally serious, but I'm off men for the foreseeable!' Marlene declared.

Thomas's expression went from horrified to crestfallen.

With that, Marlene pushed herself off her makeshift chair, which was a bale of hay covered with an old horse blanket. 'Well,' she said, glancing at Danny and Lucy and thinking that she had never seen the pair looking so serious, 'if you and Lucy aren't going to tell me what's caused Lucy to cry and you, big brother, to be in "an awfully bad mood" – to quote Jemima – then I shall push off and run myself the biggest ever bubble bath.'

As Marlene made her way back to the house, she passed Mabel coming out of the back door with a plate of Eccles cakes she'd obviously put aside. She was sure she had timed it so that she'd catch Thomas when Marlene wasn't there. Mabel might appear meek and mild, but Marlene knew it was all an act and that underneath that sugar-and-spice-and-all-things-nice exterior, Mabel was a determined young woman. And when she wanted something, she tended to get it.

Chapter Forty-Eight

Throughout the day, Angie kept an eye on Marlene's where-abouts and what she was up to, feeling the need to be vigilant for any sudden after-effects from her attack. She became angsty when Marlene went to have a bath and was in there for what seemed an age. In the end, unable to contain her concern, Angie knocked on the door to check she was all right.

'You've not drowned in there, have you?' she joked, trying to disguise how anxious she was becoming for her sister's well-being. Marlene was putting on a credibly hardy front, but Angie worried about a sudden spiral into depression.

'Don't worry,' Marlene shouted out from the depths of her bubble bath, 'I've not topped myself. I'm still alive and kicking.'

'Good to hear it!' Angie retorted, although she felt slightly perturbed that she had become so transparent.

A little later, when Marlene had gone to ring Belinda, Angie hovered around in the hallway, saying goodbye to the guests who were leaving but all the while trying to catch any snippets of conversation through the half-open door to the study.

The family of four from the Highlands had just said their farewells when Marlene emerged.

'Dear me, that was short?' Angie said.

Marlene let out one of her familiar gasps of dramatic outrage.

'Honestly, Angie, you play holy war when I'm on the phone too long – now I'm not on it long enough?'

'I wasn't meaning that,' Angie said a little defensively. 'I just thought you'd want to have a good long chat to Belinda about everything?'

'I think I'm all talked out,' Marlene said, stifling a yawn. 'I'm just going to get myself a sandwich and have an early night.'

Slightly dumbstruck, Angie watched her sister walk off towards the kitchen. She'd never thought she would ever hear Marlene utter the words 'all talked out' and 'early night' in a month of Sundays.

Angie tried not to worry, telling herself that she couldn't expect Marlene to carry on as normal after what she'd been through. She went to chat to Cora about her fears that Marlene might be permanently scarred by what had happened.

'Perhaps not scarred,' Cora said, 'but it's going to change her. It's bound to.'

Angie tried to tell herself that change could be good – positive.

After leaving Cora, Angie went to see Ida and Carl in the family room.

Knocking on the partially open door, she bustled into the room.

'Lloyd said he'd give you a tour of the grounds,' Angie said. 'We thought you might fancy a bit of fresh air.'

'You must have read my mind,' Carl said. He gave Ida a quick kiss on the lips and then left.

'Dear me, Mam, I've never seen you be kissed so much in your whole life.' Angie's light-heartedness was disguising the awkwardness she felt at seeing her mam and Carl together and how very much in love they were.

Ida ignored her daughter's comment.

'You're worried about Marlene, aren't you?' she said.

Angie sighed and sat down. *Had she become instantly readable overnight?*

'Yes, I am a bit,' she replied. 'She seems to be coping *too* well with everything that's happened.'

'Perhaps, perhaps not,' Ida said. 'But there's nothing you can do other than what you're already doing.'

Angie laughed. 'What? Stalking her?'

'Being there for her,' Ida said, knowing that Angie's need to keep checking on her little sister would ease off eventually.

Angie looked out of the window at the surrounding countryside.

'Carl's told me exactly what happened at that club,' Ida said. 'And he's one hundred per cent sure that they got to her in time. Although, by the sounds of it, *literally* in the nick of time. There was no doubting what was just about to take place.'

'Makes me sick to my stomach.' Angie kept staring out of the window, trying to replace the vile images of her sister's attack with the green patchwork of the surrounding fields and hills.

Ida nodded her agreement. 'The only positive is that she'll never let herself get into a situation like that again. I'm sure of it. It's been a hard lesson . . .' she let her voice trail off.

They chatted for a little while about Carl staying and Ida suggested that it would probably be best if he had his own room. Angie was relieved her mam had said as much.

Angie left to find Mabel so that she could get the other guest room in the West Wing ready for Carl. Then she went to see Stanislaw and Lloyd to ask if they had any clothes they could lend to their new guest, as all he had were the ones he was standing up in.

Angie knew she should have asked her mam if she wanted to ring the place in Fife and cancel her 'stay' there – but if Ida said no, Angie simply would not have the energy to argue the case for her remaining at the manor.

In the words of Dorothy's heroine, Scarlett O'Hara from *Gone With the Wind*, she'd worry about it tomorrow. *After all, tomorrow is another day.*

And hopefully, Angie prayed, one without drama or high emotion.

She didn't think she could endure another day like the one she'd just had.

By seven o'clock, everyone at Cuthford Manor was flagging. It had been a fraught, emotional day and the previous night's lack of sleep was rapidly catching up with them all.

There were only a few guests to see to, most having left

early afternoon and the next batch not due until Friday. The couple of lovebirds who had arrived in the Aston Martin seemed happy with their own company and had gone out into Durham to dine at the city's most exclusive and expensive restaurant, which overlooked the river.

Alberta had made Bertie, Jemima and Bonnie one of their favourite meals – toad in the hole – and served it up earlier than normal in the kitchen.

Marlene had taken up her own tray earlier, as she'd said she would. Angie had walked past her bedroom and heard some music playing. She forced herself not to knock and pop her head around the door.

Ida had just wanted a sandwich and a cup of tea in her room. And Danny was still in a dark mood and had grabbed himself a slice of pork pie and an apple before going straight back out to the stables.

Which left Angie, Stanislaw, Lloyd, Cora and Clemmie to welcome Carl into the fold over a supper of pot roasted rabbit with mash.

Raising a glass of French wine, Angie looked around the table.

'I'm sure I speak for everyone,' she said to Carl, 'when I say a heartfelt "Thank you" for bringing Marlene back to us.'

Clemmie, Cora, Lloyd and Stanislaw muttered their agreement.

'And for getting her away from those evil, predatory men,' Clemmie added, shaking her head in disgust.

'Yes,' Lloyd agreed, his face twitching with anger. 'I'm

still searching for a word to describe them, but I don't think one exists.'

'I wish we could bring them to account,' Stanislaw said quietly.

Seeing the set of his jaw as he forced down a mouthful of meat, Angie took his hand and squeezed it. Any violence committed on any person, particularly a woman, affected him greatly; it was hardly surprising after what had happened to his first wife and unborn child. Angie knew that Stanislaw had learnt to live with the anger, but it was easily stoked back to life. She had often wondered whether it was this that had made Stanislaw so agreeable to not having a family of their own.

There was much chatter during the course of their meal and Lloyd was keeping everyone topped up with either wine or whisky.

'So,' Angie continued, 'we want you to know you can stay here for as long as you need. It's the very least we can do.'

'That's kind,' Carl said. 'I would like to, but I need to pay my way.' He looked down at the scrumptious meal. 'I can't stay in this wonderful hotel and eat such amazing food and not give something back in return. I can turn my hand to most things, and after looking round the estate with Lloyd today, I see you could do with some extra help.'

Angie looked at Lloyd, who gave the slightest of nods.

'Okay, deal,' she said, again raising her glass. 'To the new addition to Cuthford Manor.'

'Hear! Hear!' Clemmie said, raising her glass of whisky.

Carl took a small sip of his wine.

'The only problem I can foresee,' Angie said, 'is if Mam keeps being stubborn and insists she's going off to that place in Fife—' She couldn't bring herself to say the words 'to die'.

Carl nodded.

'Yes, she can be stubborn. But I will try my hardest to make her see sense.'

Angie looked at Carl and felt the tears welling up *again*.

'Thank you,' she managed.

After dinner, Angie went to settle the three young ones, allowing them to go and say a quick goodnight to Ida.

She then checked on Marlene, who was sitting at her dressing table, putting cream on her face.

'You promised not to fuss,' Marlene told her without turning her head from the mirror.

Seeing Stanislaw going to their bedroom, Angie followed him.

'Honestly,' she said as they got ready for bed, 'I feel such a failure in the older-sister department.'

Stanislaw chuckled. Clemmie had told him with great mirth how Angie had dissolved into a flood of tears as soon as she'd clapped eyes on Marlene at the train station.

'Let me guess – because you weren't the strong, nothing-fazes-you older sister you insist on being to all your siblings?' Stanislaw asked as he climbed into bed.

'Yes,' said Angie. 'I'm the eldest, therefore I should be strongest – the one for all the others to lean on.' She got into her side of the bed and snuggled up to her husband.

'Well,' Stanislaw said, pulling his wife close, 'I spoke to Marlene, and she told me she was glad you crumbled.'

'Really?' Angie turned her head up to look at him.

'Yes. She said that sometimes it annoys her that you are so perfect – that you never seem to get upset, and that nothing ever seems to get on top of you.'

'Really?' Angie was surprised. 'I shut down for three weeks after Quentin's death. Barely stuck my nose out of my bedroom door. I don't think that's not letting anything get on top of me.'

'Funnily enough, she mentioned that,' Stanislaw said, kissing the top of Angie's head. 'But even then, she said, you didn't really let on how you were feeling. Just that you wanted to be left alone. And then when you resurfaced, it was back to the strong, resilient Angie.'

'Mmm . . .' Angie thought about that time. She'd forced herself out of her mourning for the sake of the children. She'd been like that because she hadn't wanted to make them miserable as well.

'I wonder,' Stanislaw said, 'whether sometimes a person can be too strong. Too tough.'

'I guess it's the way I was brought up. You've got my mam and dad to blame for that.'

'But that doesn't mean you can't change. It would seem your mother has. Whether that's because she's dying or because of meeting Carl, I don't know, but from what you've told me about her, she seems a very different person now to when you were growing up.'

Angie thought for a moment.

'And talking of changes,' Stanislaw continued, 'I think it's good to admit if you have changed your mind about anything ... Not feel like you have to stand by something you said, which you might feel differently about now.'

Angie pulled herself up on her elbow.

'What do you mean?' she asked.

Stanislaw turned his head to look into her blue eyes, which were still a little bloodshot from all the tears she'd spilled today.

'About having another baby. You must say if you have a change of heart.'

'Ha!' Angie flumped back down onto the pillow. 'After what's just happened, no way. I was just saying to Clemmie at the station that I was glad we'd decided not to have children. No more young lives to have to worry about. Five is enough.'

Stanislaw wanted to say that it wasn't really a decision that they had made jointly.

Angie had said she didn't want to have any more children, and he simply hadn't argued the case.

Chapter Forty-Nine

Hearing that everyone had retired for the evening, Marlene put on her dressing gown and walked down the corridor. She hadn't spoken to her mam since arriving back as she'd wanted to see her on her own.

'So,' Marlene began as she walked into Ida's room, 'Carl said you're dying?'

Ida watched as Marlene walked over to the chair by the window and sat down.

'I am,' Ida said with the same lack of emotion as her daughter.

Marlene tucked her feet underneath herself and got comfortable on the wide wingback chair.

'I'm angry,' she stated.

Ida looked at her daughter and tried hard not to show her distress at seeing the dark purple bruising of her swollen eye.

'What about?' Ida asked, knowing her daughter had much about which to be angry.

'I'm angry because you're *dying*,' Marlene said, surprised she needed to explain.

Ida laughed.

'Well, I guess that's better than being *happy* that I'm dying.'

Now it was Marlene's turn to laugh.

'Which might have been the case not so long ago,' she said, poker-faced.

'So, why do you feel angry about me dying?' Ida asked, pushing herself up in her bed.

'I'm angry,' Marlene said, 'because the little ones are going to be distraught when they find out.'

Ida sighed. 'Yes, they're going to be sad. Of course. But it won't devastate them. They've not known me long enough.' She paused, knowing how terrible those words must sound coming from a mother talking about her children. 'They'll be upset, but they'll be all right, because they have you and Angie and everyone else here who loves them and will look after them.'

'Mmm.' Marlene didn't seem massively convinced. 'I'm also angry because you've come back into our lives without a word for eight years, only for us to find out you're off again – but this time permanently.'

Ida reached over to her bedside table, where there was a glass of water, and took a sip.

'I understand why you're angry,' she said. 'But I felt it was the right thing to do.'

'You thought it was the right thing to let us think Carl was a wife-beater and not tell us the truth – that you were ill. Terminally ill.'

Ida put the glass back down.

'I didn't want you all to know immediately that I wasn't long for this life because you'd have felt a sense of obligation.'

Marlene huffed and shuffled in her chair. 'Not necessarily.'

'Angie would have,' Ida said with certainty. 'Your sister was born with a sense of innate responsibility for others.'

Marlene laughed. 'Well, she certainly doesn't get that from you.'

'That's true.' Ida smiled at her daughter's quick wit. 'And I'd be the first to admit it. But I didn't want to complicate the situation, which I would have done if I'd turned up and told you all straight off that my days were numbered. My death wasn't the important issue.'

'So, what was the *important issue*?' Marlene asked.

'Apart from my selfish desire to see you all before I go, and to tell you all how sorry I am for being such a terrible mother,' Ida spoke her words matter-of-factly, 'the main reason for coming here was that I needed to tell you about your father.'

Marlene was quiet.

'Like I said before, it felt wrong letting you live your whole life not knowing who your real father was.' Ida looked at Marlene and bit back the hurt of seeing her daughter's beautiful face so disfigured; her only solace was that it was not permanent. 'Although I have to admit that yesterday I'd have given anything not to have told you.' She took a deep breath. 'But what's happened has happened. And you've met the man who fathered you.'

Ida hesitated, unsure how to broach the subject of Jimmy coming on to Marlene.

'Carl told me . . .' she began. 'About Jimmy's behaviour at the bar in the jazz club.'

Ida watched her daughter's face for a reaction. She saw Marlene blush and her heart went out to her.

'Yeah, embarrassing or what?' Marlene said, trying to be flippant. There was an awkward pause. Marlene remembered the flash of Jimmy's hand edging its way to her bottom and his drunken come-on.

'If it had been me, I'd have been mortified. I'd have thought him a right creep.' Ida shuddered to make her point.

'Yeah, I did,' Marlene said. 'And I told him that.'

Ida's eyebrows went up. 'Good for you! What did you say?'

Marlene sat up straight in her chair.

'I got his hand and squashed it as hard as I could.'

Ida clapped. 'Well done! Oh, I wish I'd been a fly on the wall.'

'I told him I was his daughter and then I said something about how I'd wasted my time and energy trying to find him.'

Ida felt proud of Marlene, wishing that she, too, had given Jimmy a piece of her mind that day all those years ago at the Empire Theatre.

'And what was his reaction?' Ida asked, wanting to keep her daughter talking, to get it all out.

Marlene thought for a moment. 'I suppose he looked shocked.'

'I'll bet he did!'

'But I didn't hang around. I stomped off – couldn't wait to get away from him,' Marlene said, getting up and pouring herself a glass of water from the tap.

'Which is how you ended up being the target of those blokes,' Ida said, watching Marlene's reaction as she sat in the chair again. She could see the shutters going down. 'What happened wasn't your fault – you know that?' she said tentatively.

Marlene didn't meet her mam's eyes but instead looked out of the window.

The room was quiet for a few moments more before Marlene finally spoke.

'I can't believe how stupid I was,' she reprimanded herself. 'Who in their right mind goes to a club with a bloke she's never met before? I should have bailed the moment I realised his friends were coming along "for the ride".' This time it was Marlene who shuddered, remembering the words just before they entered the club.

Ida had to bite her tongue. Despite being desperate to tell her it most certainly was *not* her fault, it was more important to let her daughter speak.

'God . . .' Marlene continued looking out of the window, but instead of darkness, she saw an image of Enrico Rossi's face, '. . . I trusted him because he was good-looking and well dressed. And young. How ridiculous is that?' She let out a sigh. 'And then, even when I knew I was in danger, every part of me screaming to get out of there, *I just sat there*. Didn't move a muscle. I should have legged it as soon as I sensed they were up to no good.'

Ida waited for Marlene's anger at herself to subside. Then she said, 'I'm going to tell you something which may or may not help.'

Marlene dragged her eyes away from the window and looked at her mam.

'Anything to stop me feeling like I want to give myself another black eye for being so stupid.'

Ida felt herself stiffen at the imagery. She pushed down the anger and frustration she felt at her daughter's self-recrimination.

'When I was young,' she started, 'a little younger than you, something similar happened to me. I was taken advantage of by my mam's brother. My uncle Evan.'

Marlene's eyes widened as she twisted around a little, once again drawing her feet up under her on the cushioned chair.

'Everyone loved him,' Ida continued. 'He was a good-looking chap and the life and soul of the party. He'd visit our house regularly. For whatever reason, he took a liking to me. And not in a good way. He'd corner me when no-one was there, or when I'd gone to the outside lavvy. And every time he did, I didn't scream or shout. I didn't run and tell my mam and dad. I didn't do anything.'

Ida shook her head.

'When I look back on it, I sometimes still feel angry that I didn't *do* something. It was like I froze. Which was so unlike me.' Ida smiled at her daughter. 'I know you don't want to hear this, but you are like me in many ways. I could be a right gobby little thing, full of energy, full of fight, but when it came to my uncle Evan, it was like something happened to me. I lost the ability to move, to articulate, to function.'

Marlene was absorbed by her mam's tale, her mind

jumping back to that same feeling she'd had sat in the curtained-off booth in the club.

'After the first few times,' Ida continued, 'I wised up and made sure I was never in the house when he was there. I'd always sneak in, and if I could hear his voice, I'd sneak right back out again. And if he turned up when I was there, I'd slip out the back door, climb over the wall to the back lane and stay out until I knew he'd gone.'

'Did you ever tell your mam or dad?' Marlene asked, realising that she didn't know anything about her mam's parents. They'd died by the time she was born.

'I didn't,' Ida said, wondering how much to disclose about her childhood. 'My mam was always so busy. And so tired.' She paused. 'More than anything, though, I really don't think anyone would have believed me. Everyone loved him. He was everyone's favourite uncle.'

'So what happened?' Marlene asked. 'Did you keep avoiding him?'

'I was lucky,' Ida said, remembering how often she would pray that he suffer an agonising death. 'He moved away.'

She looked at her daughter. 'The nonsensical thing is, I blamed myself for what happened. As you are now. I even remember feeling *guilty*, which, looking back, is ridiculous. I blamed what happened on my inability to fight back – to run away. But he was the one who was to blame, who was doing the bad thing. He was the one who should have felt guilty. Not me.'

Marlene nodded, knowing what her mam was trying to say.

Chapter Fifty

Danny was lying in bed in his living space above the stables. For hours his mind had been going over and over what he could do to extract Lucy from the clutches of her controlling mother and father.

He loved everything about Lucy. She was the gentlest soul, with a heart so compassionate and caring. She never had a bad word to say about anyone. Instead, she'd make excuses for people, explaining why someone might do something hurtful or cruel. He'd told her that she was too forgiving, but she'd simply smiled and said it was to make up for all those who found it impossible to forgive. It had made Danny think of his own feelings towards his mam, and he knew he was one of those people.

Finding out that she was dying had thrown his emotions into total disarray. He'd felt angry, which had then made him feel guilty. What kind of an awful person must he be to be angry rather than sad on hearing that his own mother was not long for this world?

His thoughts had become like tumbleweed as sleep continued to evade him, rolling without direction from his mam to Lucy to Marlene.

He knew Marlene had glossed over what had happened.

What was it about his sister that seemed to draw those with evil intent to her like moths to a light? Ever since she'd been small, she'd been picked on and bullied. It was as though boys – and now men – could see her vulnerability despite her very convincing façade of confidence. It made him furious to think of what those two blokes had nearly done to his sister. *God, how he wished he could beat them senseless.*

When the red mist of anger finally started to clear, and his tired mind and body began to relax and edge towards sleep, his thoughts defaulted back to Lucy.

And particularly on what he could do to scupper her parents' selfish plans for their daughter's future.

Chapter Fifty-One

The next morning, Ida woke with a dull ache in her stomach that had nothing to do with her illness and everything to do with the dread she felt at having to tell the little ones that she would not be around for much longer.

She had lain awake most of the night wondering the best way to broach the subject. Bonnie was nearly seven. Jemima was eleven, and Bertie twelve. It pained Ida to remember how upset she'd felt on finding out she was pregnant with Bertie and how she'd hoped she would miscarry, as she had done on the occasions she'd fallen following Marlene's birth. But Bertie had stayed the course and arrived in this world in rude health. Having already hit forty, Ida firmly believed he would be her last. She'd cried tears of anger and frustration when she'd realised she was pregnant with Jemima, had prayed for another miscarriage, but those prayers had gone unanswered.

Recalling those feelings, Ida felt deep shame. Seeing how they had both grown into the most amazing, intelligent, kind-hearted children, she realised that they had not been a cruel punishment bestowed on her for some unknown mis-demeanour but a gift. She was sure they were both destined for great things in this life. They weren't old before their time as Ida had been, and for that she was grateful. But their young age and innocence also made telling them the truth that much harder.

During the night, Ida had watched the rise and fall of Carl's chest as he slept in the winged chair he had pulled next to her bed. He had been so exhausted, having not slept the previous night on the train, he'd nodded off while Ida had been chatting away to him about the children. She'd not had the heart to wake him, nor did she want to lose the feeling of comfort from having him there within arm's reach.

But despite this, her resolution to go to Fife remained strong. She wanted to leave this world with dignity and not be a burden to anyone. She'd not been there for her children, so there was no reason they should be there for her. It was time to go.

When the light started to filter through the darkness, Ida gently nudged Carl and woke him.

Seeing that he was still there, next to her, he smiled and leaned across to give her a kiss.

'I can't tell you how much it means to me to see you again. To be with you again,' he told her, taking hold of her hand.

Ida felt the dull ache deepen.

'I've been thinking during the night,' she said, looking into her love's deep-brown eyes, 'and I'm still going ahead with my plans to travel to Fife. I'm sorry.'

Carl made to object, but Ida put a finger on his lips. 'We've been through this before,' she reminded him. 'And at least we've got to see each other one last time.'

'I know we talked about it before,' Carl said, 'but things *have* changed. You have your family here. And you said yourself how nice Dr Wright is. He will be able to help. You won't be a burden.'

Carl knew he was not just arguing for himself, but for Angie too.

'*They want you to stay here,*' he stressed.

'They feel obligated,' said Ida.

'I think you're wrong,' Carl countered. 'This isn't because of a sense of duty – it's heartfelt.'

'I'm sorry, Carl, but my mind's made up,' Ida said, her tone resolute.

After breakfast, Ida asked Cora if Bertie, Jemima and Bonnie could come and see her in the family room. And would Cora mind staying? Ida had warned Angie that she was going to tell the children about her illness. A couple of last-minute bookings had just come in and Angie had told her mam that she'd join them as soon as she'd sorted out arrangements for the new guests.

Sitting on the chair next to the brown marble fireplace, which had a wonderful display of dried flowers in the grate, Ida gave a wide smile of welcome when Cora and the children entered the room.

'Nana, will you play skipping rope with us?' Bonnie asked.

'As long as I don't have to skip and can just turn the rope,' Ida said.

'Yeah!' said Jemima.

Bertie sighed. 'I guess that means I have to be the other turner.'

'Come on,' Cora interrupted. 'Sit yourselves down. Your mum's got something to say to you all.'

The three children looked at Ida, who was trying not to look too serious, or anxious about what she had to impart.

Bonnie, Jemima and Bertie did as they were told and squashed up on the sofa. Cora sat in the other armchair.

'First off, I want to say what a wonderful time I've been having since I came here,' said Ida, looking at the trio staring at her. 'And that I feel so proud of you all.' She looked at Bonnie to show her she was also included. 'You're all so bright and intelligent and altogether totally wonderful.'

The three smiled.

'But I was never going to be here forever, was I?' Ida said. The question was rhetorical.

The smiles left the children's faces.

'You're going?' Bertie asked.

'I am, I'm afraid,' Ida said.

'Why?' demanded Jemima.

'Unfortunately, it's out of my control,' Ida said, 'because I have an illness which they can't cure.'

'What illness?' Bertie asked.

Ida had hoped she wouldn't have to go into detail, but she should have guessed Bertie would want to know, and that afterwards he would go straight to the manor's extensive library to find out more from one of the medical encyclopaedias.

'It's called leukaemia,' Ida said, hoping she could leave it at that.

'What's that?' Bonnie asked.

Ida looked at Cora.

'Well . . .' Cora took over while Ida had a drink of water. 'It's when there's something wrong with your blood, which makes you unwell. And unfortunately, they haven't got a cure for it.'

Ida put her glass of water back down on the coffee table just as Angie came into the room with Carl.

'If there's no cure,' Bertie said, 'does that mean you're going to die?'

Ida glanced up at Angie and Carl, who were standing quietly in the doorway. The children were concentrating so much on Ida they hadn't noticed their arrival.

'Yes, I'm afraid it does,' Ida admitted.

Just then, Winston and Bessie came bustling into the room, their tails whacking everything in sight as they headed for Ida. As always, they started sniffing. It was only now, watching them, that Angie realised why. They sensed that her mam was unwell.

Angie clicked her fingers.

'Here!' she ordered.

The dogs reluctantly left Ida in peace.

Angie pointed her finger towards the corridor. 'Kitchen!'

Their tails stopped wagging and they sloped out of the room.

Seeing that Jemima's lower lip was trembling, Ida pushed

298

herself out of her chair and squashed up next to her to give her a cuddle.

'Come here,' she said to Bonnie and Bertie, who also looked as though they were on the verge of tears.

She wrapped all three in an embrace.

'Don't be sad. Everyone has to die sometime. And I'm quite old. I've lived my life.'

She let them all go and looked at their tear-streaked faces.

'Is that what you meant?' Bertie sniffled. 'When you said you were going?'

'Sort of,' Ida said. 'But I am going somewhere else first before I go knocking on those Pearly Gates hoping they'll let me in.' She squeezed them again and gave them a tentative smile.

'Where?' Jemima asked.

Ida didn't need to look to feel Angie's eyes boring into her.

'I'm going to a place where they will look after me until it's time for me to go properly – it's a lovely place near Fife in Scotland,' Ida said.

Bertie drew away from his mother's embrace. 'Why can't you be looked after here? It's lovely here too. You're always saying so yourself.'

Ida looked at her son and wished at this moment that he wasn't quite so astute.

'Dear me,' Cora butted in. 'What's this – the Spanish Inquisition? Why don't you go and get Cook to pour you each a glass of her home-made lemonade and see if she's got any treats going spare?'

The trio reluctantly trundled off to the kitchen, leaving just Ida, Angie, Carl and Cora.

As soon as the children had left the room, Angie pulled the door to and gave Carl a look of exasperation.

'You were supposed to change her mind,' she rebuked.

'I tried,' Carl defended himself.

'Not hard enough!' Angie snapped back.

She turned her attention to her mam.

'So, you're going to go ahead with your death trip to Fife.' Angie could hardly get the words out she was so angry.

Ida nodded. 'I am. It's for the best.'

'The best for who? It's not the best for those three poor mites who have left dazed and confused and upset as they've just been told you're dying *and* buggering off again.'

Cora's eyes widened at Angie's language. Angie never swore. At least, very rarely. 'I think I'll go and check on the children,' she said, leaving the room quickly.

'I know it's not a nice thing to have been told,' Ida acquiesced. 'But it's life, isn't it? They'll be sad for a little while, but I've not been here long, so it's not as if I'll be leaving a huge gap in their lives.'

Angie let out a gargled gasp of disbelief. *'Oh, you're only their mam! Not a particularly big gap!'*

'You know what I mean,' Ida said. 'Besides, you've been their real mother for the majority of their lives. They'll be okay because they've got you. The real tragedy would be if – God forbid – anything were to happen to you.'

Angie could feel herself starting to shake.

'And what about Marlene – and Danny – and me?' she demanded. 'Or don't we have feelings?'

'Of course you have, but you're all grown-up. You don't need me,' she said.

'Don't we?' Angie snapped back. 'God, that's so like you, Mam. Just up and leave when the going gets tough, like last time. You knew Dad would go ballistic when he found out about Carl, so you left. No worries about leaving the children – or that it was my wedding the next day! You're selfish! You're not thinking about anyone but yourself!' Angie was surprised at her inability to hold back her temper. She'd been crying her eyes out yesterday. Now here she was playing holy war with a dying woman.

Ida stared at her daughter. Stunned by her words. There was so much she wanted to say, but this wasn't the right moment.

Carl walked over to the chair by the fireplace and sat down. He leant forward, his hands clasped.

'I think Ida feels you only want her here because you feel you *should* look after her,' he said.

Suddenly feeling the energy drain from her, Angie plonked herself down on the sofa.

'You're wrong,' she said. 'I know you think I can be a soft touch, but I honestly don't feel I owe you anything, or that I am in any way obligated to look after you.' Angie knew she could elaborate but didn't. 'I want you to stay for the sake of the children. *Your* children. And your grandchild.' Angie let out a short laugh. 'God only knows why, but they think the world of you. They love you. They want you here. You heard what Bertie said – and you saw the looks on Jemima's and Bonnie's faces.'

Ida smiled back at her daughter, whose words of condemnation didn't bother her in the least. Angie was speaking to the converted. But what Angie had said about the little ones made Ida feel as though her heart was bursting with joy. And gratitude. She wanted so much to convey those feelings to her daughter, but she couldn't. She didn't trust herself not to dissolve into tears.

So, instead, she took her daughter's hand, squeezed it and smiled.

'I'll stay,' was all she could manage.

Chapter Fifty-Two

Over the next week, life at Cuthford Manor started to return to some kind of normality – or a new normality – with Carl working with Bill on the vegetable plot and in the flower garden, and Ida spending most of her days with Bertie, Jemima and Bonnie, playing whatever game they wanted and watching the occasional children's programme on the television in the family room, during which she'd normally nod off.

Dr Wright came round to talk to Ida, Carl and Angie about what to expect in the coming weeks.

'It's hard to tell how long you'll feel able to get out and about,' he said. 'It's notoriously hard to judge these things or give any kind of a timescale. When you do start to feel unwell, I'll be able to give you medication to make sure you're not in any pain – the same as the nurses in the Marie Curie Home you were intending to go to.'

Meanwhile, Marlene seemed to have taken it upon herself to oversee her mam's care, and when she could see Ida was tiring, she'd send the younger ones off on some errand, get the wheelchair Dr Wright had loaned them and take Ida for a walk around the flower garden, where Carl and Bill would show them what was coming into bloom, or any seedlings they were planting in the greenhouse.

During these times, Ida and Marlene would sometimes chat, or they'd simply enjoy their surroundings in comfortable silence, only occasionally mentioning some fleeting thought. It had become their way of communicating. There was never any small talk. And Marlene never asked Ida how she was feeling, just as Ida didn't ask Marlene how she was faring now her black eye had almost faded. They didn't need to.

For Marlene sensed a kind of peace emanating from her mother, an acceptance of her fate. And even though her mortality was looming large, her mam did not seem to be fearful. It added another piece to the jigsaw Marlene was putting together, which was beginning to show her a very different picture of her mother.

Ida also started to better understand her daughter, although she'd had a good understanding of her from when she'd first arrived at Cuthford Manor. Out of all her children, Marlene was the most like her. Ida knew that it would take time for Marlene to recover from her London ordeal; physically, she was on the mend, but the mental wounds would take longer to heal. But heal they would, and Marlene would be a stronger woman because of it.

Ten days after returning from London, just as he'd promised at King's Cross Station, Marlene received a letter from Jimmy.

Marlene had given her mam the letter – or rather the small note – to read as they walked to the paddock to watch

Danny help Lucy prepare for an up-and-coming county dressage competition.

'For someone who can talk the hind legs off a donkey, he's not very good with the written word,' Ida said, having taken all of thirty seconds to read the brief note, which simply asked how Marlene was and said that he hoped her eye was back to normal. He'd told her that he was now living back in the West End and suggested she write to him at the address at the top of the letter if she wanted to.

'He doesn't say if he's working – I guess he must be if he's paying rent,' Marlene mused.

'God only knows,' Ida said. 'He was doing some kind of magician's act last I heard.'

Marlene thought of the poster she had seen when she'd gone for a sit-down in the little park in Soho. She'd just been able to make out the word Kaplan – and another she couldn't make out in full, but which she'd thought said 'musician'.

Marlene felt her chest tighten. There it was again. The physical stab of self-recrimination. *How could she have been so stupid? So naive?*

'A magician,' Marlene murmured to herself.

'And I don't think he did his tricks in the most salubrious of places,' Ida added. Carl had told her that the Lido was technically classed as a theatre but was really a striptease club, with magic acts like Jimmy's between the shows.

'Jimmy's a chancer,' Ida said. 'He drinks too much and chases anything in a skirt, but basically he's not a bad man. You should get him up here sometime and get to know him a little.'

'I might do,' Marlene said. 'Did you love him?' she asked.

Ida let out a long sigh. 'I thought I did.'

She watched Danny encourage Lucy as she pushed Dahlia into an elegant, exaggerated trot.

'It's probably hard to believe, but back then, James was a handsome man and very charismatic. I suppose in some ways I *did* really love him, or rather, I loved the man I wanted him to be.'

Marlene was quiet as she reflected on her mother's words.

When they reached the outer perimeter of the paddock, they both sat down on a couple of hay bales that had a tartan blanket thrown over the top.

'It doesn't feel right calling him *Dad*,' Marlene said. 'Dad will always be my dad – just for the fact he was our dad growing up – even though he must be up there in line for the number-one spot of world's worst father.'

They watched as Lucy commanded Dahlia into what could only be described as a dance in which horse and rider seemed to blend together.

They were quiet for a while, entranced as Lucy coaxed Dahlia into a kind of pirouette that involved a three-hundred-and-sixty-degree turn, as though cantering on the spot.

'She's very good,' Ida admired.

'She is,' Marlene agreed. 'I *do* wish she'd tell me what's going on with her, though. Something's not right, but she won't say what. And trying to get anything out of Danny is nigh on impossible.'

Ida watched as Lucy and Dahlia completed their canter

pirouette and Danny walked across the paddock to them, sounding out his praise. She could see the ease and the love her son and his girlfriend shared, so the problem was not with their relationship. She could only assume that whatever was troubling the young couple was something to do with Lucy. Or her family, who, Ida had learnt, were incredibly well-to-do and highly regarded countywide. If Ida had to guess, she'd say that Lucy's family were not happy about her romance with the son of a miner. He would not be deemed a suitable match for their daughter.

Who was not just their only daughter.

But also their only child.

Chapter Fifty-Three

Ida rarely made it down to dinner because her appetite was minimal, as was her energy. And she wanted to conserve what time and strength she had for her children and grand-daughter. It also gave her precious time with Carl, who, having worked all day outside with Bill increasing the size of the vegetable plot, would forsake his evening meal with everyone in the dining room and instead enjoy tea and sand-wiches with Ida in her room.

During Dr Wright's last visit, Ida had pushed him to give her a rough idea of how long she had left to live.

'If you stave off infections, I'd guess – and I stress *guess* – one or possibly two months.'

'I'm happy with that,' Ida had told him. And had meant her words. She really was glad and was determined to make the most of every minute, as she still had much she wanted to impart to Angie and the rest of the children. Ida knew there was no making up for being a bad mother, but she wanted to give what little she had to them before she left. Particularly as she'd become aware of problems bubbling under the surface of their outwardly happy lives.

But the difficulty for Ida was how to stick her oar in without seeming to do so.

Still, she knew she had to try.

'If you're biding time until your guests arrive,' Ida said as she came downstairs, having heard Wilfred relay that the family from the West Country were running late, 'why don't we have a cup of tea and a catch-up?'

Seeing the tautness in Angie's face ease, Ida felt herself relax. Her daughter was clearly glad of a break. Ida waited while Angie nipped off to the kitchen and returned a few minutes later with a tea tray. They headed to the family room. It was Ida's favourite place in the manor as it was cosy, with comfortable, well-worn furniture and an entrancing view of the hustle and bustle of the stables and the rolling green landscape beyond.

'So, tell me more about you and Stanislaw,' Ida asked as she sat down in one of the armchairs by the fireplace. 'I feel like I only know the bare bones of your love story. I don't even know how you first met, other than that Stanislaw was involved in the search for your old neighbour when she went walkabouts.'

Angie put the tray down on the old oak coffee table.

'I think you know much more than the *bare bones*. I'm guessing you actually know every cough and spit of our *love story*. Knew it all well before you turned up here,' Angie said as she started to pour the tea.

Ida pulled a puzzled expression.

'I know all about your mate Niamh, who's also chummy with Pearl, who just happens to work at the Tatham, where me and my old workmates always meet for a catch-up,' Angie said with a mischievous look.

Ida narrowed her eyes. 'Who told you about Niamh?'

Angie tapped her nose and suppressed a smile.

'A little birdie.'

She handed Ida her tea.

Her mother took it, smiling her thanks.

Ida was glad Angie knew about Niamh, and how she'd been getting regular updates about them all from her. It meant Angie would understand that although Ida might have abandoned them, she had still cared and wanted to know how they all were.

'I, on the other hand,' Angie continued, 'know nothing of what you've been up to these past eight years.' She hesitated. 'But you know what I'm *really* intrigued about?'

Ida shook her head.

'You and Carl,' Angie admitted. She took a sip of her tea. 'You see, I've always seen Carl as your *fancy bit*. Some bloke you just wanted to have fun with. Especially as I thought he was quite a bit younger than you.' Angie had only just learnt that Carl was actually not that much younger than her mam. His boyish looks, slim build and mop of dark brown hair made him look much more than just five years younger than Ida. 'But now I've met him and got to know him a little, well, I guess I see him as a proper person. Not a caricature.'

Ida nodded. She had seen Angie and the rest of her children's curiosity towards Carl. No-one had really got to know him yet as he worked during the day with the groundsmen and his evenings were spent with Ida in her room, chatting, reading or playing cards, or sometimes, when Ida was tired, simply lying on top of the bed and holding her in his arms.

'What do you want to know?' Ida asked.

'Well, for starters, how did you meet?' Angie asked, settling back on the sofa with her cup of tea.

Ida thought for a moment. She did not often get an opportunity to chat to Angie on her own, and there were other topics she'd wanted to broach.

'I met Carl just after Jemima was born,' Ida began. 'At the time I was not happy. With myself. My life. I had become the woman I'd promised I would never be.'

Ida was hit by the remembrance of being cloaked in a terrible darkness, looking at herself in the mirror and seeing the eyes of her mother. Eyes which showed a soul that was defeated. Downtrodden. Dead.

Angie creased her brow. 'Who? Who had you become?'

'My mam,' Ida told her with a sad smile. 'I'd become my mam.'

Angie felt a rush of guilt. She too had promised herself when she was young that she would not become a replica of her own mam.

'Not because she was a bad woman,' Ida explained, 'she was just all mothered out – worn out – by the time I came along. Having thirteen children, two of them dying before they made it to their first birthday, I guess that's understandable. My dad didn't beat or abuse her, but he also didn't love her, barely acknowledged her presence. Her life was one of drudgery. There was no joy, no love – just existence. I'd promised myself that would never be me, but no matter how much I'd tried, I'd ended up the same.'

Ida paused and Angie saw a change in her mam. A lightness of being.

'And then I met Carl,' Ida said with a smile. 'He was working for the railways – as an engineer.'

'Is that's why he wasn't called up?'

'Yes, reserved occupation, which he was glad of,' Ida explained. 'He'd never have been able to hurt another human being, never mind kill. It's not in his nature.'

'So, how did you meet?' Angie asked.

'It was rather morbid, actually,' Ida said in a way that told Angie it was anything but.

Angie furrowed her forehead.

'I met Carl in St Peter's graveyard,' Ida explained. 'I'd gone to put a few flowers on my mam's grave. I used to go there every week. More for myself than Mam. Just to have a little bit of time on my own. And then one day I saw Carl there, putting flowers on a grave nearby.'

Angie was listening intently.

'We exchanged a few polite words. About the weather. The war. And he told me that he was tending the grave of his wife, who had died shortly before the war.'

'So he was married before?' Angie had presumed Carl had never been married. 'His wife must have died young?'

'She did,' Ida said. 'Well, relatively so. She was in her mid-thirties. The doctors had told her not to keep trying for a family as she'd had so many miscarriages and each time she'd lost a dangerous amount of blood. But she'd been desperate for a baby. Couldn't imagine life without one. So, she kept trying. The last time she'd fallen, she'd been convinced she would go full term, and she almost did, but a few weeks before she was due to give birth, she went into labour—'

'And she died,' said Angie, her heart going out to this poor woman who had sacrificed her life in her desperation to have a child. 'And the baby died too?'

Ida nodded. 'It's a terribly tragic story.'

'It is,' Angie agreed.

They were both quiet for a moment.

'It seems strange to fall in love with someone against such a sombre backdrop,' Ida continued, 'but we did. And we both admitted to having the most unusual feeling – as though we'd known each other already.'

Ida shook her head. It still puzzled her. They had joked later in their relationship that they must have been lovers in a past life.

'When I met Carl, it was as though someone had flicked on a switch and my world became flooded with light ... And it didn't take long for me to realise that I could never switch that light off. I knew if I did, I'd die.'

Ida gave her daughter a half-smile.

'I know, I'm dying now, but I'd rather die now, having had the eight years I've had, than live until I was old and grey with your dad at Dundas Street.'

Ida took a sip of her tea and fixed her eyes on her daughter, wanting her to understand and not to hate her for what she had done.

'Which is why I did what I did. Why I left you all,' she said.

Angie shuffled on the sofa. When her mam had asked to speak to her and Marlene and Danny that day, it had been to apologise for being a terrible mother, but she'd never said she was sorry for leaving them.

'At the end of the war, Carl was given notice that they were transferring him to work on the London Underground. We talked endlessly about how we could make it work.' Ida remembered the sense of irony she'd felt, having dreamed of going to London from a young child, but holding back now she had the opportunity, which was only normal. After all, what kind of a mother leaves her children?

'I wasn't worried about you and Liz. You were both grown-up, getting on with your own lives. But I couldn't leave the little ones. Not with your dad.'

Ida took a deep breath.

'And then Quentin proposed to you.'

Angie felt the familiar paradox of emotions when she thought about Quentin. The happiness they'd shared, and the grief he'd left her with when he died.

'Up until that point,' Ida admitted, 'I'd been convinced this very posh and very rich bloke would break your heart. Or, worse still, get you pregnant and then dump you. Like so many other poor young girls throughout history.'

Angie nodded. She had been aware this was how her mother felt. It was what most people had thought at the time.

'I knew you were no-one's fool – and still aren't – but love makes people do things they wouldn't normally.'

They both laughed.

'Yes, me being your perfect example,' Ida admitted. 'Anyway, then you finally brought Quentin to the house to meet us.'

Angie recalled the one and only meeting her mother and father had had with Quentin when they went to tell them they were engaged. It hadn't been exactly joyful, although her parents' lack of enthusiasm was more than compensated for when Dorothy and the rest of their shipyard workmates organised a surprise engagement party.

'And I could see that you were both in love. That you wanted to be married, to be husband and wife, to have a family. That was your dream then, and I do believe it still is now, despite you saying you don't want any more children.'

Ida held up her hand as Angie started to object.

'I'll stay on track . . . When I realised your courtship with Quentin wasn't some fly-by-night love affair – that Quentin was committed – that was when I started to think. And the more I thought, the more an idea started to take shape in my head.'

Ida paused, remembering that feeling of allowing herself to dream again.

'And the more I thought about it, the more it seemed like a perfect plan. But like all best-laid plans, nothing ever goes how you expect, as you well know.'

Ida looked at her daughter and knew she'd had to deal

with much during her life so far. The plans she had made with Quentin had been cut cruelly short.

'The idea initially was that I was going to wait until you'd at least had your wedding and honeymoon and had settled in here – in your new home. Then I was going to bring the young ones to you – or somehow get the four of them brought here, perhaps in a taxi, with a letter – and ask you to look after them for a while.'

Ida shook her head.

'I know, I was kidding myself. In reality it wouldn't be for "a while", it would be for good, but I couldn't admit that to myself. I had to force myself to believe that I would come back for them after a while . . .

'But then the day before your wedding, you came charging into the house with Dorothy, telling me that someone was going to spill the beans about me and Carl – but not just that, the first person they were going to tell was Fred. At that point there was only one outcome. I'd end up in the hospital – best-case scenario – or worse, on a slab in the morgue. Because, as you know, when your dad lost it, he really did lose it, and worse still, he had no idea of his own strength – nor of the damage it could do.'

Angie nodded. It had been why she had been so panicked that day. Why she'd felt relieved when her mam told her that she would tell her dad of the affair face to face in the pub – in a public place, so when he lost it, as they knew he would, there'd be people there to intervene.

'Everything was done in a panic. I felt awful for doing it on the day before your wedding – and I am so sorry for that – but I knew if I left and asked you to take care of the children, you would. I knew you were going to live in some kind of stately home in the country with a bloke who was loaded. It was the perfect opportunity. And I honestly didn't think anyone would suffer. Quite the opposite. Jemima and Bertie would be too young to really know what was going on, and Danny and Marlene – okay, they might have been hurt that their mam had just dumped them on you, but I honestly didn't believe for one moment they'd miss me. I'd been an awful mother, I thought they'd probably be glad to see the back of me, especially when they saw their new home.'

Angie nodded. She hated to admit it, but Ida was right. Angie's siblings had never shown any signs of missing their mam after arriving at their new home.

Ida sat back, suddenly exhausted.

'But how did you know I'd take them?' Angie asked. 'I could have left them there at Dundas Street with their dad.'

Ida shook her head. 'If there was one thing I was absolutely sure of, it was that you'd take the children with you – to your new home. I would have bet my life on it. There was no way you'd have left without them. Your conscience wouldn't have let you, but more than anything, I knew you'd *want* to take them with you. To share in your good fortune. You were always closer to them than Liz was – or than I was, their own mother. And I was right. I rang Niamh the night of your wedding and she told me how you'd made an announcement at the reception.'

Angie smiled, remembering the moment. She *had* wanted her brothers and sisters to come with her to Cuthford Manor.

'I know this might sound awful for a mother to say, but after I'd left you the note on the mantlepiece –' Ida remembered the moment as though it was yesterday '– and Carl and I had got on the train for London, there was a part of me that felt a sense of relief. Not just because leaving provided me with an escape – and I didn't have to spend the rest of my life being a duplicate of my own mother – but because in leaving the little ones, I was also saving them from the fate of those who know only poverty. This was a chance for Danny, Marlene, Bertie and Jemima to have a better life, which I knew they would have with you.'

Ida looked up at the tapestry Jemima had done of a poem entitled 'Home Is Where the Heart Is'.

'Look at this wonderful life they have. The education you've given them, their futures ahead of them. They are well fed, have a wonderful roof over their heads, they've got people around them –' she gave a crooked smile '– who are more loving and caring than many families I know.'

Ida sighed.

'The guilt I carry,' she said, her tone earnest, 'is not, as most people might assume, because I walked out on my family – but because of the time I'd had with you all before that.'

Ida took a deep breath.

'This might horrify many, but I know deep down that the best thing I ever did for the four young ones was to leave them in your care.'

318

Chapter Fifty-Four

A few days later, the annual Durham Horse Trials took place in the region's top equestrian centre just outside Crook in the west of the county. Lucy had made it to the dressage finals, which was of no surprise. The surprise would be if she didn't win by a mile. Danny was there in his capacity as head of the Cuthford Manor Riding School and to support two of his pupils who were taking part in their first-ever competition.

'Stop staring,' Lucy said out of the corner of her mouth as she dismounted.

'He's lucky I'm only staring,' Danny said, making no attempt to keep his voice down.

A couple of the other competitors walked by with their horses, and Lucy was relieved to see that they hadn't heard the anger in Danny's voice or seen the murderous looks he was giving Anthony Hetherington.

Lucy glanced over and saw that Anthony was smirking. He had the air of someone who knew he was holding all the aces. And was the undoubted winner. The prize, though, wasn't some shiny silver trophy. *She* was the prize.

'Come on,' Lucy said, coaxing Dahlia into a walk.

'I can't believe this is happening,' Danny said, stroking Dahlia's neck as they made their way over to the paddock, away from the main arena. 'I thought I had seen just about everything, but this takes the biscuit.'

Sensing the tension, Dahlia shook her mane.

'It's all right, girl.' Danny stroked her neck and breathed into her muzzle. Dahlia returned the affection with a gentle nudge.

'I'll see you back at the holding stables in about half an hour,' Danny said. 'I need to check on Sophie and Harry – they're up in about ten minutes.'

'Tell them good luck from me,' Lucy said. 'And remind them to enjoy it!'

Danny smiled. His students were nervous wrecks. The part they'd enjoy would be when they'd completed their event.

'Oh . . .' Danny jogged back to Lucy. 'Well done! You were brilliant out there! As always.'

He went to give her a quick kiss, but Lucy stepped back.

'Sorry, I'm just feeling a bit jittery at the moment. Worried about people seeing.'

Noticing the hurt on his face, Lucy stepped forwards and gave him a quick kiss on the lips, keeping her fingers crossed that no-one had seen.

'This is madness,' Danny said, the deep hurt assuaged by the kiss. 'We have to work something out.'

'We will,' Lucy said, but her tone betrayed her lack of conviction. 'Now go and see to your prodigies.'

As Danny strode off, he cast his eye around the crowds for Anthony Hetherington. Spotting him by one of the catering tents, chatting up one of the young girls serving refreshments, he made a beeline for him. Today was the first time he'd seen Anthony since Lucy had told him about her parents' plans. Plans that had come hot on the heels of their discovery that their daughter's dalliance with the 'miner's son' over at Cuthford Manor was not some flash-in-the-pan romance but serious.

Seeing Anthony today, Danny wanted nothing more than to wipe the smarmy, arrogant smirk off his face and to tell him that, contrary to what he and Mr and Mrs Stanton-Leigh might think, Lucy could not be sold to the highest bidder like some highly valued thoroughbred.

Danny watched as Anthony continued flirting with the pretty waitress.

'Anthony!' Danny called out as he marched towards him.

Pushing his mop of blond hair back with one hand, a cigarette burning in the other, Anthony the Adonis, as he was nicknamed by the county's horsey set, dragged his attention away from the object of his desire and watched as Danny approached him.

'Hello there, old boy, how's life at the *country house hotel*?' The derisory inflection in his voice when referring to Cuthford Manor made the hair on Danny's neck prickle. He forced himself to ignore the put-down. Many of those in the county with inherited wealth had made it clear they thought it 'disgraceful' that the renowned Cuthford Manor had been converted into a hotel. As though working for money was somehow to be looked down upon.

'Just to let you know,' Danny said, drawing to a halt, arms akimbo, 'it doesn't matter what anyone says – be it you, your father or the Stanton-Leighs – no-one but Lucy will decide who she does or does not marry.'

'That's good to hear,' Anthony said, glancing as a rather voluptuous dark-haired girl walked past with a tray of drinks for a group of spectators sitting around a picnic table. 'Because we all know what Lucy's decision will be – and that's exactly what her father decides. And I do believe he's made it quite clear what he wants. And he wants his daughter to marry the best.' He put his hand on his fawn-coloured jersey. 'The best being my good self.'

It took all of his reserve not to knock Anthony flat out. Instead, Danny stepped forward so that his face was just inches away from his rival's.

'Over my dead body!' He spat the words out.

Hearing the call for the next event, Danny gave Anthony one last deadly stare and marched off.

'Like you say,' Anthony shouted out after him, 'it'll be Lucy who chooses.'

As Danny reached the warm-up paddock and gave some last words of encouragement to his two 'prodigies', his head banged like a drum. The sheer anger of his interaction with Anthony was making his whole body shake.

Somehow he managed to get through the rest of the day without betraying his fury, but it was hard. Anthony's words kept repeating in his head over and over again. *It'll be Lucy who chooses.*

There was no doubt in Danny's mind that Lucy was the woman for him. That he loved her. And that he wanted her as his wife. But his love was not blind. He knew Lucy was not perfect. Her imperfections were also why he loved her so much. But, in this scenario, they could prove fatal for their love. For Lucy's father had a strange control over his daughter. Anthony's words were infuriating for the very fact that they held some truth. Lucy *would* choose. And there was a good chance that her decision would be aligned to what her father wanted.

How could he show Lucy that she did not have to do what her family wanted? That this was *her* life. And it was *her* choice who she married. No matter the consequences.

Thoughts of Lucy walking down the aisle with Anthony distracted and tormented Danny for the rest of the weekend. He tried to mask how he was feeling, but it didn't come easily. He was also trying to push thoughts of his dying mother to the back of his mind, with minimal success. He knew he had to bite the bullet and talk to her, something he'd been avoiding since Cora had strong-armed the news out of his mam the day of her planned departure two weeks ago. Since then, he'd been civil when he'd seen her about, usually with her little entourage of Bertie, Jemima and Bonnie, and more recently with the addition of Clemmie, who had discovered that Ida had worked as a char for some radical feminist she and Barbara hero-worshipped. *God, he could just imagine the reaction from both of them if they got wind of what Lucy was being coerced into doing.*

Danny promised himself that he would go and chat to his mam. Soon.

Knowing Lucy would be arriving at the stables any minute, he focused his mind back on to how he could persuade her to defy her father, whom she seemed to hold in godlike reverence, despite the fact that he was a manipulative, controlling and selfish man. He'd done a good job to get Lucy, and others he needed, on his side. His sole aim in life was to get what he wanted.

Danny had watched Mr Stanton-Leigh from afar and listened to those who knew him well. Lucy's father was a master manipulator. A good-looking, intelligent man who had no conscience. A dangerous combination. He would do anything to get what he wanted. Anything. Regardless of the hurt or damage it might cause.

Lucy must have been a walkover. Not only had he been able to manipulate her since she was a child, but all she wanted from her father – from anyone, for that matter – was kindness, love and care, and to be allowed to indulge in her love of horses. Lucy had revered her father even more when, against her mother's wishes, he had agreed she could leave the boarding school she'd been sent to and instead attend the local Durham High School for Girls, enabling her to ride early in the morning and when she came back from school in the afternoon. He'd even spent a small fortune on buying Dahlia for her sixteenth birthday.

Lucy had never been privy to the other side of her father, which, despite being told about, she refused to believe existed. She'd said to Danny before that she could not square the man she knew with claims that he was a ruthless, mercenary bully.

Danny had little good to say about his own dad, whom

he'd not seen since his mam had left them and Angie had brought them here, but if he'd had to choose between the two men, his father would come up trumps every time. What you saw was what you got with his dad. Pretending to be someone you weren't – lying to someone their whole life – was harmful, much more so than one of his dad's backhanders.

Hearing the sound of Lucy's Morris Minor, Danny went out to greet her.

'Now I can congratulate you properly,' he said, taking her in his arms as soon as she'd got out of the driver's seat and kissing her. 'Not that I had any doubt whatsoever that you'd walk away with a trophy.'

Lucy batted away his compliments.

'Talking about silverware,' she said solemnly as they walked arm in arm back to the stables. 'We had the auctioneer round at teatime pricing up the family heirlooms.'

Danny's heart dropped. He wouldn't put it past Lucy's father to have orchestrated the visit to further guilt Lucy into doing what he needed her to do.

'I know I sound like a broken record,' Danny said as they climbed the ladder to his digs, 'but your family's dire financial situation is not your responsibility.'

'"And it's not my responsibility to make it right",' Lucy cited Danny as she flopped down on the saggy leather sofa.

'The thing is, Luce, it's not up to your father to dictate who you should marry – it's *your* choice,' Danny said as he put the kettle on and dropped teabags in their mugs.

'I know, I know,' Lucy said, but her tone suggested otherwise.

'It's simple,' Danny pushed. 'You tell your father that you won't marry Anthony and that's that.'

'But it's not as simple as that, is it?' Lucy said, her eyes pleading for understanding. 'Mother and Father have made it clear to me that if I don't marry Anthony, or someone of Anthony's wealth, we will all be destitute. They'll have to sell Roeburn Hall and all the estate.'

'Destitute is a bit of an exaggeration,' Danny said. 'They're hardly going to be out on the streets with their begging bowls. It just means they'll have to buy a normal house with a garden rather than a mansion with fifty-plus acres.'

'But for people like us that is the equivalent of being out on the street with our begging bowls,' Lucy argued.

Danny felt as though they were going round in circles – again. Time to change tack.

'You say "people like us", but I don't see that you *are* like your parents – or all those others you know who claim to have blue blood coursing through their veins.' Danny handed Lucy her tea. 'I don't see you as someone who would mind living in a normal house.'

Lucy smiled. 'I'd live in a shack as long as it meant I could keep Dahlia.'

'Rather than a shack, you and Dahlia could come here and live with us – with me?' Danny put his tea on the little coffee table and looked at Lucy.

'Don't,' Lucy pleaded. 'If things were different, that would be my dream.'

'But that dream *could* be your reality,' Danny argued, trying to keep the exasperation out of his voice.

Lucy put down her tea and snuggled up to Danny, forcing away thoughts of future nuptials to a man she didn't love.

'Your parents' money woes are not your problem.' Danny spoke softly, kissing her fine blonde hair.

'But they *are* my problem. I'm their only daughter.'

Danny tried to quell his frustration and took a deep breath.

'Look, Lucy, it really *is* simple. You cannot marry someone you don't like, never mind love, just so your family can keep Roeburn Hall.'

'It's not just about keeping Roeburn Hall – it's about maintaining the family's ancestry. The Hall's been in the family since the year dot. It's not just about bricks and mortar.'

'Isn't it? Because that's exactly what Roeburn Hall is – bricks and mortar.'

Lucy sighed. She hated the class divide that existed between them. Danny would never be able to understand how the upper classes lived, or the values by which they lived.

'Lucy, you can't marry someone just to keep your home in the family. You just can't—' Danny had run out of arguments. He couldn't quite believe he was having to make the case against Lucy marrying Anthony. In his mind, it was too preposterous for words. Lucy shouldn't even be considering it – never mind behaving as though she had no choice in the matter.

'Having an arranged marriage is not that unheard of,' Lucy said. 'Look at the royal family.'

'Yes, but you're not royalty.' Danny was at his wits' end.

'I know, but it filters down to families like mine who are the rung below.'

Danny looked at Lucy and saw that her beautiful aristocratic blue eyes were filling with tears.

'Come here,' he said, pulling her close and kissing her.

'You know I love you,' Lucy mumbled. 'More than anything or anyone.'

Danny kissed her again, tasting salty tears on his lips.

'I know. We'll think of something,' he said, trying his hardest to sound hopeful when what he really felt was entirely hopeless.

Later on that evening, after Lucy had returned to Roeburn Hall, Marlene caught Danny in the kitchen making himself a late-night snack.

He was alone, apart from Winston and Bessie, who had not got up from their spot by the Aga, but had their doleful tired eyes trained on Danny – or rather, on the sandwich he was making – watching vigilantly for any bits of boiled ham that might drop onto the flagstone floor.

Marlene poured herself a glass of water and patted the dogs, who did not take their attention away from Danny, although their wagging tails indicated that they appreciated the show of affection.

'So, what's going on with you and Lucy?' Marlene asked, sitting down on the cushioned chair at the head of the kitchen table.

Danny sighed, put his sandwich on a plate and sat down next to his sister.

Marlene listened with growing outrage. Only her ire was not so much with Mr and Mrs Stanton-Leigh as with Lucy. It was hard, but she managed to keep her thoughts to herself, knowing that if she in any way criticised the woman her brother loved, he would shut down. His defence barriers would go up. And that would be it.

Instead, she empathised with his fury at Lucy's father – and railed against the compliance of her mother. Marlene had also heard how unpleasant and bullish Mr Stanton-Leigh could be and that, like his father before him, he had a great fondness for the horses; not like his daughter for the animals themselves, but for their racing form. It didn't take a genius to work out why the family was in such dire financial straits.

Marlene watched her brother slope off with his sandwich.

She had never seen him so dejected and it pained her that she couldn't help him – and frustrated her that she could not shake some sense into Lucy.

The next day, working on the premise that a problem shared was a problem halved, Marlene decided to go a step further and quietly informed Angie, Cora, Clemmie and Ida of the situation her lovelorn brother had found himself in.

Angie sympathised, but Marlene could see that her sister was run ragged with managing the business of being a hotelier, keeping an eye on the children and caring for their terminally ill mother, and therefore had not the time or the inclination to find a solution to her brother's heartache. Marlene also suspected that Angie wouldn't be too worried if

Danny's love was married off to a fellow toff, as her sister had never been a great fan of Lucy's.

When Marlene told Cora the news, she wasn't surprised.

'I feel for Danny,' Cora said, 'but that's just what folk like that do. Well, most folk like that.' Cora and Lloyd had broken the generally observed rules of the British class system and had married despite Lloyd being the son of the original owner of Cuthford Manor and Cora the housekeeper.

'Not that that makes it right,' she'd added.

Clemmie was naturally aghast at the news and Marlene patiently listened to her rant about how 'women are never going to attain the lofty heights of equality if they continue to allow themselves to be seen merely as marriage candidates for the sole purpose of breeding'.

She did not provide any kind of solution, though, other than to offer to talk some sense into Lucy, which Marlene didn't think would help. Lucy had only met Clemmie a few times and although she liked her, Marlene knew she would view any suggestions made by Clemmie as too radical.

When Marlene told Ida, she found herself answering a litany of questions: *What was Lucy's family like? How did Danny feel? Did Marlene see it as a genuine love? What was Lucy like?*

Much as Marlene didn't mind telling her mam what she wanted to know, she also didn't see how Ida could help. Especially as her mam and her brother were not exactly close and rarely exchanged anything more than pleasantries, despite the dwindling time Ida had left to live.

Chapter Fifty-Five

On Monday morning, as usual, everyone hung back after breakfast to go through plans for the week ahead.

Ida was sitting at the top end of the table in an old wooden rocking chair that had had its rockers removed. It had been piled with cushions to try and prevent the bruises she was now increasingly prone to.

Clemmie, who usually stayed over if Barbara was away on some conference or other, was sitting on the bench, adjacent to Ida, finishing off her marmalade on toast with a good slurp of tea.

Bertie sat opposite with the *Daily Mirror* laid out in front of him, scouring the articles for any news on 'foreign affairs', which had become his latest obsession. He had already told everyone about the end of the Korean War, which had gone on for the past three years and which, he relayed, 'had led to the deaths of one thousand and seventy-eight soldiers from the British Army and Royal Navy'.

Next to him was Jemima, who was thumbing her way through Alberta's *Be-Ro Recipe Book* to find something she hadn't yet learnt to bake.

And Bonnie was sitting cross-legged with the dogs on their blanket next to the Aga. Bessie had managed to edge

Winston out the way and had flopped her head onto Bonnie's lap.

Angie was just about to ask where Danny was when the back door swung open and Thomas appeared, stamping his feet on the mat to get rid of any dirt before stepping into the kitchen. He put a bundle of carrots he was holding on the side. 'From Carl. He said he's hoping they're sweeter than the last ones.'

Alberta nodded her thanks.

'Danny not about?' Angie asked, looking to the door in expectation of her brother's late arrival.

'Danny's giving one of the Travellers' kids a lesson. He sends his apologies,' Thomas said, glancing at Marlene, who, on seeing him, had suddenly got up and begun clearing the table.

'I wouldn't have thought they needed lessons,' Angie said, curious. The family had a good relationship with the local Travellers who usually set up camp during the summer months a few miles north of Cuthford Manor. Danny had bought horses from them in the past for those learning to ride for the first time.

'It's the jumps the young lad's keen on. Danny reckons he's good enough to compete nationally,' Thomas explained.

As he turned to go, Angie stopped him. 'Stay, Thomas. You can relay anything to Danny that he needs to know. Grab yourself a cuppa.'

Thomas shook his head. 'I'm good, thank you.'

'Okay,' Angie began, opening her organiser, 'it's going to be a busy week . . .'

Angie imparted whatever she had gleaned about the guests who were staying that week. The children were normally keen to hear about any families who would be checking in, and what ages the children were, but since Ida's arrival they weren't the least bit bothered.

As it was just a couple of days before the start of the grouse season – the Glorious Twelfth – there was lots to prepare and organise, on top of accommodating that week's guests.

'I really cannot understand why it's called the Glorious Twelfth as there's absolutely nothing glorious about massacring a load of beautiful birds for fun,' Marlene declared, standing with her back to the big Belfast sink where she had put all the dirty dishes.

'They're not birds, they're wildfowl – and they need culling,' Thomas retorted.

'No, they don't,' Marlene bit back, the edge to her voice more to do with Thomas's growing friendship with Mabel than the slaughter of the local 'wildfowl' population. She'd heard Mabel and Thomas yesterday evening, chatting and laughing and sounding like two lovebirds out in the backyard.

'Did you know,' Bertie chirped up, 'that some London restaurants serve up grouse on the actual twelfth? They transport what's shot in the morning down there and cook it up for the evening diners.'

At the mention of London, Marlene felt her stomach churn, along with the now-familiar but peculiar feeling of darkness that descended whenever memories of her attack came back to her. She shooed them away. They might catch her unawares, but she was quick to get rid of them when they momentarily floored her.

She caught Ida and Angie looking at her with concern and batted away their anxiety by tutting loudly and theatrically rolling her eyes.

'Perhaps,' Ida said, turning her attention to Jemima, 'our budding head chef can show me how to cook the perfect pheasant.'

'Pheasants are different to grouse, Mam, and if she does, I won't be eating it,' Marlene shot back.

'My mam's got a secret recipe for cooking fowl,' Thomas pitched in. 'I'll get it for you, Jemima, if you want?'

Jemima nodded. 'Yes, please. Tell her I promise not to divulge it to another soul.'

'I guess your mam's had plenty of practice cooking *wildfowl* – in *and* out of season,' Marlene jibed.

Thomas shot Marlene a look. 'That's below the belt.'

Seeing Ida's puzzled look, Angie explained.

'Thomas comes from a long line of local poachers, who, I hasten to add, are no longer poachers as they have gainful employment here, teaching our guests how to fish and shoot and the like.'

'Ah,' said Ida. She eyed Marlene and Thomas. You could cut the air between the pair with a knife. Just as you could feel the chemistry between them. How ironic that her 'to the manor born' daughter should fall for the son of a poacher, whereas her son, who wore his working-class roots like a badge, should love the daughter of the local landed gentry.

334

'Well,' Ida broke the tension, 'if Thomas's mam is going to be passing on her culinary secrets to Jemima, then I too need to pass on some age-old recipes from the town of her birth before I shuffle off this mortal coil.'

Angie noted how their mam never skirted the issue of her impending mortality. At first it had felt a little shocking, but these days it had become almost normal. Again, Angie was struck by her mam's wisdom. She was preparing her family for her leaving them. And, Angie noted, she was doing a good job, as whenever her illness and death were referred to, they no longer subdued the children's spirits.

'Anything but a recipe for boiled sheep's head,' Jemima said, pulling a face.

Ida shook her head in disappointment. 'You will be missing out on a rare treat – as I'm sure Thomas's mam will agree. If cooked right, it can be very tasty.' Ida had told the young ones about her own mother, the grandmother they'd never got to meet, and how inventive she could be with the very cheapest cuts of meat. Angie knew all of this because whatever Ida told the children, they invariably repeated it to her.

'I shall show you how to make pink slices,' Ida declared. 'I'll bet they're not in the Be-Ro book.'

Marlene blew out her cheeks and stretched her arms to mimic a barrel-like physique.

'What's a pink slice?' Bonnie piped up from her place by the Aga with the dogs, who were now snoring.

'It's a cross between a biscuit and a cake,' Bertie chipped in. 'And is rarely seen outside of Sunderland. It's like

335

shortbread with jam in the middle and loads of pink icing on the top.'

Ida smiled at her son. He was the most incredible little boy she had ever known. Bright as a button. A real little scholar with the gentlest of souls. Other than his dark hair, Bertie was nothing like his father. Thank God. He was undeniable proof that nurture triumphed over nature.

The chatter was interrupted by the sound of the brass bell jangling on the wall above the cooker. It usually meant that guests had just arrived.

'Ah,' Angie said, getting up and looking at her watch, 'that'll be the group from Oldham arriving.'

'Mmm,' Clemmie said, 'all that talk of pink slices has woken up my taste buds.'

'Your taste buds are never asleep,' Marlene laughed, knowing exactly what Clemmie was about to suggest. 'I'll get us a fresh pot and see if there's anything sweet stashed away in the larder.'

'Best get back to it,' Thomas said, stepping towards the door.

'Good idea . . .' Marlene mumbled under her breath. 'Before Mabel gets wind you're here and then you'll never get away.'

Thomas shot Marlene a look as he opened the heavy oak door. He hadn't heard everything she'd said, but he'd caught the gist.

'So, Ida,' Clemmie said, ignoring the verbal sparring that seemed to have become commonplace between the two of late, 'tell us more about Edith . . .'

336

Ida smiled. She was more than happy to chat about her former employer. Edith Summerskill was truly someone to aspire to. And she was pleased that it wasn't just Clemmie who was interested, but the younger ones also seemed fascinated by her stories about 'the woman politician' who had been kind to both herself and Carl. She had encouraged Carl with his poetry and told him about the Colony Room Club so that he could meet up with other like-minded poets and writers. And she had helped Ida to understand so much about herself – both as a woman and as a reluctant mother.

Chapter Fifty-Six

After welcoming the group from the north-west, who were full of apologies for checking in much later than anticipated and were all clearly in need of a cuppa and something to eat, Angie went to check on her mother in the family room.

Every day she'd noticed that her mam seemed to be that little bit more tired than the day before. Angie guessed she would be drained and in need of a rest after telling Clemmie, Marlene and the young ones about the Summerskill woman she'd worked for. Ida's routine of late was to go into the family room after breakfast, but today Angie wouldn't have been surprised if she had gone upstairs to her room for a lie-down, especially as Marlene had told her that she planned on taking the young ones into the village for a few hours to give their mam a break.

Walking along the long corridor to the back room, Angie's thoughts went to Marlene and how much she had changed since her ordeal in the capital. Her younger sister was still full of show and just as headstrong and bloody-minded – perhaps more so – but there was now also a maturity about her. And she seemed much more empathetic. Angie had seen it with her own eyes in how Marlene was with their mam – and with her lovelorn brother.

And she had stopped talking endlessly about becoming an actress, thank goodness.

Marlene, she realised, had grown up quickly in a very short space of time.

Walking into the back room, Angie saw that her mam was there, asleep in the armchair. She was amazed the new guests had not woken her as their broad Lancashire dialect seemed able to travel to the far reaches of the manor and had already caused a few disapproving glances from some of the quieter guests.

She started to tiptoe backwards and was just turning to leave when Ida woke.

'*Angie!*' Her voice was a little croaky.

'I thought you were fast asleep,' Angie said, turning and walking back into the room. 'Do you want me to help you upstairs?'

Ida shook her head. 'But I wouldn't mind a cup of tea. It's about the only thing I can stomach at the moment.'

'I'll be two ticks,' Angie said. 'I could do with a pick-me-up myself.'

Five minutes later, she returned with a tea tray and some Rich Tea biscuits. It pained Angie to see her mam like this, so wan and so skinny. Dr Wright had warned Angie that the morphine Ida was now taking would dull her appetite but was needed for the pain. Knowing that Ida was not the type of woman to disclose how she was feeling, Dr Wright had told Angie that as the white blood cells in her mam's bones and body overtook the red cells, it would cause swelling and therefore pain in Ida's bones in her arms and legs, and possibly also in her chest.

It was hard for Angie not to fuss, but she knew her mam would hate it if she caught a whiff of pity, and so she forced herself to be strong and to act as normally as possible. But, as she told Stanislaw most nights, it was hard. Very hard.

'I have a question for you,' Ida said, forcing herself to nibble on a biscuit.

'That sounds ominous,' said Angie. 'What do you want to know?'

Ida put her biscuit on the edge of her saucer, then looked at her daughter in earnest. 'I want to know the real reason you don't want to have any more bairns?'

Ida's accent had lost most of its north-east inflections, but using the word 'bairns' rather than 'children' transported Angie back to her childhood.

As if reading her thoughts, Ida looked at her second-eldest daughter. 'Growing up, you were always so natural with the little 'uns.'

Angie let out a slightly bitter laugh. 'I didn't have much choice.'

'I know,' Ida said, 'but you're not going to sidestep my question by making me take the offensive and apologise for being a bad mother. We know that. There's no changing the past. It's about the future now.'

Those last few words gave Angie pause for thought. Her mam had never been one for speaking or showing her love – but her concern for her daughter's future when she had no future herself spoke volumes.

Ida looked at her daughter.

'It just doesn't wash with me – all this excuse-making about not having the time for another child. Saying you've got all these children to look after and bring up is nonsense. They are all at school, they're all happy and like being independent, and you've got lots of others to help – I've never known children have so many people to love and care for them. And let's face it, Danny's a man now. He was always older than his age – which, yes, might have been because of his hopeless mother. And Marlene's a young woman, although it has to be said, she'll be a handful until she's old and grey – guaranteed.'

They both laughed, breaking the tense atmosphere.

'It's puzzled me from the off,' Ida said, her tone earnest again. 'You've only had one child of your own, Bonnie, with Quentin – I'd have thought you'd want to have a family with Stanislaw. He's a good man. And I can see he'd make a great father by the way he is with all the children.'

Angie took a sip of tea but didn't say anything.

'Cora told me about Stanislaw's first wife and their unborn baby.' She tried to reach her daughter with her eyes but couldn't. Angie seemed to have become entranced by the contents of her teacup. 'Surely Stanislaw must want to have a child?'

Angie looked up. 'Perhaps what happened has had the reverse effect. Made him not want to have children.' She hesitated. *Did she really think this?* 'Anyway, Stanislaw says he's not bothered. That it's about what I want.'

'Really?' Ida asked, her tone showing her disbelief. 'And you believe him? That he's not "bothered".'

Angie nodded. 'Yes, I do.'

'Or do you believe him because it suits you to?' Ida pushed.

'We're always honest with each other,' Angie defended herself.

Ida allowed herself the faintest smile. 'I don't think any married couple is always totally honest with each other – even if the dishonesty is well meaning.'

Angie's attention went back to her teacup.

'It's amazing how many puzzles you can solve by just lying in bed or looking out the window,' Ida said. 'And it came to me the other day, the real reason you don't want to have another child. Or rather, why you don't want to have a child *with Stanislaw.*'

Angie looked up at her mother, her expression curious.

'You're frightened of having a baby with Stanislaw because you feel guilty,' Ida declared. She took a deep breath. This was hard. Angie could simply walk out, refuse to hear her out. Tell her she had no right telling her what she did or did not feel. 'You just about made it over the hurdle of allowing yourself to love another man, which I know must have been hard. Cora has told me how much you loved Lloyd's son. And how much Quentin adored you.'

Ida could see her daughter's eyes had begun to well with tears.

'But thank goodness you *did* allow yourself to love someone else.' Ida brightened her tone, not wanting to open the trapdoor of grief. 'As it's clear that you and Stanislaw love each other very much.'

Ida paused.

'But my theory is that although you allowed yourself to love another man after Quentin died, you will not allow yourself to have another baby with another man. I think in your mind – in the very depths of your mind, which you might not even be aware of – you feel it will be too much of a betrayal to Quentin. You're punishing yourself for falling in love again and not mourning the loss of your first husband all your life like some women do – foolish women, I might add.'

Angie looked at her mam. She'd never been one to hold back at the best of times, but now it would seem that death's proximity had made her even more blunt and even more brutally honest.

Mother and daughter were quiet for a few moments. Ida because she had said most of what she had wanted to say to her daughter; Angie because it was taking her a few moments to process her mother's words.

'God, Mam, you sound like that Freud bloke Clemmie was telling us all about the other week. All that stuff about us not knowing what our mind's really thinking.' Angie made a sound of derision. 'Which, as I told Clemmie, I think is a load of twaddle.'

'Perhaps,' Ida conceded. 'All I know, Angie, is that we are similar in many ways. You're feisty. You don't suffer fools gladly. And you're not work-shy. But in other ways, we are complete opposites. I was never cut out to be a mother.

Never wanted to be a mother, whereas you could not be more different. You are such a naturally maternal person. Even with children that aren't your own.'

Ida could feel her energy going.

'But most of all, I think what I really want to say is, *please* don't deny yourself something you really want. And which I believe your husband also really wants.'

Ida paused.

'How old are you now? Thirty-one? Thirty-two?'

'Thirty-one,' Angie said.

'Well, you're no spring chicken. Don't leave it until it's too late. Don't blight your life – or your marriage – with regrets.'

As Angie got on with her many tasks of the day, her mam's words stayed with her. She tried to shake them off but couldn't. They'd got their claws in and wouldn't let go.

'Mam said something today which got me thinking,' Angie told Stanislaw as they got ready for bed.

'Oh, yes?' Stanislaw asked. 'What's she got you thinking about?' He tried to sound genuinely interested and not betray the irritation he felt whenever Ida was the topic of conversation. The woman might be dying, but that did not change his opinion of her.

'She was saying that she didn't think married couples were always honest with each other.'

'So she thinks marriages are based on lies?' Stanislaw said a little dismissively as he climbed into bed.

'No, she didn't mean it in a bad way, just that dishonesty

344

between a couple can be well meaning. I think she was trying to say that sometimes couples aren't always honest with each other so as not to cause upset.'

Angie climbed into bed and Stanislaw pulled her close. It rankled him to admit it, but he believed Ida might well be right.

'Do you think you've ever been dishonest with me – maybe told me what you think I want to hear?' Angie asked, her mother's suggestion that her husband did in fact want a child playing heavily on her mind.

Stanislaw shuffled as though trying to get comfortable when the discomfort he was feeling was very much mental.

'No, I don't think so,' he lied. He then asked, 'Have you?' But more to deflect the attention away from himself.

'No, I don't think so,' Angie said, her reply also a lie.

Angie couldn't sleep. It had taken Stanislaw longer to drop off than normal, but he was now snoring gently.

Angie replayed their conversation of earlier.

Was her mam right? Deep down, was she really denying herself the chance of having a child with Stanislaw?

She looked at her husband lying asleep next to her in the bed.

Had the conversation they'd just had been dishonest? *She* had been. But had Stanislaw also been dishonest?

God! Her mam had a way of really stirring things up.

And she didn't want her world to be any more stirred up than it already was. But it felt as though her mother's words had lifted the lid on Pandora's box. Forced her to look inside.

She could no longer shy away from the reality of how she was feeling deep down.

The day she'd gone with Clemmie to meet Marlene at the train station, she'd seen a mother with her children pushing a pram along the platform and had felt inexplicably angry. She'd declared to Clemmie how vehemently she felt about not having any more children because of the worry they caused. *Had she been denying her true feelings? Was the anger she'd felt really jealousy?* She'd been adamant she didn't want more children, but now she wondered if perhaps she had been *too* adamant. As though trying to convince herself, not Clemmie.

Had she been doing the same when she'd spoken to Dorothy the other day? It seemed like every time they had a catch-up these days, her best friend would subtly probe her as to why she didn't want to have a baby with Stanislaw.

'No time!' Angie had said curtly.

She'd then quickly batted the question back to Dorothy and asked her why *she* didn't want to start a family with Bobby.

Dorothy had laughed and said, 'No desire!'

Then the other day one of her friends in the village had excitedly told her that she was expecting, and Angie had made the right sounds and congratulated her, but she'd had to fight hard not to show how envious she was. She'd been hit by the memory of when she had realised she was pregnant with Bonnie. She and Quentin had been on cloud nine. A cloud she'd stayed on throughout the pregnancy despite the never-ending morning sickness and total lack of energy.

And when she gave birth to their baby girl, she had been overwhelmed by the incredible, intense love she'd felt for this tiny being.

Unlike some women who laughingly joked 'Never again!', Angie had felt the complete opposite. She'd wanted more.

Angie felt the tears come as she thought of Quentin.

And alongside the feelings of sadness, Angie realised that interwoven with her grief, as her mother had speculated, there was indeed an underlying sense of guilt.

It had been there all along, she just hadn't realised.

Chapter Fifty-Seven

As the grouse-shooting season entered its third week, taking them into September, Ida knew she didn't have long left. During his last visit, Dr Wright had said she could possibly live for another couple of months, but her body told her otherwise. She could sense the Grim Reaper's approach. But he couldn't have her yet. There was still something she had to do. Something important. Very important. If she had learnt one thing during her time on this earth, it was that there was nothing more valuable than love. Life was love. And she could not die without using what little strength she had left to help love triumph over those who sought to trample it into the ground.

The problem was those Ida wanted to help would barely talk to her, never mind listen to what she had to say with an open mind.

Ida had tried to catch Danny to chat to him, but he was always just on his way out or had to do something that couldn't wait. Her eldest son seemed set on avoiding her whenever possible.

'He's got being evasive down to an art,' Ida told Carl.

And, as a result, Lucy also had her barriers up.

Ida would not allow herself to indulge in feelings of hurt

and rejection, for she understood exactly why her son felt this way. She had been neglectful, spare with her love and care. Danny had been forced to grow up fast. He hadn't been afforded much of a childhood. And he'd had to keep his younger sisters and brothers under his wing. Never mind protect Marlene from the bullies at school.

Ida had apologised before they had known she was ill, but she had seen that her words had made no difference to Danny. His resentment held fast.

She wished she could tell him that resentments only caused self-harm. That he had to let them go otherwise he would continue to be in pain. But, at this late stage, it was unlikely she could gain his trust enough for him to listen to her words.

There was something more pressing than this, though, which Ida felt she had a small chance of being able to put right.

'I'm going out for a little fresh air,' she said, hauling herself out of the old rocking chair. She had been directing Jemima in the art of making another dish particular to her birthplace – panackelty, which involved corned beef, onions, bacon and sliced potatoes.

Winston and Bessie clambered up, sensing movement.

'I'll come,' said Bonnie, who was writing her holiday diary and keen for a distraction.

'No, you stay and finish your homework, otherwise you'll be in trouble with your teacher. You're back on Monday and you don't want it to look like you've rushed it the night before.'

'Rather than rushed it the week before,' Bertie said disapprovingly, glancing up from his book.

349

'Bertie, we're not all swots like you,' Jemima said, carefully layering slices of thinly cut potato onto the panackelty mix.

Bonnie threw Bertie a triumphant look, having been defended by Jemima.

'No bickering while I'm gone,' Ida ordered. 'And no ganging up on each other.'

As Ida made her way to the back door, the dogs clambered up from their spot by the Aga and followed her out into the yard. Shutting the door behind her, Ida stopped and inhaled deeply. She could smell the start of autumn – the new school term could not come quickly enough. Not just because Bertie, Jemima and Bonnie were starting to get niggly with each other, but because it would be good for them to have their heads filled with lessons and the ups and downs of school life when the time came for her to leave. She'd started to worry lately that the young ones had become too close to her. Ida sighed and walked towards the stables, feeling the nearness of the dogs. How ironic that this should be a worry. How lovely it had been to grow close to them, to get to know them, but now she had started to become concerned about how they would deal with her death. Ida reprimanded herself. *They would be fine.*

As Ida had expected, the stables were quiet. The riding school was closed for the day as Danny and Thomas had gone out to look at some horses that were for sale.

Walking through the open entrance to the converted barn, Winston and Bessie left Ida's side and waggled their way over to Lucy, who was giving Lucky, the pit pony, her special herbal rub to help her breathing.

'Ah, Mrs Boulter,' Lucy said, drying her hands on a towel hanging next to the stall. The dogs sniffed her hands but backed away on smelling the pungent mix of herbs.

Ida hated being called Mrs Boulter as it was her husband's name and she had not been his wife for eight years, but she knew this was simply the way Lucy had been brought up.

She looked around the large, airy stables and took in the horses glancing over at her; the sound of gentle snorting and a few hoofs stamping on the flagstones could be heard.

'I wanted to have a quick word with Danny . . .'

'I'm afraid you've just missed him,' Lucy said, closing Lucky's stable door.

As she pulled the bolt across, she turned to see Ida suddenly clutch the door frame as though she was about to faint.

'Oh God! Mrs Boulter!' Lucy ran towards her and grabbed her. 'Do you want me to get the doctor?'

'No, no,' Ida said, taking Lucy's arm to steady herself. 'It's nothing a nice cup of tea won't cure.' She nodded towards the tack room. 'I've heard you've got your own little cafeteria in there.'

Lucy laughed. 'I think that might be a bit of an overstatement.'

After helping Ida walk the short distance to the tack-cum-tea room and settling her in an old chair, the dogs making themselves comfortable at her feet, Lucy popped two teabags into the pot and poured boiling water into it from the copper urn on the side.

'Milk and sugar?'

Ida smiled and nodded. As she did so, she breathed in

the air. 'There's something lovely about the smell of leather and hay and horses . . .' she murmured as she looked around the tack room, taking in the harnesses, saddles, riding hats and all the other horse paraphernalia.

Lucy brought her tea over, feeling nervous as this was the first time she had been with Danny's mam on her own.

'People seem to either love it or hate it,' she said, sitting down on a rickety wooden chair and leaning forward to pat the dogs.

Ida took a sip of her tea. 'I'm feeling better already.'

Lucy thought Ida had indeed made a quick recovery.

'Danny's gone to buy some more horses,' Lucy said.

'Oh, of course,' Ida lied. 'Head like a sieve.'

They both took another sip of their tea, an awkward air between them – Ida wondering whether a direct or a more subtle approach would be best; Lucy concerned that it didn't look as though Danny's mam was in a rush to get back to the manor.

'Danny's done so well for himself,' Ida said, looking around. 'Who could ever have guessed he would end up with his own riding stables . . . And he deserves it. Angie has told me how hard he's worked to make it a success.'

'He has,' Lucy enthused. 'And he's a natural with the horses. And such a brilliant instructor.'

Ida could see how proud Lucy was of him and how much she loved him more than anything.

'You and Danny make a wonderful couple,' Ida declared. 'You share the same passion in life. And from what I've heard, you are both very much in love.'

Lucy blushed. 'Yes, yes, we are.'

Ida took another sip of her tea before putting it down on the upturned wooden crate. The dogs sniffed, making sure there was no food to be had.

'And would the rumour-mongers be right in speculating that a wedding might be on the horizon?' she probed.

'Oh, well . . .' Lucy hesitated. 'I'm not sure about that.'

'Really?' Ida said, her eyes now fixed on Lucy. 'Because I heard that your parents have decided that you are to marry the son of some wealthy landowner from the north of the county.' Ida creased her brow, as though trying to remember the name. 'Anthony. Anthony . . .'

Lucy didn't know what to say – or where to look. She felt cornered. 'Hetherington. Anthony Hetherington.'

'But you love Danny? Not this Anthony bloke?' Ida continued to query.

'Yes, I do love Danny, very much.' This time Lucy looked Ida straight in the eye.

'Then why have you not told your parents that you don't want to marry the man they've chosen for you?'

'It's not as simple as that,' Lucy mumbled.

'Is it not?' Ida asked. 'I'd say that there's nothing simpler. You love Danny, therefore if you are going to marry anyone, it would be him – and not someone you don't love.'

'I don't know what to say, Mrs Boulter,' Lucy said, her voice practically a whisper.

Ida took another sip of her tea.

'Can I ask you a question which might seem inappropriate?'

353

Lucy didn't say anything; she had a feeling Ida would ask anyway.

Which she did.

'Would you sleep with a man for money?' Ida asked.

Lucy went beetroot red and shook her head vehemently.

'I can see the thought is abhorrent to you, but if you marry this Anthony, isn't that exactly what you will be doing?' Ida tried to keep her voice even and non-combative. 'Sleeping with him so that your family – your mother and father and, of course, you – is able to keep Roeburn Hall?'

Again, Lucy shook her head. 'It's just what people like us do. My mother married my father because he was deemed a good match.'

'A good match meaning he had money?'

Lucy nodded. 'And because of the Stanton-Leigh lineage.'

Ida thought for a moment. 'So, because your mother married for money and social standing, you feel that you should do the same?'

Lucy didn't answer.

'If that's the case, then it would be okay for Angie to follow in *her* mother's footsteps and abandon her children when they were very small?'

Ida saw tears start to well in Lucy's eyes and a look of wretchedness on her face.

'Don't cry,' Ida smiled, knowing she could come across as rather abrupt and that Lucy was a little nervous of her. 'I've not come here to lecture you, Lucy . . .'

She waited a beat while Lucy blinked away the potential tears.

'But I *have* come here to impart some hard-learnt wisdom from a dying woman. And,' she added, giving Lucy a conspiratorial smile, 'I also have an idea I want to share with you.'

When Danny returned, he found Lucy sitting in the tack room, staring out of the window.

'Are you all right?' he asked.

Lucy shook her head. 'No, not really.'

Danny hurried over and took her in his arms. 'What is it?'

'Your mother came to see me – well, she said originally that she came to see you, but it didn't take long to realise that it was me she wanted to talk to.'

Anger flashed across Danny's face. 'What did she say? She better not have upset you?'

'No, she didn't upset me – well, not intentionally.'

Seeing his anger was still there, Lucy tried to explain.

'She didn't *upset* me, but she did *unsettle* me.'

'That seems much the same thing to me,' Danny huffed.

Lucy looked at the time. 'Oh gosh, it's later than I thought.' She forced a smile to try and reassure him. 'Don't be angry with your mam. She's just very forthright, isn't she? Calls a spade a spade.'

'That's one way of putting it,' Danny said through pursed lips.

Lucy got up.

'So, what did she say to *unsettle* you?' Danny asked.

Lucy gave another anxious look at the clock next to where the leather bridle was hanging.

'I'll tell you tomorrow,' she said, pulling on her riding hat.

As she walked out of the tack room to get Dahlia, she turned.

'You know I love you, don't you?'

Danny nodded, still perturbed by this strange mood Lucy was in. *Damn his mam.*

'And you know just how much I love you?' he asked.

Lucy nodded. 'I do. I really do, Danny.'

Chapter Fifty-Eight

Lucy rode back to Roeburn Hall at a steady trot, occasionally pulling back on the reins to instruct Dahlia to drop down to a walk. Her mind was swimming with the words Ida had spoken and the feelings they had stirred up in her. But when she reached Roeburn Hall, she felt the return of responsibility. The overwhelming sense of guilt were she to go against her family. For that was what she would have to do if she followed her heart – as Ida had encouraged her.

'It's a well-worn saying,' Ida had said, her look intense and unnerving, 'but this is a short life. And if there is anything I have learnt after the many, many mistakes I have made, it's that you have to follow this . . .' She'd placed her hand on her chest.

Ida had said many other things to her over their cups of tea, but the one that kept coming back to Lucy was that she had to 'Listen to your heart and not your head.'

It was the antithesis of the philosophy Lucy had been brought up with.

Arriving back at Roeburn Hall, Lucy hoped no-one would be about, that her mother and father had either gone out to some social event or retired to their own rooms.

Her hopes were immediately dashed when she heard her

father's cheery voice sounding out from the dining room. She inwardly cursed.

'Come in and join us, Lucy.' Her father's voice echoed around the high ceiling of the huge hallway, which made the one at Cuthford Manor seem positively small.

Lucy reluctantly went in to see her father.

Entering the dining room, her heart dropped further on seeing that her mother was also there. Her parents rarely fraternised when they were at home, limiting the time they had together to their social engagements. She immediately caught her mother's disparaging look at seeing her daughter in her riding gear, no make-up on and her hair roughly tied back in a ponytail.

'One day I'm going to see my beautiful daughter in something other than her muddy jodhpurs and a jumper covered in horsehair.'

'Darling, leave the poor girl alone – you'd be worried if she was out every night, made-up to the hilt, tripping the light fantastic.'

'Actually, I wouldn't mind at all. She is now seventeen years old and should be out mingling – not spending all her time with horses.' Mrs Stanton-Leigh took a sip of her martini.

Lucy sighed. Her mother had never understood her and probably never would.

'Sit down, Lucy.' Her father waved a hand at one of the chairs by the polished mahogany dining table.

Lucy reluctantly pulled out a chair and sat down.

'We want to chat to you, darling,' said her mother.

Lucy felt herself tense. She had a good idea what it was about. *Why had everyone decided to talk to her today?* Before this afternoon, she'd barely spoken more than a few courteous words to Mrs Boulter, and now her mother and father, whom she rarely saw together, clearly wanted to discuss something important. She sagged inwardly. She'd put money on what it was.

'We want to set a date.' Her father just came straight out and said it. 'For your upcoming nuptials.'

Lucy stared at her father and then at her mother. She'd thought they'd paired up for the purpose of talking to her about the *possibility* of her accepting the arranged marriage – not for hurtling ahead and *setting a date*!

'But I'm not even eighteen,' she said quickly. Panic coursed through her body. 'I'd presumed you'd want to wait until I'm at least eighteen – if not older – before I got married.'

'Ah, Lucy,' her father said, smiling and moving forward to pat her hand. 'We were just talking to the Hetheringtons and they are keen to see Anthony married and settled.'

Mrs Stanton-Leigh tried to read her daughter's face. Did she know of Anthony's reputation? It was why his parents were so keen to see him married sooner rather than later. Although if his parents thought that would 'cure' their son of his wandering eye and hands, they'd be sorely wrong. Judging by her expression, Lucy had no idea about Anthony the Adonis' philandering ways. Which did not surprise Mrs Stanton-Leigh. Lucy had never been interested in any kind of local tittle-tattle. Horses were her only concern.

'I think I'd rather wait until next year,' Lucy said. 'I mean, there's no rush, is there?'

Mr and Mrs Stanton-Leigh fell quiet. Lucy watched as her mother avoided eye contact and took another sip of her martini, while her father patted himself down for his cigarettes. Finding them in the inside pocket of his jacket, he took one out and lit it.

'Is there?' Lucy asked again, this time more forcefully.

Her father blew out smoke and tapped the end of his cigarette into the cut-crystal ashtray. He gave a slightly nervous cough. 'I'm afraid there is a slight sense of haste, my dear girl.' He looked across at his wife. He needed her to say the words. It would come better from her than it would from him.

'Lucy, darling,' Mrs Stanton-Leigh responded to her prompt, 'we're getting pressure from the damned banks. They're becoming impatient.'

'I'm afraid if we don't find the money soon,' Mr Stanton-Leigh waved his hand in the air, causing ash to fall around him like grey confetti, 'this place will no longer be ours. We'll be booted out of our own home.'

'Our own *ancestral* home,' Mrs Stanton-Leigh added. Seeing her daughter wilt in her chair, her shoulders drooping, she knew she had to try to put a positive spin on the situation. 'Think about what a union between our families will mean. You will be the toast of the county. *Queen* of the county. You'll want for nothing. Nothing at all.'

Seeing that his daughter was nonplussed by the prospect, Mr Stanton-Leigh cut in. 'And think of the stables you could build – and the horses you could buy. You could have

whatever you so desired. Even your own livery or equestrian centre.'

Lucy smiled at her father. At least *he* understood her.
Knew where her passions lay.

The dining room was quiet as Mr and Mrs Stanton-Leigh
waited for Lucy to say something. When the silence continued longer than was comfortable, Mr Stanton-Leigh stubbed
out his cigarette and stood up.

'Lucy, if I give you one word of advice, then it is this. You
must think with your head – and not your heart.' He paused.
He didn't have to say Danny's name. 'We'll chat about it
tomorrow, eh? Give you time to sleep on it.' His hands on
either side of her face, he kissed the crown of her head. 'I
hate to pressure you, but we really do have to start making
plans. Time's running out.'

And with those words, Lucy knew that the decision had
been made. They did not need her enthusiasm, just her
compliance.

After her father had left the room, Mrs Stanton-Leigh
moved her chair so that she was nearer her daughter.

'Darling,' she began, 'we know all about the miner's son.'

Lucy sat up straight and looked at her mother. 'He has a
name, Mother. And he might well be the son of a miner, but
he runs a successful business.'

'He runs a riding school, darling.'

Lucy stared at her mother.

'You don't really think you could have a future with
someone like that? Do you? Someone who associates with
Gypsies? And whose sister is married to a Polish refugee?

Darling, Cuthford Manor is inhabited by a family of mongrels.'

Lucy stared at her mother. *God, she hated her.*

Feeling the animosity coming from her daughter in waves, Mrs Stanton-Leigh decided to just get straight to the point.

'Darling, I'm going to speak freely. And I hope you don't mind.' She didn't wait for an answer. 'But just because you marry someone, it does not mean you have to forsake other – how should I put it – *other interests.*'

She looked at Lucy, trying to discern if her daughter understood what she was saying.

'If you know what I mean?'

'Yes, Mother.' Lucy stood up. 'I know exactly what you mean.'

Her mother's trysts, to which her father turned a blind eye, had been the foundation block of her parents' marriage.

Lucy left her mother to finish her martini on her own and with a heavy heart made her way up to her room.

She didn't think she had ever felt this desolate in her life.

By two in the morning, Lucy had given up on sleep and got out of bed, put on some warm clothes and went out to see Dahlia.

She had been brought up to believe that family was everything. That loyalty was everything for those with whom you shared blood.

And, of course, it had been instilled in her since she was

a young child how important their bloodline was. Their ancestry could be dated back to the Boldon Book.

Reaching the stables, Lucy crept quietly in. She smiled to see that Dahlia was also still awake. Noticing her mistress, Dahlia made a winnowing sound to show her welcome.

'You can't sleep either,' Lucy whispered, stroking Dahlia's forehead and resting her face against her horse's.

'What should I do?' she whispered into her beloved horse's twitching ears.

Dahlia breathed a steady stream of warm air from her muzzle, staying still as Lucy continued to ask her for counsel and confide her feelings.

The words of Danny's mam kept coming back. *'Follow your heart.'* Words of advice that contrasted with those of her own parents. In the space of just a few hours, she had been given polar opposite views on how to live her life.

Ida's advice was tempting, as it was what she really wanted to do. But at what cost?

Her parents were asking her for help. How could she refuse? How could she be responsible for her family losing their ancestral home?

Ida's advice was to act selfishly.

Her parents needed her to be selfless.

'Dahlia, tell me what I should do?' she implored.

Chapter Fifty-Nine

The next day, after Lucy got up, she waited to go downstairs for her breakfast, hoping to give her mother and father enough time to have their usual kippers, scrambled eggs and toast before going off to do whatever it was they did during the day. Neither of them worked, but both always seemed to be busy.

Trailing downstairs, tired after a restless night, Lucy walked into the dining room and stopped in her tracks on seeing that her father was still there.

'Lucy, come and sit down. You look as white as the driven snow. Let me get you a nice hearty breakfast.' He started to get up to ring the bell for the maid.

'No, Father, I'm really not hungry,' Lucy quickly objected. 'I just want a piece of toast and a cup of tea.'

She leant over and picked up a piece of toast from the silver toast rack.

'Well now, my special girl, I'm glad I've caught you,' Mr Stanton-Leigh eyed his daughter, trying to gauge if her sleepless night had led to her making the right decision, 'as I was about to leave for a meeting with the annoying blighters at the bank.'

Lucy spread butter and then spooned marmalade onto the triangle of toast, which was barely warm.

'They've become impatient of late, you see.' Mr Stanton-Leigh got out his cigarettes and pulled one out of the packet. 'I wanted to tell you this last night, but got sidetracked . . . Anyway, we've been told we have to wipe the debt clean by Christmas – if not before.'

Lucy put down her cup of tea. 'Really? That seems unfair. I mean . . .' Lucy paused to do the maths in her head. 'That's in just over two and a half months.'

Mr Stanton-Leigh grimaced. 'I know.'

He lit his cigarette.

'Which is why, my dear, *lovely* girl, we really do need you to set a date so we can get going on arranging the wedding.'

Lucy felt her heart start to beat more rapidly.

'Gosh, Father, this seems rather fast,' Lucy said. 'I thought I'd at least finish school first.' In reality, Lucy was not in the least bothered about school, but she thought it might buy her time.

'Girls don't need to do exams and get qualifications,' Mr Stanton-Leigh said, smoke swirling out of his mouth as he spoke. 'I mean, it's not as if you'll need to get a job.'

'I might *want* to get a job,' Lucy lied.

'Lucy, *my girl*, I know you only too well and the only thing on this earth that you care about is riding horses.'

Lucy looked at her father. She wanted to say that this might have been the case before. *Before she met Danny.*

'And when you marry Anthony, you will be able to spend

every minute of every day out riding. *And* building up your own stables. I know you – the first thing you will do after your nuptials is start up your own livery. Which will be the best in the county!'

Mr Stanton-Leigh did indeed understand his daughter well. Had always known where her lust for life lay. It was why he had so endeared himself to her. Unlike her mother, he had spent time with his daughter while she grew up and had given her whatever her heart desired, which had always been the same – anything whatsoever to do with horses. And, of course, to be allowed to go riding when she wanted. She would be forever indebted to him for fighting her corner and allowing her to leave her boarding school, thus enabling her to spend every free moment she had with Dahlia.

'And you can't put the bank off?' Lucy implored. 'Get some kind of bridging loan under the expectation that I will marry Anthony eventually.'

'I'm afraid not,' Mr Stanton-Leigh said. He had, of course, already suggested that himself. 'They would not take the risk. You – or Anthony, for that matter – might not make it down the aisle for some reason ... Darling, I hate to be pushy, but you know what will happen if you don't marry Anthony.' He stubbed out his cigarette as though to punctuate the point.

'I do, Father. I do,' Lucy said, feeling the weight of responsibility on her shoulders, pushing her down.

Mr Stanton-Leigh looked at his watch and got up.

'Righty-ho, I'd better be off. Go and see these wretched money men.' He pulled a long face.

366

Lucy got up to give her father a hug.

'Oh, Lucy,' he said, wrapping her in his arms. 'You are going to be this family's saviour.'

He stood back, his hands on her shoulders. 'You know we would never ask you to do this if the situation wasn't totally and utterly desperate?'

Lucy nodded and forced a weak smile.

Sitting back down and staring at her untouched marmalade on toast, she felt as if a noose had just been put around her neck.

She put her hand to her throat, feeling it tighten.

Chapter Sixty

Over the next four days, Lucy left messages for Danny telling him that she had to stay at home and prepare for the new school term. On Monday, knowing it was unlikely she would be able to come over after school finished, given that there was always some kind of do planned for the first evening of the new term, Danny decided that he couldn't wait any longer for Lucy to tell him why his mam had gone to see her. And, in particular, what she had said.

He realised that the time had finally come for him to see his mam on her own. To have a proper conversation with her.

He managed to hold back until she'd had breakfast with the children before they hurried off to their first day back at school – driven by Marlene. Thomas, in his role as instructor, was in the passenger seat, ramrod straight, jawline clenched in anticipation of the journey. Seeing the car finally making its way slowly down the driveway, the occasional crunch of gears sounding out, Danny headed to the kitchen.

There, he was glad to see that his mam was still sitting in her usual place in the old rocker, nursing a cup of tea. He had not wanted to have to go searching the manor for her. Alberta was busy clearing up the breakfast dishes. Seeing

Danny, she mumbled an excuse about having to see Bill about the vegetables for the evening meal, then hurried out of the back door to leave him and his mother in peace.

'Danny!' Ida perked up on seeing her son.

Winston and Bessie hauled themselves up to greet Danny, who gave them a quick pat.

'Don't suppose there's a spare cuppa going?' he asked.

'Of course,' Ida said, reaching for the big brown ceramic teapot. She put her hands around its pot belly. 'Still nice and hot. You just need to get yourself a clean cup and saucer.'

Danny grabbed a mug that was drying at the side of the sink unit and sat down on the wooden bench adjacent to his mam. He noticed how the dogs flumped down next to Ida, one on either side, and felt irritated that Winston and Bessie, as well as the rest of his siblings, were so enamoured of his errant mother.

Ida watched as her son poured himself a mug of tea and added milk and two heaped spoons of sugar. Judging by the serious look on his face, she had a good idea why he'd come to chat to her.

'So, Mam,' Danny began, 'I'm wondering why you felt compelled to go and see Lucy the other day on the pretence that you were looking for me?'

Ida smiled. She would rather Danny be like this – his animosity towards her open and undisguised – than pretend he felt otherwise purely because she was dying.

She took a sip of her tea and put the cup back in its saucer.

'I wanted to have a chat with her, that's all,' Ida said, knowing her answer would be unsatisfactory.

'Yes, Mam, but what did you chat to her about? When I came back after you'd had your *chat*, Lucy seemed upset.'

'Upset?' Ida asked, concerned. She hadn't thought Lucy was upset when she'd left her.

'Well, the word Lucy used was "unsettled",' he said.

'Ah,' Ida said. 'Mmm.'

She took another sip of her tea.

'What does *that* mean?' Danny asked, irritated that his mam seemed reluctant to tell him anything.

'It means,' Ida said, 'that what Lucy and I spoke about is between Lucy and me. If Lucy wants to tell you, that's fine. But it wouldn't be right for me to break that confidence.'

Danny let out a burst of hollow laughter. 'God, Mam, when did you get to be so sanctimonious?'

Ida didn't hear the accusation – just the word he used. And, more particularly, his education. She felt so proud of him. For so many different reasons. If only she could tell him that, but she knew that if she did, it would simply wash over him as he had no respect for her, or for anything she might say.

'I know you're still angry at me, Danny, for leaving you,' Ida began. Her time was running out. And she might not get this opportunity again.

Danny looked at his mam. Even though she was a shadow of her former self and knocking on death's door, he still couldn't quell the anger he felt towards her. He'd tried, but to no avail.

'Aye, Mam, I *am* angry at yer,' he said.

Ida could hear the return of his accent. It was the same

for her. If ever she was angry or perhaps a little tipsy, the sound of her birthplace would return.

'And you've good right to be,' Ida said. 'I was a terrible mam to you, and then I topped it by walking out on you all.'

Danny could feel his suppressed emotions suddenly clambering to the surface, gasping for air.

'You *were* terrible! I can't believe you could be that selfish to just dump us all on Angie. *The night before she got married.* And not just that, but you knew she'd bring us all back here. You let your own daughter bring up *your* children. God, Mam, I don't know why you ever had children if you were just going to get shot of them at the first opportunity.' Danny took a breath. His heart was racing, which made him breathless. 'And then, after you left us, you didn't even bother to make contact – not a letter, not a phone call, not a visit. Nothing!'

Danny could feel himself getting hot. All of a sudden, the kitchen was stifling.

Ida desperately wanted to say how much she had wanted to see them all that time. She had often asked herself what would be the right thing to do. In the end, she'd decided it was best to leave them be. Niamh had told her what a wonderful life they all had. How happy they seemed. They were all going to posh schools, were being well looked after, not just by Angie, but by the people Ida herself had now met and got to know.

'God, you basically made us all orphans, cos yer must have known that Dad wouldn't give two figs. I know Angie wrote to him, practically begged him to see us, but he wasn't interested. Couldn't even be bothered to come here – even though Angie offered to pick him up and bring him over.'

At the mention of Fred, Ida could feel her own blood boil. She knew she had no right to judge him, but she didn't care. She had been a terrible mother, but he had been an even worse father. And husband.

'But what makes me angrier than anything is how your actions affected Marlene – not just back then, but right up to now. I hate to think how she's going to cope after you're gone.'

Ida didn't try to defend herself. Everything her son said was true, although she believed that Marlene would be fine. She would be sad, but she was strong. She would cope. But Ida didn't say this as she knew that her son just needed to get it all out. Like most men, Danny held too much in. It needed to come out. Only then could he move forward.

She waited, wanting Danny to keep going until all his hurt and resentment and bottled-up emotions were spent.

But he stopped as swiftly as he'd started, leaving the air in the kitchen strained.

Neither mother nor son spoke, although there was still much they both wanted to say.

The silence was broken by the sound of a horse's hoofs on the cobbles out in the yard.

They both looked out of the kitchen window to see Stanislaw walking one of the horses over to a local woman who claimed going out for a trek after packing her five 'monsters' off to school saved her sanity.

Danny looked at his mother, clearly wanting but not able to say any more.

And Ida looked at Danny, wanting to say so much, but knowing that the window of opportunity had passed.

She only wished that after she was gone, her son would not let anger and resentment corrode his life, his love and his potential for contentment and happiness.

She hoped to God that, for her son's sake, Lucy would find the courage to do what was right for herself – and for Danny.

And not what was right for her parents.

Chapter Sixty-One

Over the next couple of weeks, life at the Cuthford Country House Hotel was frantic with guests; no sooner had one lot gone, than another batch arrived. Having dropped their off-spring at boarding school, many couples were making the most of their new-found freedom. There was a frenzied atmosphere behind the scenes as everyone tried to keep on top of all the things that had to be done – and to uphold the high standards that were expected and needed in order to justify the prices they charged.

Dr Wright was now visiting most days, checking on Ida and adjusting her pain medication as he deemed fit. He could see her strength was fading, although her mind remained active and alert. It always saddened him when the brain was so robust yet the body so infirm.

Angie felt her heart slowly break as she witnessed her mother's deterioration – and her frustration grow that Danny was still refusing to make peace with Ida before she died. Alberta had told her the two had 'had words' in the kitchen the previous week, and Stanislaw, pushed and prodded by Angie, had managed to squeeze out of Danny a little about what had been said.

'It's a shame,' he said to Angie as they were getting ready for bed and catching up on each other's news.

'A shame because?' Angie asked.

'Because he's not going to see the other side to his mother.'

'Well, someone's changed their tune,' said Angie, jumping into bed and wrapping the bedclothes around her, shivering.

'I think,' Stanislaw reflected as he looked out at the ink-black sky, 'I was too quick to judge. I was fortunate to have a good, loving and stable upbringing – it wasn't fair to . . . how do you say it . . . *take the high ground* with your mother. There is a part of me which still cannot understand how a mother can just up and leave her children, but then I have not experienced what Ida has in her life and therefore I cannot condemn her for what she did. If I had been in her shoes, I might have done the same – who knows. Perhaps there are reasons she did what she did which I cannot understand, because I am not her – and have not lived her life.'

Angie looked at her husband and felt the deepest love for him.

'Anyway,' Stanislaw turned from the window, lifting his voice to lighten the solemn mood, 'a man's allowed to change his mind, isn't he?' He gave his wife a mischievous look. 'Or is that only a woman's prerogative?'

Angie laughed, then became serious.

'It's allowed on the proviso that the man's change of mind is in line with the woman's thinking.'

Stanislaw pantomimed shock. 'You've been spending too much time with Clemmie and Barbara!'

Angie laughed and held open the counterpane.

'Come on, I need warming up.'

Stanislaw did a quick salute.

'Yes, ma'am! At your service and ready to oblige.'

With the change of weather, Bertie, Jemima and Bonnie managed to put on a good show of having caught a cold, which Angie knew to be fake as they only coughed and sneezed whenever she was around. Aware of how little time her mam had left, though, Angie also faked a belief that they really did have 'nasty colds' and agreed they could take Thursday and Friday off school.

They spent their time with Ida, mainly in her room, playing games and reading, only occasionally dragging her downstairs when their favourite programme was on the television. Marlene, who had also decided not to go to school, kept an eye on them all, and when she saw that her mam was flagging and needed a rest, she'd shoo the children downstairs on some errand that would earn them a treat.

Marlene was surprised by how differently she'd felt since her return from London. Whereas before she might have resented taking charge of the young ones, now she didn't. It was as though her resentment towards her mam had faded along with her bruises. As had her anger. And it felt good. She felt unburdened. And although the heaviness caused by the aftermath of the attack she'd endured was still there, there was also a lightness of being.

Her aspirations of becoming an actress had also faded fast. What she'd experienced in London had taken the rug from under her feet as she had not considered a different future for herself, but she knew she had time to work out what she would do with her life. And she'd started to have an inkling of an idea as the image of the little boy and girl begging on the streets of Soho kept coming into her mind.

Angie made sure the children were kept busy of an evening so that Carl could spend time with Ida after his day spent working in the grounds. He'd take their tray of sandwiches and soup up to her room, along with a little vase of flowers from the garden, and stay there all evening, chatting and reading poetry, which Angie had learnt was his passion. He'd fall asleep either in the armchair next to Ida's bed or on the two-seater sofa by the fire.

When Sunday came, Angie breathed a sigh of relief as the last guest left.

'We're eating in the dining room this evening,' she told everyone. 'I feel like I've hardly seen you all. And I've invited Clemmie over too. Barbara can't come as she's got her head into something "terribly important".' Which Angie was quite glad about as she didn't feel like talking politics, which normally happened when Barbara was about. She had a feeling that Clemmie was pleased too.

As everyone trooped into the dining room and sat down, Angie thought Cora and Lloyd looked a bit down in the mouth, which was unlike them.

'No Danny this evening?' Angie asked when everyone

had taken their places and Mabel had started to bring in the plates of roast beef and Yorkshire pudding.

The room fell quiet. Angie looked at Stanislaw, who shrugged his shoulders to show that he too was puzzled.

'Has something happened?' she asked, surveying the table.

Marlene looked over at Cora and Lloyd. 'You tell them.'

'Well,' Cora began, 'it would seem that Lucy has agreed to marry Anthony Hetherington. Apparently, the banns were read out today at the local church near Roeburn Hall.'

'Really?' Angie was surprised. She'd heard vague mutterings that Lucy's family were trying to marry off their daughter, but she hadn't taken the rumours seriously.

'But I thought she was keen on Danny,' Stanislaw said.

'More than keen,' Marlene said. 'Lucy's completely dotty about Danny.'

'But clearly not enough to stop her marrying another bloke,' Angie said, reaching forward and pouring gravy on her meal.

Marlene widened her eyes in exasperation. Her sister had never really taken to Lucy.

'I don't think it's as straightforward as that,' Clemmie butted in.

'Why's that?' Stanislaw was genuinely perplexed.

Bertie, Jemima and Bonnie were listening intently, their focus on the adults and not their meal. It wasn't often they got to earwig on the conversations of the 'grown-ups'.

'Simply put,' Lloyd said, 'the Stanton-Leighs, or rather Edward Stanton-Leigh, have not been savvy with their finances, and they now find themselves in a position whereby they have to forsake Roeburn Hall to clear their substantial debts.'

Angie and Stanislaw looked at each other, knowing what the other one was thinking.

'But I thought they were one of the richest families in the county,' Angie said.

'That might have been the case years ago,' Lloyd explained, 'but not any more.'

'The word on the street,' Clemmie said conspiratorially, 'is that he's gambled away his inheritance.'

Angie shook her head. 'That's terrible, but what's that got to do with Lucy marrying this Anthony bloke?'

Marlene rolled her eyes. 'Because, Angie, the Hetheringtons have money. Loads of it. The dad's some kind of hotshot in the City and has made millions on the stock market. That's what Belinda told me, anyway. She says they're *nouveau riche*.'

Stanislaw looked confused.

Marlene explained. 'They're middle-class people with enough money to allow them to live like the upper classes. But they haven't the right blood or breeding so they will never really achieve the lofty heights of the uppers.'

Marlene paused theatrically.

'Unless they marry in.'

'Well explained,' said Clemmie. 'What people like the Hetheringtons desperately want and can't buy is any kind of great ancestry or even the most tentative connection to royalty.'

'So,' Stanislaw said, 'I'm guessing this is why the Hetheringtons want their son to marry a Stanton-Leigh.'

'Exactly!' Marlene said. 'The Hetheringtons get their lineage and the Stanton-Leighs get the money they need to keep Roeburn Hall.'

Bertie, Jemima and Bonnie's eyes were going from Angie to Clemmie to Lloyd to Marlene; only occasionally did they break off to shove some roast beef into their mouths.

'Very transactional,' Cora said disapprovingly.

'Honestly, whatever happened to getting married for love?' Angie said, cutting up some of her beef. 'Come on, eat up, everyone.'

Everyone started to eat, but there was an unease.

Marlene, who was just pushing her food around her plate, looked at her older sister.

'I don't think you understand, Angie, but this is *devastating* news for Danny. He's heartbroken. Really heartbroken.'

Angie swallowed a mouthful of roast potato. 'He's young. He'll get over it. And besides, does he really want to be moping over someone who will just let herself be pushed around like that and told who she can and can't marry?'

Marlene gasped. 'Cor, Angie, and I thought our mam was hard as nails.'

She pushed her plate away and stood up.

'Well, if you don't care about your brother's broken heart, I do!'

And with that Marlene stomped out of the room.

*

When Marlene walked into the kitchen, she saw that Thomas and Mabel were sitting at the kitchen table. She forced herself not to say anything bitchy, but it was hard.

Thomas stood up. 'Where are you going?'

'Out to see Danny. Not that it's any of your business,' Marlene snapped.

She caught the look of hurt on Thomas's face and felt bad, but it hurt *her* to see him all cosied up with Mabel.

'I wouldn't if I were you,' Mabel warned.

Marlene glowered at her.

'Lucy's out there,' Thomas explained. 'She's going away for a few weeks.'

'She's getting married to that Anthony Adonis bloke,' Mabel informed.

'So I've heard,' Marlene said through gritted teeth.

She walked towards the window, keeping to the side so as not to be seen.

From this vantage point, she watched the star-crossed lovers say their goodbyes to one another. Lucy had her arms fastened around Danny as though he were being sent to the gallows and this was the last time she would see him, which was not so far from the truth, for Lucy would not be allowed within a mile of Cuthford Manor now the marriage had been announced.

Marlene felt tears prick her own eyes as she saw her brother release himself from Lucy's grip. He said something to her and wiped away a tear that was trickling down her cheek.

They then exchanged the tenderest and most romantic

kiss, which beat any that Marlene had seen on the silver screen.

And then Lucy turned and walked away.

Marlene could hear the car door of Lucy's Morris Minor shut and the engine turn over.

She saw the flicker of car lights cross Danny's stony face.

And she watched as Danny remained rooted to the spot well after the sound of Lucy's car had disappeared into the night.

Gone forever.

Chapter Sixty-Two

Over breakfast the next day, Danny told everyone that he was going away for a while.

Bertie, Jemima and Bonnie looked crestfallen.

Angie was annoyed and didn't try to hide it.

'But we need you here,' she said, putting her cup down angrily and making her tea spill over into the saucer.

Winston and Bessie clambered up from their spot by the Aga and went to Angie, sensing her mood change. Alberta quickly dried her hands, grabbed her rolling tobacco and quietly slipped out the back door.

Danny watched the dogs as they nudged Angie – looking for reassurance that she was all right.

'No, you don't need me here,' Danny told his sister. 'You're the most organised person I know. You've got plenty of staff. And as for the riding school, Thomas is going to keep it ticking over. And if he's struggling, I've told him to get Carl to help. He's good with the horses. And there's Stanislaw.'

Danny looked at Stanislaw, who nodded.

'Of course. I can keep an eye on things and step in if needed,' he said.

Angie threw her husband a scolding look.

She pursed her lips, not wanting to say what she really wanted to in front of the young ones. *That he was needed here for his siblings.* When their mother passed away, which Angie felt was going to be sooner rather than later, they would need their big brother.

'When will you come back?' Cora asked, topping up her teacup and keeping her tone from sounding accusatory, although she also felt terribly disappointed that Danny would be leaving when he hadn't made his peace with his mam yet. Cora had become close to Ida and knew how much she wanted to make things right with her son before she went.

'Where are you going?' Marlene tried to hide her own surprise at her brother's announcement when Dr Wright had warned them that their mam could go at any time. The nature of her cancer meant that she only needed to catch a cold, or pick up some germs, and it would be too much for her body to deal with.

'I'm going up north. To Scotland. There's a livery just over the border which breeds horses. I'm going to stay there a while. Learn the ropes. And buy some horses.'

'How long will you be away?' Lloyd asked. He was concerned about Danny's emotional state after just losing the love of his life to an arranged marriage. Although at the same time could understand why Danny needed to get away.

'I'm not sure,' Danny said.

'Will it be days? Weeks? Months?' Angie demanded.

'I'll ring you,' Danny said. 'When I know more.'

Angie stopped herself saying anything else, but instead turned to the children. 'Right, say goodbye to your brother and get yourselves off to school.' She turned to Marlene. 'Are you and Thomas okay to drive them there?'

Marlene nodded while the little ones quietly moaned.

Angie, Stanislaw, Lloyd and Cora watched as they said their goodbyes, saddened at the turn of events which had befallen the young man they loved and cared for so much.

After Marlene had herded the children out to the car, Stanislaw and Lloyd gave Danny a pat on the back and told him to 'take care'. Stanislaw went off to see Eugene and Ted about shoring up the log supply, and Lloyd headed for the study to go through the monthly accounts. Cora wrapped Danny in a hug and told him to keep in touch and ring them when he arrived. She then went to see Wilfred, who was manning the front reception, to tell him about Danny 'going away for a while'.

Which left Angie.

'I wish you wouldn't go,' she said, knowing that her brother could be as stubborn as she was when he'd made up his mind about something.

'Sorry, Angie, but it's something I've got to do.'

'You know there'll be others – there'll be someone else for you out there.' Angie tried to offer some solace.

'No, there won't,' Danny bit back.

Angie wanted to tell him that he was still young. And that perhaps it was for the best, but she knew this was not the time.

'Right, I'll be getting off,' Danny said, giving his sister the obligatory hug.

'Will you go and see your mam before you leave? Make everything right, you know, in case she's not here when you come back?'

Danny smiled. 'It's all right. I went to see Mam last night when you were all having your dinner.'

Angie was surprised.

'Did you? I didn't realise,' she said.

'So, are you happy now?' Danny asked.

Angie forced a semblance of a smile.

'I wouldn't say "happy", but I'm pleased you've seen her.'

Angie desperately wanted to find out if he had forgiven their mam, if their parting had been a loving one and not just something Danny felt he had to do out of a sense of duty. But Danny was through the back door before she could get the words out of her mouth.

Chapter Sixty-Three

October

The week following Danny's departure was busy, but his absence was still felt. Marlene was drip-feeding them all bits of gossip that she was picking up from Belinda, who got much of her information by covertly listening in on her mother's phone calls to her friends who were all 'in' with the Hetheringtons and the Stanton-Leighs.

'Apparently Lucy's gone down to Devon and she has to travel into the nearest town to use a phone.'

'I still can't believe she's marrying the Hetherington boy,' Lloyd mumbled, more to himself than anyone else.

Danny had only rung them once so far, to tell them he'd arrived safely.

Marlene had decided to take a break from school to spend more time with Ida. She hadn't asked permission from Angie or the school but had simply informed them both that this was what she was going to do. Neither Angie nor the headmistress of Durham High School argued the case. Just as both wondered silently if Marlene would return once her mam had passed. Marlene had always been

387

strong-willed, but since she'd come back from London, she had become even more so.

'I'm just so glad that Marlene's spending time with Mam,' Angie told Stanislaw during their usual bedtime update.

Stanislaw nodded.

Knowing what he was thinking, she added, 'I know it's a pity that it's all come so late, but it's better than never at all.'

Stanislaw pulled his wife towards him. 'I agree. And I think that goes for other things too.'

Angie smiled and responded to her husband's embrace.

On Friday, Bertie, Jemima and Bonnie returned home from school, all looking a little wan, which wasn't due to Marlene's driving as that had improved tenfold. Even Thomas had said she didn't really need him, which was met by Marlene with mixed feelings, for she had been enjoying their time together in the cosy confines of the Austin.

'You all look a little green behind the gills,' Angie said as they trooped through the back door and flung their grey school winter coats on the hooks and pulled off their regulation leather shoes.

As they nestled around the kitchen table, Bonnie was the first to sneeze, then Jemima.

Angie knew it wouldn't be long before Bertie was also sneezing, as he was guaranteed to catch anything anyone else had.

Marlene gave Angie a look that spoke of their fears.

Their mam.

'Let Alberta make you all a hot drink before you go and see Mam, all right?'

Three grumpy faces looked up at Angie.

'And I might have some of those Bourneville chocolate biscuits stashed away in the larder,' Alberta added, knowing exactly what Angie and her sister feared.

Leaving Marlene in the kitchen, chatting to the children while Alberta boiled the kettle and put a pile of biscuits onto a plate, Angie went to see Ida, who was always in the family room at this time, waiting for the children to return from their day of schooling. It was something Ida loved to hear about and she would listen enrapt as they told her what lessons they'd had, what they'd learnt, which teachers they loved and which they hated.

'Are they back?' Ida asked as soon as Angie walked into the room. Angie could see that her mother had been snoozing. 'I think I heard their voices?'

'They are, Mam,' Angie said, sitting down on the sofa and fixing her attention on her mother. 'Alberta's just sorting them out with hot drinks.'

'Oh,' Ida said, surprised. Normally they'd all charge in to see her.

'The thing is, Mam,' Angie began tentatively, 'it looks like Jemima and Bonnie have got whatever it is that's doing the rounds at school.'

'Oh, are they all right?' Ida said. 'Do we need to call Dr Wright?'

Angie realised that her mam wasn't understanding what she was getting at.

'No, no, it's just the start of winter-cold season. They'll be fine . . .' Angie paused. 'It's you I'm worried about. Dr Wright said you're to stay away from germs.'

Ida tutted. 'Oh, Angie, you are such a worrier. If I catch whatever they've got, then I do. But if you're thinking of keeping the children away from me because they've got a cold, then think again.'

Angie looked at her mam. If she agreed, she knew she'd be signing her mother's death warrant. Dr Wright had made it quite plain. A simple cold would be enough to finish her off. He had been quite forthright, at Ida's insistence, and clear about the facts.

Knowing exactly what was going through her daughter's head, Ida sat up straight.

'You can't stop me, Angie.'

Angie sighed. 'I know, Mam. When has anyone been able to stop you doing exactly what you want?'

Her words were said with love. And a growing appreciation of her mam's character, flawed though that might be.

Walking back into the kitchen, Angie looked at Marlene with sorrowful eyes. She shook her head. Angie could see her sister's eyes start to glisten with the beginnings of tears.

'Can we go and see Mam now?' Bertie said, crumbs still around his mouth.

Jemima and Bonnie weren't waiting for their sister's say-so and were already shuffling off the kitchen bench.

'Yes, you can go now,' Angie said, her voice a little shaky.

As the three youngsters charged from the kitchen to the

family room, Winston and Bessie in hot pursuit, Angie and Marlene followed in their wake with far less enthusiasm.

Reaching the family room, the two sisters watched from the doorway as Ida opened her arms as she always did on their return and gave them all a big hug.

Angie turned to see that Marlene was struggling to hold back the tears. She took her hand, her own tears threatening, and squeezed hard.

And they stood there, watching a scene which was so incredibly touching and loving and happy – and at the same time so awfully heartbreaking.

Chapter Sixty-Four

It took just days for Ida to catch the children's cold, and in no time at all, it had turned into pneumonia.

When it was clear that Ida's time had come, Dr Wright was called.

Arriving at the manor, Wilfred opened the door and offered a strained smile as he took the doctor's hat and helped him out of his coat.

They both turned on hearing the sound of footsteps on the tiled flooring.

It was Cora.

'Can I get you anything before you go up?' she asked, her hands clasped.

A solemn-looking Dr Wright shook his head.

Reaching the landing to the West Wing, he saw that Angie was sitting on a chair that had been placed outside Ida's room.

Seeing him, she immediately stood.

'Carl's in there at the moment,' she said.

Dr Wright gently knocked on the door, which was ajar, and went into the room. Unlike many rooms he'd stepped into where a patient was dying, Ida's smelled fresh and airy. It was 'nipping clean', as his wife would say, and there were flowers in a vase by the bed. The sash window had been opened a little to let some air in. Despite the cold autumnal weather outside, the room was lovely and warm thanks to a crackling log fire in the little tiled Victorian fireplace at the far end of the room. Dr Wright noted that the two-seater leather sofa near to the fire had a pillow and a couple of neatly folded-up blankets on it and presumed rightly that this was where Carl had been sleeping of late.

Carl stood up and let Dr Wright see to Ida.

Walking over to the window, he looked out at the day, knowing it was one he would never forget. For he knew it was the day he would have to say goodbye to his Ida, and he wasn't ready for it. Would never be ready for it. He had promised Ida he would live his life after she had gone, but he wasn't sure it was a promise he could keep.

As he forced back his tears, he heard Ida thank Dr Wright for all his care. Knowing the doctor was about to leave, Carl turned around and blinked back the wetness in his eyes.

'I've left the morphine here as we discussed,' Dr Wright said.

Carl nodded.

'I'll be here if needed.'

'Thank you,' Carl murmured, hardly daring to speak.

When Dr Wright walked out of the room, Angie was waiting.

'Now would be a good time for everyone to say their goodbyes,' Dr Wright told her.

He had seen many people die, but even so, he had never become desensitised to death. Despite feeling a little judgemental when he had first got to know Mrs Boulter, having heard how she had abandoned her children when they were so small, he had grown to like her over these past few months.

'I'll go and get the children,' Angie said, forcing herself to be strong and fighting back the tears.

Angie and Dr Wright walked silently along the landing and down the stairs. Both wrapped up in their own thoughts.

Dr Wright couldn't help but feel it was such a shame that Mrs Boulter had to leave her children again when he had seen with his own eyes how much love she had for them. And they for her.

Angie, meanwhile, was fighting a terrible panic. An awful sense of being out of control. She realised that she had accepted her mother was dying, but she also knew she was not prepared for the finality of her death.

'Go on then,' Angie urged the children when they reached the door to Ida's room.

The three trudged in, their faces already full of grief for what was to come.

Angie stood by the doorway and watched them each give Ida a hug and a kiss.

Her mam's words were spoken quietly, but Angie was just able to hear.

'Don't ever forget how amazing you are. Each one of you. In your own different ways.'

Angie heard Jemima sniffle.

'But you must keep your promise,' Ida said, opening up

her arms and giving them all one final big hug. 'No sad faces. Okay?'

The three nodded.

Angie stepped into the room and guided them out.

Reaching the doorway, Bertie, Jemima and Bonnie gave the woman they had come to love one last wave goodbye.

Brushing away thoughts of Danny and the sadness as well as resentment she felt that he was not here to say his final farewells to his mam, Angie took the children downstairs to the kitchen, where Alberta was busy making hot chocolate. She then went outside to find Marlene, who she'd been told was out chatting to Thomas in the tack room.

Marlene had said her goodbyes to her mam before the children, and Angie wasn't surprised that she'd gone to see Thomas, especially as Danny wasn't there.

'I just wanted to check you're all right,' Angie said.

Marlene nodded. Angie could see she had been crying.

Thomas went to squeeze Marlene's hand as more tears looked imminent, but she flinched at his attempt to touch her. There was no longer any sign of her black eye, but Angie knew there were other after-effects that would take longer to heal.

Heading back upstairs, Angie braced herself.

'It won't be long now,' Dr Wright told Angie as she came back along the landing to the room. 'Mrs Boulter has told me she'd like to say a few words to you – before Carl goes in.'

Dr Wright looked from Angie to Carl. They both nodded their understanding.

When Angie walked into the room, she forced back the tears. She did not want her last moments with her mam to be spent crying.

'I'm lucky,' Ida said, her voice raspy and quiet. Angie could hear the strength and life fading fast. 'I have been reconciled with my children . . .' She paused. 'Something I never thought possible . . . I can go in peace as I know you are all well.' She took a breath, fighting the relaxing effects of the morphine and the pull of death.

'But most of all . . .' she forced herself to carry on, speaking the words she needed her daughter to hear, '. . . I can see the burden of anger and resentment I've caused you all to carry for too long . . .' another shallow breath '. . . has gone – for you and Marlene, for sure . . . Danny too . . . I hope so.' Ida forced more air into her lungs. '*That* has allowed me to die a very happy woman.'

Angie smiled through her pain at seeing her mam like this. She looked so frail. She wasn't so sure that Danny had unburdened himself of his resentments, but she was glad her mam believed he had.

'I have something else to tell you which will make you happy,' Angie said, this time her smile reaching her eyes.

'Tell me,' Ida whispered.

Angie leant forwards and whispered in her ear.

As she did so, Ida smiled.

'The circle of life,' she said, her words so faint that Angie was only just able to make them out.

Then Ida squeezed her daughter's hand and whispered, 'Carl.' And Angie knew it was time.

'Bye, Mam,' she said, her own voice now croaky with the beginnings of tears. She kissed Ida on her cheek.

As she walked away, she felt the deep, dark sorrow of knowing that this time her mam was going for good.

Walking out of the door, tears now silently trickling down her cheeks, Angie found Carl waiting.

Seeing her distress, he took her arm and squeezed it gently.

Angie tried to give him a reassuring smile but failed. Instead, she nodded towards the door, unable to speak, for she knew if she did, she would lose control and her words would be lost in an outpouring of grief.

Carl walked into the room and left the door ajar. He went over to the bed, sat in the chair next to it and took hold of Ida's hand.

No words were needed.

Their love for one another was there, as it always had been and always would be.

After a few moments, Ida's eyes closed, and her hand went slack.

She had gone, leaving the slightest of smiles on her lips.

Chapter Sixty-Five

When Carl came out of the room, Angie got up and gave him a hug. Then she walked quietly away from the bedroom door and made her way along the landing, down the carpeted stairs to the kitchen, where her siblings had gathered.

As soon as she entered, everyone's heads turned towards her, their eyes showing they knew but still needed to hear the words.

'She's gone,' Angie said gently.

Marlene put her arms around Bertie and Jemima, who were sitting on either side of her, and pulled them close as they cried.

Bonnie shuffled off the bench to seek comfort from her mum.

Sensing their grief, Winston and Bessie hauled themselves up from their space by the Aga and nudged up to those they loved, trying to offer their own form of condolence, and in doing so, making the young ones laugh through their tears.

'Right,' Angie said after the little ones' crying had spluttered to a stop, 'can you three take the dogs out, please? The fresh air will do you all good.'

Bertie, Jemima and Bonnie nodded. Sniffing and wiping

their eyes of tears, the trio tramped to the back door, pulled on their boots and shrugged on their coats. Winston and Bessie made for the door, their tails wagging.

When it was just the two of them, Angie turned to Marlene. She looked at her younger sister and could see that she was no longer able to hold back her tears.

Sitting down next to her, Angie put her arm around her shoulders.

The sisters sat together.

Angie with tears trickling down her cheeks.

Marlene crying great sobs of sorrow.

After Angie had gone to tell the rest of the household about Ida's passing, she went to check on Marlene, who had told her she just wanted to be on her own in her room for a while.

Knocking on her door and pushing it open, she found her sister lying on top of her bed, her eyes red and swollen.

'How are you feeling?' Angie asked, sitting on the edge of the bed.

Marlene pushed herself up into a sitting position. She let out a half cry, half laugh.

'I seem unable to stop crying,' she said, before bursting into another fresh batch of heart-rending tears.

They were words Angie repeated to Dorothy when she rang her a few hours later to tell her the news that her mam had died.

It took a week to organise the funeral, and Angie ended up putting the date for the burial back in the hope that by then

Danny would have returned from Scotland. She had left a message at the place her brother was staying, informing him of their mam's death, but hadn't heard back from him personally, only from the manager of the livery where Danny had said he was lodging who had called to say that the message had been delivered. Angie felt sad and frustrated that Danny had not been there for his mam's death; she could have done with his support in comforting the young ones. And although Marlene hadn't said as much, it was obvious she had desperately wanted her brother by her side, as he'd always been there for her through life's traumas.

Later, Angie left a tetchier message relaying the need to set a date for the funeral, but when Angie had still not heard anything from her brother, she decided they couldn't wait any longer and went to see the vicar, who agreed that Ida's funeral could be held that weekend.

Ida had given Angie specific instructions about what to do following her death.

'No curtains drawn, no sad faces,' she'd demanded.

She'd told Angie that she didn't want them to 'weep or wail', but to use the occasion to have 'a bit of a knees-up'.

'If not for the grown-ups, then for the children,' she'd said. 'I really don't want them to feel sad – so will you promise me to make it a jolly occasion? Because there is much to celebrate, isn't there?'

Angie had smiled at her mam's words and nodded. It was another reason she had let a little time pass between her mother's passing and the funeral.

Angie told the vicar exactly what she wanted, insisting

her mam was buried in their local churchyard as it would be good for the children to be able to visit her grave whenever they wanted. There was also another reason, but she had not wanted to say. Not yet, anyway.

It seemed as though the weather had listened to Ida's wishes for a 'light and happy' funeral as the sun came out just before the service and, judging by the clear skies, looked intent on staying put for the remainder of the day.

As they made their way down the stone pathway to the church, Angie thought of her mam and could imagine her smiling: as requested, all the children had put on their favourite clothes. Bertie was wearing his fawn-coloured corduroys, held up by red braces, a cream-coloured shirt, a dicky bow and a blue blazer. His thick, dark hair had been slicked back with Brylcreem he had borrowed from Carl. Jemima was in a flowery dress with a tulle underskirt. She was wearing a yellow ribbon in her hair and had reluctantly agreed to put her navy woollen winter coat on as it was still cold, despite the good weather. Bonnie was wearing a pair of jeans and an Aran jumper, along with leather ankle boots. She'd refused to wear a jacket, which Angie had hoped would disguise her chosen attire.

Marlene, whose blonde hair had been twisted up into a French knot, looked like the movie star she had always aspired to be in her new crimson-coloured winter coat, a glossy black belt tied tightly to show her wasp waist. The irony was, though, that Marlene no longer yearned to be a movie star. She and her mam had talked about their love of the cinema and Ida had told her daughter about her idol, an actress Marlene had never heard of called Florence Lawrence, who had been the Marilyn Monroe of her time. Marlene had listened to how the actress had appeared in hundreds of silent movies, but that age had extinguished her sparkle. She was reduced to taking bit parts, ending up penniless and married to an abusive drunk, like the one in *Her Child's Honor*. She had died after ingesting ant poison and cough syrup and was buried in an unmarked grave.

They had talked about why they had been so enamoured of the movie stars in the many Hollywood movies they'd been to see, and Marlene had come to realise that the life many actresses led when the cameras stopped rolling was not one she wanted for herself.

But that wasn't the most affecting advice Ida had managed to impart to her daughter before her death.

She had told Marlene, with the utmost earnestness, 'Do not let what has happened to you define your life. Don't let it corrupt your future, but instead learn from it.'

They were words that Marlene had already replayed in her head many times. And she had come to the conclusion that she did not want to carry the resentments of her unhappy and neglected childhood about with her for the rest of her life, but would instead gain strength from what she had overcome. And as for the trauma of what had happened to her in London, by God was she going to learn from it. Nothing like that, she vowed, would ever happen to her again.

Seeing how much older than her age Marlene looked

today, Angie felt a flash of concern that she was growing up too fast. But then she realised that Marlene *was* grown-up. She was no longer her 'little sister'.

In contrast to Marlene's red coat, Angie had chosen to wear her favourite cream trouser suit, which had been designed by Kate and was part of her Lily & Rose autumn collection.

Cora was wearing a classy green dress she usually saved for important occasions.

Clemmie and Barbara were wearing almost identical woollen skirt suits – the only difference being their colour. Clemmie's was tartan and Barbara's a more conservative navy blue.

Stanislaw, Lloyd, Carl and Thomas all wore formal suits, but were making up for the lack of colour by their cheery demeanour. Angie knew it must be hard for Carl, but he was honouring Ida's last wishes and doing his best to make the occasion as upbeat as possible. And they were all succeeding, since any outsider looking in might guess that the reason they were all piling into the local church was a wedding or a christening, but most definitely not a funeral.

Ida had asked for the coffin to be brought into the church without much fuss so that when everyone took their seats it was already in place, covered by a beautiful floral display of yellow marigolds and violet delphiniums.

The vicar kept it 'short and sweet', as requested by Ida, for which everyone was thankful. Ida had asked the vicar to forgo the sermon and have just the one hymn, 'All Things Bright and Beautiful', and the one prayer – the Lord's Prayer.

After that, Ida was buried in St Cuthford's graveyard, which wrapped around the church. Again, Ida had asked for the burial to be kept brief, with flowers rather than soil thrown on top of her coffin.

Angie saw that Carl had forsaken a flower for a piece of folded paper. As it fluttered down onto the mahogany coffin lid, it opened a little and Angie could see it was a poem, which she guessed Carl had written himself.

'As instructed by Mam, now for the party!' Angie announced as the last flower thudded softly onto the coffin.

Everyone, including the vicar, climbed into the waiting funeral cars and headed back to Cuthford Manor.

The hotel had been closed for the weekend and Alberta and Mabel had put on a fabulous spread, including all the children's favourites. There were sausage rolls, pork pies, vol-au-vent stuffed with coronation chicken, crisps, quiche and salmon blinis. There was lemonade for the children, and champagne for the adults. The food and drink had been Angie's choice.

'Champagne rather than sherry,' she'd told Wilfred, who had been put in charge of the bar.

It had been Ida's suggestion that Angie invite her old workmates from Thompson's shipyard to the wake afterwards, and when they turned up at the manor, Angie realised why her mam had been so vehement about inviting them.

Their arrival in two cars – one driven by Rosie and the other by their journalist friend, Georgina – caused much hilarity, with all those chauffeured by their former boss climbing out of her Triumph Mayflower looking grey-faced and vowing never again to get in a car with Rosie behind the wheel. Those arriving just after – despite leaving much earlier – were grumbling that they could have cycled there quicker. A swap for the drive back was agreed.

As the party commenced with the popping of champagne corks and a toast to Ida, Angie was pleased to see that Polly's five boys and Gloria's daughter, Hope, were proving a great distraction for Bertie, Jemima and Bonnie, who had been terribly down in the mouth since their mam had died. Watching them all laughing and joking and tucking into the buffet gave Angie hope that this would snap them out of their period of mourning.

When everyone had had a chance to have some food and socialise, Angie tapped her glass with a silver spoon to get the room's attention.

'I'd like to make a brief announcement,' she began, glancing over to Carl, who gave her a nod.

The room fell quiet.

'I thought this would be the perfect opportunity to tell you all something which I know you will be glad about. Although probably for different reasons.'

Angie took a deep breath and looked at everyone's expectant faces.

'I'm pleased to say that Carl is going to stay on here and continue working with us.' She smiled at seeing everyone's faces light up. 'Which I know will be a relief to many of you!' Angie looked at Bill the gardener, who had begun to struggle with an increasingly bad back of late.

'Carl's become invaluable to us – especially as he seems to be able to turn his hand to most things.' She glanced over at Carl, who was looking uncomfortable at being the centre of attention. 'And as a city dweller who's never even needed to tend a lawn, he has proved himself to be quite the gardener. I'm sure Bill will agree Carl has been a huge help with the vegetable patch and the flower garden. And he will continue to be so.'

Bill, who was sitting next to Alberta, both of them needing to take the weight off their feet, nodded vigorously and raised his glass of single malt to show his agreement.

Angie looked at the children's faces, which had lit up on hearing the news. They liked Carl a lot and had got to know him well since Ida had died as he was about more and had started to join them all for dinner of an evening.

'So, Carl, I'd like to welcome you to the family. I think I can speak for everyone here in saying that we're over the moon you've agreed to stay. As I know Mam would be too.'

'Hear! Hear!' Lloyd said, raising his glass.

Everyone voiced their agreement.

Carl continued to look a little embarrassed and muttered his thanks.

'Before I let you carry on your conversations,' Angie continued, 'and enjoy Alberta and Mabel's wonderful spread . . .' everyone chuckled, their half-empty plates testimony to the fact they were more than enjoying the buffet, '. . . I have another announcement to make.'

Angie glanced across at Stanislaw, who was standing

next to Lloyd and Carl. As she did so, something caught the corner of her eye – something colourful.

She turned to look out of the window and saw what appeared to be a traditional Gypsy caravan coming up the driveway, pulled by two piebald cobs.

'Oh, looks like we've got visitors,' Angie said, her eyes still staring at the caravan.

'Looks like Travellers.' Stanislaw walked over to stand next to Angie.

'It looks like a man and a woman,' Clemmie said, squinting.

'Perhaps they've come to see Danny,' said Thomas.

Marlene shimmied up to Thomas whilst throwing Mabel a look.

'Oh my God!' she said. 'It *is* Danny!'

'And is that Lucy next to him?' Angie asked.

'It is!' Thomas confirmed. 'It's Danny and Lucy!'

Chapter Sixty-Six

All the guests piled out to welcome Danny and Lucy back to Cuthford Manor, their excitement heavily laced with curiosity. The entrancing vision of the couple in the beautifully painted Gypsy caravan caused much chatter as the horses made their way down the driveway.

'I thought the lad had gone north to buy proper horses, not two cobs and a caravan,' Alberta said.

'Aye, me too,' Bill agreed, 'although it has to be said it's a beautiful vardo.'

'What's a vardo?' Bertie asked.

'It's the name for a horse-drawn wagon used by Romany Gypsies' Stanislaw explained.

'I thought Lucy had gone off to Devon to stay with some school friend of hers,' Marlene said, drawing up next to them, her eyes focused on her brother and the woman he loved.

'She must have come back early,' Thomas mused.

'Or she didn't go at all,' said Mabel.

Hearing her speak, Marlene threw her a daggered look, but it was wasted as Mabel didn't notice; her big blue eyes were either looking up at Thomas or scrutinising the new arrivals.

'Well, this is a surprise,' Angie said, walking to the front of the small, welcoming crowd as the large wooden wheels of the caravan crunched to a halt on the gravel. She was still sore that Danny had gone away when it had been clear their mam had not had long left, leaving his younger brothers and sisters without his support.

'It is,' said Danny, jumping down and extending a gentlemanly hand to Lucy, who was more than capable of alighting from the caravan herself but gave him her hand anyway and stepped down.

Danny looked at Angie and then at the small crowd of people he knew were here for his mam's wake.

'I'd like to introduce you all to my wife, Mrs Lucy Boulter,' he beamed.

There was a dramatic, collective gasp.

Angie was visibly shocked. Looking down at Lucy's left hand, she could see there was indeed a gold band on her wedding finger.

'You've got married?'

Danny laughed. 'Yes, Angie. We got married yesterday. We travelled back straight afterwards to be here for Mam's funeral.'

'But I don't understand?' Angie said. 'You have to be twenty-one to get married without your parents' permission.' She was looking at Lucy, knowing that her parents would rather be tarred and feathered than agree for their only daughter to marry the son of a miner.

'Not in Scotland you don't,' Danny said, his smile still wide as he looked again at his new bride.

409

'Oh my God! You went to Gretna Green!' Marlene nudged past Thomas and Mabel and hurried over to her brother and new sister-in-law.

'How bloody romantic!' she gushed, hugging Lucy first and then her brother. 'You eloped!'

Angie looked at Danny and Lucy, the penny finally dropping. 'Well, this is a turn-up for the books!' she said, viewing them both and thinking she had not seen two people look happier. Her heart softened.

'Welcome to the family!' she declared, opening her arms and giving Lucy a hug.

She then turned to the shocked onlookers and sought out the children, who were standing stock-still, gawking at their brother and his bride and the wonderful carriage they had arrived in.

'Your new sister-in-law,' Angie said, waving them over. 'And auntie,' she told Bonnie.

The children smiled and remained standing – a little in awe of their big brother who was now a married man, and his pretty bride.

'Well, congratulations!' Stanislaw stepped forward and shook Danny's hand.

He turned to Lucy and gave her a peck on the cheek.

'Congratulations, Mrs Lucy Boulter!'

Lucy blushed. This was the first time anyone other than Danny had greeted her by her new married name.

'And welcome to your new home!' Lloyd followed suit. 'I take it you will be living here with your husband?'

Lucy nodded, a little overwhelmed by all the attention. And also by how celebratory everyone looked. Most of the guests were dressed for a party rather than a funeral. She had thought they might slip in the back way relatively unnoticed before going to lay some flowers on Ida's grave.

'That's fantastic news,' Cora said, stepping forward and embracing Lucy. She knew more than anyone what the consequences would be for Lucy running off and marrying Danny. 'Don't worry,' she whispered as she gave Lucy a hug. 'You'll be safe here. We'll make sure you are.'

Lucy blinked back tears, suddenly overcome with emotion.

'Thank you,' she mouthed.

By now everyone was walking over to the newly-weds, wanting to congratulate them both and stroke the horses.

'Can we look inside?' Bonnie asked.

'Yes, of course,' Lucy said.

The three young ones hurried to the caravan and climbed up the wooden steps.

'Wow!' Bonnie's muffled voice could be heard from inside, followed by similar exclamations of awe from Jemima and Bertie.

The rest of the guests gathered around the two runaways and offered up their congratulations. Rosie and the rest of the women who had worked with Angie at Thompson's exclaimed that it seemed just the other day that Danny was pageboy at his sister's wedding – and they all agreed that made them feel very old.

Alberta, who had held back as long as she could, hugged Danny and then his new wife, tears dripping unashamedly down her ruddy cheeks.

'Eee, I couldn't be happier for yer both,' she declared in her broad Yorkshire accent, which had become stronger, as it always did after a few whiskies.

Angie managed to coax everyone back inside while Stanislaw took the caravan round to the stables to give the horses some water and food.

'They've covered a fair few miles,' Stanislaw said, knowing that Gretna Green was around seventy miles away.

'We gave them plenty of breaks,' Lucy said. 'And we stopped overnight at Hexham.'

Stanislaw smiled. He didn't doubt the two cobs had been well looked after. He didn't know two other people whose love for horses was greater.

After congratulating Danny and his bride, Wilfred and Thomas headed down to the cellar to retrieve more champagne. They both agreed they'd never known such a joyful wake.

Cora, meanwhile, asked Mabel to get the 'honeymoon suite' ready for the newly-weds. Seeing Thomas return from the cellars with the champagne, Mabel asked if he wouldn't mind bringing her some logs from out the back so she could stack the fire.

Catching the exchange, Marlene said she would bring up some fresh flowers and a little box of confetti they always kept for their newly married guests.

As everyone headed back to the main reception room, Angie pulled Danny and Lucy back.

'I don't want to sound like a killjoy,' she said.

'But you're going to anyway,' Danny retorted.

'Sorry, Danny, but you know me, I have to say what's on my mind.'

'Let me beat you to it,' Danny said. 'You're annoyed I wasn't there for Mam's passing.'

Angie nodded, tears filling her eyes.

'And,' Danny continued, 'you think we're both far too young to get married – and you're worried about the reaction of Lucy's parents?'

'Well, yes, that's about the nub of it,' Angie acquiesced.

Just then Winston and Bessie came scrabbling down the corridor from the kitchen and into the hallway. They charged at Danny and Lucy, ecstatic at their return.

Angie watched as they enjoyed a boisterous reunion.

That was the one thing Angie *did* like about Lucy; she didn't seem to give two jots about how she looked or the fact that she was now covered in dog hair and saliva.

Having given the dogs a robust pat, ruffled their ears and told them how much he'd missed them too, Danny stood up straight.

'We're not too young,' he said. 'It wouldn't have made any difference waiting until we're older as we both know we'd still feel exactly the same.'

'And as regards my parents,' Lucy said, her hand still patting Bessie, who had pushed herself against her legs and had already stood on her foot a few times. 'Well, they can

413

huff and puff, rant and rave, they can disown me, condemn me, but they can't *do* anything as Danny and I are now legally married.'

Angie was standing listening, trying not to show how taken aback she was by Lucy's forthrightness.

Anticipating Angie's next question, Lucy added, 'And the issue of Roeburn Hall, well . . .' She shrugged her shoulders. 'If they have to sell, they have to sell. There's nothing I can do about that. And the only thing I could have done to save it, I didn't want to do.'

When Danny and Lucy, who were clearly starving, had eaten their fill of the buffet, Angie again chinked her glass.

'Well, I certainly didn't think I'd be making another toast today,' she said. 'Mam *would* be pleased. She's definitely got her wish for a very happy wake.'

Everyone chuckled.

'So,' Angie raised her glass, 'to the newly married couple, Mr and Mrs Boulter! Love and happiness!'

'Love and happiness!' the guests chorused.

The moment everyone had taken a sip of their drinks, the questions started.

Angie watched as Lucy, who was ushered onto one of the cushioned chairs near the fireplace, and Danny, who perched himself on the arm, fielded a plethora of questions: *What was Gretna Green like? Did they really get married in front of the anvil in the old blacksmith's? Was it terribly romantic?*

'So, if you weren't buying horses,' Alberta piped up,

'why were you gone for so long? Must be – what – more than three weeks now.'

Angie had her back to Stanislaw and was leaning against him as he stood with his arms wrapped around her. She had just been about to ask the same question. Again, thinking that her brother could have been here to say goodbye to his mam.

'Well,' Danny said, 'you have to be a resident in Gretna for twenty-one days before you're allowed to get married.'

There were a few *Ahhs* of understanding.

'So, that's why you didn't come back for Mam?' Angie asked.

Danny nodded.

'Your mother knew,' Lucy suddenly chipped in. 'She knew what we were going to do.'

'Really?' Marlene asked, shocked.

'What? Mam knew you two were going to elope and go off and get married in Gretna Green?' Angie asked, equally amazed. She'd barely seen Danny and Lucy say two words to Ida in all the time she had been at the manor.

Danny and Lucy laughed.

'*It was Mam's idea,*' Danny said.

Everyone looked gobsmacked.

'So, let me get this right,' Clemmie said in her usual forthright way, 'Ida suggested that you should both – despite being just eighteen and seventeen years old – elope to Gretna Green?'

'She did,' Lucy said, remembering that day when Ida

415

had pretended she had been looking for Danny, but had really come to convince her not to go ahead and marry the man her parents had decided for her, but to instead follow her heart and marry Ida's son.

'I never had Mam down as a meddler,' Marlene said.

'Me neither,' Angie agreed, although as she spoke, it occurred to her that their mam hadn't meddled with just her eldest son's love life during her time here . . .

Getting up to refill their plates, and to give themselves some respite from the onslaught of questions and attention, well meaning though it was, Danny put his arm around Lucy's waist and gently pulled her towards him.

'You coping?' he asked.

Lucy smiled and nodded.

'It's lovely everyone is so happy for us,' she said, knowing this would certainly not be the case when her own family found out the news, which was something she intended to put off for as long as possible.

'Cora's sorted out the main honeymoon suite for us,' Danny said. 'She said it's there for when we've had enough and want to escape.'

'Ah, that's lovely,' Lucy said. 'I must thank her. I keep feeling waves of guilt that everyone is being so friendly and welcoming when I've not exactly gone out of my way to get to know them before now.'

Danny nodded his understanding. It was true. Lucy had been so worried that her family would find out about their relationship, she had barely stepped over the threshold of the manor, preferring to stay out in the stables so that if anyone saw her she could say she'd gone there to meet up with other riders and to work on her dressage with Dahlia.

'*Shoo! Away with you all!*'

Danny and Lucy turned to see Marlene waving her hands at Bertie, Jemima and Bonnie, who they had not realised had also followed them to the buffet.

Jemima and Bonnie stuck their tongues out at her before hurrying off, followed by Bertie, who at least managed to grab a handful of crisps and ram them into his mouth before doing as his big sister had ordered.

'I think they're star-struck,' Marlene said to them both. 'Whereas I'm madly curious.'

Danny rolled his eyes. 'Oh God, now for the third degree.'

'I have to say, Lucy, I'm more than a little surprised.'

Lucy blushed. Then she laughed. 'Me too!'

'So, come on, I want to know *everything*. From the beginning. And you have to tell me because I'm your sister-in-law. And sisters tell each other everything.'

'No, they don't!' Danny said. 'I recall not so long ago you jumping on a train to London without telling anyone, never mind your sister *or* your brother.'

Marlene batted his words away.

'Tell me, Lucy, what made you do something so against your nature – and so incredibly romantic, I have to add.'

Lucy laughed. 'So you're saying that by nature I'm not romantic?'

'You know what I mean.' Marlene dismissed her question. 'Now, come on, spill the beans! All of them.'

As Lucy told Marlene about the day Ida had come to see her in the stables, and how she'd gone home and been confronted by her family, Danny's mind drifted off.

He knew that he had his mam to thank for Lucy now being his wife.

There had been much Ida had done wrong in her life, and he would never whitewash over that, but she had come up trumps at the end, and at a time when he had really needed her.

When Lucy had told him about his mam's impromptu visit to the stables, and about the chat they'd had, for the first time he had felt the warmth of a mother's love. His mam had done this for him, knowing how much it would destroy his life if Lucy was coerced into marrying Anthony.

She had given Lucy guidance – the kind of guidance her own mother should have given her – and told her how wrong it was to marry a man you didn't love; that it would have far-reaching consequences for many people, including any children born from the unhappy alliance.

Danny had seen how Lucy had changed after that day. In a good way.

It had been Lucy who had said she wanted to marry him, and that the only way they could do it – other than to wait four years, during which time heaven only knew what her parents might do – was to go to Gretna Green. Which, she'd told him, had been his mam's idea.

Danny knew Lucy to be a fearless rider, but on her own two feet she could often be uncertain and a little fearful.

Doing what she had done had taken courage. *A lot* of courage.

He hadn't thought it possible, but it had made him love her even more.

And now they were married, they would deal with the consequences.

They would be courageous together.

Chapter Sixty-Seven

Having satisfied Marlene's curiosity about how they came to elope, as well as fielded questions the other guests were too polite to ask, like did they spend their wedding night in their Gypsy caravan or a hotel, Danny and Lucy made their way across the room to Angie, who was chatting away to Clemmie and Barbara.

'We're just going to go and put some flowers on Mam's grave,' Danny said.

Angie was about to say that sounded like a lovely idea when Clemmie interrupted her.

'So, Angie, what was the other announcement you were going to make before our two lovebirds suddenly turned up?'

'Oh,' Angie smiled, realising that she'd never smiled as much at a wake. 'Yes, I was, wasn't I?'

Clemmie tapped her glass to get everyone's attention.

'As if we've not all had enough excitement for one day . . .' Clemmie said in her usual robust manner. 'Which I realise as I'm saying it might sound rather disrespectful to admit, this being a wake and all – but I digress, since I know Ida would actually be pleased. Anyway, we are not done with surprises on this surprisingly happy day.'

She looked at Angie.

'I'm curious, as I'm sure you all are, what exactly Angie was going to announce before the return of our two elopers.'

Clemmie stepped back and everyone's attention turned to Angie.

'Well,' Angie began hesitantly, 'I suppose there is more news to impart at this very unconventional wake . . .' She felt herself blush and, wanting her husband to be near her, stretched out her hand.

'It's happy news,' she said as Stanislaw reached her and took the proffered hand. 'And we wanted to tell you all today because I know Mam would want me to.'

Angie's mind jumped back to the day of Ida's death, when she had told her the news and her mother had smiled and whispered about *the circle of life*.

'Well, apart from having Carl agreeing to stay to live and work with us all here, *and* welcoming Lucy into the family – it also looks like we're going to have still another addition to the family,' Angie informed them.

Seeing the looks of confusion on the little ones, Stanislaw smiled. 'But I'm afraid you're going to have to wait a little while before you meet her – or him,' he explained.

Angie saw comprehension start to dawn on the faces of Bonnie, Jemima and Bertie – along with expressions of joy lighting up the faces of the others in the room.

'Yes,' Angie laughed. 'I'm expecting.' She looked at her husband, who was beaming proudly. 'We're going to have a little girl or boy. And, if my calculations are right – our new family member should arrive late spring, early summer next year.'

'Yeah!' Bonnie exclaimed, running to her mother and the man she viewed as her father. They both hugged her. 'Finally,' she said. 'A little sister.'

'Or a little brother,' Angie said.

'Well, it's about time!' Marlene exclaimed, walking over and giving her a hug. 'What made you change your mind?' she asked, knowing how vehement Angie had been about *not* having any more children.

Angie choked back a sudden outburst of tears and instead gave a slightly strangled laugh.

'Mam . . . Mam did . . . Mam changed my mind.'

Stanislaw put his arm around Angie and gave her a gentle squeeze. He hoped that Ida knew how thankful he was to her. He had tried to tell her, but she wasn't one to accept compliments or gratitude.

'She said,' Angie managed to continue, 'that I was *no spring chicken* any more and I'd better get a move on . . .'

Marlene smiled, but she had tears in her eyes.

'That's our mam,' she said, 'always brutal with her honesty.'

Angie looked over to Carl, who had given up trying to hold back his tears. He walked over, shook Stanislaw's hand and gave Angie a hug.

'Congratulations,' he whispered to her. 'And thank you so much. For everything.'

He knew that if Angie had not welcomed, or at least

suffered, Ida when she'd first turned up, so much good would not have come into being.

As Angie's former workmates bustled over to congratulate her, Gloria looked at her younger friend with a convincingly serious face.

'I hope you've told Dorothy? She'll do her nut if we've got to find out before she did.'

'Yes, I told her,' Angie chuckled. 'My eardrums are still recovering from her screams of excitement.'

They all hooted with laughter, knowing that their friend would not be exaggerating.

As Angie looked around and saw the excitement and joy in the room, she recalled the same expression on her mam's face when she had told her the news before she passed. She had been truly happy for her daughter and, smiling, had glanced down at Angie's stomach and told her unborn grandchild, 'What a lucky little baby you are – to have a mam like our Angie.'

As Angie sat in the window seat, sipping her champagne, she took a moment to watch those she loved as they rejoiced in the good news of the day.

Clemmie's occasional guffaws of laughter had gone up a notch as she chatted animatedly with Angie's old workmates, whom she had got to know over the past few years.

Barbara was in a deep discussion with Carl. Angie caught snippets of the conversation and smiled to herself to hear them chatting about who should be the next prime minister, and how Barbara dreamed of a day when the person who led the country was a woman.

Marlene and Thomas seemed to have put their differences aside and were chatting away to the newly-weds. Winston and Bessie were also nudging up and demanding attention from the new Mr and Mrs Boulter, whom they had missed these past three weeks.

The younger children were bobbing in and out of the room, playing tag or hide-and-seek, using the grand hallway as a makeshift playground.

Stanislaw was chatting to Lloyd and Cora and looked relaxed and happy. He had declared many times since Angie had told him she was expecting their child that he had never been happier.

Seeing Stanislaw go down on his haunches to chat to Bertie, Angie knew that her husband would make a wonderful father. That was something she hadn't needed to be convinced of by her mam.

Angie would miss her mam terribly, but seeing Cora and Lloyd exchange a tender kiss, she knew how lucky she was that they too had become like parents to her since she'd first arrived at Cuthford Manor more than eight years ago.

Watching Alberta and Bill sitting on the sofa, chatting away, she realised it would not be long before they would need to retire. But it was a relief that there were those waiting in the wings to take over. Mabel as cook. And Carl as gardener. She could never let Alberta or Bill go, though. They might be employees, but they were also family.

Angie put a hand on the small, firm mound of her

stomach and thought that her little girl or boy would need a nanny and Alberta might just be the perfect person. Bill could potter in the gardens for as long as he wanted and show the guests the grounds, impressing them with the Latin names of the flora and proudly showing them which vegetables they'd likely be eating that evening.

Angie knew her mam would have been pleased with her send-off. Some might say she was feeling sentimental, but she sensed her mam was still close. Thinking back to the day of her wedding anniversary, when her mam had turned up so unexpectedly, Angie's first impression then had been that there was something different about her. At the time she had put it down to the fact she had not seen Ida for eight years – reasoning with herself that of course her mam would have changed during that time.

But now she realised that the difference she'd seen was a certain serenity. An inner calmness. An acceptance of life.

With hindsight, Angie wondered if it was because her mother knew death was not far away – because she had accepted her mortality and had found a kind of inner repose, a calmness of the soul. Angie hoped that when her time eventually came, she too would be able to show such dignity and bravery, because in Angie's mind her mam had been brave – brave in the face of death, and also brave because she had fought so hard to break the cycle of servitude and poverty. Of forsaken dreams.

And she'd succeeded, but it hadn't been without sacrifice.

It was only now that Angie truly understood why her mother had not had any regrets about leaving her family.

Looking at Marlene chatting to Danny, and Bertie and Jemima playing with the other children, Angie knew they would never have been so happy, so educated and so loved had their mother not left them.

Angie had chatted with Danny after her announcement and had realised that Ida had been right when she'd said on her deathbed that she was relieved they had all let go of their resentments. Angie had doubted whether this was actually the case for Danny, but hearing how he had gone to see Ida before leaving for Scotland, and how they had made their peace, she knew he too had let go of his anger and resentment. Ida had understood her son well enough to know it would devastate his life were he to lose Lucy. She had done her best to ensure that didn't happen. And she had done so for the simple reason that she loved and cared for her son and wanted more than anything for him to be happy.

Angie thought for a moment. Her mam had been wrong about not having any maternal feelings. They might have been buried deep for many, many years, but they had surfaced at a time when her children had needed her most.

Her mam had been right when she had said that Angie was trying to bury her own maternal feelings, and that she had to stop and instead let those feelings feel the sun.

Although most would say that her mam had done the unthinkable in leaving her children, it had nevertheless been the right decision.

For all of them.

Including herself.

God did indeed work in mysterious ways, for Angie had

her mam to thank for the life she had now, a life she would not swap for the world. For the family she had around her – both her blood and also those who had become her family over these past eight years.

If her mam had not left her to look after her sisters and brothers that day eight years ago, Angie wouldn't have all of this.

All of these people in her life.

All of this joy.

All of this love.

And, of course, the child growing inside her.

Epilogue

A few weeks after the funeral, Marlene followed up her mam's suggestion and invited Jimmy to stay at Cuthford Manor. She thought she might feel some kind of innate closeness to him because he was her biological father, but she didn't. And she could tell that Jimmy didn't feel any kind of paternal feelings towards his long-lost daughter. She didn't call him 'Dad' and could tell that he didn't mind in the least.

After a few days, Marlene could see he missed the buzz and excitement of London and was ready to go back down south. When she waved him off, they agreed to write, but Marlene thought it unlikely she'd ever go to London to see him, or that he would be up for a return visit.

'He's just the most unfatherlike person I've ever come across,' Marlene told Angie. 'I can see why he never married or had his own family. He just wants to be the centre of attention. It's like he's still a child himself.'

Angie smiled. Her sister was growing into an insightful young woman. And as much as Angie would have liked to take credit for the person Marlene was becoming, she knew it was really down to the time she'd spent with their mam.

*

Six weeks later, in the run up to Christmas, Marlene was gifted an unexpected present when Bertie read them all an article that had appeared in the *Daily Mirror* about the infamous Rossi brothers, Enrico and Tony, who had been sentenced to life in prison for the murder of two rival gang members in the West End.

Carl settled quickly into his new home and workplace. Angie and Stanislaw were surprised that he didn't hanker after the hustle and bustle of the city, but nothing could have been further from his thoughts. He told them that he would be happy never to step foot in the capital again. Angie wondered whether this was because the eight years he'd spent living in London had been with Ida, and returning there would be forever shrouded by memories.

Angie also believed it brought Carl comfort being so close to the place where Ida was buried. He went to the grave a couple of times a week, always taking fresh flowers.

Marlene told Angie that she thought Carl would never love again, which Angie had said was a little melodramatic, but quietly she too thought this might be the case. She could see that the love he had inside him was given over to his poetry and to his work in the flower garden and the vegetable patch. It could be tasted in the produce he grew.

He had yet to share any of his verse with them, but Angie hoped he might feel able to in the future.

Danny and Lucy spent the months leading up to the New Year in Ida's old room until the former workers' cottages, which had stood empty since before the Second World War, were renovated and made into one dwelling.

Carrying his wife over the threshold on the day they were finally able to move in was, they agreed, 'a dream come true'.

Of course, it was not all light and laughter, for the storm that hit them after Lucy's parents found out they'd eloped had been thundery to say the least.

But the new Mr and Mrs Boulter rode it out together.

Eventually, once the Hetheringtons' wrath had been spent, the Stanton-Leighs returned their focus to the problem of their financial affairs, and in the New Year they were forced to do the unthinkable and put Roeburn Hall up for sale.

Angie's calculations were more or less spot on, and, on 21st of June, she gave birth to a healthy baby girl. A little sister for Bonnie, and a niece for her siblings.

As their daughter had been born on the day of the summer solstice – the celebration of new beginnings and change – choosing a name was easy for Angie and Stanislaw.

And so, a few weeks later, everyone gathered in St Cuthford's church for the christening of Angie and Stanislaw's baby girl – June Ida Nowak.

Dear Reader,

I'm endlessly fascinated by the mother-daughter relationship, and I really enjoyed writing about Ida – a mother who does the unthinkable and walks out on her family.

I'm also fascinated by repeated circles of behaviour that seem to be inherited by one generation to the next – and our attempts, whether consciously or not, to break free of them. And, as you are all probably aware by now, I am a champion of the belief that love really does conquer all.

And that love – in all its forms – is at the epicentre of life.

As always, I wish you Love – and lots of it!

Nancy x

Historical Notes

The actress, Florence Lawrence, who inspired Ida during her childhood trips to the cinema, was a real Hollywood actress. Born Florence Annie Bridgwood on 2 January 1886, she was a Canadian American stage performer and film actress who reached the height of her fame in the 1910s. She is often referred to as the 'first movie star' and appeared in almost 300 films for various motion picture companies. Florence also invented the first car turn signal, or 'auto-signalling arm', and the brake signal for cars. However, as she did not patent her inventions, she did not receive any profits from her work. Sadly, once the 'talkies' became popular, and Florence became older, her fame faded. On 28 December 1938, reduced to appearing in minor parts, and suffering from a terminal illness, Florence died by suicide in Beverly Hills. She was fifty-two years old.

Ida's former employer, Edith Clara Summerskill, was also a real person. Baroness Summerskill (19 April 1901– 4 February 1980) was a British physician, feminist, Labour

Sincerely Yours
Florence Lawrence.

EQUAL PAY
WITHOUT
DELAY

politician and writer. She championed such causes as equal rights and equal pay for women, birth control and availability of painless childbirth methods, and a wife's fair share of her husband's property.

The home Ida had planned to go to in Fife, Scotland, really did exist. It was the first Marie Curie Home for cancer patients and was opened in 1952. It was based in an old National Trust property called the Hill of Tarvit in Cupar, Fife. During the 1950s and early 1960s, the charity opened nine more Marie Curie Homes in adapted buildings.

THE NEW NOVEL FROM
BESTSELLING AUTHOR

Nancy
REVELL

A
DAUGHTER'S
LOVE

PRE-ORDER NOW

Discover Nancy Revell's bestselling Shipyard Girls series

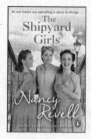   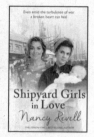

   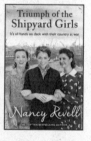

Have you read them all?